THE SECRET HISTORY *of*

TWIN PEAKS

MARK FROST

FLATIRON
BOOKS
NEW YORK

GRATEFUL ACKNOWLEDGMENT TO

Bob Miller, Colin Dickerman, Ed Victor, Paul Kepple, Max Vandenberg, Bart's Books of Ojai, John Broesamle, Bob Getman, Anthony Glassman, Stephen Kulczycki, Gary Levine, Marlena Bittner, James Melia, Elizabeth Catalano, David Lott, Vincent Stanley, Caleb Braate, David Correll, Dean Hurley, David Nevins, Rick Rosen, Ken Ross, Sabrina Sutherland ... and David Lynch.

THE SECRET HISTORY OF TWIN PEAKS.

Front and back jacket images and title page image by Clifford B. Ellis, courtesy of Susan Yake • Case cover image of Great Horned Owl © Jean Murray • Inside jacket image "A Clearing Winter Storm" © William Toti • Calligraphy courtesy of Beth Lee • All images from *Twin Peaks* courtesy of Lynch/Frost Productions • Page 30: Masonic Master Mason Apron, 1855–1865, Reason Bell Crafft, Kentucky, Collection of the Scottish Rite Masonic Museum & Library, Gift of the Valley of Lowell in honor of Brother Starr H. Fiske, 32°, 85.6.2. Photograph by David Bohl. • Page 36: Image of the Meriwether Lewis monument courtesy NPS Photos • Page 39: Image of Shahaka (Sheheke or Big White, c. 1766–1812), Chief of the Mandans, by Saint-Memin courtesy of the New York Historical Society • Page 55: Edward Curtis's photograph of Chief Joseph courtesy of the National Portrait Gallery, Smithsonian Institution/ Art Resource, NY • Page 57: Bronze statue of John "Liver-eating" Johnson courtesy of the Buffalo Bill Center of the West, Cody, Wyoming • Page 72: Image courtesy of the Grampound with Creed Heritage Project • Pages 99 – 101: Use of Kenneth Arnold article and cover of FATE Magazine, Issue 1, courtesy of FATE Magazine • Page 110: Photograph of "three tramps," Allen, William. *[The "three tramps" being escorted to the Sheriff's office]*, Photograph, November 22, 1963; (http://texashistory.unt.edu/ark:/67531/metapth184799/ : accessed April 27, 2016), University of North Texas Libraries, The Portal to Texas History, http://texashistory.unt.edu; crediting The Sixth Floor Museum at Dealey Plaza, Dallas, Texas • Page 118: Photograph of the smoke plume from the Tillamook Burn as seen from an aircraft, in August 1933. (Image: Library of Congress) • Page 134: Photograph of 1930s Man Standing in Field Holding Shotgun and Leash of Gordon Setter Dog by H. Armstrong Roberts/ClassicStock/Getty Images • Page 242: Photograph of L. Ron Hubbard seated at his desk, courtesy Los Angeles Daily News Negatives, UCLA Library. Copyright Regents of the University of California, UCLA Library • Page 268: "Rocket Scientist Killed in Pasadena Explosion," June 18, 1952, reproduced with the permission of the *Los Angeles Times*

Designed by Paul Kepple and Max Vandenberg at
HEADCASE DESIGN
www.headcasedesign.com

THE SECRET HISTORY *of* TWIN PEAKS

Office of the Deputy Director

INTEROFFICE MEMORANDUM

DATE: 8-4-2016

FROM: GORDON COLE, Deputy Director

TO: ██████████████ Special Agent

Dear Agent ███████████

The accompanying material is confidential and approved for your eyes only.

The enclosed dossier was recovered on 7-17-2016 from a crime scene that is still under active investigation. All details of this situation are classified three levels above top secret.

It is being given to you for comprehensive analysis, cataloging and cross-referencing content against all known databases under Code Red measures. We need to learn and verify the person or persons responsible for compiling this dossier and we need to know it yesterday!

Background: The content of the dossier appears to have some relationship to an investigation conducted in northwest Washington State many moons ago by Special Agent Dale Cooper, who worked under my command at that time.

The case involved a series of homicides in and around a small town called Twin Peaks, most notably the murder of a young woman named Laura Palmer. That case is considered closed but aspects of it may be relevant to your work, so we are also granting you access to all of Agent Cooper's files and tapes.

Also attached is a document highlighting previous processing of the dossier by Bureau personnel.

Roll up your sleeves and get to work on this thing—time is of the essence—and get back to me with your findings ASAP.

Sincerely Yours,

Gordon Cole

Deputy Director Gordon Cole

P.S. When you get done with this come see me immediately. By then I may have more for you to do.

DATE:	TOPIC:	SUBMITTED BY:
8/4/2016	DOSSIER PROCESSING TIMELINE	COLE, GORDON

SYNOPSIS OF FACTS:

The following dossier was recovered on ███████.

Time and location noted, but are classified as strictly NEED TO KNOW.

Field Agents ███████ and ███████ discovered dossier while on assignment in ███████ It was recovered from a crime scene that is still classified as unsolved and may have relevance to a previous crime or crimes in 1991 that is similarly classified.

Dossier was submitted to DIRECTOR on 7-17-2016.

Dossier referred by DIRECTOR to Investigations and Operations Support Section (IOSS) on 7-20-2016.

Special Agent T███ P███ will begin analysis and report on validity. All work will be conducted and dossier will be kept in clean room at FBI HQ.

STATED PRIORITY: Identify person or persons who compiled dossier.

CONFIRMED: Special Agent TP has completed all required background checks, and filed completed forms SF-86 and FD-258.

CONFIRMED: Special Agent TP adjudicated for Top Secret security clearance as of 2009 and approved for adjunct liaison with Special Task Force B███ and all related files, per Crypto Clearance 12.

CONFIRMED: Special Agent TP will report exclusively to head of Special Task Force B and to DIRECTOR.

CONFIRMED: Special Agent TP begins first analysis on 8-5-16.

All comments and annotations will be included and initialed.

APPROVED: *Gordon Cole*

CLASSIFIED

DO NOT WRITE IN THESE SPACES

SEARCHED ___ INDEXED ___
SERIALIZED ___ FILED ___
AUG 21 2016
FBI—PHILADELPHIA

COPY ON FILE

89-69-2041

ANALYST'S INTRODUCTORY REMARKS:

The following constitute my thoughts after a cursory examination of the dossier and ahead of beginning the work at hand:

Means, methodology and motivation for compilation of these documents and ephemera will be commented upon throughout and initialed (TP) as separate entries in the margins. All content is presented here in the order in which it appears in the original dossier, without revision. This order of the documents, as far as can be ascertained at first glance, appears to be chronological and as a result presents a direct, if intermittent, sense of historical narrative. As to what this narrative conveys, as stated I will present my comments throughout.

The author or authors self-identifies in the body of the MS as "The Archivist." Given the scope of the dossier and the way in which the Archivist organized it, I will attempt to offer summaries within the body of the work as I proceed.

The dossier was discovered inside a carbon steel lockbox, 17" x 11" x 3". Lockbox was not a standard size and does not appear to be of any known commercial manufacture. It also features a highly sophisticated triple locking mechanism that required extensive efforts to crack.

It is my considered opinion that this lockbox may have been personally fashioned by the person identified within as the Archivist.

The dossier itself fits snugly inside the margins of the box, further suggesting that the lockbox was custom made to accommodate it.

The dossier is contained and bound within a book-shaped ledger, which also appears to be of sophisticated self-manufacture. Its embossed cover is fashioned from boards encased in dark green cloth.

It appears well-worn, suggesting it had at
some point been exposed to the elements.
Nevertheless—fortunately—upon closer
examination once opened, a fully sealed and
vulcanized boxlike encasement around the top,
bottom and fore edges kept the ledger's
contents entirely free from damage.

The only visible ornamentation on the
entire ledger appears on the spine and
is pictured at right.

Measuring less than one-half inch and
apparently hand-tooled, it depicts a series
of triangles, the purpose or meaning of
which at first view remains unclear.

INSIDE THE LEDGER ITSELF

The documents presented inside appear to
be excellent facsimiles of the originals.
A few appear to be originals and, by virtue
of their age, fragile, but all contents
will be returned exactly as they originally
appeared.

Each page is covered by a clear plastic membrane (.02 mil thick, measured by
digital micrometer), which appears to be of standard manufacture, although the
unusual size suggests the membranes were also custom fitted.

This membrane holds each document in place. No glues or tapes were used to
affix the documents to the neutrally colored pages, which are all made from
paper of the same, uniform thickness, similar to construction paper.

INITIAL _TP_   DATE _8 128 16_

Closer examination of the edges of both the membranes and pages suggests they were cut by hand and not mass produced.

Most of the documents appear one to a page, leaving room above and below for annotations, presumably made by the Archivist. These appear regularly throughout the dossier.

The dossier appears to be divided into easily identified and sub-headed sections. They will be presented here in their original form and order. I intend to include my own comments in the margins. These will include fact checking, analysis and occasionally personal reactions or comments. Whenever possible, documents will be traced to their alleged original source and verified. Any instances of documents that prove resistant to verification will be duly noted.

It is my intention that engaging with the contents in this manner will achieve the stated and desired outcome: determining the identity of the Archivist.

Sworn and notarized before me on this day, 8-28-16,
Special Agent T█████ P██████

| INITIAL *TP* | DATE 8,28,16 |

THE DOSSIER

*** OPENING STATEMENT: [1]

A wise man once told me that mystery is the most essential
ingredient of life, for the following reason: mystery creates
wonder, which leads to curiosity, which in turn provides the
ground for our desire to understand who and what we truly are.

The search for meaning at the heart of life brings us to the
contemplation of an eternal enigma. Mysteries are the stories
we tell ourselves to contend with life's resistance to our
longing for answers. Mysteries abound. This continent, this
country, our own earthly origins are all laden with them,
underlying our existence, pre-dating all our childish notions
of "history." Mythology precedes our access to historical or
scientific fact, and, we know now, fulfilled much the same
function for earlier civilizations -- providing meaning in
the face of a remorseless, indifferent universe -- but in the
absence of scientifically verifiable fact it is necessary to
sometimes view them as one and the same.

So it is best to start at the beginning.

So signed and duly sworn:

THE ARCHIVIST [2]

[1] There is no title page,
author page, table of
contents, index or appendi-
ces anywhere in the ledger.
Nothing except the frequent
interstitial interpretative
comments by "The Archivist"
and the following opening
statement, which functions
as a kind of "foreword"
before the first "section"—TP

[2] This is the only handwritten portion of the dossier,
and block printing is
impossible to trace to an
individual. The typed
sections appear to be the
product of the same manual
typewriter, most likely a
Corona Super G, a popular,
lightweight portable model
which was first manufac-
tured in the 1970s.
  The dossier then simply
begins with the first series of
documents—TP

[1] Confirmed that this is an actual entry from the well-known published journals. The paper and ink, applied it seems with a quill, appear appropriate to the period. This is either a remarkable facsimile of William Clark's actual handwriting from his original journals—or the original itself. Have contacted the National Archives and am awaiting verification on that point—TP

[2] This passage describes Clark's first meeting with the tribe known later to us as the Nez Perce, or Pierced Noses, who were a significant presence in this part of the territory. This name was given them by early French trappers, after the tribe's affinity for jewelry and other adornments affixed through the nose.
This encounter occurred soon after the expedition passed into the eastern reaches of what is now Washington State and not far south of the present-day location of Twin Peaks. The following day these same men led Clark to meet another chief whose camp was farther downriver. This chief was called Twisted Hair—TP

I EXCERPT FROM THE EXPEDITION
JOURNALS OF WILLIAM CLARK
AND MERIWETHER LEWIS.
SEPTEMBER 20, 1805

20 September, 1805

At a distance of 1 mile from the ~~~~ lodges, I met 3 Indian boys. When they saw me, they ran and ~~~~ hid themselves in the grass. I dismounted, gave my gun and horse to one of the men, searched in the grass and found 2 of the boys. Gave them ~~~~ small pieces of ribbon, and sent them forward to the village. ▨

A man came out to meet me with great caution and conducted ~~~~ me to a large spacious lodge, which he told me by signs, was the lodge of his great chief, who had set out ~~~~ 3 days previous with all the warriors of the nation to war, ~~~~ and would return in 15 to 18 days. The few men that were left in the village, and ~~~~ great numbers of women, gathered around me with much apparent fear, and appeared pleased. They were a stout, handsome, and well dressed band.

1

2

21 September, 1805

With great cheerfulness Twisted Hair drew me a kind of chart of the river on a white elk skin. He said that the river forked a long distance above and passed through two mountains, at which place was a great fall of the water passing through the rocks. I did not reckon precise what this place would signify, but our Shoshone guide thinks it regards something like the peculiar fascination with spirits we find among the Indians of this region. I sent one man back — Reuben Fields — with an Indian to meet Captain Lewis and direct him to meet us here at this camp.

[1]

[1] I have now heard from an expert who positively verified this section as William Clark's handwriting and a known part of the historically published journals; the two commanders of the expedition had indeed split their party to hunt for provisions a few days earlier—TP

3 EXCERPT FROM A LETTER WRITTEN
BY MERIWETHER LEWIS TO
PRESIDENT THOMAS JEFFERSON.
DATED SEPTEMBER 25, 1805.

After receiving from R. Fields, I pushed my party forward to meet Captain Clark at the village of Twisted Hair. We spent the next several days gathering provisions and and resting at the camp of Twisted Hair. The first night I questioned him about the map he had drawn for Captain Clark of the falls and mountains to the north. He said that near those falls "white people" lived, from whom he had procured three strange artifacts that he showed to me. No one in our party recognized them or could divine their purpose or utility, save one.

The chief removed this ring from a small leather bag, strung on a rawhide strip, that he retreived from his lodge. Although his people wear many adornments of sophisticated design, this one appears to be of more advanced craftsmanship than any artifacts we've seen of native manufacture. The ring and setting have been expertly fashioned from precious metal or a bronze alloy, work you would only expect to find from a master smith.

As to the "white people" from whom it was allegedly obtained, it has to date

[1] This entire letter remains problematic. I can find no record of it in the original L & C journals or any mention of it among the voluminous correspondence penned by Lewis to President Jefferson.

Prior to the expedition Lewis had served as Jefferson's secretary for two years, lived in the White House and during that time became one of his most trusted confidants. Jefferson's father was a business associate of Lewis's grandfather, and the president had known Lewis since he was a boy, growing up not far from Jefferson's Virginia estate.

Because Lewis had experienced extensive contact with Native Americans during his youth, enjoyed cordial relations and often championed their cause, Jefferson personally chose Lewis to lead the Corps of Discovery. Lewis then selected as his co-commander his former commanding officer, the more experienced military man and explorer William Clark.

Jefferson's selection of Lewis was kept secret, as was the expedition itself. The Louisiana Purchase had not yet been completed during these planning stages, and the Corps of Discovery would be heading into hostile territory that three European powers—the

been our belief that no Americans or Europeans have preceded us into this part of the territory. It was also Captain Clark's prior understanding from the chief that we were the first white Americans they had encountered. This seems an assumption that we will now have to reexamine. Perhaps the chief is simply telling a tall tale and the ring was obtained through trade or barter from a French trapper moving through the area.

Twisted Hair became agitated when I pressed him for more information on this matter. He pointed to the symbol on the ring, turned it upside down and said something that our Shoshone guide couldn't fully translate about an owl, which one could say the symbol, viewed from that angle, vaguely resembles. That was all he would put forth on the matter. Our guide soon afterward told me in confidence that the chief had said the ring was related in some way to the "spirit world" they worship here. This "spirit world" is part of their pagan belief system and, from all I've gleaned to date, bears no relation to our Christian God; for instance, as I understand it, they might see an animal like an owl as in some way divine. It was my belief that not only the chief seemed to be withholding deeper information from us, as neither he nor my guide would elaborate.

Mr. President, I believe this subject may be pertinent to the matter which you and I discussed privately, prior to my departure.

It is my intention to venture north with our guide and a select group of men to find and explore the area detailed on the map drawn by Twisted Hair. Captain Clark will remain here with the remainder of our party and they will spend their time constructing canoes, employing a new method shown to us by the chief and his men. The chief has given me the ring mentioned above to take along, but with emphatic gesture indicated it should be left in its pouch and under no circumstances worn.

Yr. sincere and
obedient servant

Meriwether Lewis
— ⁀⁄⁄⁀ —

French, Spanish and English— had all targeted for their own expansionist colonial ambitions. The expedition would be fraught with danger from start to finish, security was paramount and time was of the essence.

Lewis's cryptic reference to a private conversation with Jefferson bears deeper investigation. He does elaborate, somewhat, during the following passage—TP

[2] On the face of it, it would seem this letter bears all the earmarks of an elaborate hoax … and yet, analysis does confirm this as the handwriting of Lewis to an almost certain probability. As this is one of the few "original" documents in the dossier, I have submitted it for independent carbon dating and chemical testing of both the paper and ink to see if it is in fact appropriate to the stated time frame of the early 19th century.

No mention is made of any side trip made by Lewis during this time frame in his published journals. However, the next entry in the official journals, authored by either Lewis or Clark, does not appear for six more days.

It has always been the opinion of Lewis scholars that this period of time was used for the construction of the canoes, and for rest and recovery, as many of the expedition had by this time fallen ill with intestinal disorders related to malaria —TP

[1] Let it be stated up front that there is no copy or record of this letter among the official presidential papers, but once again handwriting analysis and chemical testing of paper and ink suggest it is the work of Thomas Jefferson.

My attempt to track this letter led me to a cache of assorted and supposedly "lost" writings, a collection of unbound manuscripts discovered in the archives at Monticello in 1870 by the president's oldest living son, Thomas Randolph Jefferson. This cache was transferred to the care of the State Department at around that time, in a box labeled "Private—Unexamined."

I've accessed this collection—in the 1940s it was moved to a section of the Library of Congress that requires maximum security clearance—and was frankly astonished. Many of these writings have never been made public, as they contain the president's musings on a number of strange, disparate and esoteric subjects, among them the role of Freemasonry in the lives of the founding fathers, the "real

and present danger" to the young Republic, and Masonry itself, of Adam Weishaupt's Bavarian Illuminati—a perennial paranoid conspiracy bogeyman—and Jefferson's fascination with supernatural elements of Native American mythology.

Jefferson and Lewis were both high-ranking Freemasons of long standing, members of a fraternal organization that emerged in the 15th century. Its original purpose seems to have been regulatory, setting qualifying professional standards for stonemasons while serving as an intermediary for them with clients or authorities, much like a modern guild or union. Over the centuries, Freemasonry evolved into a worldwide fraternal body and expanded its membership far beyond craftsmen into statecraft and even the foundation of governments, including America's own, taking on an air of secrecy and even mysticism. Its closely guarded rituals and symbolism make it one of the longest-standing "secret societies" in known history.

continued on page 19

4 EXCERPT FROM A JOURNAL FOUND IN THE PRIVATE PAPERS OF PRESIDENT THOMAS JEFFERSON. UNDATED: LATE 1805 (?)[1]

No news from Lewis for a number of weeks, as his dispatches since April make their way back toward civilization at the merciless vagaries of various and irregular riverboat traffic, then onward and east by stage from Saint Lewis.

And then, among the packet I received today, this. What to make of it?

One can only assume it bears some relation to this: In addition to the Corps of Discovery's explicit and publicly stated mission, under confidential instruction from me, L. was to remain alert to the chance to explore any opportunity which might provide insight into the spiritual or shamanistic traditions of the northwestern tribal people he would encounter.

This instruction arose in part from our mutual study of certain volumes in the possession of the A.P.S. library that suggested anomalous and peculiar geological arcana might be encountered once one traveled farther west beyond the border of the Louisiana Territory into the uncharted lands of Oregon Country. In this instance, L. appears to have exceeded the letter of this secondary objective to an alarming degree.

Having read his dispatch a half dozen times this morning, I remain firmly convinced this must have been composed while in the grip of fever, perhaps even after partaking of some herbal or vegetative compound, either accidentally, or one given to him by some unidentified natives he encountered.

How else to explain these rambling and often incoherent ravings?

It begins with a more or less direct account of traveling three days due north from the main body of the Corps to a "certain location" that Lewis says was revealed to him on a recently drawn native map. At which point I am then treated to a disjointed assortment of passages that defy categorization, i.e.:

"Lights from the sky, the silvery spheres... music, like some heavenly choir... fire that burns but does not consume... colors unseen or unimagined, flowing from all things... gold, all gold, bright and shining...."

All of it written in a rapid scrawl. Many of the words illegible. Nearly a page of lunatic ranting about "the secret deep within the color red." Puzzling references to classical statuary, black lines and a thoroughly incoherent discourse on the "mysterious force B. Franklin had stumbled upon." Finally, the fragmented and feverish mention of an uncanny encounter with a "silent man."

His last words in this vein, at which point L. appears to have altered course and sailed back toward reason:

"I should have heeded his warning."

He goes on to write that he has destroyed the native map and all other record of his passage north.

Which warning, I wonder, and whose? The Indian chief "Twisted Hair"? Or the "silent man"?

In the next dispatch I received from him — not for many months later, one hastens to add — L. writes:

"Reunited with Clark, Oct 3rd. All our men getting better in health and at work at the canoes. We will soon press on westward. I have made no mention of what I have experienced above the falls. No one else who accompanied me appears to recollect any part

of it. At times, it nearly slips from my
memory, like a silvery glimpse of fish in
a river. I could have returned it to the chief,
but I have decided, for now, to keep it."

I am not at all certain what he refers to as "it"
here. But it otherwise appears as if L. at this point is
once again back within the confines of his sound mind,
a result I was heartened to have confirmed by the
subsequent dispatches I have just received from him,
nearly one year afterwards.

Whatever might have occurred during L.'s
"diversion," after months of strenuous but often
inconclusive wayfaring, within days of his return
the expedition resumed their journey to the west
with unerring certainty. In a matter of days they
made swift and certain passage on to the Columbia
River and within weeks found their way to the
Pacific Ocean. Now, nearly two and a half years
after their departure, they have arrived safely back
in Saint Louis.

ARCHIVIST'S NOTE

The principals of the Corps of Discovery returned to
Washington in 1807, where Lewis and Clark were greeted as
heroes. The vast collection of plant and animal specimens they
brought back with them kept scientists engaged for years.
Their celestial and geographical observations filled in the
map of what would soon become the western United States. The
expedition was judged a spectacular success.

As an immediate reward for his years of service, in 1807
Jefferson appointed Lewis as governor of the Upper Louisiana
Territory, a position he returned to St. Louis to fill. Two
troubling and difficult years followed.

Two sharply divergent narratives emerge from this period:
either Lewis began a steep descent into alcoholism and
incipient madness, or he became the target of an elaborate and
effective plot by powerful enemies already entrenched in the
developing Western territories to undermine his position.[4]

continued from page 14

While preparing for the expedition, at the direction of the president, Lewis had spent extensive time studying at the library of the American Philosophical Society in Philadelphia, founded by Benjamin Franklin—a high-ranking Mason himself. Lewis spent weeks there studying various physical sciences he would use on the expedition, and who knows what else. The Society at this time was rumored to also have collected the largest and most extensive library of ancient esoteric literature in North America, dating back centuries, on such occult subjects as alchemy and "transmutation."

But in none of the aforementioned archives, either public or private, did I find any other copy of the entry shown here. Which leaves the intriguing possibility that the copy in this dossier may be a previously undiscovered original—TP

[2] An update appears on an adjoining page, and if taken at the president's word, was written approximately one year after the previous entry—TP

[3] Does "it" refer to the ring described, and drawn, by Lewis in his earlier post?—TP

[4] Two additional entries in the dossier pertaining to Lewis's time in that office follow—TP

5 THE MISSOURI GAZETTE,
SEPTEMBER 2I, I808

BY THOMAS MASTERSON

It has been announced that on this date a charter has been granted for the founding of the first St. Louis Masonic Lodge, Lodge III. Meriwether Lewis, famous explorer and current Governor of the Upper Louisiana Territory is noted on the charter as its first Master.

The other thing that is now

This appeared on the bottom of the third page of the paper, as a minor news item. Not long afterward Lewis initiated William Clark into the St. Louis Lodge. Clark later founded Missouri Lodge I2 and remained active in Masonic circles during the remainder of his life. Jefferson may have initiated Lewis into the secretive fraternal order personally. [1]

These theories suggest that there were two esoteric organizations vying for future control of the developing nation: one with positive democratic intentions for its citizens (Freemasons) and the other malign (the Bavarian Illuminati), interested only in enriching its elite class at the expense of the general populace. Opposing ideologies, it might well be said, which continue that struggle to this day.

It should also be noted that Lewis financed and organized the publication of the Gazette, the territory's first newspaper, soon after his arrival, bringing a civilizing influence to a rough frontier colony that at the time of his arrival numbered no more than 300 people. Which suggests he may well have written the article shown here personally. [2]

I have occasionally underlined passages that seem to me pertinent to consistent thematic details.

[1] Theories about the arcane influence of the Masons on the early development of the American government abound. For instance, it's often suggested that the design for the country's Great Seal—the pyramid-and-eye-symbol that appears on the one-dollar bill—was passed to Jefferson one dark night by a mysterious hooded figure who just as quickly vanished. Almost a third of our presidents have been Masons. As I've discovered, one could fill a library with books written on the subject—TP

[2] What significance the creator of the dossier ascribes to the two men's participation in Freemasonry is difficult to yet fully ascertain, but may be hinted at by the following entry—TP

[1] No official headings identify who conducted this "inquiry," close to 200 years after the incident. The Archivist emerges as the most likely candidate—TP

[2] This was a common complaint of appointed officials serving in the western territories; the fledgling U.S. government was perpetually short of funds at this time and the new capital's bureaucrats were notoriously slow to make reimbursements—TP

[3] This references a traitorous plot conducted by Jefferson's disgraced former vice president, Aaron Burr—who had fled west after killing former Treasury secretary Alexander Hamilton in a notorious duel on the New Jersey Palisades—and various co-conspirators, which was exposed in 1805. This faction planned to seize control of a large area in Texas, Mexico and Louisiana in order to create a new and separate republic to be ruled by Burr as feudal monarch.

6 FINDINGS OF AN INQUIRY CONDUCTED
INTO THE DEATH OF
MERIWETHER LEWIS, 1989 [1]

On the evening of October 10, 1809, arriving alone on horseback, Meriwether Lewis took shelter for the night at an inn along the Natchez Trace, a primitive trail carved through the Tennessee wilderness, seventy miles southwest of Nashville.

Still the *governor* of the Upper Louisiana Territory, Lewis had left St. Louis and was en route to Washington, D.C., for two purposes: the first was to personally protest and, he hoped, overturn State Department denials of various reasonable expenses spent out of pocket in the discharge of his office, leaving his financial affairs in a precarious state. [2]

Lewis planned to attack this predicament directly: he had finally organized all of his and Clark's journals from the Expedition of Discovery. He was on his way to deliver them to a Philadelphia publisher and collect delivery money promised by a contract arranged prior to his departing for St. Louis to assume his job as governor.

His second and more secret purpose -- according to recently uncovered sources -- was to deliver to Jefferson and his newly elected successor, President James Madison, evidence of a conspiracy of corruption and usurpation being waged by the young country's political enemies in the Louisiana Territory. [3]

This correspondent now believes that while serving in St. Louis, Governor Lewis discovered that General James Wilkinson -- who had exposed Burr's plot to Jefferson -- had in fact been a principal in this traitorous cabal and exposed Burr's treachery only to save himself.

Wilkinson, the commanding general of the United States Army, had for decades been working as a double agent for the Spanish crown, during which time he ruthlessly destroyed the careers of multiple rivals through the use of forged poison pen letters, slander, secret ciphers and other means. None of this would come to light until Wilkinson's death in 1825.

He had also, previously, attempted to murder Meriwether Lewis. Wilkinson had betrayed Jefferson's confidence by revealing to his Spanish handlers the Corps of Discovery's secret expedition. While Lewis and Clark were in the field, Spain ordered Wilkinson to stop them by any means necessary. Three different times companies of Spanish assassins, over 200 in number, ventured north after the Corps of Discovery, once missing them near the Platte River by less than two days. If these men had succeeded in finding them, the subsequent history of the United States would have been drastically altered. [4]

Lewis left St. Louis carrying extensive evidence he'd uncovered of Wilkinson's past and present treachery, which he intended to deliver to Jefferson and Madison. Lewis had originally planned to travel downriver to New Orleans and from there by boat to Washington. So concerned was he about his real intent being discovered by Wilkinson -- then commanding officer of corrupt New Orleans -- that Lewis abandoned his route to Washington mid-journey, left the river at Fort Pickering -- near present-day Memphis -- and set off on horseback into the wilds.

Lewis wrote a letter to President Madison from Fort Pickering to explain his change in plan: "my fear of original papers relative to my time in office falling into the hands of our enemies induced me to change my route and proceed by land through the state of Tennessee to Washington." [5]

General James Wilkinson, commander in chief of the country's armed forces—before presidents regularly assumed that title—and Lewis's predecessor as governor of the Upper Louisiana Territories, had written to Jefferson, warning him of the plot, which resulted in Burr's arrest and trial for treason in 1807—TP

[4] I can verify this charge has been substantiated. A Revolutionary War hero who served as commander in chief under three presidents, Wilkinson is now described by historians as "the most consummate artist in treason the nation ever produced." Along with Burr and Benedict Arnold—both of whom Wilkinson knew well, conspired with and got the better of—they represent a triumvirate of treachery and deceit unsurpassed in the next 200 years.
All of these men are also, invariably, associated with the Illuminati strain of conspiracy—TP

[5] Verified. This letter exists—TP

The man who accompanied Lewis from Fort Pickering, as his guide and protector until Nashville, was Major James Neely. Neely had recently been named agent in charge of relations with the Choctaw Indian Nation in western Tennessee.

A recent posting that had been made -- unbeknownst to Lewis -- by none other than General James Wilkinson.

*LEWIS'S LAST NIGHT

On the evening of October 10, 1809, Meriwether Lewis arrived alone at the log cabin lodging known as Grinder's Stand -- the home of John Grinder, who was away on business. His wife, Priscilla Grinder, admitted Lewis. His servants, whom Lewis had sent out to recover pack animals that had run off earlier that day, arrived later. Mrs. Grinder noticed Lewis was armed with two pistols, a rifle, a long knife and a hatchet worn in his belt.

While eating little of the dinner Mrs. Grinder prepared, Lewis appeared agitated. After the meal, according to Grinder, he paced back and forth in front of the cabin, smoking a pipe and talking to himself. Mrs. Grinder described him as "talking like a lawyer" and ranting about his "enemies."

She also saw him continually "worrying" a small leather pouch he kept around his neck on a rawhide loop.

This went on past dark. When Lewis stepped inside, he appeared lucid and spoke kindly to her. But when she prepared a bed for him, Lewis refused to sleep on it, and instead made a pallet against a wall facing the front door with a buffalo robe, his pistols at his side.

After setting up Lewis's servants in the barn, Mrs. Grinder went to bed with her children in an adjoining cabin. She was awoken at three o'clock

in the morning by the sound of a struggle from next door --
heavy objects falling to the floor, cries, then a gunshot,
followed by another.

She heard Lewis shout "Oh Lord!" -- but claimed she was too
terrified to come to his aid when he then called to her for help
and water. She also claimed she saw him through cracks in the
cabin wall staggering around outside in the moonlight.

Mrs. Grinder roused his servants at first light, and they
found Lewis still alive, lying in a pool of his own blood. He'd
suffered two gunshot wounds, to the back of the head and the
abdomen, and his throat and arms had been slashed with a knife
or razor. Mrs. Grinder claimed that Lewis begged them to use
his rifle to finish him off before falling quiet and dying
shortly afterward.

The Indian agent who'd served as his escort, Major James Neely,
arrived at the inn before noon that morning. He identified
himself to Grinder as an associate who had been traveling
with Lewis since Fort Pickering but had stayed behind the day
before -- at Lewis's insistence -- to search for two horses that
had strayed into the woods. Why he arrived a full 12 hours
after Lewis's servants -- who'd been charged with the same
task -- was not asked or answered.

Making no effort to alert local authorities, Neely surveyed the
scene, claimed all of Lewis's possessions and supervised his
burial in a hastily built coffin on the property nearby. A few
days later, Neely wrote this to Thomas Jefferson and posted it
from Nashville: [6]

Nashville Tennessee
18th October 1809

Sir,

It is with extreme pain that I have
to inform you of the death of His Excellency,
Meriwether Lewis, Governor of upper Louisiana,
who died on the morning of the 11th and
I am sorry to say by Suicide.

Major James Neely

Jefferson published a public statement in response, which accepted Neely's tragic version of events without questioning. As a result suicide was quickly then and has ever since been assumed as the cause of Lewis's death.

Jefferson's opinion was based exclusively on Neely's account of the testimony given him by Mrs. Grinder, the sole witness to the tragedy. And, later, on one other.

*THE RUSSELL LETTERS

Jefferson's opinion of Lewis's troubled state was reinforced by only one source: a letter unavailable to the public for almost 200 years describing Lewis's journey from St. Louis to Nashville. The letter was written to Jefferson and signed by the commander at Fort Pickering, Lewis's friend Major Gilbert Russell, and dated two years after Lewis's death.

According to this letter, Lewis had arrived at the fort from St. Louis in a "state of mental derangement" brought on by despair about his economic troubles and compounded by bouts of heavy drinking. Russell states that the ship's captain told him Lewis had attempted suicide twice between St. Louis and Fort Pickering. Lewis had attempted to take his life yet again since his arrival, so Major Russell had seen fit to incarcerate him until he was "completely in his senses," at which point the letter concludes with Lewis, having regained his equilibrium, departing for Nashville with Major Neely.

The tone and style of this letter is completely at odds with an earlier letter written by Russell and received by Jefferson in the weeks after Lewis's death. This earlier letter makes no mention of suicide attempts or "derangement" and instead paints a warm portrait of Lewis consistent with everything known about him, saying that in the weeks before his death he appeared thoughtful, strong-minded and purposeful. Near the end of this letter, Russell refers to Lewis's death as a "murder."

The first letter Jefferson received has been thoroughly authenticated as being written in Russell's hand. [7]

A grand jury investigation into the death of Governor Lewis conducted recently by the state of Tennessee conclusively determined that the second Russell letter, discovered two centuries afterward, is a forgery.

Not only was the second letter forged, but this damning document came directly from the office of General James Wilkinson. Handwriting analysts found an exact match to the hand of Wilkinson's clerk, who wrote all his correspondence. The forged letter was not only sent to Jefferson, a copy was made and placed in Wilkinson's files, a common practice in the days before automated copying. That's where it remained until its recent discovery. [8]

So why was this second letter sent over two years after Lewis's death? There's a cold-blooded logic to it; it was written while Wilkinson was being court-martialed for treason over his own role in the Burr conspiracy, a charge ultimately dismissed for lack of evidence.

While Wilkinson escaped conviction on this and two other treason charges during his lifetime, it finally came to light after his death in 1825 that he had been serving as a double agent for Spain since 1787.

So, a reasonable conclusion: After being charged with treason, Wilkinson forged this letter to falsely establish that during his journey Lewis was in a suicidal state of mind, in case Wilkinson should ever be questioned about what role he might have played in his tragic death. [9]

*LEWIS'S POSSESSIONS

Major Neely and the trunks holding Lewis's possessions reached Nashville a week after his death. The trunks were sent on to Monticello, where they arrived at the end of November. A man named Thomas Freeman—operating under the orders of his longtime superior officer, General James Wilkinson -- conveyed them to Jefferson's estate.

[7] Verified—TP

[8] Confirmed—TP

[9] This sounds reasonable to me as well. I'm embarrassed to confess that I didn't know any of these details about Lewis or Wilkinson—and I was a history major—TP

Only one inventory of Lewis's possessions survives, one taken by Jefferson's secretary, Isaac Coles, after they reached Monticello. Coles's list makes no mention of the $220 with which Lewis was known to have left Fort Pickering. Nor does it include any mention of Lewis's pistols, hunting knife, two horses or gold watch.

Major James Neely kept Lewis's best horse after his death and was seen in public wearing Lewis's knife and pistols on his belt, as well as his gold pocket watch. (May we presume he also kept the cash? Affirmative.) This somehow made the local papers and was brought to the attention of Lewis's family. Shortly afterward, Neely was confronted by Lewis's brother-in-law, who requested the return of these personal items. He secured only the horse before Neely slipped from sight and from history.

Also missing from the inventory: a substantial percentage of Lewis's papers, which Coles described as having been "thoroughly rifled through." This includes the evidence of Wilkinson's corruption in Louisiana that Lewis referenced in his letter to Madison -- along with many of his journals from the Expedition of Discovery. It is firmly established fact that Lewis left Fort Pickering with these writings in his possession.

Also missing was a sophisticated cipher device, of Jefferson's own design, that Lewis had used for years to encode messages he sent to Jefferson. [10]

Most of the papers that went missing have never been recovered. When the "definitive" edition of Lewis and Clark's journals was published no mention or explanation was offered about the peculiar absence -- covering more than half of their two-year mission -- of so many entries written by the man of letters in charge of the mission. [11]

Also listed in the inventory: small leather pouch found hung around the governor's neck -- empty. [12]

Last among the possessions that were inventoried remains the most curious: Found stuffed in the pocket of his coat, the Masonic apron of the governor, bloodstained.

[10] Verified—TP

[11] The definitive accounts of the Lewis and Clark expedition were published in 1814. According to numerous scholars, many of the private diaries Lewis was known to have written during the expedition have never been recovered—TP

[12] This seems to describe the pouch that earlier may have held the jade ring—so it seems likely that Neely stole the ring as well—TP

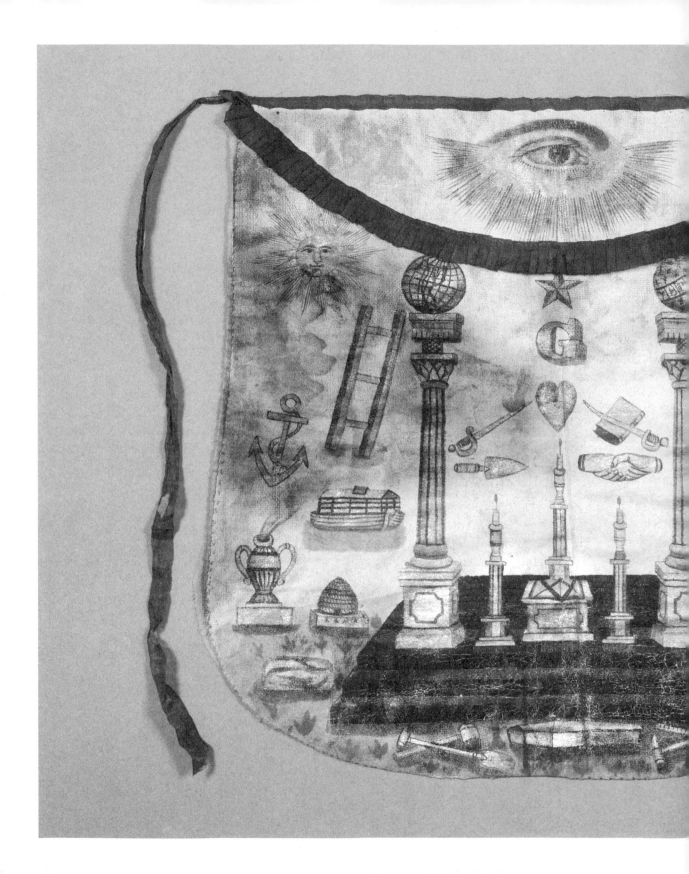

* Meriwether Lewis's bloodied
  Masonic apron today

A word of explanation: A version of this ceremonial garment is given, upon entry, to every initiate accepted into the Masonic Order. A symbolic version of a craftsman's tool belt, or in the parlance of the day an "apron," this object is worn during all Masonic meetings and rituals and is supposed to remain in the possession of the initiate at all times. Made from silk, backed with linen and hand-painted with the Order's arcane symbols -- including the "all-seeing eye," which also adorns the one-dollar bill.

This highly personal object was returned by Jefferson -- a fellow Mason -- to Lewis's mother. It was passed down through three generations of descendants before being given to the Masonic Grand Lodge in Helena, Montana, where it remains on display to this day. Its provenance is unshakable.[13]

With the permission of the Lodge, this correspondent was able to gain possession of the apron in order to perform a complete examination. Tests conducted on the bloodstains still visible on the garment yielded the following results:

DNA testing confirms -- through detailed comparison with samples from living relatives -- that the blood on the apron is not that of Meriwether Lewis. The blood on the garment belongs to two other individuals -- unidentified.

Is it possible that, after murdering him, his assailants wiped their own blood on this garment, sacred to Lewis as a Mason, as an act of desecration? Did this act betray some underlying antipathy to the organization that hints at their identity or motive?

*OFFICIAL INQUIRIES INTO LEWIS'S DEATH

Although no documents of the proceedings survive, a local Tennessee county inquest into the matter was conducted after Lewis's death. Surviving oral histories from county residents claim that a charge of murder against the Grinders and

[13] Verified—TP

"parties unknown" was returned but then dropped for reasons attributed to the jury's "fear of retribution." [14]

Shortly afterward, the Grinders disappear from Tennessee. After, it is said, having come into "a substantial sum of money."

*IN CONCLUSION

At the time of his death, Meriwether Lewis was 35 years old, a strong, sturdy individual, toughened by years in the military and the wilderness. He had survived deprivations unimaginable by modern men. During the expedition he defended himself and his men courageously in battle with hostiles, in one instance killing four attackers single-handedly. He performed one of the more remarkable services ever rendered to his nation, and his personal friend and patron Thomas Jefferson, in our history. You would need to combine Charles Lindbergh, John Glenn and Neil Armstrong to conjure a 20th-century figure with a comparable impact on the national psyche.

Proving himself an able political leader during his time as governor, Lewis might one day have succeeded his mentor as president, a job for which many believe Jefferson was grooming him. One has to look ahead to the assassinations of Lincoln and Kennedy to find a more shocking loss of such a universally admired public figure.

Under confidential orders from the president, Lewis traversed an untamed wilderness and returned triumphant. Based on my recent findings it is reasonable that Jefferson sent Lewis not only to find a "Northwest Passage" to the Pacific -- history's standard narrative -- but to investigate many strange rumors and claims stemming from this region: an unknown tribe of "white Indians," the existence of fabulous gold and silver mines, the possible existence of mastodons, sea monsters and other quasi-mythical beasts, as well as traces of ancient, vanished civilizations, including a mysterious race of giants. [15]

[14] Confirmed—TP

[15] I can verify that there are dozens of 19th- and early-20th-century newspaper stories from across the country detailing the recovery of various "giant skeletons"—usually seven to nine feet tall—most often from ancient burial mounds. These are believed to pre-date any previously known North American civilization. Curiously, in most instances, the bones were apparently collected by the Smithsonian Institution . . . and never seen again—TP

16 From which we conclude, as we build a profile for him, that the Archivist has personal knowledge of the region—TP

17 Another crucial glimpse into the mind of the Archivist. Determining this person's identity remains priority number one—TP

18 Both verified—TP

19 Agreed—TP

20 To which I would add: what happened to the ring in Lewis's pouch after Neely apparently took it? And what happened to Neely himself, who vanished for good a few months afterward? Why did Twisted Hair warn Lewis about not putting on the ring?

The section concerning Meriwether Lewis left me determined to know more. I can report that at the urging of Lewis's living descendants a grand jury was finally convened by the state of Tennessee in 1996, presumably after the dossier was compiled. After hearing expert testimony from two dozen witnesses in forensic,

On at least one occasion, referenced earlier, it seems Lewis encountered mysteries peculiar to this corner of the world, the upper Northwest. Mysteries that, this correspondent can personally confirm, persist to this day. [16]

With all humility, by the authority vested in me by my own confidential charter, this correspondent has endeavored to carry on the work begun by Captain Lewis: the spirit of fearless inquiry into enduring mysteries applied in the search for ancient truths that transcend and defy conventional wisdom. This dossier represents the fruits of that labor. [17]

As to the governor's "suicide"? Based solely on slanderous "accounts" offered by political enemies, this notion became by default the prevailing narrative of Lewis's tragic end. Mental illness was so poorly comprehended in his time that a more shameful fate for a hero of his stature is impossible to imagine. This shocking notion cast such a pall over his reputation that it nearly obliterated inquiry.

But not quite.

A U.S. congressional committee ordered an investigation into the matter in 1848. They also voted to erect a monument over his grave, which stands there to this day. Prior to placing the monument, his coffin was recovered, identified and briefly opened. A doctor engaged by the committee viewed the body, at that point still remarkably well preserved, and testified in the official report that "Governor Lewis almost certainly died at the hands of an assassin."

As scientific techniques improved in the 20th century, Lewis's descendants have pressed the government to exhume his remains for comprehensive forensic study, which may well reverse the 200-year-old calumny his reputation has suffered.

Two last telling details from that congressional inquiry: Mrs. Grinder testified that she witnessed Lewis crawling outside, begging for water, in the moonlight. I have examined records of the phases of the moon for that year: there was no moon that night.

Also: the carpenter who fashioned the crude coffin in which Lewis was hastily buried later told the committee that he had viewed the body and testified that he saw a wound in the rear of Lewis's skull. [18]

Which raises this question: Governor Lewis was renowned as one of the great marksmen of his era, so are we to believe that while attempting suicide, he would shoot himself in the back of the head ... and fail? That he then shot himself in the chest and again failed to finish the job, leading to several final hours of almost incomprehensible suffering?

It seems far more likely that Lewis had good reason to fear pursuit, as his behavior suggests, when he arrived at Grinder's Stand. It seems equally likely he suffered an assault at the hands of unknown assailants that night, suffering grievous and fatal injuries. The slashes to his throat and arms sound like what forensic science would classically describe as "defensive wounds." [19]

Given that the blood of two unknown men was found on his Masonic apron, it appears Lewis fought to defend himself against multiple attackers with every last fiber of strength in him.

Final questions: What motivated General Wilkinson and the Spanish to pursue the extermination of the Corps of Discovery? What were they so afraid of Lewis and Clark finding in the Pacific Northwest?

Did Lewis write about some darker secret in his missing journals? Was there something besides incriminating evidence he was conveying to Washington that inspired assassins to track him down in the wilderness, brutally murder him and then frame his death as suicide to deflect inquiry? [20]

ballistic and criminal investigation disciplines, the jury returned a finding that the remains of Governor Lewis should be exhumed and examined for the purpose of identifying the exact cause of death.

After initially denying this request, the National Park Service reversed its ruling in 2008 and recommended the exhumation proceed. In 2010 the Park Service reversed itself again and declined the grand jury's order to retrieve the remains. The only explanation they offered was that it would cause "untold damage" to a cherished historic monument. What such an examination could do to help restore the reputation of the man this monument was erected to honor goes unremarked upon.

So two centuries after his death the body of Meriwether Lewis, national hero, lies moldering in the grave, just off the ancient road known as the Natchez Trace. A seldom-visited site in a still-remote stretch of American wilderness, a more melancholy "tribute" would be hard to imagine—TP

* Here we see the broken column of the monument,
  designed to symbolize the tragedy of a
  remarkable life cut short.

* (L) Meriwether Lewis (R) The traitorous
  General James Wilkinson

*ARCHIVIST'S FINAL THOUGHT

I have recently verified one last curious aspect of this story. When Jefferson sent Lewis to the Northwest, he ordered him to keep an eye out for various strange phenomena often mentioned in rumors of the region, among them a tribe of "white Indians" and a race of giants. I have found dozens of strange references in the 19th-century American press to the recovery of skeletons of men in burial mounds that are between seven and nine feet tall. For instance, just one of many:

[21] All verified, and, I must concur, very very strange indeed.

The dossier continues on the following page, signifying the start of a new "section"—TP

WISCONSIN MOUND OPENED.

SKELETON FOUND OF A MAN OVER NINE FEET HIGH WITH AN ENORMOUS SKULL.

MAPLE CREEK, Wis., Dec. 19.—One of the three recently discovered mounds in this town has been opened. In it was found the skeleton of a man of gigantic size. The bones measured from head to foot over nine feet and were in a fair state of preservation. The skull was as large as a half bushel measure. Some finely tempered rods of copper and other relics were lying near the bones.

The mound from which these relics were taken is ten feet high and thirty feet long, and varies from six to eight feet in width.

The two mounds of lesser size will be excavated soon.

There is also no dispute that when Lewis and Clark returned east, they brought with them a chief of the Mandan tribe from the Dakotas named Sheheke-shote, aka "Big White." The Mandan are often mentioned in connection with a pervasive rumor from the early expansionist era: that somewhere in the upper Midwest dwelt a tribe of Welsh-speaking "white Indians," alleged descendants of a 12th-century Welsh prince called Madoc—

in Welsh, Madog ab Owain Gwynedd -- who sailed to America and followed the Mississippi north, founding a series of colonies along the way. Evidence for this is offered in the houselike structures in which the Mandan lived, which look like early Welsh villages, and the unusual boats they used, which closely resemble the Welsh seagoing "coracle."

This much is fact: Chief Sheheke-shote was very pale complected, with blue or green eyes, and he stood at least six feet ten inches tall. Sheheke and his wife and son traveled with Lewis and Clark all the way to Washington, D.C., where Lewis introduced him to Thomas Jefferson.

After an absence of two years and two attempts to return him to his people that required an army escort of more than 600 soldiers through hostile territory, Sheheke finally made it back to his Mandan village.

Sadly, it is said that his people did not believe the chief's stories of this powerful new civilization and its leaders that he had encountered. As a result Sheheke lost his standing with his nation and, a shattered man, died in a Sioux raid a few years later. [21]

*** NEZ PERCE HISTORY:

I THE STORY OF
     CHIEF IN-MUT-TOO-YAH-LAT-LAT
     (CHIEF JOSEPH) OF THE NEZ PERCE

In the 1870s, white prospectors discovered gold in the Wallowa Valley in the Pacific Northwest -- now central Washington State -- the traditional homeland of the Nez Perce, the people first encountered by Meriwether Lewis. Soon afterward, claiming that the U.S. government had already acquired the rights to their valley in a treaty with another tribe, General Oliver Howard was dispatched with a full brigade to escort the Nez Perce to a reservation. This was a direct violation of the government's existing treaty with the Nez Perce.[1]

[1] I can verify that the following is the statement made by Chief Joseph in direct response to Howard's demand that he must abandon his land and lead his people onto a reservation—TP

41

64   PLIGHT OF THE NEZ PERCE

"Perhaps you think the Great Spirit Chief sent you here to dispose of us as you see fit. If I thought you were sent here by the Great Spirit Chief, I might be induced to think you had a right to dispose of me. Do not misunderstand me, but understand fully with reference to my people's affection for this land. I never said this land was mine to do with as I choose. The only one who has a right to dispose of it is the one who has created it. I simply claim a right to live on my land and accord you the privilege to return to yours.

"In treaty councils the commissioners have claimed that our country had been sold by another to your Government. Suppose a white man should come to me and say, 'Joseph, I like your horses, and I want to buy them.' I say to him, 'No, my horses suit me, I will not sell them.' Then he goes to my neighbor, and says to him: 'Joseph has some good horses. I want to buy them, but he refuses to sell.' My neighbor answers, 'Pay me the money, and I will sell you Joseph's horses.' The white man returns to me and says, 'Joseph, I have bought your horses, and you must let me have them.'

"If we sold our lands to the Government, this is the way they were bought." [2]

Chief Joseph was surrounded in the Bear Paw Mountains of north

The Nez Perce had never before been a "hostile tribe" toward American settlers. After Joseph's refusal, in spite of his efforts to keep the peace, hostilities escalated and the cavalry were mobilized to finish the job. To avoid being slaughtered where they lived, or forced onto a reservation, Chief Joseph led his people -- a group of over 700 men, women and children, including only 200 fighting men -- on a desperate flight toward Canada.

2 CHIEF JOSEPH'S SPEECH TO
HIS PEOPLE BEFORE THE RETREAT,
SUMMER 1877

"I have tried to save you from suffering and sorrow. We are few. They are many. You can see all we have at a glance. They have goods and ammunition in abundance. We must suffer great hardship and loss.

"I will go now to the place known to our ancestors, seldom visited, the place of smoke by the great falls and twin mountains, to seek the aid of the Great Spirit Chief in this time of need." [1]

This sounds like a reference to one of their principal myths, common to many nations in the Northwest region, that refer to ancient relationships with mysterious beings they refer to as "Sky People."

Chief Joseph had never before been called to serve his people as a military leader. His role was closer to that of a spiritual leader or elder. Despite this lack of military experience, when he returned from this mysterious "pilgrimage" Chief Joseph led his people on one of the great tactical retreats in history, during which they engaged in a series of 13 battles or skirmishes against more than 2,000 soldiers, cavalry and artillery under the command of General Howard.

[1] This sounds similar to the place visited by Lewis and Chief Twisted Hair, an ancestor of Joseph's—TP

3 DISPATCH FROM GENERAL OLIVER HOWARD
TO COLONEL NELSON MILES AT
FORT KEOGH, AUGUST 1877

"Joseph and his band have eluded our troops and he is now continuing his retreat toward British Columbia. I shall never forget the actual pass through which he made his exit into Clark Basin near Hart Mountain. He seemed to travel through the mountain itself-- by way of the dry bed of what was usually a mountain torrent, with such precipitous walls on either side that it was like going through a gigantic rough railroad tunnel. According to my scouts there had been water running through that channel just days before.

"I had troops stationed at Hart Mountain in accordance with instructions, ready and watching for them, but at daybreak, a giant cloud of smoke or dust appeared to the east. My men rode in pursuit, believing that Joseph's whole body had got past him, and followed this long dust trail, abandoning the mouth of the pass. Once they had passed on, Joseph led his people out of the tunnel through the mountain. By the time we reached the spot a day later, a river once again flowed through that channel.

"We believe he is aiming at refuge with Sitting Bull. He is traveling with women and children and wounded at a rate of about twenty-five miles a day; but he regulates his gait by ours. We will lessen our speed to about twelve miles a day and he will also slow down. Please at once take a diagonal line to head him off with all the force at your command, and when you have intercepted him send word to me immediately and I will by forced marching unite with you." [1]

[1] Verified—TP

4 THE TURNING POINT, ACCORDING TO
    COLONEL MILES, THE COMMANDER WHO
    CUT OFF JOSEPH'S RETREAT

"At a desperate point in our pursuit, our forces encountered a mountain man, a familiar figure who had lived for decades in these parts named 'Liver-Eating' Johnson. Johnson, who claimed to have knowledge of Indian ways and what he called 'the source of Joseph's power,' led us a roundabout way in forced march to a position in the Bear Paws that put us in position to cut off the line of Joseph's northerly retreat."

Liver-Eating Johnson

After II weeks, having never lost a battle against this vastly superior force, only 30 miles from the Canadian border and freedom, Chief Joseph was surrounded in the Bear Paw Mountains of northern Montana. After a five-day battle, only 87 of his warriors remained. Rather than risk the lives of the surviving 350 women and children, Joseph chose to surrender.[1]

[1] Verified—TP

[1] Verified as Captain Wood's account of Joseph's surrender. If I may, a personal reaction here: This seems to offer a clear mythologizing—i.e., expansion—of Chief Joseph's authentically heroic struggle. We're asked to believe that a "pilgrimage" to consult with some totemic deity—perhaps one of the "Sky People" referenced earlier?—gave Joseph the power to travel through mountains and create traveling clouds of smoke to misdirect their enemies. He seems to be referring to the same or a similar location earlier visited by Lewis—which prompted the hallucinogenic encounter he wrote about to Jefferson—allegedly in the Twin Peaks vicinity.

For the record, let me state that I am secular and a skeptic by nature. Intimations of the supernatural are always easier to report or suggest than verify, particularly with events that took place over 150 years ago. Show me the science, please—TP

5 CHIEF JOSEPH'S SPEECH AT THE SURRENDER TO GENERAL HOWARD, OCTOBER 5, 1877[1]

Thus ended the last war between the United States and a Native American nation.

Chief Joseph *(left)* pleaded his case to General Howard *(right)*.

Joseph threw himself off his horse, draped his blanket about him and, carrying his rifle in the hollow of one arm, changed from the stooped attitude in which he had been listening, held himself very erect, and with a quiet pride, not exactly defiance, advanced toward General Howard and held out his rifle in token of submission. Although he spoke good English, in order to be understood by his own people Joseph spoke to Howard through an interpreter:

"Tell General Howard I know his heart. What he told me before, I have in my heart. I am tired of fighting. Our chiefs are killed. The old men are all dead. My brother who led the young men is dead. It is cold and we have no blankets. Our little children are freezing to death. My people, some of them, have run away to the hills and have no blankets, no food. No one knows where they are—perhaps freezing to death. I want to have time to look for my children and see how many I can find. Maybe I shall find them among the dead.

"Hear me, my chiefs. I am tired. My heart is sick and sad. I have fought, but from where the sun now stands, I will fight no more forever."

```
*6*  STATEMENT  BY
     GENERAL  HOWARD'S  ADJUTANT,
     CAPTAIN  CHARLES  ERSKINE  WOOD
```

Joseph and 400 followers were taken on unheated railcars to Fort Leavenworth, Kansas, where they were held in a prisoner-of-war camp for eight months. The following summer, the survivors were taken by rail to a reservation in Oklahoma that was little more than a concentration camp. By that time, over half of the Nez Perce had died of epidemic diseases.

For the next 3I years, Chief Joseph fought for his nation's cause and met with three different presidents to argue his case. Captain Erskine Wood, good as his word, tried to carry on the fight for justice for them. He resigned from the army, practiced law in Portland and fought to get the matter before Congress. He eventually raised the money to bring Joseph to Washington to speak for himself.[1]

[1] Verified—TP

Colonel Miles had had two conferences with Joseph before we arrived. In them he had promised in clear terms that if Joseph surrendered, he and his people would be returned to their own country. If Miles promised this, it unavoidably became a condition of any surrender; that he must return the Nez Perce to their former lands. Every excuse made for not doing so—that it was for the welfare of the Indians, that the whites would take revenge on them, that it would bring on another Indian war—though perhaps good reasons in a way, clearly broke faith with the Indians and repudiated the conditions of the surrender.

General Howard instructed me to take Chief Joseph as a prisoner of war into camp and see that he was well treated, but carefully guarded against escape. I had Chapman translate this to Joseph and I nodded pleasantly to the chief and tried to look as if it were all friendly. I beckoned him to come with me, and he promptly came forward, and we started to walk back. When we reached his tent I told him I, myself, would see him again. I wished him good luck and hoped his troubles were over, and then left him.

It will be observed that, true to Indian custom, Joseph had not spoken for any of his other chiefs. That night Chief White Bird with his family and a few of his band escaped and finally joined Sitting Bull in Canada.

General Howard maintained that by permitting this escape Joseph had violated the terms of surrender, and so the government was no longer bound to return the Indians to their own land.

General Howard and I constantly differed on his position. He maintained that he had no authority to make any specific terms, that it was entirely up to the secretary of war and the president; and that Joseph had violated the terms in permitting White Bird to escape. I never have thought and do not now think these arguments sound.

Before he departed from the camp the mountain man Johnson told me the white man had awoken "powerful medicine" in Nez Perce territory by violating the many promises made to Chief Joseph. As a result, for the people who established claims and settled in the stolen Nez Perce territory, he claimed there would someday "come a reckoning."

[1] All verified. A more profound definition of the meaning of freedom is hard to imagine—TP

7 SPEECH MADE BY
CHIEF JOSEPH IN LINCOLN HALL,
WASHINGTON, D.C., 1879[1]

A PLEA FOR
PEACE & EQUALITY

IN-MUT-TOO-YAH-LAT-LAT

"CHIEF JOSEPH"

of the

NEZ PERCE INDIANS

speaks at the

LINCOLN HALL
WASHINGTON CITY, D.C.
14th JANUARY, 1879

Chief Joseph addressed a full house of cabinet members, diplomats, and congressmen at the Lincoln Hall auditorium in Washington City, D.C. For nearly an hour and twenty minutes he relayed the history of his people, the many broken promises, and the hardships and horrors his people face.

This transcription of Joseph's eloquent and moving speech is distributed as a public service message by

INDIAN RIGHTS ASSOCIATIONS

Philadelphia, Pennsylvania

Printed by LEA & BLANCHARD, Chestnut street.

"MY FRIENDS, I have been asked to show you my heart. I am glad for a chance to do so. It does not require many words to speak the truth. I want the white people to understand my people. Some of you think an Indian is like a wild animal. I will tell you about my people and then you can judge whether an Indian is a man or not. I believe much trouble and blood would be saved if we opened our hearts more. IT DOES NOT REQUIRE MANY WORDS TO SPEAK THE TRUTH.

My name is In-mut-too-yah-lat-lat, Thunder Traveling over the Mountains. I am chief of the Wal-lam-wat-kin band of Chute-pa-lu, or Nez Perce. I was born thirty-eight winters ago. My father was chief before me. He died a few years ago. He left a good name on earth.

The first white men of your people who came to our country were named Lewis and Clark. They brought many things which our people had never seen. THEY TALKED STRAIGHT and our people gave them a great feast as proof that their hearts were friendly. They made presents to our chiefs, and our people made presents to them. We had many horses of which we gave them what they needed, and they gave us guns and tobacco in return.

All the Nez Perce made friends with Lewis and Clark. Our chiefs told them how to speak to the Great Spirit Chief about the many mysteries of our land. With his blessing my people agreed to let them pass through this country and never to make war on white men. This promise the Nez Perce have never broken.

Our fathers gave us many laws, which they had learned from their fathers. These laws were good. They told us to TREAT ALL MEN AS THEY TREATED US; that we should never be the first to break a bargain; that it was a disgrace to tell a lie; that we should speak only the truth; that it was a shame for one man to take from another his property without paying for it.

We were taught to believe the Great Spirit sees and hears everything, and that he never forgets; that hereafter he will give every man a spirit-home according to his deserts: if he has been a good man, he will have a good home; if he has been a bad man, he will have a bad home. This I believe, and all my people believe the same.

If the white man wants to live in peace with the Indian, he can live in peace. There need be no trouble. TREAT ALL MEN ALIKE. Give them the same laws. Give them all an even chance to grow and live.

All men were made by the Great Spirit Chief. He has made his heart known to me. WE ARE ALL BROTHERS. The earth is the mother of all people, and all people should have equal rights upon it. You might as well expect all rivers to run backward as that any man who was born a free man should be contented penned up and denied liberty to go where he pleases.

I have asked your Great White Chiefs where they get their authority to say to the Indian that he shall stay in one place, while he sees white men going where they please. They cannot tell me. I only ask to be treated as all others are treated. If I cannot go to my own home, let me have a home in a country where my people do not die so fast. WHEN I THINK OF OUR CONDITIONS, MY HEART IS HEAVY. I see men of my own race treated as outlaws, driven from country to country, or shot down like animals.

We only ask to be recognized as men. Let me be a free man, free to travel, free to work, free to trade where I choose, free to follow the religion of my fathers, free to talk, think and act for myself — and I will obey every law or submit to the penalty. WHEN THE WHITE MAN TREATS THE INDIAN AS THEY TREAT EACH OTHER WE SHALL HAVE NO MORE WARS. We shall all be brothers of one father and mother, with one sky above us, and one country around us, and one government for all.

Then the Great Spirit Chief who rules above will smile upon this land and send rain to wash out the bloody spots made by my brothers' wounds upon the face of the earth.

FOR THIS TIME, THE INDIAN RACE IS WAITING AND PRAYING."

—IN-MUT-TOO-YAH-LAT-LAT
"Chief Joseph"

[2] To these intriguing anomalies, or coincidences, I will add one of my own. According to my research the mysterious mountain man referred to in Captain Wood's statement as "Liver-Eating Johnson" is the man on whom Robert Redford's character was based in the 1972 movie *Jeremiah Johnson* (an excellent movie, by the way).

After a life spent in the wilderness, the real Johnson died in an army veterans' home in Santa Monica, California, in 1900. His body was returned to Cody, Wyoming, for reburial in 1974—soon after the movie came out, not a coincidence—where the grave site is marked by the memorial shown on the following pages.

One final observation for me: After the surrender of Chief Joseph, Johnson told Captain Ernest Wood that because of the army's treatment of the Nez Perce, there would one day "come a reckoning." I believe the nature of that reckoning will eventually be revealed—TP

ARCHIVIST'S NOTE

In an agonizingly slow response to Joseph's appeal, six years later his people were allowed to move from Indian Territory in Oklahoma to a reservation in northeastern Washington. Once they arrived, the Nez Perce discovered they would be forced to live alongside the broken remnants of II other tribes. Joseph and the people of his nation were never allowed to see their homeland in the Wallowa Valley again.

Joseph died in Washington State in 1904, at the age of 64. According to his doctor, he died of a broken heart.

*IN CONCLUSION

Joseph's mysterious "pilgrimage" prior to his retreat replicates or echoes the "vision quest" experience of Meriwether Lewis in the "place by the falls and the twin mountains."

Is it possible that both Lewis and Chief Joseph may have had some sort of congress there -- physical, metaphysical or otherwise -- with "the Great Spirit Chief who rules above"?

If so, was this a direct encounter or did it require traveling to a sacred place that may have been indicated in the ancient Nez Perce map shown to Lewis? [2]

EDWARD CURTIS TOOK THIS PHOTOGRAPH OF

JOSEPH IN SEATTLE, IN 1903

JEREMIAH JOHNSON,
aka "Liver-Eating Johnson"

THE BURIAL PLACE
OF "LIVER-EATING
JOHNSON"
in Cody, Wyoming

[1] The Archivist's focus now
shifts to the history and
development of the town
itself. The following excerpts
appear to be taken from an
original handwritten journal.
Its author and the incident
discussed I can find no other
verification for, although it
appears to be the work of a
base and criminal character.
New entries are not marked
by dates, merely preceded
by a dash. The page and ink
both authentically date from
the period around 1875–80
—TP

*** THE TOWN OF

T W I N   P E A K S :

I OWL CAVE

Moving forward in time, it is important that we learn to
distinguish between mysteries and secrets. Mysteries precede
humankind, envelop us and draw us forward into exploration
and wonder. Secrets are the work of humankind, a covert and
often insidious way to gather, withhold or impose power. Do not
confuse the pursuit of one with the manipulation of the other.

In some instances, for clarity when the handwriting is
obscure, I have typed out the entries for ease of reading.[1]

— Six days north out of Spokane. Picked a good camp site near a big fast stream. ~~The~~ Panned it for placer and found traces of gold. Set up the tent and built a lean-to out of pine, of which there is much about. DB is ~~████~~ surveying the land here about, and we'll file claim with the land office soon. Don't know where DB picked it up but he knows the ropes.

— A week of searching for this mine and it sure ain't where it said so on ~~██~~ that map we took off that fella in Yakima. A cave with vanes of gold, thick as bridge cable, he tole us. No such luck yet. But there's landmarks on that map

we seen already, so whoever drawn
it up — and we ~~know~~ no it
weren't him; he said an Injun
give it to him — no doubt they ~~had~~
been in these parts previous. Denver
Bob thinks this means they wrote
down where the cave was a bit off
the mark so no jasper who just
stole a glance at it could find it.

This is Injun country, no doubt.
No runins with em yet ~~#~~ but we seen
plenty a strange shit in these woods,
like scarecrows and stones all set in a certain
strange way and up in high places these
four-legged platforms made of timber,
lashed with leather. Denver Bob thinks
they're graves or some religious shit.
Might be. Two of em had bodies on top,
shriveled like mummies, picked clean,
eyeballs and all, by vultures which we
also seen plenty.

-- Still got stores fer three weeks, and there's game about and fish in the crick. Searched bout five square miles, no luck yet but DB says this work needs patients so we'll keep at it. Lots of caves about in these hills so we'll find it sure one day.

-- Found something but we don't know what. Might could be the mine we think. A deep cave, connected inside to many like passages. Up in the high woods a mile east of camp, at the base of a cliff. Opening's hid by woods, and there's rocks piled up at the entrance so it sure seems somebody was trying to hide it. Found one of them queer platforms near the entrance, that's how we found it. No body on it, but plenty of Injun shit, bundles of sticks and herbs, bones of some small animals. Not so smart, maybe, putting it so close to the cave like at, but what you expect from an Injun. Took most of the damn day to move them rocks out the way so we're worn out. DB tried to take a compass read to mark the spot -- had a hard time with it, the damn needle just spun around. Which to DB meant some kind of metallic deposit nearby, which he said was good.

Nightfall by that time, but tired as we was Denver Bob could not be bothered to wait. Gold fever, I call it, cause I got it to. We fired our lanterns up and Denver Bob went in first. Stank like hell. Followed that cave down a long snaky passage, a hunerd feet in. No gold in the rock, at least not here. Looks like this passage was dug out, though. Axe or chisel, maybe. Real deep dark in here.

Okay. The passage opens into a big ass chamber. Couldn't see the ceiling by the lantern light, that's how big. Natural cavern, we think. Bob got real close to the wall with his light on one side, I took the other.

No gold but DB called me over and we both held up our lights. On his side the whole wall's covered with painting I guess you'd call it. Different colors. Not like one picture, but a whole mess a strange shapes and symbols, kind of primitive. Injun work, no doubt, and they can't draw fer shit. Don't add up to any sense we can make of it.

I pull out the Yakima map and sure enough some of them same looking figures are on it. We figure we're onto it good now but who the hell knows what this shit means — there's no gold in it, thats for certain. Denver Bob ~~lit~~ lit a fire with some scrap wood while I draw some of it down proper in my notebook:

Two human figures, one big, one small. Two mountains. Some rain or a waterfall. maybe a lake. A bunch of circles everywhere, one that looks like the sun, one the moon, maybe. A symbol like fire. A circle of what could be trees.

This symbol shows up a few times:

Looks like a bird, maybe, but who know, its like a damn kid's scribbles. Coulda saved us a lotta trubble if them Injuns learned to write proper English and spell shit out. What the--

-- Damn, something screeched back in there then flue out of dark at us like a bat out a hell. We run all the way out, nearly beat my brains in on the wall once. DB dropped his damn lantern. Felt that thing right behind us breathing on our necks. Got out of there and night was thick on us. Thing passed straight over our heads and we hit the ground. Bird for sure, maybe a bat. DB thought an owl. If it were, it's the biggest damn owl I ever seen, and I don't care to see it again.

-- Moved camp down close to a river cause we heard from that cave a real peculiar whistling and what I thought was like moaning. DB thought it were voices and he got spooked. I tole him could be the wind to settle him but I don't think so. Every time I try to sleep I see that thing's eyes. Strange cause I can't recollect seeing em then, but I see em now looking at me when I close mine.

-- Woke up and Denver Bob was gone. Just cleared out during the night, I think. All his gears here, including his rifle, and he never went nowere without that Spencer. Figure I'll hold it for him. Fuck this shit. Still got my compass and I know the trail. Heading back for Spokane pronto.[2]

[2] I find a reference in Agent Cooper's original case notes to a similarly described location near Twin Peaks called Owl Cave—TP

ARCHIVIST'S NOTE

This journal was discovered buried in the stacks of Spokane's
Masonic temple. According to their records some loggers came
across it at an abandoned campsite in 1879, in a saddlebag on
the desiccated corpse of a starved mule. No human remains were
found at the site. A Spencer rifle with the initials DB carved
on the stock was in the saddle, but it's since been lost.

The "Yakima map" referred to in these entries was not found.
There's no name on the journal, but one Spokane local recalled
seeing that saddlebag on a horse belonging to a man named
Wayne Chance, a lowlife drifter from out of the territory who
often traveled in the company of another man known as Denver
Bob Hobbes. Neither man was ever seen again, which was judged
as no great loss to the community.

The cave referred to is now known to me as Owl Cave, in the
mountains east of Twin Peaks, part of what is now Ghostwood
National Forest. It had long been known to native people, but
as Lewis never mentions it this appears to have been the first
discovery of it by settlers. Geologically, it is part of an
extensive chain of lava tubes related to long-dormant volcanic
activity in the local mountain chain. To this day, much of it
has never been explored. [3]

Why the journal ended up in a Masonic lodge -- as opposed to
a local library or historical society -- is uncertain. Masons
established an early presence in the region, which, as in many
other places down through the centuries, led to whispers of
their participation in strange, ancient rituals. Perhaps they
were making investigations of their own. Interestingly, the
symbol most often employed by the Masons' nemesis "lodge" -- the
aforementioned Illuminati -- is the owl. [4]

[3] Another indication that
the Archivist has personal
knowledge of the area—TP

[4] This is confirmed, and the
image depicted is authentic
—TP

2 LOGGING MANIA

With the arrival of "civilization," inevitably, the exploitation
of the land by its new inhabitants commenced.

1

THE QUICKSILVER ADVANCE of regional industry over the past few decades is a story well known to all. The key to its success to the advancement of our community is no closely held mystery, any half-soused saloon puzzle wit can recount the tales of pioneer bravery, pluck and fortitude. The unvarnished truth, as usual, is a more bitter pill; a forced march conducted to a drumbeat marking the widespread rapine of our fair state's most vibrant and ubiquitous natural resource: the lush green forests which adorn our landscape.

Imagine a mantle of woods so deep and rich, stretching as far as any man can see; this was the arcadia which greeted our predecessors to the region. And with dollars in their eyes, they fell upon the forests with jack, hook and band saw like starving revenants gorging themselves on a wedding banquet.

The reaping continues unabated. What rapacious man could not harvest by hand, they have despoiled through caprice and carelessness. The infamous Yacoit Burn, of not so distant memory to the west of here, burned 200,000 acres of prime acreage, killed 38 mortal souls, and in the process destroyed 12 billion board feet of timber.

Let us also not forget, prior to this logging boom, the once bountiful fur trade in these parts that within three generations has reduced the local beaver and pine weasel populations to a fraction of their former abundance. Add to this dire ledger the perpetual gold and silver fever that to this day still holds this region in its grip.

The moment has come to pause and ask ourselves: What shall be done to curb this mad dash for Mammon and preserve our precious local treasures? Some few years ago, the Northern Pacific Railroad sold to German-born lumber baron Friedrich Weyerhaeuser one million acres of our magnificent forests. Employing many of our brothers—and by most accounts treating them fairly—while boldly bringing industry to far-flung corners of our state, has filled the coffers of the timber barons and the banks of many of our fine smaller communities. But in the dawning years of this new century, have we at last reached a point where it seems prudent to look within and query ourselves: At what price?

Case in point, the calamity that recently beset a nascent rural community north of Spokane. There in Twin Peaks, rival saw-mills, operating on either side of the river, both used to bringing their logs to market, each became caught up in a frenzied drive to outdo the other. Two houses, Packard and Martell, neither alike in dignity, directed their swarming minions to fill the river with their spoils, in the process denuding the surrounding hills. 2

And in so doing overwhelmed that waterway with a logjam of such girth and capacity that it reached back some seven miles, all the way to the well-known falls,

---

[1] This appears to be an early editorial from an unidentified newspaper, most likely the *Spokesman-Review* from Spokane, but no author is identified, and neither is the paper—TP

[2] The Packards and Martells were two of the prominent founding families of Twin Peaks—TP

while rendering the river below them virtually impassable to all other traffic.

This waterlogged stalemate persisted for two weeks, resistant to every remedy the companies employed. And then, one unseasonably warm winter's night, as a dazzling display of the Northern Lights painted the sky with colors the likes of which residents said they had never seen—cobalt and vermillion are not traditionally considered part of the Aurora's paint box—a catastrophic spark. Most say dry lightning from a passing storm struck. Other witnesses claim columns of fire descended from the sky, but whatever the source, the result was the same: that static flotilla of fir and pine soon erupted in flame.

Like a dire Biblical prophecy, visible for miles, the river burned for seven days and seven nights. Its coruscating glow could be glimpsed on the horizon, it is said, from neighboring states, even across the border into Canada.

Once the wind came up the fire spilled onto the shores on either side. The wretched town folk, deploying only a meager volunteer fire brigade to combat the conflagration, watched helplessly as the fire raced up the tinder-dry hills from the river's bank, destroying all in its wake.

Over half the wooden structures in the town of Twin Peaks—a community of hardy pioneers, merchants and home-steaders, barely three decades old—were lost. Six people died in the fire and large numbers of livestock and livelihoods alike perished in the blaze. At last, on the eighth day, the rains came and finally put an end to the blaze. The only positive to come from it, one might add, was the utter destruction of the logjam that had befouled that river. But at what cost?

In the aftermath, as is the human way, multiple fingers pointed in myriad directions, eager to attach blame. No doubt the consequences will play out in our court-rooms for years to come. Some souls were even quick to ascribe the calamity to a medicine man's curse supposedly laid upon these lands, or so the legends go, when they were purloined by our government from the native tribes.

But there is a more pernicious curse that has afflicted mankind from our origins that emerges as a much more likely culprit: the beast we call greed that resides, however dormant, in every human heart. The late Chief Joseph once asked how can the white man hope to survive in this land if the love of money fills their breast. The gravest battle we must fight as our new state and nation face the future must surely be the one between this ravenous beast that dwells within and the better angels of our nature. If Chief Joseph was correct in saying "we are all of the Great Spirit and we must listen when the Great Spirit speaks," will it one day be too late to change our path to the future?

EMPLOYERS

* The Night of the Burning River; man-made calamity or ancient curse?[3]

3 I have verified from other existing records that the event detailed above did in fact take place outside the then-unincorporated town of Twin Peaks on the night of February 24, 1902. The logjam on the river caught fire, spread onto land and the death count later rose to eight, as two victims died from complications a few days later TP

3 ANDREW PACKARD

The following story was published in the town's
first biweekly newspaper, the Twin Peaks
Gazette, in May I927.

TWIN PEAKS
GAZETTE

15¢

Issue 18, Volume 5   TWIN PEAKS, WASHINGTON   *May 14, 1927*

OUR STRANGE CAMPING TRIP

by Andrew Packard

N EARLY SPRING camping trip for our local Boy Scout Troop 79 turned into a bigger adventure than the six boys and Scoutmaster Dwayne Milford, 21, had counted on when they shouldered their packs and marched into the back country two weeks ago. Scout First Class Andy Packard, 16, penned the following account exclusively for the Gazette upon their return:

We set out early Friday morning and hiked up the trail into the Ghostwood about twelve miles and then turned left at Fat Trout Stream. We were heading to our traditional campsite near the Pearl Lakes where we planned to spend the weekend fishing, exploring and working on our Merit Badges.

It was a beautiful spring day and the weather looked promising; not too warm during the day, cool but not too cold during the night. After stopping to enjoy a refreshing lunch, we followed

Local Scout Andy Packard (16) finds something strange in the woods.

the stream north and reached our camp by the shores of Big Pearl Lake at three o'clock. We put up our tents, gathered wood for the fire and took a refreshing swim in the lake, which was still plenty cold, let me tell you.

A couple of us, your author included, were looking forward to completing our camping Merit Badge with the weekend's activities. We each brought a checklist of tasks we

needed to complete, determined in a friendly spirit of competition to achieve Star, Life and Eagle Scout rank before the end of the year. We split into two groups and while the first group worked on setting up the tents, gathering wood and organizing dinner, Scoutmaster Milford led this author and two of my fellow Scouts on a climb further up into the woods.

As we were hoping to fulfill the badge requirement of hiking an additional 1,000 vertical feet after making camp, Scoutmaster Milford led us up a steep slope to the east. This required a patient and careful ascent, as we followed a well-worn path that switched back and forth across the incline, varying from 7 to 10 degrees of vertical.

After reaching the summit we entered a stand of thick woods on a long, wide plateau following a path that Scoutmaster Milford said was an old Indian trail. Just before a clearing in the woods, he asked us to take a compass reading and record it on the maps we were making as part of our badge assignment.

This was the first strange thing we encountered: none of us could take a reading. The needles were swinging wildly from one side to the other—mine was nearly spinning in a circle—and they would not settle down. Scoutmaster Milford said he had observed this before during a scouting trip here once and not to worry; probably some kind of magnetic disturbance, maybe from nearby mineral deposits.

"Camping Trip" continued on pg. 6

PACKARD MILL ON THE

as business at the mill is as solid as

"Camping Trip" continued from pg. 1

We entered the clearing, where we planned to stop for some refreshment. A circle of trees stood in its center that we identified as sycamores. Not fully grown, more like striplings, twelve in number but uniform in size. There was also a strange smell in the air, like burning oil from a seized-up engine with a hint of sulfur to it. I noticed a small seeping pool of thick black sludge in the center of the circle and confirmed this as the source of the odor we'd noticed. We speculated that it must be a discharge from some kind of petroleum deposit. [1]

After only a few moments of standing in the circle, Rusty and Theo complained of feeling lightheaded, so Scoutmaster Milford moved us out of the circle and back to the edge of the woods.

At this point, a swift-moving bank of dark clouds slid in from the west above the plateau. It looked like a storm might be in the offing, even though none had been forecast, so we put on our rain ponchos. Scouts, you may know, are always prepared for such occurrences.

The air around us grew noticeably darker. It also suddenly got much colder—on my thermometer I recorded a drop of over ten degrees—and then the wind came up, strong and gusty, stirring the trees around us.

I looked back and noticed what appeared to be something moving in the thick woods on the far side of the circle of trees. Scoutmaster Milford suggested it might be best to head back down to camp. I said it might have been the wind moving the trees. He agreed, but said calmly that since bears, wolves and even an occasional cougar are seen in these parts, it was better to be safe than sorry.

(Scoutmaster Milford, it should be noted, always maintains a calm demeanor under any circumstances, and I predict that one day he will be a leader not just of scouts, but of men.)

We made our way back down the slope toward camp as the rain began to fall. I heard a peculiar whistling sound coming from the woods above, and when I pointed it out the others heard it too. I could not identify it as any bird song I was familiar with, which surprised me, as I already have a Merit Badge in

something fierce. Thunder rumbled, and peeking out a flap, we saw lightning fire up the dark sky; it was heading our way. The surface of Pearl Lake danced with hammering rain.

We passed the time by recounting the story of our hike. Scoutmaster Milford lit a Coleman lantern and entertained us with a local ghost story involving Owl Cave and a one-armed stranger, but when Sherm, our youngest scout, became visibly distressed, he wisely declined to recount its colorful conclusion. (I

"Scoutmaster Milford...always maintains a calm demeanor under any circumstances..."

Scoutmaster Dwayne Milford (21)

Wilderness Survival requiring extensive knowledge of local flora and fauna.

We made it back to camp at approximately 1700 hours, to find our fellow scouts had reacted in admirable scout fashion to the rapid and unexpected storm. All our provisions had been secured and we repaired to the larger of our two tents as the rain began to fall in sheets. (I joined them but not before setting up a rain gauge outside.)

The cloudburst that proceeded to assail us soon reached deluge proportions, rattling and shaking our tents

had heard this story on a previous campout and can attest that it is an entertaining, but spooky one.)

Two hours later the rain had hardly abated and it became clear we would have to do without a fire for our evening meal. We proceeded to lay out a spread of tinned meats and sardines and a few leftover sandwiches. Our impromptu meal received a delightful kicker when Scoutmaster Milford revealed he had carried in a six-pack of Nehi orange soda for us, and had earlier submerged them to cool in the lake. (Typical of his thoughtful nature, he had brought one for each of us and never for a moment thought of himself.)

I volunteered to retrieve the sodas, put on my poncho and made my way down to the lake where Scoutmaster Milford had specified. I noticed that it was getting on toward sunset, although with the heavy storm clouds it was nearly black as pitch already.

I found the Nehi orange sodas just where Scoutmaster Milford had said I would, protected by a circle of rocks from the turbulent water. As I pulled the last bottle from the lake, a startling lightning strike snaked out of the sky and struck the crown of a towering Douglas fir by the shore not fifty yards from where I was standing.

As I looked up, in the flash of the strike I caught a glimpse of someone standing at the edge of the tree line, not far from where the bolt had scorched the fir and briefly set it aflame. The figure appeared to be a man, although the image quickly vanished. He looked extremely tall, at least seven feet by my estimate. I did not notice what he was wearing but in the darkness it didn't really register.

What I remember most is that the figure was looking directly at me. His eyes possessed a peculiar intensity, as if lit from within. He didn't seem even the slightest bit startled by the lightning, which had struck much closer to him than to me, nor by my presence there. The tall fir beside him, which had caught fire before being doused by the rain, illuminated him for a moment longer and in that moment I saw the man turn and vanish into the woods behind him.

My first thought, as I struggled to make sense of this, was that he must be a lumberjack caught out in the storm, which I realized later didn't make sense; we were a great distance from the nearest logging area. I quickly gathered the sodas in my arms and hurried back to the tent, but in my haste I dropped one of the bottles, shattering it.

Once inside, I told the others about what I'd seen as I distributed the Nehis. My account was met with the usual skepticism and youthful joshing about "seeing things," but Scoutmaster Milford took a keen interest in my account and pressed for more details. Stealing a glance out of the tent flap, I noticed him undo the snap on the holster of his field knife. He shined his flashlight across the tree line but the beam made only the dimmest impression from this distance and neither he nor I noticed anything out of the ordinary. Although I still felt unnerved by the whole affair, I endeavored to put it out of my mind as I sat down to enjoy our "tin can" supper. (As the one responsible for the broken Nehi, I distributed the bottles to the other scouts and made do with water from my canteen.)

As we dined it continued to rain without interruption. We spent the remainder of the evening playing cribbage and studying our scout manuals, before retiring promptly at ten o'clock. I confess that even after the stimulating events of the day I had difficulty falling asleep. Once or twice I thought I heard a deep rhythmic thudding sound outside, like someone beating a distant drum that seemed to faintly shake the rocks beneath us, until eventually the steady patter of the rain escorted me to dreamland.

I was the first scout to awake. Checking my watch, it was a few minutes past 0600 hours. I slipped on my boots and stepped out to answer the call of nature. The storm had passed, leaving the landscape refreshed and aglow in early morning light that carried the promise of a pleasing day.

Scoutmaster Milford stood near the fire pit we'd never had occasion to use the night before, looking at something on the ground nearby. I joined him and we studied it together.

Although we'd set the tents on sheets of a high patch of flat granite near the lake, the fire pit had been dug nearby on a patch of dirt, surrounded by stumps for seating. Beside the pit, impressed into ground freshly muddied from the rain, was a footprint. Not any ordinary footprint, but one of immense proportion that might suit, say, a figure of over seven feet in height. It formed a depression four inches deep in the mud, suggesting a significant amount of force and weight. As we walked toward the woods, we noticed other similar footprints in the mud, but the distance between them suggested a vast stride exceeding even what one might allow for such an oversized figure. Scoutmaster Milford calmly asked me if I'd brought my Brownie camera along, and when I replied in the affirmative he asked me to fetch it.

Reproduced here is the photo I took of the first footprint we noticed:

I offer this story and my photograph not as unshakable evidence to persuade anyone to accept without question my account as the truth of these events. I encourage each reader to make up their own mind about such unlikely things. But for myself, I know I am left with a lasting impression that, to paraphrase the Bard Shakespeare who we studied in Mrs. Loesch's English class this year, there is definitely a lot more on heaven and earth than we dream about in our philosophy.

—*Scout First Class (and hopefully soon Eagle) ANDREW PACKARD* [2]

PIONEERING

as people from around the country

[1] There is a similar location in Cooper's case notes, a place called Glastonbury Grove. I have also checked all geological source maps and there are no known oil reserves in the area described—TP

[2] I can confirm that Andrew Packard was indeed a Twin Peaks High School sophomore that year. He came from a prominent local family, often referred to in local accounts as one of the "first families of Twin Peaks."

The Packards had founded, in the late 1880s, and still owned the biggest sawmill in the area, the Packard Mill, which was referenced earlier in the story about the "burning river." By the time this story was published, and for decades to come, the Packard Mill would be the largest employer in the township.

Andrew was by all contemporary accounts considered an upstanding, reliable individual. He

would later serve for decades as president of the Packard family business, and take many prominent roles in community organizations, including the Rotary, the Chamber of Commerce, the Optimists Club, the Elk Lodge, and—interestingly—the local Masonic Lodge—TP

[3] The majority if not all of which, needless to say, turn out to be false or outright hoaxes—TP

[4] According to town records, beginning in 1962, Dwayne Milford began serving 14 consecutive two-year terms as the mayor of Twin Peaks, a pillar of the community by any definition—TP

[5] Noted that the Archivist claims to have known Packard well enough to recognize his signature; a first. I have also looked into this curious "first death" reference and initial results were unsuccessful, but let's see if it surfaces again—TP

ARCHIVIST'S NOTE

As to the veracity of Andrew's encounter with this alleged "Bigfoot"-like humanoid, I offer no encouragement or confirmation. It probably sold a lot of newspapers. The Northwest would soon afterward become known as the home of the myth of Bigfoot, a reclusive giant usually offered up as some remnant of a "missing link" between humans and primitive man. Native people of the region, and for that matter around the world, tell many stories of such creatures, usually describing them as demonic beings like the wendigo of the Algonquian peoples or, in Asia, the yeti. Sightings continue periodically to this day.[3]

Much later in life, Andrew's path would take a strange and drastic turn toward the malfeasant, which may throw some shade on this youthful encounter, but let's reserve comment for the moment.

As for Scoutmaster Dwayne Milford, he also went on to a prominent local career. He worked for many years in the town pharmacy founded by his family and, after the death of his father, took over as owner and pharmacist shortly after World War II. This is far from the last we will hear about either man.[4]

The following excerpt was discovered among the personal papers of Andrew Packard, following his first "death" in 1987. This correspondent can verify, from personal experience of this individual, that the handwritten section across the top of the page was penned by Packard himself.[5]

6/21/1927

Dear Diary
This is the section of my
story that they left out of
the printed edition in the
Gazette. They told me at the
time that they ran out of
space, but I think it probably
had a whole lot more to do
with the fact that Douglas
Milford was, at the time,
living in sin with Pauline
Cruyo, the estranged daughter
of the owner of the Gazette.

We examined the footprints in the mud, and I took my photographs. Scoutmaster Milford, looking off into the woods, now told me a story about a camping trip his younger brother Douglas had taken in the same location six months ago.

Although both brothers had worked with the Boy Scouts for years, Douglas no longer served as a scoutmaster. Scoutmaster Milford told me the reason was that Douglas had recently been asked to leave the scouts after an unseemly incident -- having to do with said camping trip -- which Scoutmaster Milford said highlighted a "lamentable defect" in his brother's character. It was no secret among scouts that the Milford brothers had a complicated relationship, so I listened and asked no questions.

Earlier that year, Douglas came back from said camping trip with a wild story about having encountered what he called a "giant" in the forest. Given that Douglas had always been prone to "fanciful and chronic exaggeration," this latest example of a "tall tale" was discounted by Dwayne and everyone else.

That provoked greater protestations from Douglas, including an even more outlandish claim that on the same trip he'd also come across a "walking owl" that he told Dwayne was nearly as "tall as a man." Douglas also swore he'd captured photographic evidence of both creatures, but it turned out the film in his camera had been prematurely exposed. He blamed this on the darkroom at the Milford family pharmacy, suggesting that it was Dwayne's fault for improperly mixing the chemicals.

Douglas also said having the pictures didn't really matter because he had a photographic memory -- which Dwayne confirmed; his brother does have near total recall -- and remembered every last detail. In the weeks that followed, Douglas would sometimes vanish from home for days. Dwayne believed his brother might have been sneaking up to these woods again.

The next month Douglas brought this incident up at a Regional Scoutmaster Council in Spokane, interrupting the proceedings and demanding that unless the scouts launched an all-out investigation into the matter he would bring it before the National Scoutmaster Council. Dwayne tried to calm down his agitated brother, but sadly the evening ended with Douglas decking Dwayne with a right cross, at which point he was removed, kicking and shouting, from the Scout Hall.

This was followed by the council passing a unanimous motion to strip Douglas of scoutmaster rank and expel him from the organization. The resulting "brouhaha" brought deep consternation to the eastern Washington scouting community--not to mention within the Milford family--and all there agreed to strike it from the minutes of the meeting.

Scoutmaster Milford then confessed to me that since this episode, he and his younger brother had barely spoken. He told me Douglas had always been the "black sheep" of their family, showing no interest in the family business and flunking out of pharmacy school in Yakima, but sucker-punching his brother in front of twenty-three members of the senior regional council represented a new level of rebellion. Since that incident, Dwayne said that his brother's life had continued to spiral downward; Douglas was now managing a pool hall down by the river flats on the wrong side of town, where he'd "shacked up with a fallen woman," and I think I have a fair idea of what he meant by that.

But now, after what we'd witnessed ourselves, Scoutmaster Milford wondered if he'd judged his brother too harshly, and it was clear this weighed on him. Either that or, he said, maybe Douglas had followed us into the backcountry and staged the incident for spite, which, he allowed, "I wouldn't put past him."

I said that unless Douglas had figured out a way to broad jump 15 feet 12 times in a row while wearing size 22 shoes, I didn't see any way he could have staged what was in front of us.

I also added, for what it was worth, that whatever I had seen in that flash of lightning standing beside the burning fir tree, I did not believe it was his brother wearing a pair of stilts.

5 DOUGLAS MILFORD[1]

Many in town to this day believe it was no phantom "Bigfoot" in the woods that derailed the life of Douglas Milford, but the demon rum. Anecdotal evidence from residents during this period frequently mention Douglas and booze in the same breath, and this was during the height of Prohibition to boot. For a while there in the late 1920s, to state it more plainly, the younger Milford brother became the town drunk.

Douglas left Twin Peaks after the crash of '29 when the Depression hit, riding the rails, drifting from city to city, a man without a home, a family or any apparent purpose, a not uncommon fate for the rootless during that dire decade of the 1930s. Little is heard from Douglas until he next turns up in San Francisco, where he enlisted in the Army the day after Pearl Harbor in 1941. He spent the war years in a quartermaster's brigade in the Army Air Corps, island-hopping across the Pacific as the Allies turned back the tide against the Japanese.

In November of 1944 -- although his records throughout the war are frustratingly incomplete -- it appears that while stationed on Guam, now-Sergeant Douglas Milford was brought up on serious charges of black market trafficking of stolen Army property, primarily liquor and cigarettes.

But rather than endure the normal protocol of a court-martial, it appears D. Milford accepted instead an offer to "volunteer" into a special detachment stateside. [2]

After vanishing from the ranks in the Pacific, he next turns up as a buck private in Alamogordo, New Mexico, at the White Sands Missile Range in 1945. [3]

What exactly he was doing in this "special detachment" remains unclear, but one theory rises above the others. Although their

[1] A section on the "wayward" brother, Douglas Milford, now follows—TP

[2] I can confirm that those charges were dismissed— although he was demoted— and Milford was transferred to the base mentioned below—TP

[3] White Sands was the site of the first atomic bomb testing in the late stages of WWII—TP

U. S. AIR FORCE VOLUNTEER

AIR FORCE ENLISTMENT FORM

(Class..................one..................)

1. Surname .... MILFORD
2. Christian Name .... Douglas
3. Present Address ...... Box 12 San Francisco, California
4. Military Service Act Letter and Number 800255
5. Date of Birth .... August 11th 1909
6. Place of Birth .... Twin Peaks, Washington
7. Married, widower or single ...... married.
8. Religion ...... R. C.
9. Trade of Calling ...... Logger
10. Name of next-of-kin ...... None
11. Relationship of next-of-kin ...... —
12. Address of next-of-kin ...... —
13. Whether at present a member of the Active Militia ...... No
14. Particulars of previous military or naval service, if any ...... No
15. Medical Examination under Military Service Act: ...... —

(a) Place San Francisco   (b) Date 8 December '41   (c) Category A2

DECLARATION OF RECRUIT

I, __Douglas Milford__ , do solemnly declare that the
above particulars refer to me, and are true.

Douglas Milford (Signature of Enlistee)

DESCRIPTION ON CALLING UP

Apparent Age .... 32 yrs 4 mths.
Height .... 5 ft 9 1/4 ins.
Chest Measurements { fully expanded .... ins.
                     range of expansion .... ins.
Complexion ...... Fair
Eyes ...... Brown
Hair ...... Brown

Distinctive marks, and marks indicating congenital peculiarities or previous disease.

nil

RIGHT THUMB PRINT

O. C. .... Depot Btin.

.... Regt.

Place San Francisco   Date 8 December 1941

M.B.W 133
500M—8.17
1772—39—1158

existence has never been acknowledged, this may have been the unit assigned to various hazardous duties around the Manhattan Project, bearing the risk of possible radiation exposure.[4]

If that is indeed the case, Douglas survived the ordeal intact, because he next turns up at the Army air base in nearby Roswell, New Mexico, in July of 1947. Records indicate he was working at the base's PX at the time, now a corporal in the Army Air Forces, but questions remain about what he was actually doing there.

What is clear is that he was present on the base at the time of the infamous Roswell "UFO crash," and his name appears on a list of people who were interviewed by military officers in the days after whatever happened out there happened.

What follows is the only transcript of that interview with Douglas Milford this correspondent, through strenuous effort, has been able to obtain. [5]

The interview was conducted on July 8, shortly after the "crash." The interviewer appears to have been a regular Army lieutenant, but is not specifically identified in the fragment obtained. It also seems clear that, at the time, Douglas was being held in some kind of informal custody.

[4] Unconfirmed, but then the existence of this unit has never been officially verified—TP

[5] Verified as authentic—TP

[6] Milford may here be referring to his common-law wife, the aforementioned Pauline Cuyo, whom he had left behind in Twin Peaks at least 15 years earlier. I find no indication that Milford ever formally married anyone else in the interim —TP

000-73

INTERVIEW FORM
INT-F-000399

REFERENCE # 221-912

INTERVIEWER

DATE 8th JULY 1947

INTERVIEWEE CPL. DOUGLAS MILFORD

INTERVIEWER: Please state your name and rank.

DOUGLAS MILFORD: Corporal Douglas James Milford, Army Air Forces.

INTERVIEWER: Where do you reside?

DOUGLAS MILFORD: Here on the base, Roswell Field.

INTERVIEWER: Are you married, Mr. Milford?

DOUGLAS MILFORD: I'm married, but I wouldn't say I'm a fanatic about it. (chuckles) [6]

Hey, pal, can I have some java? What they're serving in the brig is like cat piss.

(pause; sound of pouring coffee)

INTERVIEWER: Please tell us of your experience in the early morning of July 5, 1947.

DOUGLAS MILFORD: Well, I'm working the early shift on the register, right, and all through the pre-dawn rush we're hearing scuttlebutt that some sort of top-secret test craft, or something even stranger, had crashed out in the desert during a thunderstorm—

INTERVIEWER: From whom did you hear this?

DOUGLAS MILFORD: Everybody really, nobody in particular, anyone coming into the PX. Word was they'd been tracking some strange bogeys on radar the past few days, but this was something extra heavy, you knew that right away. Then, about an hour before

[1]

dawn, the MPs and some hot-shot flyboy rush in and shut down
the whole cantina. Hush-hush. Mum's the word.

INTERVIEWER: Did you notice this officer's name or rank?

DOUGLAS MILFORD: Major, I guess, judging by the brass on his
collar, but none of us knew the guy and if he was wearing a
name tag I didn't notice it.

INTERVIEWER: What did you do then?

DOUGLAS MILFORD: I helped close up shop, then went out back for a
smoke, but found I couldn't stop thinking about this. Always
been that way. Curiosity eating away at me. The whole base had
a tit in a wringer, high alert. So I borrowed a Willis from the
motor pool, snuck out the back gate and drove out there myself
for a look-see.

INTERVIEWER: How did you know where to go?

DOUGLAS MILFORD: There was a convoy of vehicles scrambling out
that way, heading northwest. It was still dark so I just fell
in and followed 'em at a discreet distance.

INTERVIEWER: How far did you travel?

DOUGLAS MILFORD: Maybe thirty-five miles. You could see lights
over the hills ahead so once I got close, I slipped off
the road and came in a back way onto the sheep ranch where
everybody was headed.

INTERVIEWER: What did you see, Mr. Milford?

DOUGLAS MILFORD: Well I came over this rise—off-road at this
point—and looking down I saw this debris field stretched out
across a low plain for two, three hundred yards.

INTERVIEWER: What sort of debris field?

DOUGLAS MILFORD: A crash site, that was obvious. A big shallow
trench had been gouged into the ground, as long as a football
field. You could hear the hum of a generator and all around
it lights they'd set up were picking up pieces of bright shiny
metal, strange material, unconventional looking to say the
least. MPs were scrambling to set up a perimeter, and off in

[2]

RA

the distance, I spot a big clusterf*** of Air Force personnel
bunched around something.

INTERVIEWER: Could you see exactly what they were doing?

DOUGLAS MILFORD: Hey pal, can I bum a smoke?

   (pause; sound of cellophane rattling, the pop and hiss of a
   lighter, a long exhale of smoke)

Thanks. Now, I was a good distance away, over a quarter mile, but
they were gathered around some kind of intact craft that had
gone nose up into an embankment. Looked kind of like a flying
wing shape, like an old Curtis. I pulled out a pair of field
glasses and zeroed in. Saw they were trying to lift this thing
with a crane out of the embankment and move it onto a flatbed.

INTERVIEWER: Was it a plane?

DOUGLAS MILFORD: Couldn't tell.

INTERVIEWER: (pause) What else did you notice?

DOUGLAS MILFORD: Soldiers milling all around, real chaotic scene,
   and I noticed they're all wearing gas masks. Some of them were
   combing through the debris trail, but others were moving around
   things lying on the ground closer to the wreckage.

INTERVIEWER: Could you identify what they were?

DOUGLAS MILFORD: (a long pause) Your guess is as good as mine. Or
   better.

INTERVIEWER: What did they do with these things?

DOUGLAS MILFORD: They were loading 'em into the back of some
   ambulances that were waiting nearby.

INTERVIEWER: You never saw what they were.

DOUGLAS MILFORD: No, sir. But some of them they were putting into
   bags, and a couple they were loading onto stretchers. Then a
   big black car with a motorbike escort jams up and parks nearby.
   By this time they'd loaded the craft onto the flatbed and

were covering it with a tarp. This guy hops right out, ramrod straight, takes a gander at the craft, then marches right over to the ambulances.

INTERVIEWER: Did you recognize the officer?

DOUGLAS MILFORD: I didn't say it was an officer.

INTERVIEWER: (pause) Did you recognize the man who exited the car?

DOUGLAS MILFORD: Not at first. But when I got back I realize his picture is hanging up in the PX.

INTERVIEWER: Who was it?

DOUGLAS MILFORD: Is it okay to say?

INTERVIEWER: Just state what you saw, please.

DOUGLAS MILFORD: Looked to me like it was General Twining.

INTERVIEWER: General Nathan F. Twining? Commander of Air Materiel Command?

DOUGLAS MILFORD: Yes, sir, that General Twining.

(The recording is interrupted here, and then resumes with:)

INTERVIEWER: What did the general do when he first arrived on the scene?

DOUGLAS MILFORD: He takes a quick peek inside the ambulance then starts barking orders. They closed up the doors and drove off. No siren, but they left in a hurry. Then he walked over toward the wreckage. At that point, a wave of MPs pour over the hill behind me and I get knocked on the head. Next thing I know I'm wearing cuffs in the back of a paddy wagon. (Long pause.) Listen, no disrespect, sir, but would you mind if I spoke briefly to your superior officer?

INTERVIEWER: Why?

DOUGLAS MILFORD: You could tell him this isn't the first time I've seen something like this.

[4]

ARCHIVIST'S NOTE

The transcript stops there, leaving us to wonder what Milford was referring to here -- the incident at Pearl Lakes, perhaps? What happened when, or if, Milford went on to speak to the lieutenant's superior, and how far up the chain of command did this climb?

The presence of General Nathan Twining at the scene of the crash comes as no surprise. One of the most decorated officers of WWII, in the aftermath of Roswell he was closely involved with the formation of Project Sign in September of 1947, the first of three Air Force task forces dedicated to the official investigation of unidentified flying objects. [7]

From what we know of what was about to happen to Douglas Milford, it's probable that he may have turned a conversation -- perhaps with General Twining himself -- into a position with the group that was about to become known as Project Sign.

Their work began with an immediate effort to alter public perception of what actually happened at Roswell. Initial reports after the incident included details that no military officials in their right minds would ever have authorized for public release, including mention of the wreckage of a "large metallic disk" and the recovery of unknown bodies. Within days all those reports were walked back, witnesses were silenced through intimidation or bribes, and the entire incident was now explained away as "the crash of a top-secret air balloon." This debunking machinery would soon become standard operating procedure, and Doug Milford was right in the middle of it. [8]

Milford's life was about to take a drastic turn; as the reader shall see, he becomes a kind of Kilroy of esoteric phenomena. And because of a chain of strange events that occurred in the weeks just before Roswell -- detailed below -- Milford would very soon find himself returning to his home state of Washington.

For a very specific reason, and in a very different role. It begins here:

[7] I can confirm that shortly after the Roswell incident, General Nathan Twining helped compile and analyze the Roswell data for the first serious report on UFO phenomena, which led to the formation of the program described above, which was officially known as Project Sign.

Twining was later named chief of staff of the Air Force in 1953 and served as chairman of the Joint Chiefs of Staff—TP

[8] I can verify from internal Air Force documents that there was legitimate panic within the entire military that the crashed "vehicle" they found was actually a Soviet spy plane, of an advanced technological nature unknown to the West. Secrecy and cover-up, in the context of mounting Cold War tensions between our nation and theirs, seems much more likely than a "saucer from outer space" —TP

[1] I've confirmed that the following story appeared in the June 25, 1947, edition of the *Pendleton East Oregonian*, on the bottom of page one—TP

*** LIGHTS IN THE SKY:

I THE KENNETH ARNOLD INCIDENT

In December of 1946 a U.S. Marines transport plane
disappeared and presumably crashed in heavy weather on
Mt. Rainier. Ever since, military and volunteer civilian
pilots in the region had been searching for the wreckage...
and the $5,000 finder's fee offered by the military.
One of those pilots was Kenneth Arnold. [1]

there was "not much possibility, | checkup. Fourth Army head- | .... the evidence

Continued on Page 20, Col. 6 | quarters announced that a trial | justified trial by court-martial.

IMPOSSIBLE! Maybe, but Seein' Is Believin', Says Flier

Pendleton, June 25—

PROMINENT Idaho businessman Kenneth Arnold, who was working with the fire control at Boise and flying in southern Washington yesterday afternoon in search of the missing Marine plane from last year, stopped here en route to Boise today with an unusual story—which he doesn't expect people to believe but which he declared was true.

He said he sighted nine saucer-like aircraft flying in formation at 3 p.m. yesterday, extremely bright—as if they were nickel plated—and flying at an immense rate of speed. He estimated they were at an altitude between 9,500 and 10,000 feet and clocked them from Mt. Rainier to Mt. Adams,

arriving at the amazing speed of about 1,200 miles an hour. He judged their wingspan to be at least 100 feet across.

"It seemed impossible," he said, "but there it is—I must believe my eyes."

He landed at Yakima somewhat later and inquired there, but learned nothing. Talking about it to a man from Ukiah in Pendleton this morning whose name he did not get, Arnold was amazed to learn that the man had sighted the same aerial objects yesterday afternoon from the mountains in the Ukiah section!

He said that in flight they appeared to weave in and out of formation. "The first thing I noticed was a series of flashes in my

eyes as if a mirror was reflecting sunlight at me. I saw the flashes were coming from a series of objects that were traveling incredibly fast. They were silvery and shiny and seemed to be shaped like a pie plate. What startled me most at this point was that I could not spot any tails on them.

"I counted nine of them as they disappeared behind the peak of Mount Rainier. Their speed was so great I decided to clock them. I took out my watch and checked off one minutes and 42 seconds from the time they passed Mount Rainier until they reached the peak of Mount Adams. All told the objects remained in view slightly less than two minutes from the time I first noticed them."

ARCHIVIST'S NOTE

Occurring less than two weeks before Roswell, Kenneth Arnold's UFO sighting was picked up by the newswire services and quickly made national and international headlines.

Once again Army Intelligence and, in this instance -- for the first time -- FBI personnel were dispatched to investigate. The lead investigators filed this report, which has never been made publicly available:

SECRET
COPY

LOCATION: Hotel Owyhee, Boise, Idaho

INCIDENT: 4AF 1208 I

INTERVIEW
CONDUCTED: 12 July 1947

MEMORANDUM FOR THE OFFICER IN CHARGE:

      1.   On 12 July 1947, Mr. Kenneth Arnold, Box 387, Boise, Idaho, was interviewed in regard to the report by Mr. Arnold that he saw 9 strange objects flying over the Cascade Mountain Range of Washington State on June 25th. Mr. Arnold voluntarily agreed to give the interviewer a written report of exactly what he had seen on the above-mentioned date. The written report of Mr. Arnold is attached to this report as Exhibit A.

AGENT'S NOTES: Mr. Arnold is a man of 32 years of age, being married and the father of two children. He is well thought of in the community in which he lives, being very much the family man and from all appearances a very good provider for his family. Mr. Arnold has recently purchased a home on the outskirts of Boise, and recently purchased a $5,000 airplane in which to conduct his business, all of which is explained in the attached exhibit.

It is the personal opinion of the interviewers that Mr. Arnold actually saw what he stated that he saw. It is difficult to believe that a man of Mr. Arnold's character and integrity would state that he saw objects and write up a report to the extent that he did if he did not see them. To go further, if Mr. Arnold can write a report of the character that he did while not having seen the objects that he claimed he saw, it is the opinion of the interviewer that Mr. Arnold is in the wrong business, that he should be writing Buck Rogers fiction. Mr. Arnold is very outspoken

continued

SYSTEMATICALLY REVIEWED
BY JCS ON
CLASSIFICATION CONTINUED

SECRET
COPY

TOP SECRET SPECIAL HANDLING NOFORN

and somewhat bitter in his opinions of the leaders of the U.S. Army Air Forces and the Federal Bureau of Investigation for not having made an investigation of this matter sooner. To put all of the statements made by Mr. Arnold in this report would make it a voluminous volume. However, after having checked an aeronautical map of the area over which Mr. Arnold claims that he saw the objects it was determined that all statements made by Mr. Arnold in regard to the distances involved, speed of the objects, course of the objects and size of the objects, could very possibly be facts. The distances mentioned by Mr. Arnold in his report are within a short distance of the actual distances on aeronautical charts of this area, although Mr. Arnold has never consulted aeronautical charts of the type the Army uses.

Mr. Arnold stated that his business had suffered greatly since his report on June 25 due to the fact that at every stop on his business routes, large crowds of people are waiting to question him as to just what he had seen. Mr. Arnold stated further that if he, at any time in the future, saw anything in the sky, to quote Mr. Arnold directly, "If I saw a ten-story building flying through the air I would never say a word about it," due to the fact that he has been ridiculed by the press to such an extent that he is practically a moron in the eyes of the majority of the population of the United States.

    1 Incl. Exhibit "A"

    .FREDERIC NATHAN, SPECIAL AGENT FBI

    DOUGLAS MILFORD. S/A CIC 4TH AF [2]

ARCHIVIST'S NOTE

The presence of Douglas Milford as one of the investigators --
listed as a Special Agent for Continental Air Command, a unit
that supplied many of the personnel who went on to work for Project
Sign -- confirms that he was now swimming in deeper waters.

So we can surmise the following: Milford was immediately
recruited and commissioned in some unspecified capacity in the
aftermath of the Roswell incident -- and sent north at once to
investigate the recent Arnold incident. A memorandum from a July
8 meeting in the office of Chief of Air Force Intelligence orders
that "saucer reports be investigated by more qualified observers
of flying disks." A description for which Doug Milford, since
Roswell, appears to qualify.

2 KENNETH ARNOLD AND EDWARD R. MURROW

Shortly after the sightings, Ken Arnold was interviewed on radio
by respected CBS newsman and radio personality Edward R. Murrow.
The interview was heard nationwide. I've transcribed it here:

ARNOLD: I never could understand at that time why the world got
so upset about nine disks, as these things didn't seem to be a
menace. I first assumed that they had something to do with our
Army and Air Force.

MURROW: On three different occasions, then, you were questioned
by military intelligence. They expressed doubt as to the
accuracy of some of your reported observations.

ARNOLD: That's right. Now of course some of the reports they did
take from newspapers, which did not quote me properly, and in the
excitement of it all, one newspaper or another got it so snarled up
that nobody knew just exactly what they were talking about, I guess.

MURROW: But this is how the name "flying saucer" was born?

[2] Verified; the previous memo is authentic. Leading one to believe that "The Archivist" must possess some level of government security clearance – TP

ARNOLD: Yes. These objects more or less fluttered like they were, oh, I'd say, boats on very rough water or very rough air of some type, and when I described how they flew, I said that they flew like you'd take a saucer and skip it across the water. Most of the newspapers misunderstood and misquoted that too. They said that I said that they were saucer-like; I said that they flew in a saucer-like fashion.

MURROW: That was an historic misquote. While Mr. Arnold's original explanation has been forgotten, the term "flying saucer" has become a household word. Few people realize, Mr. Arnold, that you've also since that time reported seeing these same strange objects in the sky on three other occasions.

ARNOLD: Yes. Some pilots I know in the Northwest have reported seeing them on eight separate occasions.

MURROW: What is your own personal opinion now on the nature of what you and the others had seen?

ARNOLD: I don't know how best to explain that. But if they were not made by our science or our Army Air Forces, I am inclined to believe they're of an extraterrestrial origin.

MURROW: Extraterrestrial origin? You mean you think there's a possibility they may be coming out of space from another planet? I suppose that's pretty hard for people to take seriously.

ARNOLD: Well, I'll tell you this much -- myself and all the other pilots, none of us appreciate being laughed at. We made our reports to begin with, essentially, because we thought that if our government didn't know what they were, it was our duty to report it to our nation. I think it's something that's of concern to every person in the country, and I don't think it's anything for people to get hysterical about. That's just my frank opinion of it.

MURROW: So that's how it all began; that was the trigger action. Kenneth Arnold's story went scudding over the newswires. Radio and newspapers picked it up, and then within days the country broke out into a flood of "flying saucer observations." [1]

[1] I have verified that this interview was indeed broadcast nationally on CBS Radio. One is left to wonder how much of Arnold's apparent bitterness was colored or shaped by his interactions with Milford—TP

BUICK		CHEVY

BOB J. HART

PHONE SE7-0775

12528 28th ave NE, Seattle, WA 98125

PHONE SE7-0775

CUSTOMER'S ORDER NO. _____ DATE ___ **July 14** ___ 19 **47**

SOLD TO· **Douglas Milford**

ADDRESS **Twin Peaks**

Washington

SALESMAN **Bob J. Hart**

	MDSE. SOLD			MDSE. RETD.		REC'D ON			
CASH	CHARGE	C.O.D		CASH	CREDIT	ACC'T	NOTE		

QTY	PARTS NUMBER	DESCRIPTON	PRICE	AMOUNT
I		1947 Buick Roadmaster 4Dr. Sedan		
		motor # 14787169		1,949.00
		Carlsbad Black		
		Helical 3-spreed Manural Trans.		
		Air. Cond. & Htr.		
		Down Payment		1,949.00
		Amount to be Financed		0
		Title & Tag Fee		8.75
		price includes WA state tax		

RECEIVED BY

TOTAL **$1957.75**

554   ALL CLAIMS AND RETURNED GOODS MUST BE ACCOMPANIED BY THIS BILL.

ARCHIVIST'S NOTE

Shortly after interviewing Arnold in Boise, Doug Milford
apparently flew to Seattle. This correspondent has located
a sales receipt for a new 1947 black Buick Roadmaster sedan,
purchased at a dealership outside of Seattle on July 14.
The buyer was Douglas Milford, and he paid in cash.

What was Milford doing in the Seattle area? And where'd he get
the cash for a new car? Read on:

3 OTHER SEATTLE SIGHTINGS

It is worth noting that during the next few weeks in the
summer of 1947 over 850 reports of UFO sightings appear in the
collective U.S. media. Many of these may be attributed to so-
called "copycat sightings" -- a well-documented psychological
phenomenon. But over 150 of them survived closer scrutiny to
make it into the files of Air Force Technical Intelligence, the
office that would soon oversee Project Sign. [1]

Among those cases deemed legitimate was a sighting on July 5.
A veteran United Airlines pilot named Emil J. Smith, flying
a commercial DC-3 flight from Boise to Seattle, spotted nine
silvery disks -- the same number Arnold spotted -- flying in
formation nearby and monitored them for over ten minutes.
Smith's copilot and stewardess observed them as well. We'll
come back to Smith in a moment.

4 MAURY ISLAND

A few days before Kenneth Arnold had his encounter near Mt.
Rainier, an incident with even more disturbing consequences
was reported to the west, on the water in Puget Sound Harbor
between Seattle and Tacoma, near Maury Island. This is where
the story of all the 1947 sightings can be said to begin, and
where the role of Douglas Milford starts to assume firmer shape:

[1] One of these cases,
pertinent to this dossier, is a
UFO sighting in early
September 1947 involving
"flying disks" over Twin
Peaks, Washington. Initiating
further research—TP

On June 2I, a licensed Marine scavenger named Harold Dahl, his I6-year-old son Charles and their family dog were salvaging orphan logs -- a hidden menace to shipping; logging operations paid a healthy fee for their recovery -- from Puget Sound near Maury Island. At around II that morning they noticed six round unidentified aircraft hovering in the sky high above them. Alarmed, Dahl immediately made for shore and observed the disks through binoculars from there, also taking a number of photographs.

As reported by Paul Lantz in his story that appeared the next day in the Tacoma Times, Dahl described the crafts as a metallic gold or silver color, with a ring of six porthole windows around the perimeter. The crafts made no sound, had no visible means of propulsion and he estimated each of them to be approximately 200 feet in diameter: [1]

up in the sky," he says.

"Five of the craft were flying around the sixth, which appeared to be in distress and losing altitude," said Dahl. "Then an explosion erupted from the damaged ship, and a huge volume of two different substances fell to the water, raining down all around us. One of them was a thin, white metal that appeared light and almost looked like newspapers. The other was a hot, black lava-like rock, tons of it. Some landed on the boat, smashing the wheelhouse, cracking my windshield and knocking off the horn. One of the rocks grazed and burned my son's arm, and another directly struck and killed my dog.

"As I watched, the other ships sailed down after the damaged vehicle, which was fluttering like a falling leaf, looking as if in some way to assist it," Dahl went on. "One of them touched the falling ship with its hull— in what I would describe as a 'jump-start' maneuver. The craft stabilized and then all six of them soared up rapidly into the air, without making a sound, and disappeared."

Dahl collected samples of both substances from the boat and out of the water, then immediately made for shore and reported the incident to his supervisor, Fred Lee Crisman. He brought with him and showed to Crisman a number of the metallic fragments he found on board his ship that he'd collected inside a large Kellogg's Corn Flakes box. He also turned over the film he had taken to Crisman.

That same day, a local stringer in Tacoma for the United Press named Ted Morello picked up Lantz's story and put it out on the UPI newswire, where it gained traction nationally.

Fred Lee Crisman took possession that day of the metallic and rock fragments from Dahl. Dahl's son was treated that afternoon for second-degree burns to his right arm. After calling the Tacoma Times and giving the story to police beat reporter Paul Lantz, Crisman also immediately contacted a friend of his in the Midwest named Ray Palmer. [2]

5 RAY PALMER

Ray Palmer was the editor of a popular nationally distributed pseudo-scientific pulp magazine out of Chicago called Amazing Stories. The previous year Palmer had enjoyed his highest circulation by publishing a series of sensational articles by one Richard Sharpe Shaver, a Pennsylvania welder and former hobo, who claimed he had acquired secret knowledge of an earlier "progenitor" race of beings he called "Lemurians." Palmer called these stories, collectively, "The Shaver Mystery."

Shaver claimed it began in the early 1930s, when a peculiar frequency emanating from his welding gun allowed him to hear the thoughts of his coworkers. Not long afterwards he started picking up more sinister telepathic signals -- in effect "downloading" extended dialogues almost like transcripts -- from the aforementioned Lemurians.

Shaver's strange narrative claimed that these Lemurians lived in vast underground cities -- accessible only by caves and lava tubes, frequently set deep below dormant volcanoes throughout the world. Among these, supposedly, are Mt. Shasta and Mt. Rainier. They were a cruel, cold-blooded race in possession of incredibly advanced technologies that they used to closely observe human life, often interfering with and even

[2] No relation to the Palmer family of Twin Peaks—TP

tormenting, torturing and occasionally dining on humans. Chief among various other assertions Shaver made about their powers was telepathy, the ability to communicate silently to the minds of others, even at a great distance -- which was the method by which Shaver stated he had come to learn about them. [1]

Shaver wrote that the Lemurians had also developed advanced weapons he quaintly called "ray guns" that sound a lot like the concentrated light of lasers, which are now commonplace, but were at that time still 15 years away from human invention.

Even more dangerous than the weapons, Shaver claimed, was the creatures' telepathic ability to influence the minds of humans without their knowing it, forcing them to take actions against their will. The stories also claimed that the Lemurians had forever been opposed by a second race of peaceful aliens -- called "teros" -- with whom they were locked in eternal battle. Hailing from somewhere in the distant constellation of the Pleiades, these "teros" individuals were allegedly human-like enough in appearance to live unnoticed among the human race. He wrote that they would occasionally reveal themselves and confide in humans in order to enlist our help in the battle.

Soon after the Lemurian stories appeared, about a year before the Maury Island incident, Ray Palmer published a letter in Amazing Stories from Fred Lee Crisman. In it, Crisman claimed that during his service in World War II, while on a top-secret mission, he stumbled across one of these so-called "Lemurian caves" in Burma, and barely escaped with his life.

[1] Given that he exhibited classic symptoms of paranoid schizophrenia, it's not surprising to learn that Richard Shaver spent a fair portion of his adult life in and out of mental institutions. Which doesn't, necessarily, discount his stories, but encourages a distinct lean toward the skeptical. Shaver died in 1975, at the age of 68—TP

MYSTERY OF THE CAVE

Sirs:

I flew my last combat mission on May 26th, 1945. I was shot up over Bassein and ditched my ship off Cheduba Island. Captain ███████ and I hoofed it to Rudok through the Khesa Pass to the northern foothills of the Karakoram. We found what we were looking for. We knew what we were searching for.

For heaven's sake, drop the whole thing, you're playing with dynamite. My companion and I fought our way out of the cave with submachine guns. I have two nine-inch scars on my left arm from something that came at me in perfect silence. The muscles were nearly ripped out. How? I don't know. My companion had a hole the size of a dime in his right bicep. It was seared inside. How we don't know. But we both believe we know more about the Shaver Mystery than any other pair. You can imagine my fright when I picked up the magazine and saw you splashing words about the subject.

Do not print our names. We are not cowards, but we are not crazy.

This is indeed an important bit of infor-

[2] I can confirm that Fred Crisman was in fact an OSS officer serving in Europe and Asia during the war, and a licensed pilot in the Army Air Force Reserve at the time of the Maury Island incident—TP

I have been able to verify that Fred Crisman served in the OSS -- the precursor U.S. intelligence organization to the CIA -- during the war in various locations and flew scores of combat missions in the Far East. At the time of the Maury Island incident Crisman was still an active officer in the U.S. Army Air Force Reserve and, in addition to his marine salvage business, was working for the Department of Veterans Affairs.[2]

So, as result of this letter, Crisman and Palmer became acquainted. When Crisman told Palmer about the metallic fragments from Dahl's ship, Palmer asked Crisman to mail him some of the artifacts they'd recovered from the wreckage, which Crisman did that same day. Palmer also suggested they fly in pilot and businessman Kenneth Arnold -- who had just been in the news because of his UFO experience at Mt. Rainier -- to consult with them about it.

What follows is Kenneth Arnold's account of their meeting, subsequently published in the premier issue of Fate, a new Ray Palmer magazine that appeared in Spring 1948:

FATE

SPRING 1948 25¢

VOLUME 1   NUMBER 1

Many Other Startling Articles And Features

The FLYING DISKS

KENNETH ARNOLD
IN TACOMA

3 Verified. Smith's sighting
was mentioned in the Air
Force report cited earlier—TP

4 See earlier reference to
Paul Lantz, as the reporter
who broke Dahl's story
locally—TP

5 I have verified these
details of the B-25 crash.
As the crash occurred after
midnight on the day that the
Air Force became a separate
service branch, Davidson and
Brown entered history as the
first official casualties
suffered by the USAF. Why
they weren't able to follow
the others and parachute to
safety from the damaged
plane remains unclear—TP

6 The reader will recall
the purchase of a black
Buick prior to this by
Douglas Milford. The
physical description of the
man, however generalized,
could also pass for one
of Milford at the time—TP

I received a call from Ray Palmer in Chicago, who I did not know, asking if I'd be willing to investigate a recent incident in Tacoma and write a story about it for Palmer's magazine. I accepted his offer of $200 for the assignment. Without telling anyone other than my wife, I flew to Tacoma late on Wednesday afternoon, July 30th, and checked into Room 502 at the Winthrop Hotel. A reservation was waiting in my name, although I had not called ahead to make one.

I immediately called Fred Crisman and I met with Crisman and Harold Dahl in my hotel room that evening, and after hearing their story, and viewing the rocks and white metallic fragments they had retrieved from the site, I suggested we share the story with someone else who was used to investigating such things. They agreed and I contacted an experienced United Airlines pilot friend of mine named Emil J. Smith, who had recently had an in-flight disk sighting of his own, to share the information with him. 3

I also thought it best to contact the investigators from Military Intelligence and the FBI—Milford and Nathan—who had recently questioned me at my home in Boise about my experience near Mt. Rainier a few days earlier.

The next morning I flew to Seattle to pick up Captain Smith and bring him back to Tacoma. By the time we returned, two other Military Intelligence investigators, who had been contacted by Milford and Nathan and had flown up from their base in San Francisco—Captain Davidson and Lieutenant Brown—had arrived and were waiting for us in the lobby. That night we all met with Fred Crisman in my room at the Winthrop and he shared the story again with the four of us. Harold Dahl declined to join us for this meeting, but the reason why was not immediately relayed to us.

After Crisman left, we were discussing the strange events of the day when I received a phone call at 12:30 AM from a man who identified himself as "Paul Lantz from the *Tacoma Times*." 4

Lantz said he was calling to warn me that an anonymous informant had just contacted him at the newspaper to say that a meeting regarding the disk fragments from Maury Island was taking place in Room 502 at the Winthrop. He went on to describe everything we had discussed with

I'll never go into the air again without a camera!" declares Kenneth Arnold standing beside his plane the day after observing a train of nine mysterious flying disks.

4

Crisman in the room that evening, as well as what Davidson, Brown, Smith and I had just been discussing after Crisman's departure. Lantz's information was eerily accurate, as to the content of our discussions, and we were grateful for the warning. After we hung up, alarmed, Davidson and Brown suggested we move into the hall, as they suspected our room was under electronic surveillance.

Davidson and Brown, sufficiently alarmed, suggested that we give them the 25 to 30 metallic fragments for safekeeping. They told us that they planned to immediately launch a full investigation into the matter, but needed to fly back to their home base of Hamilton Field in California, north of San Francisco, that night in order to be present for ceremonies the next day, August 1st, which marked the official transfer of the U.S. Army Air Forces into a new and independent military branch, the U.S. Air Force.

After giving them the corn flakes box with the metallic fragments, we said our goodbyes and Davidson and Brown immediately left for nearby McChord Field, where they planned to take off for California in a B-25 at approximately 1:00 AM.

I was woken in my hotel room early the next morning by a call from a distraught Fred Crisman. He tells me he'd just heard on the radio that the B-25 carrying Captain Davidson and Lieutenant Brown had caught fire within half an hour of take-off. At an altitude of 10,000 feet the only two other people on board—one the crew chief, the other a sergeant on leave catching a ride home—had parachuted to safety, but the plane had shortly thereafter gone down near Kelso, Washington, with both Davidson and Brown on board. Deeply troubled, I told Captain Smith what had happened, and we decided to wait at the hotel for Crisman to join us. This news came to us a full 12 hours *before* the Air Force made the names of the victims publicly available. [5]

When he arrived Crisman told us that he had spoken again to reporter Paul Lantz of the *Tacoma Times*, who told him he had received *another* anonymous call early that morning, informing him that the B-25 which had gone down that night had been sabotaged or shot down. The informant also claimed that the Marine transport plane that had crashed on Mt. Rainier the previous December—the one I had been looking for when I first spotted the flying disks days earlier—had also been shot down. Crisman called Lantz and he immediately came to the Winthrop to discuss this news with me and Captain Smith. Lantz had already written an article about the anonymous call and the crash, to be published later that day, which he then shared with us. He also told us that during both times he'd spoken with him the caller would not stay on the line for longer than 30 seconds, apparently worried that the call was being traced. He also said that the military had already sealed off the B-25

Kenneth and Mrs. Arnold beside the Callair, three place plane used on his historic "saucer" flight.

crash site as well as the surrounding 150 acres, allowing no civilians, not even the Civil Air Patrol, into the area.

Crisman also recounted to us startling information he had received from Harold Dahl the night before, which explained his absence from last night's meeting:

Dahl said that the morning after his initial meeting with us, a man in a black suit had shown up at his door. Claiming to be some kind of government official who was investigating the Maury Island incident—Dahl seemed to think FBI, although no credentials were offered—the man persuaded Dahl to accompany him to a nearby coffee shop. Dahl described the man as of average height and average appearance. They drove there in the man's brand-new black Buick sedan. [6]

Over coffee the man told Dahl in such detail about the experience he'd had on the boat that it was as if he'd been there to witness it. "You were not supposed to see this," Dahl said the man told him. He went on to say that if Dahl "loved his family and didn't want anything to happen to his or their general welfare then he would not discuss his experience." And if anyone in the future were to ask him about it, he should admit that he had "made the whole story up." After the man drove him home Dahl discovered his son Charles was missing from the house.

The local United Press stringer, Ted Morello, also called in during this meeting, to verify information about the crash and our meeting with Brown and Davidson, and to tell us he had also received an anonymous call early that morning telling him the B-25 had been shot down. The caller went on to tell him to warn "Arnold and Smith that the same thing could happen to them." At this point, looking frightened, Fred Crisman quickly left the hotel.

ARCHIVIST'S NOTE

Young Charles Dahl would remain missing for five days until he allegedly called his father, collect, from a motel in Missoula, Montana. After safely returning to Tacoma, Charles said that he'd been in Missoula a few days and "had no idea how he'd gotten there." [7]

About an hour after Crisman left, Arnold and Smith received a notice from the hotel, slipped under the door of Room 502, that the Cooks, Waitresses and Bartenders Union, Local 61, American Federation of Labor, had declared a strike and that hotel services, including the elevators and switchboard, would be suspended indefinitely. Picket lines soon appeared outside the front entrance, prohibiting traffic in and out. Aside from a few remaining guests, the hotel was virtually empty.

From this point on, certain they were under surveillance -- and perhaps in physical danger -- Arnold and Smith locked the doors to Room 502, turned on all the faucets, turned the radio to maximum volume and spoke only in low voices. Arnold left the hotel only once that day, to buy a copy of the afternoon paper. As he had told them it would, Paul Lantz's article appeared on the front page of the evening edition of the <u>Tacoma</u> <u>Times</u>, under the headline shown on the opposite page.

At 5:30 that afternoon, Arnold and Smith received another call from reporter Ted Morello, who said he had just gotten off another call from the same anonymous informant. Arnold and Smith requested to meet Morello in person to discuss it, as they no longer trusted holding conversations on the phone or in their room. They checked out of the Winthrop Hotel and traveled to meet Morello in a back room at local radio station KMO, where Morello also worked part-time.

Taking them aside, Morello told them his informant had called to tell him he'd learned that Fred Crisman had been taken into custody by military personnel that afternoon and had "just been put on an Air Force transport headed for Alaska."

[7] If I read this correctly, in the timeline of UFO history, this is the first recorded appearance of one of the so-called "men in black," mysterious individuals who, allegedly, appear to UFO witnesses after sightings and intimidate them with veiled threats about what might happen if they reveal what they've seen. The clear implication here is that the man in black engineered the disappearance of Dahl's son to coerce Dahl into silence.

And, if so, one also has to ask: Is it possible this first "man in black" was Douglas Milford?—TP

The Tacoma Times

THE ONLY INDEPENDENT NEWSPAPER IN TACOMA.

TACOMA, WASHINGTON, THURSDAY, AUGUST 1, 1947

SABOTAGE HINTED IN CRASH OF ARMY BOMBER AT KELSO

By Paul Lantz

THE MYSTERY of the "Flying Saucers" soared into prominence again yesterday when the *Tacoma Times* was informed that the crash of an Army plane at Kelso may have been caused by sabotage. The *Times's* informant, in a series of mysterious phone calls, reported that the ship had been sabotaged or "shot down" to prevent shipment of flying disk fragments to Hamilton Field, California, for analysis. The disk parts were said by the informant to have come from one of the mysterious platters that nearly plunged into the Sound near Maury Island recently.

The two crash survivors have said that one of their engines burst into flames and that the fire apparatus installed in the engine for such emergencies failed to function.

Smith immediately called a contact at McChord Field and learned that an Air Force transport had taken off for Alaska within the hour, but he was unable to obtain a passenger list. They were also unable to reach Crisman at home. They called Harold Dahl, who said he had not heard from Crisman. Then, in extreme distress, Dahl hung up after telling them he didn't want to hear from them anymore, said he was sick of the whole business and if authorities ever asked him about it again he would deny having seen anything in the harbor, and claim it had been a hoax all along.

Morello then told Arnold and Smith the following: "You're involved in something beyond our power to find out anything about. I'm giving you some sound advice. Get out of this town until whatever it is blows over.

I think you're nice fellas and I don't want anything to happen to you if
I can prevent it."

After leaving the station, Smith and Arnold drove to Harold Dahl's address
to question him one last time. When they arrived they were shocked to find
the house at the address he'd given them earlier in the week deserted and
vacant, unlocked and covered with cobwebs; it was clear no one had lived
there for months. Deeply shaken, the two men drove directly to McChord
Field. During this trip, Arnold noticed that they were being followed by
a black Buick sedan.

Before leaving town, they had arranged one last meeting with an Army
Intelligence major at McChord. Treating the whole matter casually, the
smiling officer nonetheless took all of the remaining pieces of rock Fred
Crisman had given them, saying he would be sure to have them analyzed
"for the sake of being thorough." Arnold still had a piece in his hand and
was about to pocket it, when the officer held out his hand: "We don't want
to overlook even one piece."

"I handed him my piece," said Arnold. "This major was a smooth guy, but
not smooth enough to convince me that these fragments weren't important
in some way. I suddenly felt that no one had played a hoax on anybody."

They then drove directly to the civilian airfield. Arnold flew Smith up
to Seattle, dropped him off, then took off again and flew east, headed
back home to Boise. This is his account of what happened next:

6 KENNETH ARNOLD'S FLIGHT HOME

I started my airplane, warmed it up good, checked both my magnetos at full throttle, checked my gas lines, fuel valves and so on. Everything seemed to be in perfect order. Although it was rather late in the day it was only about a four-hour flight to Boise. When I got the weather sequence on my radio I knew I would have a twenty-to-thirty-mile-per-hour tail wind at the higher altitudes.

I was anxious to get going! I shoved the throttle clear to the instrument panel and took off, feeling a little unsteady about everything but glad I was going home at last. As I circled the airport, I could still see Captain Smith looking up at me. I headed for home.

I climbed to an altitude of eight thousand feet. I felt a lot better after crossing the Cascades and started to let down over the Columbia River with the intention of landing at Pendleton, Oregon, to get gasoline. Everything was running smoothly.

I landed at Pendleton and the boys there gassed up my airplane. I got out of the cockpit to stretch my legs but stayed close to my plane. I signed my credit slip and with a full gas tank was ready to take off again for home. I wasn't tarrying as the hours of daylight were numbered. I had navigation lights but didn't have a battery in my ship to operate them so had to make it home before dark.

I recall flipping my controls to indicate to the tower operator I was going to take off. The tower operator knew me and knew I had a receiver. He always came over the receiver to me if for some reason I should hold. Everything seemed fine. My plane was running well. Again I shoved the throttle clear to the stop. My engine roared and I was off the ground.

I reached an altitude which I would judge was around fifty feet. My engine stopped cold. It was as if every piston had been frozen solid. It never even gave a dying bark.

To take off and have an engine stop at that low altitude is probably the most dangerous thing that can happen in an airplane. You don't have enough speed to sustain you for a normal landing. Your only choice for putting her down is straight ahead, with no power and little or no lift from your wings.

Instinctively I dove the plane straight at the ground until I must have been within ten feet of the runway, then came back on the stick as fast as I dared in an attempt to level off without causing an abrupt stall. My little airplane came through. I was sinking fast but I set it down on all three points.

The shock was pretty hard. My left landing gear was badly bent and my left spar was broken in two. At the moment I didn't know what had happened. I thought the engine had frozen. I was unhurt. I jumped out of the cockpit, ran around to the front of the plane and turned the propeller. It was loose and easy. People came running out to see what was the matter.

I was curious to see if my engine would start again. I scooted around the wing and back into the cockpit. There I discovered what had caused my engine to stop. Until this writing, I have kept this a secret to myself. My fuel valve was shut off. I knew instantly there was only one person who could have shut that fuel valve off—and that was myself.

I turned the valve back on. One of the fellows swung the propeller. My engine started immediately and ran smoothly. I taxied my plane rather limpingly into the hangar. I was scared stiff.

I didn't tell anyone what had happened for the simple reason that no one would believe me. I was in no respect accustomed to turning my fuel valve off. I only did so when my plane was either leaking gas through the carburetor float or when I put it away in storage. I elected not to say anything to anyone until I had some logical reason within my mind to explain how I could do such a ridiculous thing. The care and precautions I had always exercised before taking off and which had become an established habit with me for over three years had somehow failed.

The possibility that my thoughts or mind in some peculiar way was being controlled or dictated to do this, or that some external force could have caused this to happen would seem perfectly preposterous to anyone who had not experienced what I had just experienced.

ARCHIVIST'S NOTE

After repairs to his plane, Arnold made it home safely, and for the next few years -- until publishing his book in 1952 -- kept largely quiet about his experiences. He later ran unsuccessfully for lieutenant governor of Idaho in 1962 and died in 1984.

7 HAROLD DAHL

Harold Dahl moved away from Tacoma after Maury Island, and lived peacefully until his death in 1982. He never spoke again publicly about these events, other than to maintain his posture that he had made it all up. [1]

8 FRED CRISMAN

Crisman returned to the Tacoma area from his mysterious trip to Alaska and the following month, on September 8, the Air Force revoked his reserve commission. [1]

A few months after his return, Crisman penned a second letter to Ray Palmer's magazine Amazing Stories in which he claimed that sometime during this trip to Alaska he discovered a second "Lemurian"-style frozen cave while in the company of a soldier he identified only as "Dick" and, once again, barely escaped with his life. But this time, he claimed, his companion "Dick" was not as lucky, perishing from wounds from a "ray gun" wielded by whatever beings they encountered. [2]

Crisman wrote a third letter to Palmer's second magazine, Fate, in 1950, in which he vehemently denied the Maury Island incident was a hoax and that the crash of the B-25, and the death of the two officers, proved it. He also claimed he'd given the two officers photographic evidence of the disks that Harold Dahl had shot on the day he first saw them. No trace of these photos or fragments of the Maury Island materials were ever recovered from the wreckage.

[1] One nagging thought I keep coming back to with Harold Dahl: Maybe it was all a hoax or maybe it wasn't, but would anyone have injured his own son and killed his own dog in order to sell the story?—TP

[1] Suggesting that Crisman suffered a rebuke or punishment from his reserve unit as a result of his involvement in the incident. I have verified that there were military brigs in Alaska during this period that were used for the kind of "off the grid" questioning more familiar from techniques employed in the early 21st century—TP

[2] Just an opinion: If it was all a hoax, Crisman strikes me as the man who orchestrated it—TP

[3] While researching Fred Crisman, I came across a strange detail that may be of interest only to me: Throughout the '40s and '50s there are repeated references to Crisman having a "working telephone" concealed under the dash of his car. Decades before such equipment was commonplace, how did Crisman have access to one?

Which leads me to wonder: What if Crisman himself had been the unidentified caller to both Lantz and Morello? It wouldn't be out of character, if the following is true—TP

[4] This appears to have been the conclusion of Ray Palmer as well, who tied Crisman in a later editorial to the assassination of the president of South Vietnam, Ngo Dinh Diem, three weeks before Kennedy was shot in 1963—TP

[5] The same can be said for Garrison's benighted and controversial case—Shaw was acquitted—dismissed by history as prosecutorial overreach and remembered more now as the focus of Oliver Stone's movie *JFK* in 1991. But there's no doubt Garrison stirred up a toxic, corrupt stew of conspiracies, right-wing fringe groups,

Although his military commission had been revoked, Crisman was recalled to active duty during the Korean War and served as a fighter pilot for two and a half years. After returning again to civilian life, during the remainder of the 1950s and '60s, Crisman worked as a teacher, school administrator, freelance writer and speechwriter for many political figures. He also hosted a radio talk show in Puyallup, Washington, using the pseudonym Jon Gold, usually promoting far-right-wing causes.[3]

Although this correspondent has been unable to confirm this as fact, rumors of Crisman's involvement with CIA as a deep cover operative -- from WW2 through the 1970s -- continued throughout his lifetime. If this is the case, it appears Crisman may have functioned as a handler, or "black bag go-between," a discreet conduit facilitating access between official higher-ups and freelance field operatives, offering deniability to both sides of any dubious transaction. In agency parlance, these men were known as "extended agents." [4]

Bearing this in mind, Crisman later became a "person of interest" in the investigation of the assassination of John F. Kennedy. When maverick New Orleans District Attorney Jim Garrison arrested local businessman Clay Shaw in 1967 for conspiring to kill the president, it was reported that the first person Shaw called after he was taken into custody was Fred Crisman, with whom he had apparently served in the OSS during WWII.

Garrison's grand jury subpoenaed Crisman shortly afterward. He appeared before them and was questioned about relationships he had with a surprising number of the Garrison investigation's targets. What emerged were a few more strange details about Crisman's shadowy activities: He had flown back and forth from Tacoma to New Orleans and Dallas 84 times in the three years prior to the JFK assassination. He held a diplomatic passport, vouched for by a senator on the Intelligence Committee. It also turns out that Jim Garrison had worked for the FBI after the war, in the Pacific Northwest, at the time of the Maury Island incident.

But aside from those details little came of Crisman's testimony in New Orleans and no charges of any kind were brought against Crisman by the grand jury. [5]

At the age of 56, Fred Crisman died in 1975 at the Seattle Veterans Hospital of kidney failure. An autopsy was ordered, for reasons that remain unexplained.

Three years after his death, Crisman's name surfaced again during the 1977 House investigation into the JFK assassination. A key witness in those hearings identified Crisman as one of the infamous "three tramps," a trio of vagrants who were arrested behind the grassy knoll above Dealey Plaza shortly after the shooting. Photographic analysis concluded, and this correspondent concurs, that Crisman did indeed resemble the shortest of the three men to a more than reasonable degree. [6]

Those who maintain that shots were fired from the knoll traditionally believe the "tramps" may have been the assassins. Although they claimed to have been "riding the rails" and had spent the night in a homeless shelter, all three men were well dressed and clean-shaven at the time of their arrest. All three men were also released not long after being taken into custody, and Dallas police claim to have since lost their arrest records.

Testimony from colleagues at the high school where Crisman was teaching at the time in Rainier, Oregon, seemed to provide him with a posthumous alibi for 11-22-63.

Whatever "official" role Crisman may have played as an operative -- and at this point the trail is too tangled and diffuse to reach absolute conclusions -- there is no doubt he remains a cog in the machinery of many enduring mysteries and conspiracies through the second half of the 20th century. [7]

Cuban exiles and whispers of unholy alliances between gangland figures and espionage agencies, all hovering around the pale ghost of Lee Harvey Oswald—TP

[6] At various times, Watergate burglars and former undercover operatives E. Howard Hunt and Frank Sturgis—who fit the same shadowy black-bag profile as Crisman—have also been identified as two of the "tramps." Along with, strangely, a career criminal and alleged mob hit man named Charles Harrelson—now deceased. Before dying in prison he actually confessed to the killing of JFK, although few gave the confession much credence. He was also the estranged father of well-known actor Woody Harrelson!—TP

[7] I have verified some of this. In recently declassified CIA documents, Fred Crisman has an extensive file—heavily redacted—which confirms that he did work as an active agent in the OSS during WWII as a liaison to British Royal Air Force, and later as an active CIA agent, assigned as a "special investigator at large" in the Pacific Northwest. His return to

continued on page 112

* The three tramps in Dealey Plaza,
  November 22, 1963

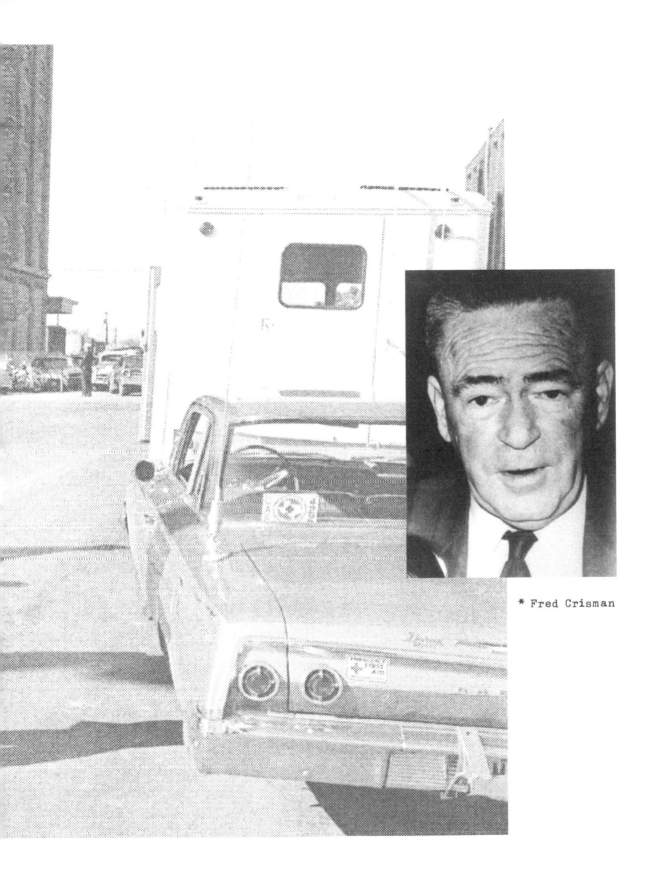

* Fred Crisman

continued from page 109

service as a combat pilot in the Korean War was largely a cover for his varied espionage assignments in the region, including Japan. The teaching and school appointments he later took on in civilian life were also selected as ideal cover for his ongoing CIA activities, as was a position he took at the Boeing Company for two years in the early 1960s. The list of black-bag or "dirty tricks"–style operations he was involved in is extensive. Knowing this makes his motives in the Maury Island case seem more than suspect—TP

[1] A personal note on Palmer: For his role in popularizing science fiction through his magazines, Palmer was memorialized by DC Comics, who in 1961 gave his name to the alter ego of a new superhero, the Atom—TP

[2] Leading one to ask: Had Douglas Milford made his way to Chicago?—TP

9 RAY PALMER

Chicago magazine publisher Ray Palmer, who died in 1977, adds one last detail worth noting. [1]

Just after the Maury Island incident, Fred Crisman mailed Palmer a cigar box filled with some of the metallic objects and rocks Harold Dahl had recovered. A few days after the crash of the B-25, Palmer claimed, a single intelligence agent visited him at his office unannounced. If the man mentioned which agency he represented, Palmer did not specify. He described the man as "average looking" and wearing a black suit, and that he "casually questioned me about the Maury Island incident and the Shaver-Lemurian articles."

Palmer said he showed him the box Crisman had sent him, but the agent -- whom Palmer did not identify by name -- seemed "remarkably uninterested" in it and Palmer replaced it in a locked file cabinet. The next morning, Palmer discovered that his office had been burgled, and the box and its contents had been stolen from the file cabinet, "where the agent had watched me place it." [2]

10 THE CRASH OF THE B-25

An extensive Air Force investigation into the crash of the B-25 yielded few satisfying answers. For instance: After the two other crew members parachuted, at an estimated altitude of between seven and ten thousand feet, why did Captain Davidson and Lieutenant Brown not follow them out and instead die in the crash? It's also worth noting that they never attempted to notify anyone by radio that their plane was in distress. Perhaps they didn't have time to react, or whatever caused the fire took out power to the com systems as well.

The surviving crew chief stated that "all persons aboard were in readiness to bail out after efforts to extinguish the fire proved fruitless." It seems most likely that a true Air Force man like Captain Davidson stayed with the plane simply to steer it away from populated areas to avoid civilian casualties, and lost control before they could abandon ship. In which case he is not only the first Air Force casualty, but a true American hero.

And as to what caused the left engine fire that resulted in the crash? The report concluded: "The cause of the fire could not be determined."

II WHAT WAS IN THE CORN FLAKES BOX?

Two types of material were recovered by Harold Dahl from Maury Island: black slaglike rock, and the previously mentioned thin white metal.

Although the sample Crisman sent to Ray Palmer in Chicago in the cigar box was stolen, and whatever was in the corn flakes box disappeared in the crash of the B-25, reporter Ted Morello wrote one last story on a third batch of samples that Dahl gave to him soon after the crash for safekeeping.

Morello turned these fragments over to a chemistry professor at the nearby College of Puget Sound for analysis. On August 8, reporter Paul Lantz wrote about the professor's findings in the Tacoma Times:

not known.

Although the rock was found to be common slag, the other metallic substance cannot be explained by any metallurgist. It does not exist naturally on Earth, nor can it be duplicated. The two mystery ingredients are calcium, which in this concentration would offer protection against radioactive material by absorbing radium, and titanium.

It is not clear exactly what

Although discovered in 1791, titanium was not extracted and isolated from compound ore into its pure, usable form until 1925. At the time of the crash in 1947 it still had few, if any, industrial or commercial uses.

Shortly after the B-25 crash, with the advent of the Cold War in the 1950s, both the Soviet Union and the United States began using titanium extensively in military aviation. The U.S. at that point designated it a "strategic material" and began to collect it at the Defense National Stockpile Center.

In both nations' aerospace industries, titanium quickly became a key component in developing rockets, missiles and craft strong enough to withstand the atmospheric stresses of space exploration.

12 PAUL LANTZ

This tragically turned out to be one of the last bylined stories ever written by reporter Paul Lantz. A few months later, on January 10, 1948, at the age of 29, Lantz died suddenly and without warning.

Many years later, the widow of Paul Lantz revealed in a letter to her husband's friend and fellow reporter Ted Morello this story, about an incident that she said took place at their home sometime in the fall of 1947:

One Sunday afternoon, after we returned from church and were just sitting down to lunch, Paul was visited by two men, dressed in black, who came to the house and identified themselves as FBI agents. I thought I might have seen one of them before but I wasn't sure. I left them to speak privately in the living room and went in to make coffee. A short while later, concerned after hearing raised voices from the other room, I tried to listen in on their conversation, which went on for over an hour. I heard the two men warning Paul to stop — I couldn't make out what they meant by that, but it wasn't hard to figure — but Paul defiantly told them he would do no such thing and that no one could prevent him from doing his job. The two men left the house soon after that, angry, apparently after realizing that their attempt to intimidate my husband into silence wasn't going to work.

Lantz, a small, brave man who had survived a serious case of polio as a youth, had made many friends while working the police beat in Tacoma. His funeral was attended not only by family, friends and colleagues but by most of the Tacoma Police Department. His tragically premature death remains cloaked in mystery. [1]

13 DOUGLAS MILFORD'S SHADOW

He flickers through the Roswell and Maury Island stories like a shadow. Knowing what we do now, this appears to have been by design, and we can start to infer his intentions.

Milford is, by July 1947, clearly working for someone. It is, almost certainly, an organization or agency, not an individual. The most likely candidate appears to be the emerging Project Sign, investigating sightings but also suppressing information, intimidating witnesses, and stifling inquiry. At the worst he's guilty of sabotage and even murder.

He remains inscrutable. Was he, like Fred Crisman, a licensed provocateur, swimming in slipstreams of interconnected conspiracies and double- or triple-dealing? Or was his purpose more pointed and single-minded?

We will follow his trail from here to see what it tells us. And it leads, inevitably, back to his hometown of Twin Peaks. [1]

But first, let me offer an alternate theory regarding the Maury Island incident that is worth considering, which also may account for the strange behavior of Fred Crisman.

One of the first nuclear production complexes to produce weapons-grade plutonium is located at Hanford, Washington. Located 200 miles east of Tacoma around a bare, desertlike stretch of the Columbia River, the Hanford Ordnance Works -- often more benignly referred to as the Hanford Engineering Company -- is nearly half the size of Rhode Island. In 1942,

[1] If an autopsy was performed on Paul Lantz, I was unable to locate it. Contemporary accounts state that Lantz died after a "short unspecified illness" that apparently puzzled his doctors. The official cause of death offered on Lantz's death certificate is meningitis, but none of the accounts I've found even mention this—TP

[1] Milford was working for Project Sign—TP

the government seized this land by exercise of eminent domain, a constitutional right most citizens don't even know exists. Over 1,500 people were "relocated" from two nearby farming communities, creating ghost towns that exist to this day. [2]

They also removed people of three Native American nations, including Lewis and Clark's old friends the Nez Perce. Yes, this was reservation land, and therefore judged "ideal" by the powers that be for their purposes. Having fleeced the Nez Perce out of their land in their 19th-century treaty, it proved even easier to do it a second time. With a world war on this time, patriotism trumped reason; even the "Indians" couldn't refuse pitching in to save the world. Once the Manhattan Project split the atom, the B Reactor the government built at Hanford produced most of the plutonium used in the bomb dropped at Nagasaki, as well as in most of the nuclear weapons America continued to manufacture throughout the Cold War. [3]

As a result Hanford also produced a massive amount of nuclear waste, a threat of contamination to the area's groundwater and other resources, before the country had developed a coherent plan on how to store or contain it.

So what did they do with it? Recently declassified documents reveal that in 1949, soon after the war, officials at Hanford covertly released massive amounts of raw, irradiated uranium fuel into the local environment. Levels monitored in a 200-mile area around Hanford exceeded the established daily limit of iodine-131 by over 1,000 percent. [4]

The water and land rights that had been granted to the Nez Perce were fouled for generations to come. But there would be no relocations this time; citizens in the area were, instead, routinely tested to see what effect these contaminants would have on them, and in the next few years thyroid disease and cancer rates soared, at which point officials at every level denied that any radiation above acceptable levels had ever been released. I wonder what Chief Joseph would have had to say to the government about that.

[2] Verified—TP

[3] Verified – TP

[4] Confirmed—TP

* The Hanford nuclear facility

In the light of this revelation, is it possible that what Harold Dahl encountered that day in Puget Sound were <u>American</u> aircraft -- the size and origin of which I'll deal with momentarily -- engaged in the illicit "dumping" of nuclear waste in the Puget Sound? This could explain the "burns" suffered by Dahl's son and the death of his dog. It could even explain why the photographs taken by Harold Dahl that day were fogged and overexposed. It appears no one ever thought to test the samples he retrieved for radioactivity. Is it possible that the samples taken on board the B-25 may have played a role in disturbing the electronic systems on the plane, thereby contributing to the crash?

When Dahl first went to Fred Crisman with his story, what if Crisman was given an assignment by his CIA handlers to "obscure" the truth with an even more sensational cover story of "flying saucers"? Kenneth Arnold's UFO story was all over the local news at the time, and would have presented a perfect misdirection. This might explain many of Crisman's actions -- Dahl might not even have known his true motives -- as well as why the military closed ranks around the whole affair. It might even explain all of Milford's subsequent actions, particularly the silencing of Dahl and the attempted intimidations of Paul Lantz and Ray Palmer.

As to the "flying saucers," there are indications in Crisman's CIA file that right after the war he was intimately involved in what was known as Project Paperclip, the covert postwar effort by Allied forces to bring to America key Nazi scientists who were involved in Hitler's missile and jet programs. Many of these scientists -- most famously Wernher von Braun -- became leading figures in the U.S. rocket and space program, which was based at White Sands Missile Range in New Mexico. In exchange for changing sides, none of these men were ever prosecuted for their potential war crimes. [5]

[5] Verified—Project Paperclip did exactly that—TP

But there were a few others -- most notably the Horten brothers, Walter and Reimar -- who resisted the West's overtures. One of the Hortens and many other hard-core Nazis escaped to Argentina after the war. In the opinion of many they were the most talented and advanced aeronautical engineers in the world. Late in the war they had designed a jet-powered flying-wing aircraft called the Horten Ho 229. Although it arrived too late to see active service for the Luftwaffe, this aircraft was the source of rumors that in the war's final months the Nazis were developing "alternate aircraft," including saucer-shaped and flying-wing fighters. It is not hard to study the surviving Horten prototypes and look ahead 40 years to the B-I and B-2 bombers. [6]

Many of these same scientists also went to work for the Soviets. Most of the UFO intrigue and subterfuge in the U.S. military was driven by the fear that these unknown and superior craft suddenly appearing over Western skies could be Soviet aircraft. If the Russians did possess them, from a Cold War Soviet perspective, the strategy makes perfect sense:

Send in waves of technologically advanced aircraft to operate openly over America, against which we had no possibility of defending ourselves, as a way to intimidate us and deflate confidence in our new atomic weapons -- which the Soviets did not yet possess. Whatever these craft were, there's no question they created panic and uncertainty in the military.

What if the "weather balloon" narrative out of Roswell was a rushed, clumsy attempt to cover up the crash of one of these Soviet spy planes? Could the UFO stories in the Northwest similarly have been a cover for squadrons of these craft operating openly over our airspace? [7]

There is, of course, another, however improbable, possibility: What about the original conclusion of Project Sign that these mysterious aircraft were of "no earthly origin"? That their technology was "outside the scope of U.S. science, even that of German and Soviet rocket and aircraft development"?

[6] Verified—which makes me wonder the following: What if the U.S. got its hands on these designs and was attempting to develop "flying-wing" aircraft of its own at White Sands, New Mexico, or Hanford in the Pacific Northwest? Could "flying-wing" prototypes have been the objects seen in the sky by Kenneth Arnold, Emil Smith and countless others? And if they were American in origin, could the military have been using these craft—which perhaps had the ability to fly and hover, as many contemporary aircraft do—to discreetly dispose of nuclear waste from Hanford in the Puget Sound? Is that what the Archivist is hinting at here?—TP

[7] All sound reasoning, except . . . a wave of similar stories about UFOs over Russia date from that same time frame. Rumors also exist that the Nazis recovered a crashed flying saucer in 1937, and that technology recovered from that crash formed the basis of their "fixed-wing" aircraft program. It's a hall of mirrors.

I've also just found a recently declassified report from Fourth Air Force Headquarters in San Francisco that there were at least three UFO sightings directly over the Hanford site as early as January of 1945, described by the pilot who gave chase to one of them as a "bright ball of fire, so bright you could hardly look

continued

121

directly at it." The brass moved to install batteries of searchlights after the incident and deployed additional fighters on constant night patrol over the area. At least one more sighting occurred after taking these measures—TP

[8] Verified—TP

[9] Verified—TP

[10] There are, in fact, verifiable accounts of all incidents he mentions. Which, of course, doesn't make them facts—TP

[11] I'm assuming all of this is best explained as describing the exterior of an aircraft itself—TP

[12] Okay, I will admit my mind is reeling. It's after three in the morning and I feel like I'm teetering on the edge of a mine shaft . It seems clear that the Archivist, by walking the reader through these more reasonable theories—and then logically discounting them—is nudging us toward acceptance of the impossible, but I'll need more time to process this before I start embracing meta-theories that shatter the foundation of my Western education and philosophy. I'm going to have to start drinking either a lot more or a whole lot less coffee. Another chapter tomorrow—TP

There are numerous references to earlier sightings of strange airships in 1946 over Northern Europe, then Greece, Portugal, Spain and Italy. Pilots at the time called them "ghost rockets," of which over 200 sightings are on the record, all registered by radar. [8]

Then there are the "foo fighters," strange flying balls of light and other aerial phenomena witnessed by Allied pilots that were presumed to be some kind of Axis secret weapon -- until it turned out, after the war, that German and Japanese pilots at the time were seeing them too. [9]

And it doesn't stop there. In the 1970s, a European author named Erich von Däniken -- often derided, for good reason, as a fraudulent hack -- provided an authentic missing piece to this conundrum. He connected the UFO phenomenon to the oldest sources on record. Turns out there are even earlier references -- to sightings, going back to biblical times -- check out Ezekiel's encounter with "angelic chariots" in the sixth century B.C., in what is now Iraq -- up through the Dark Ages and the Renaissance, in virtually every country in the world, including "mystery airships" that appeared soaring over the American West in the 19th century, strange tales of abductions, crashes in Texas and Missouri six years before Roswell, and massive sightings over Los Angeles in the early 1940s.

The point about the whole subject is this: Once you open the top on this thing, the genie won't get back in the bottle.[10]

The following is a modern translation of Ezekiel (1:4-1:21) -- which I somehow missed in Sunday school -- if you need something to keep you up at night:

4 I looked, and I saw a wind-storm coming out of the north, an immense cloud with flashing lightning and surrounded by brilliant light. The center of the fire looked 5 like glowing metal, and in the fire was what looked like four living creatures. In appearance their form 6 was that of a man, but each of them had four faces and four wings.

7 Their legs were straight; their feet were like those of a calf and gleamed like burnished bronze. 8 Under their wings on their four sides they had the hands of a man. All four of them had faces and 9 wings, and their wings touched one another. Each one went straight ahead; they did not turn as they moved.

10 Their faces looked like this: Each of the four had the face of a man, and on the right side each had the face of a lion, and on the left the face of an ox; each also had the face of an eagle.

11 Such were their faces. Their wings were spread out upward; each had two wings, one touching the wing of another creature on either side, and two wings covering its body.

12 Each one went straight ahead. Wherever the spirit would go, they would go, without turning as they went. [11]

13 The appearance of the living creatures was like burning coals of fire or torches. Fire moved back and forth among the creatures; it was bright, and lightning flashed out of it.

The creatures sped back and 14 forth like flashes of lightning.

As I looked at the living crea- 15 tures, I saw a wheel on the ground beside each creature with its four faces.

This was the appearance and 16 structure of the wheels: They sparkled like chrysolite, and all four looked alike. Each appeared to be made like a wheel intersecting a wheel. As they moved, they would 17 go in any one of the four directions the creatures faced; the wheels did not turn about as the creatures went. Their rims were high and 18 awesome, and all four rims were full of eyes all around. When the 19 living creatures moved, the wheels beside them moved; and when the living creatures rose from the ground, the wheels also rose. Wherever the spirit would go, they 20 would go, and the wheels would rise along with them, because the spirit of the living creatures was in the wheels. When the creatures 21 moved, they also moved; when the creatures stood still, they also stood still; and when the creatures rose from the ground, the wheels rose along with them, because the spirit of the living creatures was in the wheels. [12]

548

*** TWIN PEAKS SIGHTINGS,
    DISAPPEARANCES AND ABDUCTIONS:

I PROJECT SIGN

Mysteries are as much a part of nature as sunrises. They may
not yield to us, but they are freely available for all to wrestle
with. The hoarding and withholding of "secret" knowledge is the
trademark of covert societies and governments, for the purpose
of concentrating power and resources within a powerful elite,
the few against the many. These polarities stand in direct
opposition to one another; mysteries enliven existence, secrets
strangle it. The battle continues to this day, and the flow of
information -- in any "free" society -- depends on the outcome.
Regarding the UFO phenomenon, this conflict was about to be
enacted within the U.S. government and military.

Our minds are wired by nature to detect patterns. I have
disciplined mine for decades to recognize and draw out patterns
where none might first seem apparent. But even the untrained eye
begins to sense the emergence of a peculiar pattern particular
to a specific geographical area like Twin Peaks. A comparable
sample size taken from any other similar community's history --
I've compiled over a dozen, at random, as an exercise -- yields
nothing like the catalog of misfortune in evidence here.

The challenge is to trace it, if possible, to its origins. That
becomes a search for common threads. One of those threads, in
the person of Douglas Milford, we've already identified. Let's
follow it.

In the aftermath of the Maury Island incident in 1947, Douglas
Milford next turns up a few months later at the newly minted
Wright-Patterson Air Force Base in Ohio, for the first
"official" meeting of Project Sign.[1]

[1] This document is authentic—TP

SUMMARY OF INFORMATION

SUBJECT:

CLASSIFIED

First meeting of technical research and development division (T-3, or AMC Engineering) project designated Operation Sign.

The meeting is called to order at 0800 hours, December 9, 1947. Conference room C, Command Wing, Wright-Patterson Air Force Base, Dayton, Ohio.

Present: Acting Commanding General, USAF Gen. Hoyt Vandenberg; Chief of Air Base Materiel Command, Gen. Nathan Twining; Director of Intelligence, (AFOIN) Office of Intelligence Gen. Charles Cabell; Director of Intelligence AMC, Col. Howard McCoy; Chief Executive Collections Branch, Col. Robert Taylor; Collections Officer, Lieut. Col. George Garrett; Analysis Officer, Maj. Aaron J. Boggs; Analysis Officer, Maj. Douglas Milford; Analysis Officer, Maj. Dewey Fournet; FBI Liaison Officer, Special Agent S.W. Reynolds

The meeting begins with a report from Lieut. Col. Garrett:

Lieut. Col. Garrett: For purposes of analysis, eighteen of our most reliable reported sightings of "Flying Disks" were selected for breakdown into detailed particulars. None have been preliminarily explained away as natural phenomena. Each report was assigned a number and each number appears in the left-hand column of the data on the following pages.

Four reports, Numbers 2, 4, 17, and 18, have not yet been fully analyzed. The subject headings on which the breakdown has been made are:

CONFIDENTIAL

REPORT	DATE	*HOUR	LOCATION
1	19 May	1215	Manitou Springs, Colorado
2	22 May		Oklahoma City, Oklahoma
3	22 June	1130	Greenfield, Massachusetts
4	24 June		Mt. Rainier, Washington
5	28 June	2120	Maxwell Field, Alabama
6	29 June	1330	Near White Sands, New Mexico
7	1 July		Bakersfield, California
8	4 July	2015	Emmett, Idaho
9	6 July	1345	Clay Center, Kansas
10	6 July		Fairfield-Suisun, California
11	7 July	1145	Koshkonong, Wisconsin
12	7 July	1430	East Troy, Wisconsin
13	8 July	1550	Mt. Baldy, California
14	9 July	2330	Grand Falls, Newfoundland
15	10 July	1600	Harmon Field, Newfoundland
16	12 July	1830	Elmendorf Field, Alaska
17	4 September	1930	Twin Peaks, Washington
18	8 September	1430	Twin Peaks, Washington

*Local Standard Time

REPORT	OBSERVER'S NAME	OCCUPATION	OBSERVED FROM
1	███████████	Railroad Employee	Ground
		" "	"
		" "	"
2	███████████	Businessman-Pilot	Ground
3	███████████	*Not stated	Ground
4	███████████	Businessman-Pilot	Air
5	███████████	Captain, AAF	Ground
		" "	"
		" "	"
		1st Lieut., AAF	"
6	███████████	Employee, NRL	Ground
		" "	"
		" "	"
		Wife of ██████████	"
7	███████████	Civilian Pilot	Ground
8	███████████	United Air Lines Pilot	Air
		" " " Co-Pilot	"
9	███████████	Major, AAF	Air
10	███████████	Captain, AAF	Ground
11	███████████	CAP Instructor	Air
		CAP Student	"
12	███████████	CAP Pilot	Air
		CAP Passenger	"
13	███████████	1st Lieut., ACCNG	Air
14	███████████	Constable, Newfoundland Constabulary	Ground
15	███████████	TWA Representative	Ground
		PAA "	"
16	███████████	Major, AAF	Ground
17	███████████	Captain, AAF	
18	███████████	Major, AAF (present)	

*From letter received, observer is obviously well educated.

REPORT	DEVIATION FROM STRAIGHT FLIGHT	COLOR	SIZE
1	Climbed, dove, hovered overhead, resumed original course	Silver	Apparently small
2	███████████████	███████████	██████████████
3	None reported	Silver, very bright	Small
4	███████████████	███████████	██████████████
5	Zig zag course "much like a waterbug"	Brilliance slightly greater than a star	Not stated
6	None reported	Some solar specular reflection	Not stated
7	██		
8	None reported	Almost dusk; could not distinguish	Impossible to determine
9	None reported	Very bright and silvery colored	30-50' in diameter
10	None reported	Reflection from sun	Comparable to a C-54 at 10,000'
11	Descended edgewise, stopped at 4,000' and assumed horizontal position. Proceeded in horizontal flight for 15 seconds, stopped again, then disappeared	Not stated	Not stated
12	None reported	Not stated	Not stated
13	None reported	Of light-reflecting nature	Apparent depth of a P-51
14	None reported	Phosphorous color	Not stated
15	None reported	Silvery	Same span as a C-54 at 10,000'
16	Followed contours of mountains five miles away from observers	Resembled a grayish balloon	Approx. 10' in diameter
17	Pursued by fighter pilot for 20 minutes, evasive actions taken	Silvery white	60-100' in diameter
18	Rapid ascent, disappearance	Silver	Big as a f****** house

REPORT	SHAPE	SOUND	TRAIL	WEATHER
1	No definite shape could be determined	None	None	CAVU
2	▓▓▓▓▓▓▓▓	▓▓	▓▓▓▓	▓▓▓▓▓
3	Irregular; round, Did not appear particularly disc-shaped	None	None	Not stated
4	▓▓▓▓▓▓▓▓	▓▓	▓▓▓	▓▓▓▓
5	None stated; seemed like a bright light	None	None	Clear moonlight
6	No details other than that shape was inform with no protuberances	None	Possible vapor trails	CAVU
7	▓▓▓▓▓▓▓▓▓▓▓▓▓▓▓▓▓▓▓▓▓▓▓▓▓▓▓▓▓▓▓▓▓▓▓▓▓			

REPORT	SHAPE	SOUND	TRAIL	WEATHER
8	None definite, but seemed flat on base with the top slightly rough in contour	None	None	CAVU
9	Round, disc-shaped	None	None	CAVU
10	No shape could be distinguished	None	None	Sunny
11	Not stated, but report refers to "saucer" several times	None	None	CAVU
12	▓▓▓▓▓▓▓▓	None	None	CAVU
13	Same as Report No. 11	None	None	Not stated
	Flat object, of light-reflecting nature which appeared to be without			
14	vertical fin or any visible wings	None	None	CAVU
15	Egg-shaped, or like barrel head Circular in shape, like wagon wheel	None	Bluish black trail approx. 15 mi. long	Clear with scattered cumulus at 8 to 10,000'
16	Resembled balloon	None	None	Not stated
17	Disc shaped	None	None	Clear and unobstructed
18	None	None	None	High clouds

REPORT	MANNER OF DISAPPEARANCE	REMARKS
1	Climbed very fast and out of sight	No definite shape could be determined and even with the aid of 4 to 6 power binoculars object could not be brought into focus
2	██████████████████████████	
3	Obscured by a cloud bank	From letter this observer wrote, it is obvious he is a well-educated person. Seeks no publicity.
4	██████████████████	
5	Lost in brilliancy of the moon	Observers (2 rated, 2 air intell.) phoned Field Ops to ascertain no scheduled experimental a/c were in vicinity. Sky chart attached to re[port?]
6	Cannot explain, except that reflection angle may have changed abruptly	Observer is Admin. Asst. in the Rocket Sonde Sect. of NRL. Two other "scientists", and wife of one, were in party and made same observation
7	████████████	███████████████
8	Don't know whether they put on a tremendous burst of speed, or disintegrated. However, they did disappear into sunset	Observers were Pilot, Co-Pilot, of scheduled UAL DC-3. Stewardess also saw objects. Suggest reading of very detailed statements.
9	Unexplained	When first sighting object near horizon, observer looked at chart in his lap to check position. When he looked out window again, object was off his left wing at 11 o'clock.

REPORT	MANNER OF DISAPPEARANCE	REMARKS
10	Disappeared at an angle of about 30 degrees above the earth's surface	Rolled from side to side 3 times in its path across the sky. Sun reflected from top side, but never from underside, even when turning
11	Unexplained	None
12	Unexplained	None
13	Pilot (at 300 MPH) attempted to keep object in sight, but unable to do so	Observer contacted bases in area w[hich?] reported no a/c in air at time
14	Unexplained	First 4 discs flying line-a-trail
15	Unexplained	Seemed to cut clouds open as it passed thru. Trail was like beam seen after a high-powered landing light is switched off.
16	Unstated	Object was observed paralleling the course of a C-47 then landing.
17	Pilot unable to keep up	Stopped and started
18	Vanished into clouds	Clearly metallic, variable speed, fast as s***

REMARKS

From detailed study of reports selected for their
impression of veracity and reliability, several
conclusions have been formed:

(a) This "flying saucer" situation is not all
imaginary or seeing too much in some natural
phenomenon. Something is really flying around out
there.

(b) Lack of topside inquiries, when compared to
the prompt and demanding inquiries that have
originated topside upon former events, give more
than ordinary weight to the possibility that this
is a domestic project, about which the President,
etc. know.

(c) Whatever the objects are, this much can be
said of their physical appearance:

> 1.   The surface of these objects is metallic,
> indicating a metallic skin, at least.
>
> 2.   When a trail is observed, it is lightly
> colored, a blue-brown haze, that is similar
> to a rocket engine's exhaust. Contrary to a
> rocket of the solid type, one observation
> indicates that the fuel may be throttled,
> which would indicate a liquid rocket engine.
>
> 3.   As to shape, all observations state
> that the object is circular or at least
> elliptical, flat on the bottom and slightly
> domed on the top. The size estimates place
> it somewhere near the size of a C-54 or a
> Constellation.
>
> 4.   Some reports describe two tabs, located
> at the rear and symmetrical about the axis
> of flight motion.
>
> 5.   Flights have been reported, from three to
> nine of them, flying good formation on each
> other, with speeds always above 300 knots.
>
> 6. The discs oscillate laterally while flying
> along, which could be snaking.

A lot to unpack here: First of all, Milford is now listed as a USAF major. He's obviously been promoted, perhaps for his effective service during the Maury Island incident.

Kenneth Arnold's sighting is #4 on this list; his friend the airline pilot E. J. Smith's is clearly #8. We also notice that the confounding Maury Island incident does not make the roster. Make of that what you will.

Far more interesting to this correspondent are the final two sightings on the list, which occurred in or around Twin Peaks in early September -- because the minutes make it clear that the witness to incident #18 was in the room that day: none other than Doug Milford himself. [2]

Searching deeper for secondary accounts of these two sightings, a check of Twin Peaks' local biweekly newspaper yielded the following:

[2] I've identified a number of high-ranking Air Force officers who claim to have personally witnessed UFOs. They tend, perhaps not surprisingly, to be the most sympathetic among military personnel to the possibility of extraterrestrial origins —TP

TWIN PEAKS

GAZETTE

SINCE 1922

ONLY 35¢

Issue 252, Volume 25   TWIN PEAKS, WASHINGTON   Saturday, September 6, 1947

LOOK TO THE SKIES

**by *Gazette* Staff Writer
Robert Jacoby [3]**

A LOCAL RESIDENT walking his dog on the evening of September 4 enjoyed more than one of our famed "golden moment" sunsets last Thursday. Retired mill worker Einer Jennings (63) was making his way along the hiking trail near Sparkwood and Highway 21 when he looked to the west and noticed a bright shiny object, perhaps reflecting the sun's dying rays, as it streaked across the sky from south to north. The object moved silently and swiftly, said Jennings, and appeared to wobble slightly in the air.

Moments later he heard the powerful rumble of jet engines and a USAF fighter plane roared out of the south along the same flight path at low altitude, close enough for Jennings to read the insignia on its fuselage. It appeared to him that the fighter, which Jennings identified as a McDonnell FH Phantom, was pursuing the first object. Stopping to watch, Jennings said that the first object showed a startling ability to stop suddenly, change directions and accelerate to top speed almost instantly. The fighter jet, on the other hand, had to maneuver, roll and turn much in line with what Jennings termed "the basic rules of gravity," and as a result had great difficulty keeping up.

Einer Jennings (63) and his dog, Rover.

"It was almost like a game of keep away," said Jennings, "or an old-style dogfight without any shooting. And it was clear to me that the jet didn't have a chance of catching this thing. It looked to me almost as if this other object, whatever it is, was toying with the fighter."

Jennings said he watched this strange pursuit unfold in front of him, back and forth across the horizon, over what he estimated was about thirty seconds. At that point the silvery object simply accelerated straight up into the cloudless sky and disappeared. The jet tried to climb after it, but after some ten seconds Jennings said he saw it turn and head back to the south in the direction it had come from, presumably toward Fairchild Air Force Base.

At least half a dozen other people on that west side of town report hearing or seeing the jet over our area that evening—hardly a regular occurrence—but no one else has, as of yet, mentioned sighting the silvery object.

Mr. Jennings cut short his walk and headed home. Although since his recent retirement friends say he is a well-known fixture at local watering holes, Jennings swore on his mother's life to this reporter that at the time of the sighting he hadn't yet imbibed a drop, but freely admitted to repairing to Woody's by the Water afterwards to share his experiences with fellow regulars over an adult beverage or two.

Whether this incident is in any way related to the recent rash of what some have termed "unidentified flying objects" across our state is unclear. Our calls to the information officer at Fairchild Air Force Base proved unfruitful with regard to the first object, however they did confirm that a fighter jet from the base did fly through our region Thursday evening on what they termed a "routine patrol."

If anyone else has stories to share about this or any other "objects in the sky," please feel free to contact this reporter at the *Gazette*. Your help is always welcome and your anonymity is guaranteed.

REPORTER ROBERT JACOBY
as a young man

³ I have confirmed that the reporter for this story is the older brother of Dr. Lawrence Jacoby, a psychiatrist who figures prominently in Agent Cooper's notes on the Laura Palmer case.

The Jacoby family had moved in 1939 from Twin Peaks to Pearl Harbor, where the father, Richard, was stationed in the Navy. He and his wife abruptly divorced in 1940. The next year Richard returned to Twin Peaks with the older son, Robert, while the younger, Lawrence, remained in Hawaii with his mother, Esther, who shortly after the divorce officially changed her first name to "Leilani" —TP

ARCHIVIST'S NOTE

No other local eyewitnesses came forward, but this article is a clear reference to incident #17 on Project Sign's list, what became known as the "UFO dogfight." The pilot of the Phantom was Lieutenant Dan Luhrman.

I have transcribed here an excerpt from his account in Project Sign's files:

> "I was ten minutes into my patrol when I spotted a brightly lit object on the horizon due north of my position, flying at approximately the same altitude. After determining there were no other known aircraft on radar in the area I gave pursuit to determine its identity. Reaching full power I realized the object was maintaining the same distance from me, and was too fast to catch in a straight run, dropping in altitude by this point down to around 500 feet. I engaged in a series of turns, trying to cut the object off, but it continued to elude me with a series of effortless maneuvers. When it went into a sudden vertical climb I tried to follow, until my plane stalled out at 14,000 feet. The object passed out of my visual range and I returned to base."

After curiosity swelled in the local press, Fairchild's information officer released a statement that the jet had been pursuing the by now familiar, all-purpose Air Force standby, a "derelict weather balloon." [4]

Established in 1942 as a repair depot for damaged aircraft returning from the Pacific theater in WWII, in the summer of 1947 Fairchild Air Force Base was turned over to Strategic Air Command, which made it home to the 92nd and 98th Bomb Groups. Located 15 miles west of Spokane in southeastern Washington -- less than half an hour by jet from Twin Peaks -- it became home to the B-29 Superfortress bomber, a key component of U.S. air defense during the Cold War. There were also rumored to be ICBM nuclear missile silos on the base. [5]

The second confirmed sighting in Twin Peaks occurred four days after Jennings's encounter, on September 8. As we shall soon see, this event made the local paper only indirectly, but it is the subject of this report offered by Major Douglas Milford during that first Project Sign meeting at Wright-Patterson AFB: [6]

[4] Verified—TP

[5] This is one of the first of what soon emerges as a clear pattern over the next two decades of UFO sightings over nuclear missile silos—TP

[6] I am curious how the Archivist gained access to these confidential files—and what that tells us about his identity—TP

DEPARTMENT OF THE AIR FORCE
TASK FORCE MJ-12

PROJECT SIGN
Lt. Col. Milford

INCIDENT #18 FIELD REPORT

LT. COL. GARRETT:
The following report by Major Milford will now be presented by
him and entered into the minutes. Major?

MAJOR MILFORD:
After the "dogfight" sighting on September 4 made the local paper,
I immediately flew to Fairchild from Seattle and drove from there
to my hometown of Twin Peaks. As I had known the sole eyewitness,
Einer Jennings, since childhood--he was a schoolmate of my
father's, and father to one of my own school chums, Emil Jennings--
I decided not to approach him in any official capacity, but as an
old family friend.[7]

After listening to Einer's story, by now embellished by a few star
turns on the barstool, I gently cautioned him, speaking as a friend,
of the dangers experienced by some individuals who had witnessed
sightings in western Washington--Dahl, Arnold, et al.--who
afterwards had been shadowed or threatened by "mysterious visitors,"
stressing the case of Arnold, who narrowly avoided death due to
apparent sabotage of his airplane.

Einer turned pale, and by the end of our conversation I mentally
checked a box beside his name marked "mission accomplished."
Since Einer was among the leading candidates for "town drunk"--
the Jennings clan had long been a "no account" family in these
parts and, if the rap sheet Emil has already compiled is any
indication, always will be--I gathered his tale wasn't gaining
traction with locals in any case, particularly after Fairfield
issued their "weather balloon" story.[8]

To satisfy my curiosity, the next day--September 8--I visited
the area of his sighting and retraced Jennings's steps. Spotting
no physical evidence, I was walking back to my car when a mental
image of a location miles away on the other side of town seized my

C1

mind with an alarming intensity. It was an area near the Pearl Lakes in the Ghostwood National Forest that I knew intimately from my Boy Scout days, and with it came back memories of a strange experience I'd had there 20 years earlier that I had, unconsciously I believe, long suppressed.

I felt compelled to drive and then hike up to the location immediately, and it is no exaggeration to tell you that I almost felt as if I had no choice in the matter.

As I ventured into the woods, atop a plateau above Pearl Lake, although I perceived no change in the weather, this clear fall afternoon turned as black as night. I heard a strange, pulsating electric hum fill the air, all other sound diminished and I sensed more than saw movement in the trees 50 yards ahead of me. This was followed by a bright--almost blinding--cluster of lights that burst into view overhead, different colors, red, white, green, swaying and rotating in what seemed to be swift and regular patterns. Alarmed, I knelt down and crept forward behind a felled log and was able to determine that the lights were hovering above a clearing that was illuminated intermittently by the moving beams.

From my closer vantage point, I could also see that the beams were issuing from an object in the air, stationary, about 25 feet above the clearing, but below the tree line. I could only infer its shape from the darkness it generated-- large and round, maybe a hundred feet in circumference-- as the lights themselves were so dazzling I had to slip on my aviator shades in order to see anything at all. I believe this shape could have been a craft or ship of some kind, with its power source the pulsating hum that appeared to issue from its direction as well. Then, in the clearing directly below this enigma, perhaps because

02

[7] If he did not present himself to Jennings as an Air Force officer, he nevertheless ends up performing a similar function: intimidating a witness—TP

[8] Milford was spot-on about Emil Jennings running out a bad string of the local gene pool: In 1964, he passed out drunk and drowned in the steel tub of his basement beer-brewing apparatus. His only son, Hank Jennings— onetime football hero at Twin Peaks High, according to its 1968 yearbook— compiled an even more impressive rap sheet in his postgraduate career, including a stint in the Washington State Penitentiary for vehicular manslaughter—TP

my eyes had adjusted with the darker lenses, I noticed someone
standing there.

Three someones, actually. Children. Two boys and a girl, each of them
no more, I would estimate, than seven or eight years of age. Their
backs were to me, motionless, arms at their sides, and they appeared
to be looking up at the dark shape above them. Within moments, all the
varied lights appeared to merge into a single large and steady strong
white beam, pointing straight down at the three figures like a
Hollywood searchlight, but a hundred times brighter--even with my
dark glasses on I had to close my eyes and look away or risk being
blinded. The oppressive hum changed now as well, rising in pitch and
intensity to such a degree that I had to cover my ears. Then, suddenly,
the sound stopped, and the beam of light disappeared. It took a few
moments for my eyes to adjust, but I realized it was because I was
wearing my shades; when I took them off I realized it was suddenly
daylight again. My surroundings now looked completely ordinary.
Whatever had been hovering in the air above the clearing was gone.

And so were the children. I scoured the area for them, but found no
trace of anyone's presence. Nor did I come across a single piece of
physical evidence indicating that a ship or craft the size of the
one I thought I had witnessed had been there. I realized the
compelling thoughts that had seemed to direct me so urgently to
this place were gone from my mind as well. I had enough presence
of mind to use my Minox camera to take pictures of the area, which
at this point I realized I knew well from my childhood. I had
visited this clearing a number of times before and on one occasion
had an uncanny experience there. Not far away was the entrance to
an ancient cave my pals and I used to explore during our early
years, reported to be an old Indian dwelling with ancient drawings
and pictographs on the walls. We called it Owl Cave.

Seized by an extreme feeling of dread, my pulse racing as a host of
unpleasant memories flooded back into my mind, I rapidly left the
area and returned to my vehicle.

03

ARCHIVIST'S NOTE

So Douglas Milford's personal UFO experience went considerably beyond the other 17 entries on Project Sign's initial list to conclude with what appears to be the first officially recorded instance of a UFO "abduction," or in the parlance of the later Project Blue Book, a "close encounter of the third kind."

There is unfortunately no record of how Milford's story was received by the other officers in the room at Wright-Patterson. Nor is there any mention of whether Milford showed them any of the photographs he'd taken that day in the woods, or if, in them, he had captured anything of interest.[9]

[9] Was this an actual "UFO" encounter, or something else altogether? Milford never mentions actually seeing a craft or ship, only a dark space that he infers is something of the kind. Did he have an observational bias to find what he was seeking? As subjective as it sounds—and given Milford's earlier reputation for fanciful exaggeration—I find it problematic to accept his account at face value. Independent corroboration is required—TP

2 THREE STUDENTS VANISH

<u>TWIN PEAKS GAZETTE</u>
FRIDAY, SEPTEMBER 12, 1947

Issue 266, Volume 26   TWIN PEAKS, WASHINGTON

ALL'S WELL THAT ENDS WELL

by *Gazette* Staff Writer Robert Jacoby

THEY'RE SAFE and sound! The drama that had our town in an uproar Monday evening ended happily on Tuesday just before noon. The three elementary school students who had vanished without a trace from a third grade nature walk safely emerged from the woods near Pearl Lake, a few miles from where they had disappeared but none the worse for wear.

The three children—two boys and a girl, whose names have been withheld at their parents' request—wandered away from their class. By the time their teacher and chaperones noticed their absence, only minutes later, a frantic search failed to find them. Word was conveyed to police and the forest service and soon search and rescue teams and dozens of volunteers were combing the woods for them all through the night. A pair of bloodhounds was dispatched from Wind River to aid in the effort.

The exhausted team continued their efforts until daybreak and beyond and were about to expand the scope of their search when, lo and behold, the trio of youngsters were spotted by a sharp-eyed team of Eagle Scouts from local troop 541 near the Pearl Lake campground. Scoutmaster Andrew Packard and his boys made a game of it and quickly carried the youngsters on piggyback the rest of the way down the mountain.

Although hunger and thirst were their only complaints, the children seemed in good health and fine spirits, and were happily reunited with their families. They were taken to the hospital for a quick check-up, where it seems they're all in the pink. According to one source, the kids were slightly confused and seemed to think they'd only been gone for an hour or so, had little or no recollection of spending a night in the woods alone and were genuinely surprised to learn that it was Tuesday!

Yet another testament, as if we needed one, to the resilience and pluck of our local youngsters! This reporter will have more details for you and a longer look at this story in the *Gazette*'s edition next Tuesday.

1

VERY GREEN MOON

One other local source confirms the basic chain of events
in this story, and also provides a hint to the identity of at
least one of the three children in the woods.

1 When Major Milford writes how this event brought back a "flood of memories" and what sounds like the onset of a panic attack, a question arises for me: Did Douglas Milford experience something like a "close encounter" of his own at this same location back in 1927? The one mentioned in his brother Dwayne's account where he claims to have encountered a giant and "a walking owl as tall as a man" that resulted in his falling-out with the scouts' regional council as well as his brother Dwayne?

Also: No follow-up article appears in the next or any other edition of the *Gazette*, leaving one to wonder if Douglas paid a subsequent visit to reporter Robert Jacoby—TP

CALHOUN MEMORIAL

HOSPITAL

DAN HAYWARD, MD

TWIN PEAKS, WASHINGTON
INCORPORATED 1925

DATE & TIME _____ 9/9/47 4:30 PM

PHYSICIAN'S INTAKE EXAM

PATIENT	Margaret Coulson - who goes by "Maggie"		DATE OF BIRTH	10/10/40
GENDER	AGE	HEIGHT	HEIGHT	
F	7	54"	65 lbs	

Patient has no physical complaints, other than hunger and a seemingly unquenchable thirst. After a night in the woods, she appeared to have suffered no symptoms of exposure -- a balmy Indian Summer night, where the temperature dropped no lower than 58 degrees, helped in that regard.

Patient appears to be moderately dehydrated. She drank at least a pint of water while in the exam room, which patient claimed did little to ease her thirst.

Physical examination: Temperature and lymph nodes normal. Reflexes normal. Pupils normal, not dilated.

No visible injuries or wounds, aside from minor abrasions on both knees and elbows and this: recently raised or abraded skin on the back of her right knee, centered in the middle. Reddened or irritated marks that present in straight thin symmetrical lines that also form an unusual, but perhaps random pattern, seen below:

INITIAL _____ DATE 9/9/47

PHYSICIAN'S INTAKE EXAM
CONTINUED

Patient says she feels this as slightly painful, but does not remember what caused it or when it happened. Could be a scratch but it appears more likely to be the result of a slight burn, as if she backed into something hot, although that seems hard to figure given circumstances.

Also unusual that patient does not remember most details of this night spent in the woods. Children sometimes have a tendency to block out traumatic experiences, but the fact that the two boys also report no memory of the night is certainly unusual. Other similar cases suggest that perhaps memories will return over time.

As I was leaving the room, patient asked me if I thought "the owl was coming back." When asked about this patient did not elaborate. Seems more than likely the children may have heard or seen an owl in the woods at night, so memory may already be resurfacing.

Attending physician: Dr. Dan Hayward [2]

ARCHIVIST'S NOTE

The medical evaluations of the two male children could not
be located, but I was able to ascertain their identities: Carl
Rodd and Alan Traherne, both of them third grade classmates
of Margaret Coulson at Warren G. Harding Elementary School in
Twin Peaks. Carl Rodd and Alan Traherne graduated from Twin
Peaks High School, along with Margaret, in 1958.

*THE SECOND CHILD

After two years of community college in Spokane, Alan Traherne
moved to Los Angeles, where he worked for a number of years
as a sound technician in the motion picture and television
industry.[3]

Before this correspondent could question him about this event
in his childhood, Traherne passed away in 1988 from cancer.

*THE THIRD CHILD

Carl Rodd joined the Coast Guard the year he graduated from
high school and eventually climbed to the rank of boatswain's
mate, serving on a patrol boat under heavy combat during the
early years of the Vietnam War.

This correspondent was able to locate a photograph of Carl Rodd
during his Coast Guard service that suggests he had a similar
tattoo or marking to the one Margaret received on the back of
his right knee.

[2] I've determined that this
Dr. Hayward was the father
of Dr. Will Hayward, who at
this time was attending his
first year of medical school
at Washington University in
St. Louis.

In 1952, after completing
his postgraduate work at the
University of Washington in
Seattle, Will Hayward took
over the family medicine
practice his father had
founded in Twin Peaks in
1925. He later figures
prominently in Agent
Cooper's notes of the Laura
Palmer case—TP

[5] Medical records indicate
Traherne suffered from PTSD
and there is evidence he
attended a "survivors group"
of abductees in the early
'80s—TP

Rodd was later reported missing while on duty off the Alaskan coast during the devastating Anchorage earthquake and ensuing tsunami of 1964. He was rescued by a Native American fishing crew, but Rodd's patrol boat and the bodies of his shipmates were never recovered. Rodd lived with the Aleuts who rescued him for five months while he regained his strength. It was often later said by Rodd himself that he underwent a spiritual conversion while in their company that "saved his life," adopting their deist or animist form of shamanism. He married a young Aleut woman during his time with them, but the following year, after her and their baby's tragic death in childbirth, Rodd abandoned the Aleuts and, for a time, wandered the trackless wilds of the Yukon, British Columbia and Northwest Territories.

He eventually settled in the town of Yellowknife, working as a tracker for hunting expeditions. During this time he was known to write poetry and songs, and occasionally appeared as a folksinger at local cafes, performing his own compositions. He was also hired to perform stunts in a few movies that occasionally shot on location in the area.[4]

In the early 1980s Rodd returned to his hometown for the first time in nearly 30 years and took up residence outside Twin Peaks in a brand-new trailer park. He eventually became the manager of this park, and part owner as well. He quietly gained a reputation there and in the rest of the community as a sensitive, caring and, despite his meager means, generous soul. He lives there in the park to this day.[5]

3 OWL CAVE

The facts of Project Sign's Incident #18 present many hallmarks of classic "abduction" cases, which at this time had not yet been widely experienced or reported. The reference made to an owl by the girl, which unfortunately the doctor did not more aggressively pursue at the time, may indicate the presence of what are now commonly referred to as "masking memories," that is, a memory constructed by the mind -- or, according to some, implanted by an external source -- to supplant a real and much more disturbing encounter with something that also possesses oversized eyes. Douglas Milford, as we know, had had his own experience with something in these woods 20 years earlier.[1]

The nearby presence of "Owl Cave," and the numerous depictions of owls in its pictographs, suggest that Native Americans in the area may have had similar experiences with this phenomenon during prior millennia.

[5] Carl Rodd's new home was the Fat Trout Trailer Park, outside Twin Peaks on the way to Wind River, a town that was later listed as a place of interest in an ongoing FBI investigation of some kind during the late '80s and early '90s. It is a classified file of the highest order and I need time to obtain sufficient clearance to examine it.

I also find mentions of Carl Rodd in the *Twin Peaks Post* [formerly the *Gazette*] dating from the late 1980s. They would occasionally print a small slug at the bottom of columns in the letters section called "Carl Said It," apparently quotes he would share with younger friends over coffee, a few examples included below—TP

CARL SAID IT:
It's all connected

CARL SAID IT:
What is, is. What was, was.

CARL SAID IT:
All there is is now.

———

[1] A number of indicators lead me to conclude that there is a 96 percent probability that the dossier's Archivist is, him or herself, a resident of Twin Peaks—TP

[2] Okay, I have found literally dozens of volumes containing theories and speculations about owls as metaphors and symbols—including one for the aforementioned Illuminati—"screen memories" for aliens in abduction cases, guardians of the underworld, messengers of the subconscious and even more outlandish hooey. There's one whacked conjecture that they show up as harbingers of some weird phenomenon I can't even figure out called "reverse speech," which is supposed to offer some sort of window into the deepest parts of the unconscious.

Personal bias: I don't like owls. They're merciless predators that have always creeped me out; ever watched a YouTube video of one gobbling down an intact live rat? That's guaranteed to destroy your appetite for a while—but the notion that three kids stuck out in the woods for a night might run into an owl doesn't strike me as anything out of the ordinary. Even Douglas Milford's saying he once saw a walking owl that was as big as a man doesn't seem that strange to me. Some breeds of owls stand well over three feet tall and they all plump themselves up when confronted to appear more threatening. It's dark out there, the primitive brain stem senses danger everywhere, your nervous system is cranked up like an overstrung mandolin, your eyes can play tricks.

Sometimes an owl is just an owl.

Also, the Archivist doesn't elaborate here, but it's likely that the "Maggie Coulson" referenced in this case grows up to become Margaret Lanterman, a noted Twin Peaks eccentric often cited in Agent Cooper's files, whom the locals referred to as "the Log Lady."

If she is one and the same, it would not surprise me to learn that she once got lost in the woods overnight as an impressionable kid and later developed an entire menu of debilitating mental or emotional symptoms related to logs—TP

4 PROJECT GRUDGE

A few months after that meeting at Wright-Patterson AFB, in late 1947 the Air Force unit known as Project Sign produced a finding for their superiors. Titled, blandly, "An Estimate of the Situation," the paper concluded with a matter-of-fact working hypothesis that UFOs were most likely of extraterrestrial origin.

This document worked its way up the entire Air Force command ladder intact unopposed, until the man at the top -- General Hoyt Vandenberg -- rejected their conclusion outright. Not only that, he ordered all copies of the report destroyed.

He also ordered that Project Sign be shut down immediately. It was followed by the formation of its successor, Project Grudge -- using essentially the same personnel and engaged in essentially the same work, but with an entirely different mission. [1]

The express purpose of Project Grudge was not only to investigate and report, but to actively debunk any and all UFO sightings as mundane phenomena or outright hoaxes. A public program of disinformation was now conducted using the U.S. media, disseminating the general idea that the whole notion of extraterrestrial life zooming around our skies in impossibly advanced crafts was crackpot stuff. Grudge was a purposeful institutionalized attempt to squelch public curiosity about these strange and rapidly proliferating incidents and sightings. [2]

[1] Verified. I can also confirm that, although it is often talked about, no copies of this document, "An Estimate of the Situation," are known to exist. Vandenberg never spoke about his reasons for taking this action—TP

[2] Verified—TP

Although Project Sign -- through the work of Doug Milford and others -- had occasionally been in the business of discouraging witnesses, the debunking machinery deployed by Project Grudge represented a different order of magnitude. For experts in the field in years to come, Grudge would be looked back on as the Dark Ages of UFO inquiry.

While Project Grudge proceeded publicly, General Nathan Twining -- at the direction of President Truman -- allegedly helped organize and served as part of an insider group of 12 scientists, government officials and high-ranking officers known by various names but most often as Majestic 12 (MJ-12). This group received the highest level of security clearance in American military history. The order to radically change the direction of the Air Force position on UFOs allegedly came from them, but since any and all public acknowledgment of MJ-12 has been disavowed ever since as a matter of policy, its very existence remains in question. [3]

We will return to Douglas Milford and Project Grudge shortly. For reasons that will soon become clear, a deeper look into the underlying dynamics of power and influence in his hometown are in order.

[3] I am unable to confirm whether a star chamber panel like MJ-12 ever actually existed, its multiple depictions in modern pop culture notwithstanding. It is a wildly controversial subject and may be as mythical as a unicorn.

But it is worth considering that the Archivist may be speaking here from firsthand knowledge—TP

*** N O T A B L E   L O C A L   F A M I L I E S :
    Packards, Hornes, Jenningses,
    Hurleys and Martells

I   T H E   B E G I N N I N G

Twin Peaks possesses all the traditional sources of information
available to any small town -- library, hall of records,
newspaper -- but beyond that also exists a unique and even more
insightful resource called the Bookhouse, which will be explained
in the body of the next excerpted document.

Entitled "Oh, What a Tangled Web . . . ," this slender volume was
commissioned by the Twin Peaks town council in 1984 and written
by reporter Robert Jacoby of the Twin Peaks Gazette -- which in
1970 changed its name to the more up-to-date Twin Peaks Post.[1]

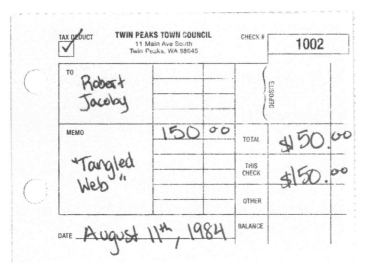

[1] According to its foreword, "Tangled Web" was written in order to "set down for posterity the story of our foundational years, while many of this marvelous saga's original voices, however dimmed by time, can still be heard." For which, according to the receipt below from city records, the town paid Jacoby the princely sum of $150, plus expenses—TP

OH, WHAT A
TANGLED WEB...

— ROBERT JACOBY —

ONE

OUR TALE BEGINS when three families originally tied their fortunes to the fair, abundant forests which mantled the virgin hills and byways that lay between White Tail and Blue Pine mountains.

James Packard arrived first, eldest son of a Boston shipping family, alerted by his Harvard roommate—one of the Weyerhaeuser boys—about the wealth of natural resources that lay west of the Rockies and north of the Columbia River. Inspired by a vision, Packard traveled west and, moved by its natural beauty and untouched trees, laid claim to ten thousand acres around White Tail Falls in 1890. Once the railroad built a spur line from Spokane to connect Packard's mill to the Northern Pacific, the Packard Timber Company became the economic engine for the town that sprang up around his burgeoning business: the town of Twin Peaks.

When Friedrich Weyerhaeuser purchased a million acres in the state of Washington from the railway interests in 1900, he organized the "Weyerhaeuser Syndicate," a confederation of lumber companies that took dominion over his new kingdom. James Packard became one of those partners and the Packard Timber Company grew along with the Syndicate, a beacon of industry attracting waves of northwestward pioneers to seek their own fortunes in the Northwest.

One family already in the area wasn't too thrilled with the Packards' staking their claim. The Martells, descended from

French trappers who'd worked the area's beaver population fifty years earlier, had founded their own modest lumber operation along the river three years before James Packard set foot here. Underfunded and outmaneuvered, the Martells couldn't compete with the Packard operation, particularly after Packard bought the land surrounding every side of their 150-acre claim. Bad blood arose between the families as a result, escalating from threats to legal action to an infamous attempted murder in October of 1914.

During the annual Lumber Days Festival, Ersel Martell —second son of patriarch Zebulon Martell—and a shady confederate from across the northern border, Jean Jacques Renault, accosted James Packard's oldest son, Thomas, outside the Grange Hall's annual square dance. Some say it was about a girl, others say it started with a slight from Thomas about Renault's "rough manners." It ended in a knife fight behind the barn, with Thomas clinging to life. The assailant Renault fled back to Canada, eluding capture, where his fugitive status led him down a wayward path to a life of crime as head of the infamous Renault Gang, which would soon amass a fortune running Canadian whisky across the border during Prohibition. (Some old-timers claim that bootlegger traffic was so thick on Black Lake, you could buy a drink from the next canoe.)

Although he hadn't personally wielded the knife, Ersel Martell took the fall as an accessory to Renault's assault and stood trial. Despite maintaining his innocence, Ersel spent the next three years atoning in the Washington State Penitentiary at Walla Walla. Thomas Packard, in the meantime, fully recovered and soon afterwards married Minnie Drixel, the gal who—so it's said—had been the focus of their barn dance dispute. Ersel returned to town after his release from prison, sullen and embittered, with the Packard–Martell feud now turned up to a permanent simmer.

Their feud seemed at an end when the Depression hit bottom in 1933, after the Martell family harvested the last of the old-growth timber on their land. Their fortunes steeply declined and the next spring, on his deathbed, old Zebulon Martell sold the family's acreage and timber rights to Thomas Packard. "Old Zeb" promptly passed on, with pen still in his hand and a scowl frozen on his face.

Thomas Packard, magnanimous in victory and eager to forge a permanent peace, hired all of Martell's old workers, and in 1939 he closed and eventually tore down the Martells' antiquated sawmill.

The third family that prospered mightily in Twin Peaks during the early twentieth century was the Horne clan. Patriarch Danville Horne had founded a mercantile company in San Francisco that banked its first million during the California gold rush. The promise of the timber industry attracted one of Danville's sons to the area in search of their next fortune; Orville Horne arrived in 1905 and opened a well-financed general store and dry goods business that soon eclipsed the motley local competition—one of which, legend has it, suspiciously burned down. By the 1920s, as the bounty of the logging boom blossomed, that general store grew into a three-story anchor of the business district known as Horne's Department Store. Soon, valley residents were treated to a selection of products as fine as the splendid offerings available in Seattle, San Francisco or even New York!

Representing the pinnacle of luxury values, the Packards and Hornes provided a vital sense of social aspiration to the fledgling community. Together they became principal investors in building the Bijou Opera House, a 250-seat jewel box on the main square that upon opening in 1918 became the centerpiece of local entertainment and civic pride. It served not only as a venue for high culture—visiting opera legends like Enrico Caruso and musicians of the first rank like Paderewski often adorned the marquee—it also served as a vaudeville house on the Orpheum circuit: The Marx Brothers and a young juggler named William Claude Dukenfield (aka W. C. Fields) were only two of the great acts who early in their careers graced its splendid stage. During the 1920s the Bijou did triple duty as the

15

OH, WHAT A TANGLED WEB...

town's first movie theater, and was the first in the region to be outfitted for sound when the "talkies" came along. The debut of *The Jazz Singer* in 1929 made unfortunate headlines, however, when one elderly patron—the town's last living Civil War veteran—heard Jolson's singing voice issue from the speakers and succumbed to a fatal rictus.[2]

[2] According to local records, the impetus to build the Bijou began in 1915 when, during a swing through the provinces, Caruso refused to play Twin Peaks, dismissing it as a backwater venue unworthy of his presence. Three years later, suitably impressed—and in possession of a fat check from the Packards—Caruso sang at the Bijou's premiere—TP

16

The Hornes, on the wings of these rising fortunes, a short time later created the town's first grand hotel, the Great Northern, built on the bluffs above White Tail Falls, a short hop down a spur line from the railway station. In awe of the Great Northern's grandeur, most of the local hotels and rooming houses that had once attracted the tourist dollar immediately folded their tents.[3]

But hard times lay ahead. The people of our town survived the Depression through sheer grit, stout character, and the country's unquenchable appetite for wood. Then, along with the rest of America, Twin Peaks and Washington State put their shoulders to the wheel to aid the war effort when World War II shattered global peace. The constant threat of attack from the Japanese to the west and infiltrating Hun saboteurs from the north heightened tensions. The local premiere at the Bijou of the 1941 film *49th Parallel*—which features an attack by a rogue Nazi raiding party in western Canada—sent local enlistment soaring and led to the formation of a volunteer watch that tenaciously defended the border until war was declared after Pearl Harbor.

Spearheaded by popular law enforcement leader Sheriff Frederick Truman, the group that rallied to defend our territory was officially known as the Citizens Brigade, and counted among its ranks our fittest and finest young men. For their service during the war years they soon passed into local lore as the Bookhouse Boys, named for the old one-room schoolhouse out on Highway 21 that Sheriff Truman selected as their meeting place. (Since being displaced by the town's first official school system in 1918, it had served as a lending library.) When America officially entered the war, many of that first generation of Bookhouse Boys went on to serve with honor and distinction in every branch of our military, more than a few of whom made the ultimate sacrifice. The names of the fallen adorn the World War II Memorial in Town Square across from the Giant Log.

But the surrender of the Axis powers didn't mean the end for the Bookhouse Boys, who have maintained their admirable tradition of community service and the twin ideals of justice

[3] According to the *Gazette*, once again—a coincidence surely—the week before the Great Northern opened, their biggest competitor went up in flames. Below is an excerpt from the *Gazette*—TP

"A fire of unknown origin destroyed the Sawmill River Lodge Tuesday night, one of the oldest establishments in town. No injuries were reported, but as proprietors Gus and Hetty Tidrow viewed the wreckage in the cold gray of dawn they were heard to say they will not attempt to rebuild."

17

and literacy ever since. Proud members of the group's next generation included the sons of Sheriff Truman, Franklin and Harry—named for Presidents Roosevelt and (no relation) Truman, respectively. Twin Peaks is indeed fortunate that both boys grew up to follow their father in service as our local sheriff. After Frank served with the Green Berets in Vietnam he returned to take the job after their father retired, and later a job with law enforcement in western Washington, where his wife's family hails from. His younger brother Harry, already a deputy, assumed the office from Frank in 1981, ensuring that a fifty-plus-year tradition of a "true-man" wearing the Twin Peaks sheriff's star continues to this day.

Some believe the Bookhouse Boys' most remarkable achievement came in 1968, when its members made up the entire starting lineup on the Twin Peaks High School seven-man football squad. That hard-nosed crew went undefeated for Coach Bobo Hobson during the regular season, a first for our small community—the misprint on the old town sign notwithstanding—and then thrilled their die-hard fans when they rumbled through the local, sectional and regional playoffs to reach the Washington State championship game. That epic contest ended in a heartbreaking loss to the Kettle Falls Cougars, 9–6. Thus ended, to this day, the best and only chance Twin Peaks High has ever had at hanging a statewide championship banner from the rafters of Hobson Hall.[4]

And finally, regarding that feud between the Packards and Martells? Well, I'm delighted to report that it found a happy ending. Although both houses may not have been *exactly* alike in dignity—to paraphrase the Bard—they did eventually fashion a storybook ending straight out of *Romeo and Juliet*.

In 1958, the eldest son of Ersel Martell, affectionately known as Pete—winner of six straight Lumberjack of the Year awards at the Packard Mill—tied the knot with the youngest daughter of Thomas Packard, the deceptively lovely Catherine. After she returned home at the end of her senior year at Sarah Lawrence,

[4] That starting roster, engraved on a plaque beside the trophy case in Twin Peaks High's main corridor, includes the following names: Frank Truman, Harry Truman, Ed Hurley, Tommy "Hawk" Hill, Henry "Hank" Jennings, Thad "Toad" Barker and Jerry Horne, who was apparently the placekicker, punter and return specialist. Ben Horne is listed as the team's student manager. At the bottom is a special thanks to "our number one booster, Pete Martell."

I've also come across a cryptic reference in a *Twin Peaks Post* column by Robert Jacoby in 1970 that suggests that something about how that championship game went down wasn't completely kosher—TP

18

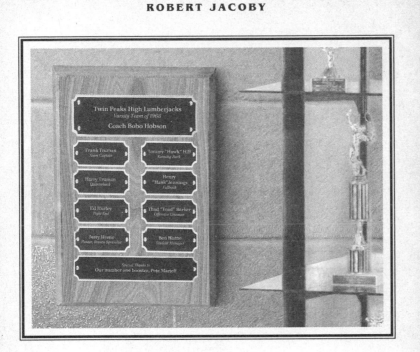

Catherine and Pete got reacquainted at the annual square dance during Lumberjack Days, where, according to tradition, the newly crowned Lumberjack of the Year can ask any woman present to dance a waltz; he chose the comely Catherine, whom he'd apparently had his eye on for some time. (This was the same event, mind you, where the attack by Pete's father Ersel on *her* father Thomas had taken place over forty years before.) As they tripped the light fantastic, folks said you could see sparks flying from as far away as White Tail Falls. Before the week was out, Catherine had set aside her plans to study in Europe for a year and the happy couple announced their engagement.

Who said true love only happens in the movies? [5]

[5] For anyone not yet convinced this amateurish slice of Chamber of Commerce civic puffery is pure fiction, the *Romeo and Juliet* reference should put those doubts to rest. See the following—TP

19

* The Bookhouse, circa 1987

2 CATHERINE AND PETE MARTELL

By this time an enormous class divide had developed between the two families, given how sharply their fortunes had vectored since the Martells sold their mill to the Packards. If the Packards/Capulets were now the Vanderbilts of Twin Peaks, the Martells/Montagues had devolved into something closer to the Kramdens.

There must have been sparks flying at that barn-burning hootenanny -- Pete and Catherine clearly produced, at first, a high level of chemistry that resulted in their hasty trip to the altar -- but according to everyone around them it wouldn't be long before sparks changed to daggers. (Although they never had a child, there were, at the time, inevitable rumors of a bun in the oven that necessitated their nuptials.)

The loveless arrangement that resulted between these "star-crossed lovers" deserves a niche in the matrimonial hall of shame. Whatever affection survived between them issued almost entirely from the husband, a well-liked and simple fellow; Pete played checkers, not chess. Catherine played nothing but hardball.

Despite his woeful fate, Pete's feelings for Catherine never wavered, decades after his return on that investment dwindled into unrequited longing and, from her end, chronic contempt. His friends marveled at Pete's undying devotion to his Lady Macbeth of the Sawmill. While in a local diner, I once overheard him explain to a friend in these exact words his formula for a successful marriage:

> As long as whatever both halves of a couple
> give to each other adds up to I00 percent?
> Don't really matter how they divvy it up.

Pete estimated his part of that equation at 70 percent, by the way, which most who knew them would agree underestimates his actual contribution. He also, once, in a rare moment of candor brought on by a few single-malt scotches, admitted that "Catherine is plain hell to live with." [1]

[1] So the Archivist admits to firsthand knowledge of Pete Martell. Confirms that the Archivist is or was in some way part of the community. We will eventually identify this individual—TP

If Catherine Packard Martell had redeeming personal qualities, she kept them to herself. She did possess an icy Titian beauty and the temperament to match, while inheriting all of her family's most ruthless instincts and none of her gender's mitigating compassion. A local wag referred to her as "a Packard by name, a Medici by inclination." [2]

Only a few years into their marriage Catherine entered into a permanent dalliance with the scion of the town's other most prosperous and prominent clan, Benjamin Horne -- married, at the time, with children -- someone with whom she shared a cutthroat approach to business and pleasure.

She also remained unhealthily devoted to her older brother Andrew, acting as his hammer in business while he served as the friendly public face of their company. While they always got along, it seemed to irk Catherine no end that Andrew was also fond of Pete, whom she considered their social inferior. But Andrew appreciated Pete's lack of pretension and Pete always made him laugh.

The two siblings -- and "third wheel" Pete -- shared different wings of Blue Pine Lodge, the Packard compound on the shores of Black Lake near the mill. That arrangement persisted for over three decades, until Andrew married for the first time, late in life -- at age 70 -- and that changed everything.

3 ANDREW PACKARD REVISITED

The document excerpted below, author unknown, was found in the Bookhouse. [1]

[2] More confirmation that the Archivist has personal knowledge of or contact with these people. There were no similar references in the early historical sections, which suggests the Archivist was or still is a contemporary of these people. Or could it have been someone from out of town with the ability to observe them with fresh eyes?—TP

[1] Confirmed. One of many volumes found there, all of which were cataloged by Agent Cooper in his notes. I've also confirmed that this one was typed on a vintage Underwood that permanently resides in the Bookhouse—TP

THE

ANDREW PACKARD

CASE

3/15/89

A lifelong bachelor, who'd always played the field while devoting his life
to business, Andrew in 1983 did something completely out of character:
he lost his heart to a young Asian woman during a business trip to
Hong Kong. Andrew traveled there on a two-week state-sponsored trade
mission to sell hardwood to emerging Eastern markets. He returned with
a blushing bride, and nearly a child bride at that.

Josie Packard. Her passport claimed she was from Taiwan, but she was
born and raised in an orphanage in a provincial region of mainland
China. Her marriage license states she was only nineteen at the time
of their betrothal. Since she claimed not to speak English, no one in
Twin Peaks ever knew too much about her, which wasn't helped by her
spending most of her time alone. The only friend Josie made here was
Pete Martell, who shared not only their large and empty house but also
a lack of daily structure. (Pete's "management job" at the mill, for
which he was well paid, had by this point become ceremonial.)

Not long after she arrived, Pete made it a pet project to teach English
to Josie. She got fluent so quickly, anyone more curious than Pete
would have asked whether she knew more than she was letting on from the
get-go. The same thing happened when he tried to "teach" her tennis.
How to handle rackets of every variety turned out to be second nature
to his new sister-in-law, but Pete was always the last to read the
writing on any attractive female's wall.

The truth was that, in Josette Mai Wong--not her real name--Catherine had
met her match in cold-blooded calculation. That Josie was able to hide
her long-play intentions under the placid mask of an innocent immigrant
bride, while playing every side around her against the other, made her
far more dangerous than anyone could have imagined. Catherine, who never
trusted her and was always on the lookout for any hint of scheming in her
rival, didn't even see what was coming until it was too late.

This is part of the jacket on Josie put together by Interpol in Singapore,
just before she showed up in Twin Peaks:

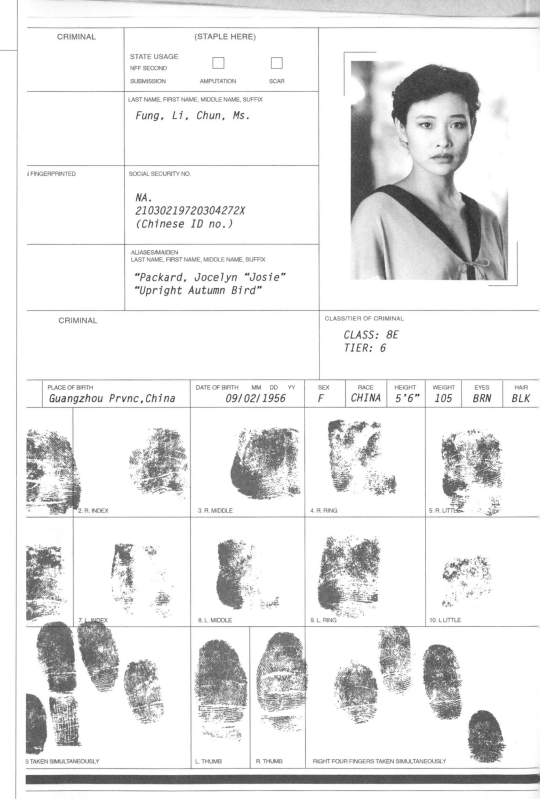

CRIMINAL   (STAPLE HERE)

STATE USAGE

NFF SECOND   ☐   ☐

SUBMISSION   AMPUTATION   SCAR

LAST NAME, FIRST NAME, MIDDLE NAME, SUFFIX

Fung, Li, Chun, Ms.

N FINGERPRINTED   SOCIAL SECURITY NO.

NA.
21030219720304272X
(Chinese ID no.)

ALIASES/MAIDEN
LAST NAME, FIRST NAME, MIDDLE NAME, SUFFIX

"Packard, Jocelyn "Josie"
"Upright Autumn Bird"

CRIMINAL   CLASS/TIER OF CRIMINAL

CLASS: 8E
TIER: 6

PLACE OF BIRTH	DATE OF BIRTH MM DD YY	SEX	RACE	HEIGHT	WEIGHT	EYES	HAIR
Guangzhou Prvnc,China	*09/02/1956*	*F*	*CHINA*	*5'6"*	*105*	*BRN*	*BLK*

2. R. INDEX   3. R. MIDDLE   4. R. RING   5. R. LITTLE

7. L. INDEX   8. L. MIDDLE   9. L. RING   10. L LITTLE

S TAKEN SIMULTANEOUSLY   L. THUMB   R. THUMB   RIGHT FOUR FINGERS TAKEN SIMULTANEOUSLY

[2] Verified with Interpol sources. I believe it's also likely, the tone being consistent with what I've seen of his case notes, that *Agent Cooper himself may have put together this untitled volume*—TP

INTERPOL

SUBJECT'S real name is Li Chun Fung, which roughly translates as "upright autumn bird."

Born September 2, 1956, in Guangzhou province. (Subject later claimed she was born in 1962.) Father was a high-ranking "RED POLE" enforcer in the Siu-wong triad, mother was a legendarily beautiful prostitute known as the "Lace Butterfly"—deceased shortly after her daughter's birth from a heroin overdose. During her childhood, her father rose to the position of "Deputy Mountain Master," or second in command, for the largest triad in the region. Subject was raised and trained by her father; she studied criminality the way a street urchin in the Peking Opera learns acrobatics. A brilliant if disinterested student, she attended an exclusive private boarding school in Shanghai, where at sixteen she organized and ran her own drug and prostitution ring, entrapping and extorting members of the administration and faculty in a brazen blackmail scam. Fearing her father's muscle, none of the victims would testify against her, and she graduated with honors.

Beautiful enough to work as a runway model, after graduation she climbed to the top of the Hong Kong fashion industry, and founded her own fashion label. It served as the cover for a cocaine sales and distribution system that spread into every corner of the emerging music, film and entertainment industry there in the 1970s. She was identified as a person of interest in connection with a series of "accidental" overdoses during the second half of this decade, which eliminated many of her dealer rivals and a fashion designer with whom she'd conducted a public feud. During this time it is believed she was initiated into her father's triad by blood oath, an unprecedented step for a female. By this point subject was fluent in six languages, maintained half a dozen aliases in different countries and is still wanted for questioning in major cases throughout the Asian Rim. Her net worth by the age of 21 was believed in be in excess of fifteen million dollars U.S. She was as much feared for her ruthlessness as she was admired for her beauty.

In 1980, during an escalating inter-triad gang war, her father was gunned down inside his Guangzhou nightclub. When rumors surfaced that subject had either arranged or carried out the hit herself in order to inherit her father's operations, her luck finally ran out. With this violation of the triad's most sacred oath—don't kill your boss—the triad's senior council turned against her and a contract was issued on her life.

At which point, subject abruptly vanished from Hong Kong and has not been seen by reliable sources since.

THE ANDREW PACKARD CASE / CHAPTER ONE   3/15/89

Enter Andrew Packard. We now know that Josie was actually 27 by the time she met her soon-to-be American husband, not the 21 she claimed. When the two met during a state-sponsored black-tie "mixer" at the Hong Kong Trade Center, Andrew believed Josie was an art and design student from a local university, hired to work as a hostess for the evening. He was also sufficiently swept off his feet to buy that she was Josette Mai Wong, a plucky orphan girl from the slums of Taiwan, not a patricidal sociopath looking to escape a death order. Meanwhile, Josie had stashed whatever remained of her ill-gotten fortune somewhere offshore, while retaining enough ready cash to pull off her desperate gambit.

To set this up, and make her escape from the vengeful triad prior to Packard's arrival, Josie bought protection from a Hong Kong import-export man, a South African emigré named Thomas Eckhardt,[3] using herself as collateral. During Andrew's business trip, Eckhardt made a successful play to become Packard's local contact in Hong Kong. When Packard left to head home, Eckhardt thought that Josie would be staying with him in Hong Kong; her disappearance seemed to take him by surprise. If he knew that she'd left for the Pacific Northwest to join Packard, Eckhardt took years to find her there. Which is one of the reasons to suspect Eckhardt knew her intentions all along, as part of a comprehensive plan he and Josie had devised.

According to Pete, Josie told him she had refused Andrew's first proposal in Hong Kong as too impulsive, but then showed up at their door in Twin Peaks unannounced three weeks later and accepted, saying she'd needed some time to think it over. She apparently made that midnight entrance wearing only high heels, a mink coat and Chanel No. 5.

Blindsided by this seductive interloper parachuting into her life, Catherine thought her brother had gone mad; Andrew hadn't even mentioned Josie when he returned. When she failed to dissuade him from going through with the marriage--without even the prenup she begged him to make Josie sign--her shock turned to slow-burning rage; her grip on the Packard fortune was in trouble.

THE ANDREW PACKARD CASE   /   CHAPTER ONE

While Josie played the part of the fragile bird with a broken wing to perfection, she mesmerized the guileless Pete and slowly and subtly undermined Catherine's influence with Andrew. Josie also cast her hooks into the new community around her. Local lout Hank Jennings fell under her spell--clearly no match for her charms-- and began working as her accomplice in various ways.

The next victim Josie foozled was more pragmatic, and her success even more surprising: Sheriff Harry Truman. A man of more pristine character in the region is impossible to come by, but Josie's charms were world class, and Harry was a small-town guy who'd never found the right woman. The wrong one found him first. It's not known exactly when their romance began; I believe it happened after Andrew Packard's "first death." [4]

Like many of his class, Andrew Packard was a boating enthusiast, and his prize possession was a 1936 40-foot mahogany-hulled classic Chris-Craft Sportsman, harbored in a boathouse on the Packards' family estate--the Blue Pine Lodge--and rechristened the "JOSIE" just after their wedding. Andrew could be seen at her helm during the season tooling around in his peacoat and captain's cap with Josie at his side. Until one afternoon in September of 1987 when Josie stayed home with a migraine and the JOSIE exploded in the boathouse the moment, apparently, that Andrew fired up the ignition.

Local police concluded that although there were plentiful human remains at the scene, the explosion had been so violent--it leveled a sturdy timbered boathouse that had stood for 60 years--that no identifiable human tissue could be found. Since Pete and Catherine had both seen Andrew enter the boathouse moments earlier, from the kitchen window inside, the report concluded Andrew had

[3] Thomas Eckhardt

[4] I've been waiting for this subject to resurface. Sometimes patience is rewarded—TP

Sunday Edition
$2.50

PUBLISHED
IN THE STATE OF
WASHINGTON
SINCE 1922

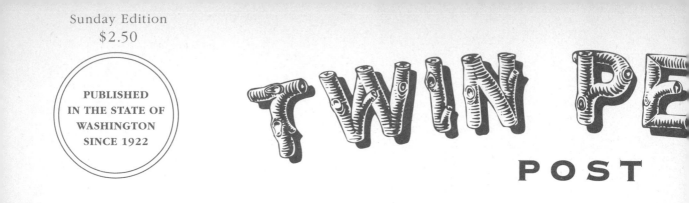

TWIN PE

POST

VOL. 65, NO. 270   TWIN PEAKS, WASHINGTO

TRAGEDY AT BL

by CYRIL PONS, *Staff Reporter*

A BOATING accident yesterday claimed the life of local businessman **Andrew Packard, 75**. Shortly after 9:00 AM an explosion rocked the boathouse at the Packard estate, Blue Pine Lodge. According to family sources, Mr. Packard had left the house to take his customary morning boat ride in his favorite runabout. Moments later, apparently when he started the engine, a blast erupted that was powerful enough to destroy the boathouse and shatter windows in the main house

Pata Cut Paduaad ac Dra

AKS

SUNDAY, SEPTEMBER 27, 1987

ACK LAKE

over fifty yards away. Fire and police arrived within minutes and pronounced Mr. Packard dead at the scene.

Mr. Packard was believed to be alone at the time, and no one else at the scene was injured. Mr. Packard is survived by his wife, Josie, and his sister, Catherine.

Mayor Dwayne Milford issued this statement a few hours later from City Hall: "Our community today is shaken to its core at the sudden and senseless death of one of its most outstanding citizens. I've known Andrew his entire life—I was once proud to call myself his scoutmaster—and I cannot find the words to describe my profound shock and sense of loss. Andrew was like a younger brother to me. Like the brother I never had." [5]

[5] A curious statement from someone who, as we know, MOST DEFINITELY HAD a younger brother—TP

It's been a long time since a market-

been the only casualty. Josie claimed not to have
seen the blast, but only heard it from her bedroom
upstairs. [6]

Because so little evidence remained, the only conclusion
insurance investigators could draw was that a leak in
the fuel line near the ignition prompted the explosion.
Since there was a seven-figure life insurance policy
involved, as well as Andrew's recently redrafted will
designating a new sole beneficiary--guess who--Josie
became a figure of significant interest not only to
the insurers but also Andrew's bereaved, suspicious and
coldly vengeful sister. In cold black ink: Andrew had
left the Packard Mill, and all his assorted businesses,
exclusively to Josie.

Josie now wore the veil of the grieving widow to
perfection--she fainted at the funeral--and not a hint of
impropriety came close to sticking to her. No connection
to her criminal past in Asia ever surfaced. She possessed
a rare and ethereal beauty that was almost otherworldly,
one that women--Catherine excluded--were not threatened
by, and that most men felt an impulse to protect. The
Twin Peaks community mourned with her. Near the end of
her period of "mourning," around the time the insurance
companies took a harder look at the accident, Josie
first ensnared the good and decent Sheriff Harry Truman
in her web, as an insurance policy of her own.

No coincidence, then, that at this point in the
investigation their interest began to drift away from
Josie in the direction of Hank Jennings--the henchman
Josie had hired and paid handsomely to arrange Andrew's
"accident." Josie was also gently nudging Sheriff Truman
in Hank's direction--an aside here, a suggestion there--
but it turned out that Hank had (conveniently) been
arrested two hours before the explosion on suspicion of

[6] It just occurred to me that the film *Body Heat*, which came out a few years before this, has a strikingly similar plot twist. Maybe she saw the movie? Still worth watching, btw—TP

[7] Emil was the son of Doug Milford's erstwhile UFO witness—TP

vehicular homicide; a hit-and-run involving Hank's truck on a highway near the border. All part of Josie's plan.

A first-rate lawyer from Seattle--way out of Jennings's price range--bargained that charge down to a guilty plea on one count of vehicular manslaughter. Hank never stood trial and began serving a five-year stretch in the state pen, knowing he had the cash Josie paid him stashed and waiting for him on release.

A brief look at how Hank Jennings's criminal disposition developed is in order.

It's tempting to see Hank as a bad seed that germinated into a nasty piece of rotten fruit on a warped family tree. His father, Emil, was a ne'er-do-well souse about whom no town resident has a good word to say, since he owed most of them money. [7]

Emil's uncle Morgan died in 1914 when he fell down drunk in a Spokane street after a three-day bender and was run over by a beer wagon. Hank's mother, Jolene, was a hardworking, hash-slinging waitress at the Double R for 35 years. Hank was her only child with Emil, and Jolene doted on him, filling him with a confidence that surpassed the borders of his actual qualities by a wide margin.

Hank grew up strong and sturdy and was a more than competent athlete, which kept him out of trouble for most of his teenage years. The innate ferocity of football suited his temperament; he became a standout two-way player for Coach Hobson's Lumberjacks at Twin Peaks High. He also benefited from membership in the Bookhouse Boys--recruited by the Truman brothers--where his somewhat surprising love for American literature blossomed. (He favored Kerouac, Irwin Shaw and, more useful to his later career, the collected works of Raymond Chandler and James M. Cain.) Hank and Harry were close during their high school years, fullback and quarterback, respectively.

The first sign of moral rot emerged during the 1968 state championship football game.

TWIN PEAKS

SINCE 1922

GAZETTE

ONLY 75¢

Issue 318, Volume 46   TWIN PEAKS, WASHINGTON   *Thursday, November 14, 1968*

Distraught fullback Jennings (#80) hides his face after his game-losing fumble. Coach Hobson, tight end Hurley (#65) and quarterback Truman (#45) look on concernedly.

FROM THE JAWS OF VICTORY

by *Gazette* Staff Writer Robert Jacoby

TRAILING BY A field goal with less than a minute to play, the Twin Peaks High Lumberjacks were driving down the field for what it seemed would inevitably become the touchdown that brought the school and our town its first state championship banner. Then, on second and goal from the two-yard line, fullback Hank Jennings took a handoff from quarterback Harry Truman and headed for a hole on the right side you could have driven a logging truck through, which tight end Big Ed Hurley had opened with a tremendous bone-crunching block . . .

. . . and without being touched, Hank coughed up the pigskin, pulled up short and watched it bounce to the turf, where two Kettle Falls players fell on it at the one-yard line, which brought down the final curtain on the team's and the town's golden hopes and dreams.

Jennings, who appeared stunned after the game, confirmed that he hadn't even been touched by a member of the opposition. He explained, repeatedly, to anyone who would listen, that the ball had simply "squirted out of my hands like a pumpkin seed."

"I must have tried to hold onto it too tight," said a downcast Jennings. "Trying to protect it. Trying to protect it too hard."

"It was a good play," added junior quarterback Truman. "Just like Coach drew it up. Sometimes the ball just doesn't bounce your way."

Team captain and senior Frank Truman, Harry's older brother, offered only this: "We were so close. This close. It's almost a crime what happened out there."

A few of the players, and many students and citizens in the crowd, were seen shedding many a tear after the game. Twin Peaks coach Bobo Hobson, in his fortieth and some believe final year of coaching the Lumberjacks, remained philosophical after the game. "I should have invested in my brother's bar when I had the chance. While the town drowns its sorrows tonight, he's going to make a small fortune. And I can assure you, I will be among them."

1 DEAD, 2 INJURED IN LOCAL ACCIDENT

One man was killed and two others are hospitalized with critical injuries in a head-on crash involving two go-carts Saturday night. Eyewitnesses on the

Reports came in at 12:25 P.M. of a serious crash on trail 6F near Parker Road, and sheriff deputies along with the Twin Peaks fire department re-

THE ANDREW PACKARD CASE   /   CHAPTER ONE

A few in the crowd that night grumbled along the lines
of "what else would you expect from a Jennings." The rest
seemed to accept it as yet another lesson in the bittersweet
human condition in general, and life in Twin Peaks in
particular.

A few years later a more unsavory scenario for Jennings's
mishap emerged. A visitor to the brothel and gambling
establishment known as One Eyed Jacks, just across Black
Lake on the far side of the Canadian border, heard a story
one night that turned the accepted version of events on
its ear.[8]

Jean Renault--oldest son of deceased family patriarch Jean
Jacques Renault--was overheard bragging during a poker
game that he'd placed a substantial wager on underdog
Kettle Falls in that game and then "fixed" the outcome.
When asked why he'd go to all that trouble to corrupt a
high school football game, Jean laughed and was heard to
say, in thickly accented English: "Because I can."

Given Renault's amoral viciousness, that's easy to believe,
but in pulling that string he also made an investment in
the future loyalty of Hank Jennings. A few months later,
after Christmas, Hank was driving around town in a brand-
new, tricked-out cherry red Chevy pickup. When asked how he
came by it Hank explained that he'd used savings scrapped
together cooking short order at the Double R over the
holidays.

You don't need to be Perry Mason to connect these dots.

A few months later, Hank and Harry Truman had an abrupt
falling-out--a fistfight that erupted at the Bookhouse
when Harry confronted him about the "fumble." Harry's
older brother Frank and Big Ed had to pull Harry off Hank
or he might have pummeled him to death. Did Harry connect

[8] One Eyed Jacks figures prominently in an investigation conducted by Agent Cooper just after the Laura Palmer case—TP

the dots himself? I think so. But neither Truman told
their father, the sheriff, about it and the truth
stayed buried inside the Bookhouse. Hank and Harry were
no longer friends, and Hank's slide to the dark side
accelerated.

That summer Hank began making runs across the border
working for Jean Renault, a postgraduate education in
professional crime. His personal morality followed a
similar downward trajectory: It wouldn't be long before
former teammate Big Ed Hurley had his own reasons for
wanting to pummel Hank.

During senior year Big Ed and classmate Norma Lindstrom
had become an item. Norma was head of the cheerleading
squad and homecoming queen, a dazzling beauty from a
modest family on the shabbier side of town--that is,
where most everyone not named Packard or Horne lived.
The Hurleys had been Packard sawmill employees for two
generations--Ed's uncle had lost two fingers there--and
Ed's brother Ernest followed in their footsteps, but Big
Ed's teenage obsession with cars, trucks and motorcycles
indicated a different path lay in store for him. Norma's
father, Marty Lindstrom, had worked for the railroad for
many years, before retiring to open an unassuming diner
in the heart of Twin Peaks.

This diner, and its extraordinarily good coffee and pie,
has become, I admit, something of an obsession for me.
Included is a short history which can be found on the
inside of their menus. [9]

[9] Verified. Cooper must have really been into this place
—TP

Welcome to the Double R!!

Opened in 1938, this restaurant was first known simply as the Railroad Diner, serving the sort of hearty fare they used to dish up on the Northern Pacific dining cars worked by founder and owner Mr. Marty Lindstrom. From the day they opened its doors, one of the main attractions were Mrs. Ilsa Lindstrom's famous pies, many of them family recipes from her Swedish relatives, including such time-gone-by favorites as gooseberry, lingonberry and strawberry-rhubarb. Mr. Lindstrom put up a big sign and thought that folks would refer to his place as "Marty's Railroad Café," but it wouldn't be long before people started calling it the Double R. After the war years, Marty yielded to popular opinion and added the neon RR that adorns the sign to this day.

Beverages

Coffee or Tea	1.75
Milk	1.75
Orange Juice	2.50
Milkshake	3.50
Rootbeer Float	3.50
Malts	3.50
Soda	2.25
Ice Tea	1.75
Lemonade or Orange Whip	2.25

Breakfast

2 Eggs · Any Style	4.00
The "Double" R	7.00
Omelette with Cheese	5.25
French Toast	6.50
Pancakes or Waffles	5.75
Lumberjack Pancake Stack	6.25
Steak and Eggs	9.95
Woodcutter's Combo Breakfast	9.50
Oatmeal	4.50

All above served with Toast, Hash Browns, Bacon or Sausage

Sandwiches

Quarter Pound Hamburger	7.85
Barkburger Special	7.95
Turkey Club	8.49
Roast Beef	8.10
Ham and Cheese	5.95
B. L. T.	6.75
The Redwood	8.00

Sides

French Fries	3.49
Onion Rings	3.00
Salad	3.49
Soup of the Day	3.35

Dinners

B.B.Q. Ribs	10.95
Corned Beef	8.95
Steak "T" Bone	12.95
Beef Stew	8.49
Chicken Fried Steak	10.50
Spaghetti with Meat Sauce	7.95
Veal	14.40
King Crab	Market Price
Fish Dinner	10.95
Catch O' the Day	Market Price

Desserts

Our Famous Cherry Pie	2.50
Huckleberry Pie	2.50
Gooseberry Pie	2.50
Lingonberry Pie	2.50
Strawberry-Rhubarb Pie	3.00
Ice Cream	2.00

Breakfast • Lunch • Dinner — Served Anytime!

After speaking with all the principals, I believe I've discovered why
Big Ed and Norma, who were so obviously in love, never married. Again,
I find Hank Jennings is responsible. Here's how:

With American involvement in the Vietnam War at an all-time peak,
Big Ed Hurley enlisted in the Army after graduation and headed out of
town for basic training. Everyone assumed that Norma and Ed would marry
first, but Big Ed--displaying a tendency to hesitate at crucial personal
moments that never showed up on the football field--neglected to pop the
question before embarking for Fort Dix. Norma hadn't yet realized that
reticence was as much a piece of Big Ed as his inability to articulate
his reasons for it. Sweet-natured Norma, who'd stuttered as a child and
suffered from low self-esteem, simply assumed she wasn't good enough.
That fall Big Ed left the States to begin a two-year hitch in the
command HQ motor pool in Saigon.

With Big Ed out of the picture, Hank--who'd gone out with Norma briefly
during junior year--began circling his prey. Hank's own mother, Jolene,
had been one of the original Double R waitresses, and he'd worked there
himself all through high school--where Norma was now pulling shifts on
the weekends while attending community college--so they'd known each
other all their lives.

Hank approached her as a friend who shared her sorrow at the absence of
Big Ed. That struck a chord with Norma. Like any good sociopath, Hank
could simulate sincere emotions, without actually feeling them; with
Norma, "empathy" and "sincerity" went a long way. Hank was also patient
and armed with a surplus of dirty money, which he wasn't shy about using
to impress her. Norma grew to like the attention and by November they'd
progressed from weekly lunches to occasional dinners, and then Norma
invited Hank over to the house for Thanksgiving.

Norma claimed later that by then the daily letters she'd been getting
from Big Ed by military post had stopped; she hadn't heard a word
from him for over six weeks. A period during which Big Ed later said
he dropped her a line every day, addressed to the diner, and couldn't
figure out why his best girl wasn't writing him back. It wasn't in Big

Ed's nature to write his friends back home to check on Norma. Ed assumed
the worst, that he wasn't good enough and her affections had changed.
I believe it's because, at this point, you could add a felony charge of
"tampering with the U.S. mail" to Hank's criminal résumé.

Big Ed was supposed to come home for Christmas leave, but since he
hadn't heard from Norma he canceled the trip. He wrote one last letter
asking for clarity, but Norma never got it, so while Ed spent the holiday
drowning his sorrows in a Saigon PX, Norma was in the arms of Hank
Jennings at the annual tree-lighting ceremony in the Twin Peaks town
square. That night, as the townsfolk sang carols and a fresh sprinkling
of snow dusted the square's magnificent old 60-foot-tall Douglas fir,
Hank slipped Norma a small present in a beautifully wrapped box. Inside
was a big fat diamond engagement ring--no doubt stolen and fenced.

She said yes.

Norma's Dear John letter reached Big Ed three weeks later. Big Ed
thought long and hard about writing back, but was so brokenhearted and
prone to self-doubt that his thoughts got all tangled up and, after
a dozen false starts, decided he couldn't express a word of what he
actually wanted to say. So Ed hesitated, dithered and then declined to
act at all. Not that, as we know, such a letter would have ever made it
to Norma, but at least he could have truthfully said he'd written one.

Big Ed learned about their marriage after the fact, when a letter from
Harry finally did make it to him--an intimate affair at the Chapel-in-
the-Woods, attended by both families and not a single Bookhouse Boy--but
by then it was too late. Hank took Norma by train to San Francisco for
a swank honeymoon, then drove down the coast in a rented convertible
to Los Angeles, where they saw the sights and attended a taping of The
Tonight Show, with Johnny Carson, who, as he did every year, had taken
his show to the West Coast for a couple of weeks.

When they returned home, Norma threw herself into finishing her degree,
with the intention of becoming a nurse--but life had other ideas. Her father,
Marty, was diagnosed with heart disease, and her mom left the diner to care

Hi Mam and Dad from beautiful
downtown Burbank! (ha-ha)
Los Angeles is so much fun! we
took a movie studio tour today —
Hank wanted me to take a fake
"screen test" but I was too shy!
Then he somehow got us tickets to the
Tonight Show! Johnny Carson is so
funny and handsome! Sammy Davis
Junior was on the show and he sang
and danced and told funny stories
about his friends and so was this
really funny overweight actor named
Victor Buono who read some of his
hilarious poems! we're having so
much fun!

            Lots of love,
            Norma (and Hank!)

POST CARD

Mr. and Mrs. Lindstrom
508 Parker Road
Twin Peaks, WA 98065

for him. Then Hank's mother, Jolene, took ill--lung cancer--
so Norma helped care for her while taking over management of
the Double R. (Hank was by now spending most of his days "on
the road," working for Jean Renault.)

With her vitality and vision, Norma transformed a serviceable
greasy spoon into a place worth a special trip out of
your way. She revamped the menu and opened a small bakery
next door to produce her mother's pie recipes in greater
numbers, selling them as a side business, and eventually
by mail order. She also redesigned the waitress uniforms-
-the crisp, distinctive white-trimmed aqua dresses they
still wear today--and slowly turned a taken-for-granted
community hangout into a source of local pride.

(Let me reiterate that the food, and particularly the pies,
at the Double R--and did I mention the coffee?--are truly
something special.)[10]

Norma lost her dad in 1978. Her mom came back to work
at the diner afterward, and Norma loved working side by
side with her--especially with Hank's long and frequent
absences--but Ilsa never got over losing Marty. The
prospect of grandchildren helped sustain her, but Ilsa's
health declined and she passed suddenly one night in
her sleep in 1984. The whole town turned out for Ilsa's
funeral, but Hank didn't make it--out of the country, and
unreachable, on "business" again. At which point Norma
realized there weren't going to be any children either.
They'd settled into a distant and loveless routine. Every
time Norma thought of ending it, Hank would do something
just kind or affectionate enough to keep her growing
feelings that they were finished at bay.

Until three years later, when Andrew Packard was vaporized
in his boathouse, and a few weeks later Hank pled guilty to
hit-and-run.[11]

[10] Yes, definitely Agent Cooper – TP

[11] The first "chapter" of Cooper's narrative ends here.
    My first question is: Why did he write this? He obviously had become fascinated with, and fond of, the people and places of the town. Based on the date at the front, this was after the Laura Palmer case was closed but apparently before he left town. Cooper had some time on his hands, so he turned his investigative skills to clearing up a couple local mysteries, like a concert pianist practicing the scales to stay in form.
    It's only my opinion, but it also seems possible he did this as an act of friendship—as a way to tell his new friends hard truths about the losses or trouble in their lives without confronting them. I believe he may have then just left these pages in the Bookhouse in the hope that his friends Sheriff Truman and Big Ed Hurley—both Bookhouse Boys—might come across them.
    No way yet of knowing if they did—TP

1 Verified. This one was
written by Sheriff Truman's
chief deputy at the time,
Thomas "Hawk" Hill—TP

TOMMY HILL,
circa 1987

4 LOVE TRIANGLE

In addition to fostering interest in reading, the rules of the
Bookhouse encouraged "journaling" in its members. A second
"journal" from a local source, also found at the Bookhouse -- in
the Local Interest section, on the shelf right next to Cooper's
work -- picks up Big Ed's story from there.[1]

THE BALLAD OF
BIG ED AND NORMA
AND NADINE

BY

HAWK HILL

MY PAL BIG ED HURLEY came back to Twin Peaks a few months after Saigon fell in 1975. I hooked up with him there once in fall of '73 during shore leave. (I was a gunner's mate on a PBR, patrolling the Saigon River delta. Talk about a flat-out shit suicidal detail, but that's another story. Remind me to tell it to you sometime. And remind me, next time I see him, to kick the ass of the jerkweed who talked me into that recruitment center in the first place, if I can ever remember who that was. Hank.)

After a bottle of 90 proof brain grenades loosened up his tongue, Big Ed confessed he was still carrying a Statue of Liberty–sized torch for Norma. Now I love the big dumb SOB like a brother, okay, but breathe a word about Norma and the dude goes into full-out mope mode like a twelve-year-old Girl Scout who lost her cookies. I grabbed him by the shoulders, told him to buck up and stop acting so beaucoup dinky-dow about his stale old stateside sob story. Nobody in our immediate vicinity—and by that I meant the closest two thousand miles—gave two shits. The statute of limitations had expired on that heartbreak and there was a surplus of local nookie in our current clique to help his "little-brain-housing unit" achieve a permanent state of amnesia vis-à-vis what's-her-name. He came out of it, slightly, but the evening crashed for good, as I vaguely remember, with Big Ed getting goony-eyed over some Frankie Valli tearjerker that dropped on the jukebox—"That was our song," he said, I kid you not—and that's when I split the scene. A firefight up the Mekong on my PBR sounded good compared to this episode of Queen for a Day.

We exchanged a few letters over the next couple years. I punched my ticket home six months before Big Ed, courtesy of some VC shrapnel I absorbed with my gluteus maximus when some FNG (military slang for "fucking new guy") lieutenant ordered us up the wrong fork of the river, thereby nearly introducing us all to the Beautiful Round-Eyed Woman who takes you to the Big Base Camp.

Back in Twin Peaks, next letter I get from him Big Ed tells me he was about to sign up for another hitch and go career Army—the action he saw in the HQ motor pool wasn't exactly hot—when he learned that family obligations were calling him back home.

Ed had this sad sack younger brother Billy who'd been hurt at the mill—a stack of logs fell off a truck and crushed one of his legs. For the record, becoming the third generation of Hurley to get himself maimed on the job. They called it Hurley Luck. You know those safety signs they put up in the workplace? The one in the mill read: " ___ number of days since a Hurley was injured."

(My old man worked thirty-five years in the field for Packard, in way hairier circumstances, and never came down with a hangnail. And by the way, don't ever call those guys "lumberjacks" or it'll really piss 'em off. They're loggers. Lots of Native people did that job. We built the skyscrapers in New York too, but it wasn't 'cause we were "fearless Indians" either. Not enough white people were desperate enough to want those jobs.)

That injury crushed Billy's spirit, too, what was left of it. Confined to a wheelchair, he went on disability, and started investing those checks in local water holes. Billy and his wife Susan had a young son named James, still in elementary school, and Susan pleaded with Ed that the boy needed his help and she needed him to read Billy the riot act. Well, Big Ed was up for that job and the Army lost a hell of a mechanic.

Many moons ago during the Depression, Big Ed and Billy's parents had opened a roadside stand outside town selling eggs, fruits and vegetables from the family farm. (Best corn in the valley, by the way. Well worth the drive.) After WW2, when rationing ended and motorists hit the road again, Big Ed's old man Ed added some gas pumps and lucked into owning a viable business. (For clarity: Big Ed had been born Ed Junior, but he came into the world as one enormous fucking baby so they started calling him Big Ed even when he was little, which wasn't for long.)

Big Ed also came in with this weird gift for figuring out how shit worked. Five years old, his mom would come home to find out he'd field stripped the toaster or her vacuum cleaner. She whupped him so good that pretty soon he could put all that shit back together the right way, too. By the time Big Ed got to high school he could assemble a Volkswagen blindfolded and was working as chief mechanic at the garage his old man added to what by now folks were calling Ed's Gas Farm. Me, I just called him the "engine whisperer." And good thing he knew how mechanical stuff worked, 'cause when it came to the human heart, the poor bastard didn't have a clue.

Big Ed didn't tell a soul, even me, when he was coming home from 'Nam. Two weeks after the last chopper got out I walked into the Bookhouse and found him sitting there with a 16-ounce Olympia in one hand and a copy of *Catch-22* in the other. (Big Ed's one-line review of Joseph Heller's masterpiece: "This guy was definitely in the Army.") For a while Big Ed kept to himself at the Gas Farm, working his butt off, taking care of his nephew James, and spent what few spare hours he had at the Bookhouse, trying to get James interested in reading. He tried everything, man. Twain, Tarzan, hell, even Doc Savage. Good kid, James. Not a reader.

Our former teammate Frank Truman, who'd taken over from his old man as sheriff, tried to talk Big Ed into joining the force as a deputy. After pondering the decision for a month, he decided to stay on at the Gas Farm to help his old man, who had a bum wheel of his own, courtesy of, you guessed it, another Hurley mishap at the mill when he was a teenager. It's an ill wind that blows nobody some good, as some old white guy said, so in his place Frank hired another of his high school teammates and fellow Bookhouse Boys, yours truly.

(Let me add here that, at the time, I still had some resentment toward Frank, since he was the one who first hung the "Tommy Hawk" nickname on me in junior high. Back then, white people still found condescending shit like that funny. You know, like *F Troop* or casting a Jewish guy from Brooklyn named Jeff Chandler as Cochise.)

At the time I was seriously considering moving to Alaska to work on a deep-sea fishing trawler—yes, I did need to have my head examined, and knew it, and courtesy of the VA, I booked an hour in the company of their on-duty shrink, to sort out some shall-we-say issues about Frank and my decision. Six minutes into my soul-searching monologue, the Doc shoots me a look and says: "Wait a second, you want to work on a fishing boat in the Arctic? I'm from Alaska. Are you fucking nuts?" For that wake-up call let me just say, for the record, "Thanks a heap, Doc." And so began my own career in local law enforcement. [2]

Although Norma knew he was back in town, Big Ed waited a year before going into the Double R for a cup of coffee. I was at the counter myself that day. The moment Big Ed saw Norma behind the register he went all pale and gulped in air—his chest swelled up like a water balloon—but Norma was hitched to Hank now, and Big Ed's vocal cords shut right down. Norma's heart probably skipped a beat when Big Ed walked through the door, too—life with that punk Hank was no bed of roses—but, as usual, she took her cue from Ed, and he didn't give her one, so they smiled politely, and stood there mumbling small talk so tiny you couldn't find it with a microscope. The sight was so pitiful I ordered a second piece of pie just to break it up.

That's how it stayed. A creature of habit, Big Ed started and ended every day with a cup of joe at the Double R, and usually ate lunch there too. A blind man could see that Norma's marriage to Hank was shakier than hell, and Big Ed had 20/20. He wasn't going to do anything about it, but knowing it pumped enough fuel to keep the pilot light on that torch burning for years.

Then, one Saturday in late 1984, he ran into Nadine Gertz.

When Ed's father passed in 1983, Big Ed took over the business. He put up this big new neon sign that he designed and built himself. Had a big glowing egg on it, a tribute to the family's old farm stand, and a mallard that he said symbolized his father's love for hunting—and he renamed the place Big Ed's Gas Farm. His nephew James, who by this point was like a son to him, worked weekends pumping gas.

Nadine had been a couple years behind us in school, although I can't say I remembered her. Maybe Big Ed did, I don't know. She was

[2] A detail of interest: Tommy Hill was a full-blooded Nez Perce whose parents left their reservation years earlier—just before the Hanford nuclear site came online, lucky for them. His father, Henry, was a fearless, legendary tree-topper—guys who climb the highest trees with cleats on their boots and trim the tops. Henry tree-topped for the Packard Mill his entire career—which is, according to the Department of Labor Statistics, the most dangerous job in the world—without ever suffering an injury—TP

[3] Verified—TP

BIG ED'S GAS FARM

driving her father's John Deere lawn mower to the Gas Farm that day for repairs at about 3 MPH. I'd just pulled my cruiser in to the pumps and James was about to fill 'er up. Big Ed was backing up his tow truck out of the garage and Nadine was riding so low he never saw her coming and backed right into her. James and I heard the crunch. Tipped the John Deere right over, but Nadine leaped off that thing like an acrobat before it hit the ground. She'd been a gymnast in school, but I didn't remember that either.[3]

Big Ed jumps out and runs over to help her, terrified and concerned, and she saw that expression on his face and, I guess, mistook it for something like, who knows with her, romantic longing? I guess nobody'd looked at her exactly that way before. She keeled right over and Big Ed caught her before she hit the ground. So I hurry over in my official capacity, since I'm an eyewitness, and I saw her jump clear right before impact and stick the landing so I know she's not injured. But Big Ed doesn't know that, and he's stricken, like he's crippled or killed this poor girl, and there goes his business and everything he's worked his whole life for. So he's holding her, eyeballing her face for signs of life with all those concerns ping-ponging around in his head, and her eyes flutter open and she sees Big Ed's dreamy rugged-handsome mug staring down at her. And it's not like Nadine is unattractive or anything. She's actually kind of exotic-looking, feline-like, and dressed beatnik fashionable with a silk scarf and a low-cut leotard thing going on.

And the first thought that goes through my mind is, well, that's that, she's in love with him now. And my second thought is, maybe this'll take Ed's mind off

Norma. I'm concerned for my friend, right, I want him to be happy. This is all before any one of us—little James is standing there, too—realize who this person is.

So the first thing she does is hug him, 'cause she knows exactly who he is—we find out later she'd had a crush on Big Ed since junior high, like most of the girls—and Big Ed's just so damn relieved she's alive he hugs her right back. And I know, instantly, watching the medicine flow between them, what with his vitality and her rocking gymnast physique, this thing is gonna end up between the sheets and fast. I get this big grin on my face, like an idiot, and James is staring at me like, what's up with you? I tell him I'll explain later.

Big Ed keeps asking her if she's sure she's all right, and she keeps telling him she is, and he keeps apologizing and she tells him it's okay, the mower needed fixing anyway, and then she kisses him, impulsively, and he breaks into this goofy grin, since when's the last time that happened, and at that moment he realizes he's got a hot little live wire in his arms and all the lights are green. And we still don't, neither one of us, remember who she is.

So, exercising my official capacity, I ask, "What's your name, miss?" and she says Nadine Gertz, and that rings a bell for Big Ed and it's a good memory—he remembers her in a gymnastics meet, vaulting over a horse. The name rings a dim bell for me, but I can't quite place her, so I go on to obtain her vitals: her dad lives a quarter mile away, and she'd been living down in Spokane for a while, working as a seamstress, which is why we hadn't seen her around town, but she was thinking of moving back home and opening a shop so she was staying at her dad's and noticed his lawn was overgrown and he told her the mower was on the fritz so that's how she came to drive the John Deere to the Gas Farm.

Big Ed tells her not to worry about that, it's all his fault—like he's never said *those* words before—and he'll fix the mower for free. So in my official capacity, given that both parties are in resolution, I declare there's no need to file an accident report, and since they're still stuck to each other like Siamese twins, I suggest they exchange contact information, and then I nudge James and have him help me push the John Deere—which wasn't that badly dinged up—into the garage.

What's going on? James asks quietly, once we got it inside, glancing back at his uncle. Both he and Nadine are on their feet now, shaking hands, and neither one is letting go. They're feeling the mystery, I tell James. What mystery, he asks. The mystery of life, I say, which you'd know about if you'd read more books like your uncle tells you. James grins like he gets it now. Good kid, James. (Except his favorite book is still *Charlotte's Web*.)

Ed and Nadine got hitched three weeks later, at the Chapel-in-the-Woods. Boom, just like that. Same place Norma and Hank got hitched.

All the Bookhouse Boys turned out for this one, minus Hank, who's permanently scratched from the roster. Turns out the rest of the fellas vaguely remember

DEPUTY ANDY BRENNAN

Nadine from school, too, but it's not until the reception at the Grange Hall after that the new guy Sheriff Truman just brought in as deputy, Andy Brennan—a few years younger than the rest of us, and greener than grass—whispers to me he was in Nadine's class at school and, oh my gosh, don't I remember what happened back then? I say no, Andy, I was too busy getting my ass shot off in 'Nam by some tiny dude in black pajamas.

Andy waves me outside, like anybody was gonna hear him in the Grange Hall with the rented cover band playing the greatest hits of the Young Rascals. Nadine's mother, Andy tells me, had "health problems of the mental variety," and her father wasn't a picture of stability either. Big drinker. They moved to town from somewhere in Idaho when Nadine was in seventh grade, and when she was a sophomore Nadine had "an actual, honest-to-gosh nervous breakdown" and had to take off school for the spring semester. Really, I say, watching her slow dance with Big Ed through the window.

Yes, says Andy, she went away to one of those places where people go to rest up and collect themselves. I say, you mean the puzzle house? Not the state one, says Andy, a privately owned facility—her parents had a little money; her old man had invented some kind of industrial flame retardant way back. How long was she gone, I ask. She came back for the fall, so I guess about six months, says Andy, but nobody ever knew why. She wore a beret and a scarf all the time and told everyone she'd been a foreign exchange student in France. How'd you find out about it, I ask him. Andy says, I don't know, people just have a way of telling me things.

(Andy, it turns out, owns some kind of ninth-degree black belt in gossip, which is about his best quality as a law enforcement officer, and I mean that as a positive. Or as he put it to me later, "You know, Hawk, I never think of myself as a gossip. I think of myself as an oral historian.")

Do you think your friend Big Ed knows about Nadine's history? Andy asks me.

I doubt it, I said, my heart sinking as I watched them dance—she had her feet on his and he was twirling her around like she weighed a feather.

No, Big Ed didn't have a clue about what was ticking away inside his sparkly new bride. And even though he now devoted himself to her happiness without a glance backward, it wasn't long before, somehow, Nadine put two and two together about Big Ed and Norma and his old torch, and hairline cracks started showing up in Nadine's psyche. Small remarks at first, then an endless stream of questions, followed by angry outbursts—a few of them public—that totally buffaloed him, since the only thing he was guilty of was having a life before he met her. And then she started following Ed whenever he went to the Double R. Just staring at him and Norma through the window while he's at the counter minding his own business. By now he's getting the idea his little firecracker might be carrying an extra load of powder, and of course he doesn't know what to do about it or who to talk to, so he doesn't tell anybody.

That fall, Big Ed and Sheriff Truman go bird hunting, like they do every season. Nadine followed Big Ed then, too, fifteen miles into the woods, thinking—who knows what—that he was sneaking off to meet Norma at four in the morning for a rendezvous at a duck blind?

That's when Big Ed accidentally shot out her eye. He had no idea she was even out there, creeping right into their line of fire, and she startles a bunch of ducks and they rise up and shoot and a single stray pellet of buckshot catches her smack in the eye. How was he supposed to know? A big fat heaping load of Hurley luck. Harry was right next to him when it happened, so everybody knows it was a righteous accident, including Nadine. But Nadine lost the eye.

Of course Big Ed blames himself, when the only thing he did wrong was marry Nadine before doing his due diligence, but now he's bonded to her by industrial-strength super guilt. He nurses her back to health and devotes himself twice as hard to making her happy. But the loss of Nadine's eye put a permanent zap on her head. She starts wearing that pirate eye patch, and gets stuck on this idea she's going to invent something like her old man did, to help save the world, and help save Ed from a life of drudgery at the Gas Farm. Except she doesn't realize that's the only life he wants, the one he chose and made for himself, and that included her. And now he had to live with it.

So we have a confluence of events: Andrew Packard blows up in his boathouse, and Hank gets arrested and sent up the river and two months later Nadine loses the eye and most of whatever remained of her grasp on reality. One night, then, at the Double R, Big Ed is sitting at the counter, the weight of the world on his shoulders, and Norma sees him, for the first time, like she hasn't really seen him in years. It's a slow night and she comes over with two cups of coffee and an extra piece of pie and the two of them get to talking. Really talking, like

BIG ED AND NORMA AT THE RR

they haven't talked in years, not since Ed came home. Commiserating. Consoling each other, about Hank, about Nadine. About what a hash they've both made of their lives and their marriages.

It's starting to snow outside, the first big storm of the season, about three days before Christmas, and over the next hour and a half these two fall in love all over again—no, not even that, actually. They both realize they've never been *out* of love. Ed finally pours his heart out to her about all the letters he sent from Vietnam, and she tells him she never got them, and she looks down where that day's mail is sitting next to the register—where Hank used to work—and she puts it all together. I know, I was there, in a back booth grabbing a bite after my shift, watching it happen with a big old grin on my face.

They don't take any action, of course. No stepping out, no sneaking around. Big Ed stays "true" to his burden. But he and Norma are in it—whatever it is—together from here on out, no doubt about that. He starts coming into the diner almost every night, after the evening rush, and they have these long conversations. Nadine's stopped following him by this point 'cause she's back in her workshop like a mad scientist—okay, poor choice of words—working on her invention, a "completely silent set of drape runners," around the clock. And Ed and Norma tell themselves it's only a matter of time before things work out and they're finally together again.

We'll see. Knowing Ed, he might even get around to doing something about it in another fifteen years or so.

5 DOCTOR AND PATIENT[1]

After losing her eye, while recuperating in Calhoun Hospital, Nadine was assessed for the first time in her adult life by a licensed psychiatrist. Dr. Lawrence Jacoby had returned to Twin Peaks from the island of Oahu in Hawaii in 1981, after the death of his mother, Leilani, and established a private practice in town, as well as a consulting residency at the local hospital.

Jacoby had garnered a controversial reputation in the 1960s and '70s after publishing a series of research articles and then a book based on his work entitled The Eye of God: Sacred Psychology in the Aboriginal Mind.[2]

In the book, Jacoby proposed a theory for the evolution of spirituality in early native people through the ritualistic use of psychotropic plant life by shamans or tribal healers. The book developed over a decade of anthropological fieldwork Jacoby conducted with aboriginal tribes all over the South Pacific and South America. Work that he freely admitted -- the sound you hear is Margaret Mead rolling in her grave -- included his participation in the rituals he describes throughout, including at one point a short-lived marriage to a chief's daughter. (The list of drugs the tribes shared with him, including peyote, ayahuasca and various Amazonian mushrooms and rare frog venoms, would be enough to knock anyone's cerebral cortex into the next dimension.)[3]

Here is a small example, from the medical establishment's perspective, of the kind of long thin branch Jacoby was crawling out onto in his book:

[1] I'm getting tempted to visit the Bookhouse myself. No telling what else you'd find on those shelves.
   The Archivist now picks up the story again—TP

[2] Verified—TP

[3] All verified as "local" hallucinogens. The ingestion of which, I might add, might well encourage a hasty "marriage" to an Amazonian princess—TP

THE EYE OF GOD:

Sacred Psychology in the
Aboriginal Mind

DR. LAWRENCE JACOBY

KURTIS
BOOKS

"Jacoby talks the talk and he definitely walks the walk."
— DR. TIMOTHY LEARY

Drawn from years of field experience among a wide variety of native and aboriginal people, *The Eye of God* takes the reader on a journey of discovery unrivaled in modern sociological/psychological literature. A visionary tour into the spiritual richness of pre-Columbian, tribal existence, Jacoby's findings offer a stark and bracing contrast to the presumptions and mores of the modern world.

"I felt like I was right there with him— maybe I was."
— JERRY GARCIA

"I'm speechless."
— MEHER BABA

DR. LAWRENCE JACOBY

Dr. Lawrence Jacoby is a trained and licensed Jungian psychiatrist who grew up, and has established an active practice, in both Hawaii and the state of Washington. He has also spent over a decade in the field working with and studying aboriginal people on three continents. This is his first book.

photo by Harvey Trufant

/IK KURTIS BOOKS
a division of AMESLEY PUBLISHING CO.

One of the strangest components of the tribe's pharmacopeia was a thick liquid compound they would let me try only once. It was reserved for the use of veteran shamans and I only earned their trust to sample it after many weeks of attentive study and participation in their daily rites. They called it *ayahuasca*, and never would reveal its source to me, although from what I observed as they prepared it—a daylong process which involved both rendering and cooking—it seemed to me to include both plant and animal extracts. I was the only person to use the substance on this occasion, with the shaman and two apprentices attending me, and only after a two-day fast as the sun went down on the second day.

At one of their holiest places, near the river, I was instructed to strip to a loincloth and kneel, while both my wrists were secured in loops of rope that were held by the two apprentices. The substance, contained in a gourd, was raised to my lips by the shaman as he uttered an indecipherable chant. It gave off an odor that was almost unendurably foul and I gagged once as it neared my face; one of the reasons for the fasting, I realized. Tilting back the gourd, he poured the substance into my open mouth all at once and I quickly choked it down, attempting with all my might to ignore the urgent signals my body was giving me to reject it. I realized the other reason for the fasting; it hit my empty body with paralyzing force and speed. My nervous system immediately felt as if I'd set it on fire and sweat seemed to simultaneously squirt from every pore of my skin. I closed my eyes in terror, my heart pounding, and as the substance overwhelmed my conscious mind I lost all track of time, or of even being in time. I believe I almost immediately vomited but no longer possessed any way of knowing how quickly this happened, or, indeed, if it did happen.

When I opened my eyes, two things occurred: I realized that I was no longer where I thought I had been, and at the same moment no longer knew who "I" was. My vision was both clouded and somehow enhanced, and at some level I registered that what I was "seeing" was not what was physically in front of me. I also knew that the veil of "reality" had been rent, split or torn away and that I was looking into a different or perhaps deeper dimension, one that either underlies ours or that coexists with it side by side, separated by the thinnest margin imaginable, one that our relatively primitive neurology prevents us from perceiving.

As I "looked" deeper—an inadequate description for a kind of seeing that involved all my senses, although not necessarily on the physical level—I realized there were living beings before me in this field of energy. As they drew closer to me, I realized that they could "see" me as well and that my presence had drawn their interest. This alarmed me slightly, as I could not discern their intent. They might have been angelic or demonic, or perhaps hybrid creatures, and there were many of them moving toward me, tall and humanoid. I realized that their interest in me felt cold, reptilian, neutral but shading toward malevolence, lacking all compassion.

A shining figure, much taller than the others, suddenly appeared in their midst and it gave off a violet light so bright and powerful it washed away everything else in my field of vision, nearly "blinding" me. I cannot honestly remember anything else about its appearance, which may or may not have been humanoid—my memory holds it closer in shape to a sphere that emanated a powerful impression of "beauty," but in an almost purely abstract sense. The other figures seemed to either defer to this figure or recoil from it in fear; it occurred to me that the figure might have been drawn to me by some protective instinct. As the other figures withdrew or receded, the new figure moved closer, and as it neared, all my own fears subsided and I felt a benevolent calm wash over me, an energetically soothing rush of peace and then a sense of joy that swelled up in my chest until I thought it might burst. A wholly inadequate phrase arose in my mind at that precise moment to fully describe this experience, and it was this: I am in the presence of "god" energy.

The next thing I remember: waking, lying facedown in the mud beside the river, alone and naked, the ropes still loosely attached to my wrists. It was dawn, light filtering through the forest canopy. I rose and staggered back toward the village, shivering and drained, but still carried and filled by the joyous wonder I had experienced. The shaman welcomed me by the village's central fire, smiling, and they wrapped me with a blanket, sat me down in the shaman's hut and gently let me sip from a bowl of water and fed me some kind of bland root paste. I felt weak as a foundling and unable to speak. The shaman sat down beside me and leaned in and repeated the same phrase to me, more than a few times, which, roughly translated, I heard as: "You are reborn into a new world."

ARCHIVIST'S NOTE

As a result of provocative material like this, Jacoby's book
was fiercely attacked by the American medical establishment
as lacking scientific rigor, but he rejected their criticism
on the basis that their traditional methods and standards were
outmoded. "Scientific objectivity is one of our most deeply
held, and crippling, illusions," he wrote. He also claimed that
all true spiritual insights and experiences were by necessity
profoundly disrupting, and deeply personal to the individual
and therefore entirely subjective. For some visionary
sociologists and anthropologists, and a big percentage of the
then-emerging "New Age" culture, Jacoby's work became one
of the signature works for a new way of comprehending human
psychological evolution, and it enjoys cult status to this day. [4]

Jacoby claimed that one of the main reasons he returned to
his hometown was to continue his studies with Native American
tribes in the region, along with the need to care for his older
brother Robert, the veteran reporter for the Post, who by this
time had been diagnosed with multiple sclerosis.

But accepting a conventional job with a hospital, as can
be seen in this evaluation of Nadine, was no guarantee that
Jacoby's methods would be any less unusual.

[4] Not with me. I tried to
plow my way through his
"magnum opus," but it reads
like an encyclopedia of
meandering gibberish,
though I'll concede it would
probably make a lot more
sense if you were on
drugs—TP

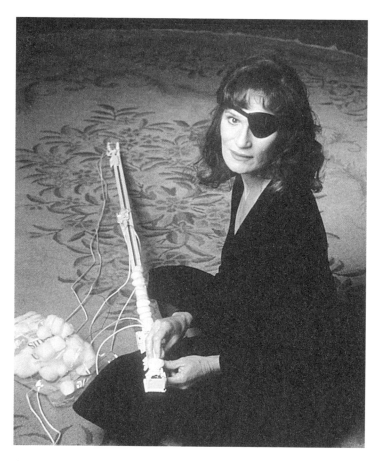

* Nadine, drapes

CALHOUN MEMORIAL HOSPITAL

DEPARTMENT OF PSYCHIATRY

PSYCHIATRIST Dr. Lawrence Jacoby		**DATE, TIME**	11/29/87 4:30 PM
NAME, MARRITAL STATUS Nadine Gertz Hurley, Married			
DOB 1/25/1950	**GENDER, AGE** Female / 37	**HEIGHT, WEIGHT**	5'6" / 112 Lbs

Wow. Patient is really whacked out, poor thing. I mean she is hip deep in the shit. Husband shot out her left eye a couple of weeks ago--hunting accident, or at least that's their story about it, and it doesn't ring altogether true so there's plenty of room for skepticism once you get past the particulars.

Husband's the sturdy, stolid patriarchal type, classic blue collar, strong-silent, upstanding. Vietnam vet, but noncombatant. Not to suggest for a second that he shot her on purpose but someone made a choice here, and my money's on Nadine. She's a thwarted creative--with severe blockages and neurotic adaptations, no doubt from family history, which I will try and take some time to inventory.

Working hypothesis: The left eye is wired to the right side of the brain so--in the event a choice was made--patient has chosen to shut down the optic pathway to her intuitive side. One possible interpretation would be that she was sensing something going on around her that she didn't want to see. The injury will likely prompt a period of intense suffering, as it seems she was already predominantly left brain dominant and the right side is now literally "flying blind." Since we also know there's no such thing as an "accident" and there's a positive side to every negative choice, let's dance with the idea that perhaps she willed the loss of her eye to stimulate internal growth in her area of greatest deficit? We all choose our fate even if, to quote Beatle Paul with St. Paul, the road to Damascus is long and winding, but if she can be led to embrace what she's unconsciously chosen for herself maybe she's got a chance.

The family has an extensive file here at the hospital. Ah-ha! Mother was diagnosed "manic-depressive" at this very institution about ten years ago and shipped off for state psychiatric care. Dad signed the papers. (She was sent to a former fort built in 1871, by the way, that had been converted to a mental ward, where she

page __1_/_3_

initial ___*LJ.*___

42p1642-P32

underwent shock treatment, straitjackets and "hydrotherapy," which involved pounding
subjects with cold water from pressurized hoses. For a more primitive means of treating
this "illness" you'd have to refer back to the Victorians and Bedlam. Astonishing.)

It gets worse: The daughter was herself admitted for "comprehensive treatment for
depression" about two months after Mom was sent to the snake pit. Nadine froze in
school one day, standing at her locker. Couldn't move. They found her locked in place
between classes and had to carry her like a mannequin to the nurse's office. Not a
full break, it turned out, but a debilitating one requiring six weeks of treatment,
including such classics as "sleep and art therapy," and a soupçon of Thorazine.
After which she was released to spend another six weeks in at-home supervised care,
with Dad--the undiagnosed alcoholic--as her primary. (Whereas, in a native village,
the entire population would have cared for her equally and compassionately around
the clock. And they're the primitives. Don't get me started.)

At which point, Mom came home from Western Psychiatric. Assuming they'd pumped her
full of Miltowns until she was thoroughly numb and told her to take up
needlepoint--at the time, on treatment protocol priority lists, "housewives" were
one step above livestock--you can sense the unspoken shame filling up that
household like a slow leak from a toxic well.

The mother passed five years ago. Although patient made an attempt to break away and
start life on her own in Spokane, it proved unsuccessful and when she felt herself
sliding she returned home to live with her father again. The "manic" side is manifesting
in the daughter now too. A hasty, impulsive marriage, which all too soon resulted in
the wound to the eye. By which point patient was already in the grip of a mania about
"silent drape runners" in which she spends every waking moment trying to design and
build the perfect prototype. She shared some of her drawings for it with me--it's a
whole portfolio really, and she's quite skilled--as she's constantly revising them.
This is a new decompensation on me, but then each one is like a snowflake, isn't it?

Come to think of it, what better way to deny and conceal the shame you feel is all
around you than by silently covering it up? Not unlike the way she's now "pulled the
curtain closed" on her left cerebral optic pathway.

initial _____L.J._____

Proposed treatment plan and prognosis: This could take a while. We're going to
start with nature walks, silent meditations, lots of peace and quiet. Massage,
maybe some Rolfing to release the patterns locked into her fascia. A lot of time
looking at trees, listening to the wind. Wean her off the pain meds and the drape
runners and engage in gentle mythical/metaphorical truth telling. With the hope
that eventually she'll be ready to probe the underlying pain.

Final thought, a regret really: Patient would have been a perfect candidate to test
my new optical integration system. Glasses with one red polarized to test my new
optical integration system. Glasses with one red polarized lens for the right eye,
one blue polarized lens for the left. My working theory being that the red spectrum
slightly suppresses activity in the left or logical hemisphere, while the blue
spectrum does the same in the spatial/intuitive side of the brain and that when
worn together--although it does tend to give "reality" a slightly purple tint--the
patient tends to experience increased integration between the two spheres by
increasing activity within the corpus callosum and encouraging the two sides to
work together. They work for me, but that's preaching to the choir. She would have
been a perfect candidate for testing.

It really is a shame she lost the eye.

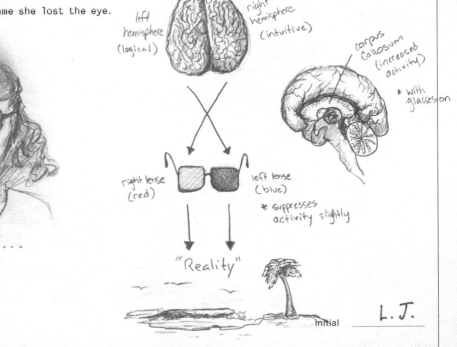

poor girl...

"Reality"

initial L.J.

[1] Agent Cooper's investigation into the "cold" Packard
case continues—TP

[2] Yep. *Body Heat.* But I guess
it was Andrew who saw the
picture, not Josie. Or maybe
they both saw it separately
and that's what tipped him
off?—TP

6 ANDREW PACKARD REVISITED (AGAIN)

We now return to the second installment of the
Andrew Packard saga, also found in the Bookhouse.[1]

Andrew Packard did not die in the explosion at his boathouse. Josie's plot, with Hank as her henchman, failed. Andrew had either been tipped off or sensed Josie was about to do him in and left the boathouse that day undetected, before the explosion.

Extensive planning on his part preceded this: Since we know human remains were found at the scene, a body was clearly in the boat at the time of the blast. One has to surmise that role was played by a bum or drifter whom Andrew drugged or killed and stashed in the boat the night before. Someone who wouldn't be missed; Andrew got all of it dead right.

So how exactly did he die the second time?[2]

Assume Andrew got away clean and went into hiding. Maybe he didn't know exactly who'd planted the bomb although hard to imagine he had a better suspect in mind than Josie but from then on he stayed a step ahead of her. Assume he found out about her plot beforehand, giving him plenty of time to set up his escape and hide enough cash to pull off a disappearing act. Once he realized he'd fleeced both Josie and the police, he created a new identity, and traveled back to Hong Kong to dig up the truth about Josie that he'd missed the first time.

He soon fingered his old "partner" Thomas Eckhardt as Josie's accomplice, realizing he'd been played for a patsy by both of them, to kill him and take possession of his fortune. Andrew waited three years to put his revenge into play and didn't reveal himself until all the players--including Hank, when he got out of the pen--were gathered on the stage.

The only person he trusted to help pull this off was the one he'd trusted the longest, his sister Catherine. Once Andrew knew the hit was coming all the rest was a setup--the "accident," the new will--to catch Josie. Once Andrew split the scene, Catherine became his eyes and ears. Josie was patient, playing a long game; she waited almost 2 years to make her move. Josie was smart as a snake, but once his mind got clear about who she really was, Andrew was smarter. And as soon as Josie tried to sell the mill and tens of thousands of

The Secretary of State
of the United States of America
hereby requests all whom it may concern to permit the citizen/
national of the United States named herein to pass
without delay or hindrance and in case of need to
give all lawful aid and protection.

Le Secrétaire d'Etat
des Etats-Unis d'Amérique
prie par les présentes toutes autorités compétentes de laisser passer
le citoyen ou ressortissant des Etats-Unis titulaire du présent passeport,
sans délai ni difficulté et, en cas de besoin, de lui accorder
toute aide et protection légitimes.

SIGNATURE OF BEARER/SIGNATURE DU TITULAIRE

NOT VALID UNTIL SIGNED

PASSPORT PASSEPORT	**UNITED STATES OF AMERICA**
Type/Catégorie **A**	Code of issuing / code du pays émetteur State **USA**
Surname / Nom **WALBROOK**	PASSPORT NO./NO. DU PASSEPORT **031585130**
Given names / Prénoms **ANTON DAVID**	
Nationality / Nationalité **UNITED STATES OF AMERICA**	
Date of birth / Date de naissance **01 MAY/MAI 19**	
Sex / Sexe **M**	Place of birth / Lieu de naissance **SEATTLE, U.S.A.**
Date of issue / Date de délivrance **11 DEC/DEC**	Date of expiration / Date d'expiration **10 DEC/DEC 96**
Authority / Autorité **PASSPORT AGENCY SEATTLE**	Amendments/ Modifications SEE PAGE **24**

```
A<USAWALBROOK<<ANTON<DAVID<<<<<<<<<<<<<<<<<
031585135BUSA1905012M9612196<<<<<<<<<<<<<<<4
```

62-103581--17

adjoining Ghostwood Forest acreage to Ben Horne for a
speculative real estate venture--behind Catherine's and
Josie's "partner" Eckhardt's back--Andrew showed up in
town again.

Andrew informs Josie that, since he's obviously not
dead, the mill is no longer hers, so there's no sale.
They toy with Josie for a while--brother and sister-
-punishing and humiliating her, treating her as a
servant. They were like that, the two of them, the
way they looked at people, like kids burning ants
with a magnifying glass.

Then Andrew sends word to Eckhardt about where he can
find Josie, letting him know how Josie has played him
as well. Eckhardt first sends an emissary to take her
out, but Josie shoots that man in Seattle. After that
she tries to kill an FBI agent who is on to her--yours
truly--with the same weapon.[3]

Then the noose begins to tighten. Andrew plays both
ends against the middle. He tells Josie he knows she
only tried to kill him because Eckhardt forced her
to. He warns her the law is about to catch up with
her, for that and all her other crimes. That much,
at least, was true.[4]

[3] Verified. During the Palmer investigation, a previously unidentified assailant shot Cooper in his room at the Great Northern Hotel. His notes reveal that Cooper, expecting the assault, was wearing a Kevlar vest that saved his life—TP

[4] This is the end of the typewritten material. What follows is handwritten on the same page—TP

[5] I've determined there's a 96 percent probability this is the handwriting of Sheriff Truman. Given how shaky it appears, my guess would be that he was drinking heavily at the time, which accounts for the 4 percent disparity.
   Truman must have written it after finding these chapters in the Bookhouse, just as Cooper had apparently intended him to do. Probably after Cooper left town, by the way.
   The following excerpt from the coroner's report could have been added by either Truman or the Archivist—TP

I was there, Coop. Andrew told her he forgave her cause he couldn't
help himself, he still loved her and that Eckhardt was coming to take
her away and help her escape the law, with his blessings. Maybe she
believed him, I don't know.

Then Eckhardt showed up, and Andrew told him that Josie warned him
about the attempt on his life years earlier, betraying Eckhardt.
Like that was the only reason he'd survived in the first place.
Josie sleeps with Eckhardt, then shoots him in his room
at the Great Northern. I got there moments later. Josie
swore she shot him in self-defense. And like always,
I believed her.

Then she just died. Like her heart failed, broken to pieces
by all the lies she'd kept living for so long. Right there in
my arms. Most of her died a long time ago. She already
felt like a ghost.

Thank you, Coop. It's better to know than not to know, [5]
that's what you always said, right? Someday I'll probably
agree with you ...

TWIN PEAKS, WASHINGTON

CALHOUN MEMORIAL HOSPITAL CORORNER

CALHOUN MEMORIAL HOSPITAL

AUTOPSY REPORT

EXAMINATION REF. NO.

1989-03/11-01

PACKARD, JOSIE

On the morning of March 11, 1989, an autopsy was completed on the body of JOSIE PACKARD.

Visible Injuries: None

Internal Injuries: None

Cause of Death: Unknown

Anatomical Summary:

External Injuries Female (Front and Back):

CAUSE OF DEATH:

Unknown.

No visible wounds or injuries. Internal organs appear healthy and functional. No drugs or alcohol in stomach or bloodstream.

CURIOUS ANOMALY:

Body weighs much less—at least 25 pounds—than physical appearance would indicate. I have no explanation for this.

DATE AND SIGNATURE OF EXAMINER

3/11/89   Dr. Will Hayward.

76a3402-A12

ARCHIVIST'S NOTE

Days after his death, an associate of Eckhardt showed up in Twin Peaks
and made arrangements to transport both Eckhardt's and Josie's bodies
back for burial in Hong Kong. Neither Andrew Packard nor anyone else
objected to the arrangement.

The associate also left a gift with Catherine, one that Eckhardt apparently
wanted her and Andrew to have: an elaborate Chinese puzzle box. Inside that
box they found another identical but smaller box, and inside that one an
even smaller steel box. When Andrew, Catherine and Pete succeeded in opening
that one, they found a key to a safe deposit box at the Twin Peaks Savings
and Loan. Eckhardt had visited the bank and left something there for them.

Pete and Andrew went to the bank the following morning together to
check it out.

[1] Kind of quaint, isn't it, how news was still being disseminated in print during these last days before the Internet. If it weren't for all the murders and explosions and dizzying double-crosses, I'd be tempted to say it seemed like a more innocent time —TP

7 RECENT DEVELOPMENTS

*** TWIN PEAKS POST [1]
MARCH 28, 1989

Weekday Edition
$1.00

PUBLISHED
IN THE STATE OF
WASHINGTON
SINCE 1922

TWIN PEAKS
POST

VOL. 67, NO. 87   TWIN PEAKS, WASHINGTON   TUESDAY, MARC

EXPLOSION AT BANK:
THREE DEAD, ONE INJURED

by CYRIL PONS, *Staff Reporter*

A **DEADLY EXPLOSION RIPPED** through the downtown offices of the Twin Peaks Savings and Loan at 9:25 this morning. Details are still coming in, and police, fire and rescue crews remained on the scene as this edition went to press. Our staff reporters are still on the scene as well, gathering facts, and the bank has yet to issue an official statement. In speaking with law enforcement, and the few witnesses we've been able to locate, here is what we know:

The blast appeared to have occurred in the bank's basement, in the area of the vault and the safe deposit box room. The most extensive structural damage was confined to this lower level of the building but all of the windows on the main floor were blown out, causing chaos—but no serious injuries, thankfully—on Main Street. A shower of

"Explosion" continued on pg. 18

Audrey Horne (18), injured; Pete Martell (52), dead; Delbert Mibbler (79), de

Wagon Wheel Bakery Opens Second Loca

"Explosion" continued from pg. 1

money was also blown out into the street, which added to the confusion.

At approximately 9:15 this morning, Twin Peaks High School senior Audrey Horne (18), daughter of prominent local businessman Benjamin Horne, entered the bank for reasons that are still unknown.

At approximately 9:20, a witness at the bakery across the street noticed two men enter the building. One she recognized as Pete Martell (52), manager of the Packard Mill. The second man, who she described as older, silver haired and wearing a suit, she did not recognize.

The cashier on duty upstairs, Mrs. Dorothy Doak (49), who was severely shaken up by the incident but not injured, was taken to the hospital for observation and was not available for comment.

After the blast, Miss Horne was found unconscious but alive in the rubble of the basement. She has been transported to the ICU at Calhoun Memorial Hospital, where she is listed in critical condition. Another witness reported that when she was carried out to the ambulance on a stretcher, they noticed a pair of handcuffs attached to one of her wrists. A first responder later confirmed to this reporter that Miss Horne had been found near the open vault door, but that it may have shielded her at least partially from the explosion.

He also confirmed that Miss Horne may have been intentionally shielded by one of the victims in the blast, Pete Martell, who was found lying on top of her.

Mr. Martell was pronounced dead at the scene. He is survived by his wife, Catherine Martell.

The second victim, whose body we're told was found on the stairs to the first floor, was the bank's longtime assistant manager, Delbert Mibbler (79). A beloved presence in our downtown community, and the grandson of one of the bank's founding partners back in 1906, Mr. Mibbler was believed to be less than a week away from officially retiring after 58 years at his family's institution.

The third victim, who has yet to be identified, and was apparently the closest person to the actual blast, is believed to be the silver-haired man who was seen earlier entering the bank with Mr. Martell.

By midmorning, a rumor was circulating through the crowd outside that this man might have been Andrew Packard—who a few people swear they have seen around the Great Northern during the past few weeks, despite the well-known fact that Mr. Packard perished in an explosion in the boathouse of his estate on Black Lake several years ago.

Another rumor making the rounds is that several news organizations received word from an unknown source earlier this morning that something big was going to happen at the bank today. News crews were actually on their way there when the explosion occurred.

The *Post* will publish a second special edition this evening to bring you all additional details as they are made available.

"Soon even

Polluti
Ruinin
Beaut

LIKE MOST projects, the fac go a review pr officials to pr Environmental (EIS), a process opportunities The first phase "scoping" docu parameters of t Officials outline project in a

ARCHIVIST'S NOTE

That bomb at the bank provided a punctuation mark to the end of the final sentence of the final chapter of the Packards' prominence in Twin Peaks. Thomas Eckhardt played the last card in their game after all. Authorities never did publicly identify the "third victim" who died at the bank, so Andrew Packard rose from his grave only to be sent hurtling back there by a second explosion. Given that Cooper had figured this all out, and passed the information on to Truman, it must have been decided somewhere in the corridors of power that some truths were simply too inconvenient to reveal.

This time Andrew stayed dead. The explosion was explained away as the tragic outcome of a gas leak from an antiquated boiler meeting an opportunistic spark. The Packard Mill and all its properties passed back into the sole possession of Catherine Martell, the grieving sister, and her grief was genuine, make no mistake about that. Survivors bear the brunt of tragedy, especially if they had a hand in creating it.

She was the only resident of Blue Pine Lodge now, and with no living heirs or relations, Catherine became a recluse. She never spoke or wrote about what had happened, so one question remains unanswered: Who exactly was she grieving for? All of them, perhaps; brother Andrew, certainly; husband Pete, for all his shortcomings -- at least in her eyes -- probably; maybe even Josie, the worthy opponent who had tested her like no other.[2]

Given her amorality and cold contempt toward people, it's difficult to view Catherine Packard as a sympathetic figure. She was, however, tragic in the tradition of Greek drama, as one highborn with many gifts who falls victim to her own hubris.

[2] As the last of the old-growth forests were harvested, the lumber industry around Twin Peaks had been declining for years. Soon after, Catherine abruptly closed the Packard Mill—the town's largest employer throughout the 20th century—after a fire, strangely, gutted its central facilities. As the town's largest employer, the mill's closing dealt a devastating blow to the local economy.

A few weeks after the fire, Catherine sold the mill and its associated properties to her former paramour, Benjamin Horne, and his investors in the Ghostwood Development, the plan he'd been pursuing for years.

225

* The Packard Mill, circa 1989

Name   TWIN PEAKS REGISTRAR
PO Box/   PO. BOX 451
Address
City & State   TWIN PEAKS, WA 98065

_____ (SPACE ABOVE THIS LINE FOR RECORDER'S USE) _____

ASSIGNMENT OF CONTRACT
SALE OF REAL ESTATE

KNOW ALL MEN BY THESE PRESENTS: That _____ BENJAMIN JOSEPH HORNE

of _____ TWIN PEAKS, WASHINGTON _____ for and in consideration

of the sums of _____ THIRTY THREE MILLION AND NO/ _____ Dollars

lawful money of the United States, to _____ CATHERINE MARTELL _____ paid by

TWIN PEAKS BANK _____ of _____ TWIN PEAKS

Country of _____ UNITED STATES _____ State of _____ WASHINGTON

do by these presents, sell, transfer, assign, and set over unto the said contract for the sale of certain real estate described as follows, of wit:

     THE PACKARD MILL, INCL. BUT NOT LIMITED TO
     IT's ASSOCIATED PROPERTIES
     FL. # 3550537
     TWIN PEAKS COUNTY

Made and recorded on the _____ 23rd _____ day of _____ MARCH 1989 _____ in Book _____ SB#333927

Page _____ I _____ of _____ 5 _____ in the office of the County Recorder of said County in which said contract

was made and executed by _____ HON. M.J. KAFFEE ESQ.

County of _____ TIMBER LULL _____ State of _____ WASHINGTON

and bears date the _____ 23rd _____ day of _____ MARCH 1989

TO HAVE AND TO HOLD, for the same unto the said.

     Assignor represents and warrants to Assignee that this Assignment is a true and complete copy of the Purchase Agreement, Assignor's interest in the Purchase Agreement is free and clear of any prior assignment and of any lien or security interest, Assignor has good right and lawful authority to execute and deliver this Assignment and to assign to Assignee all of Assignor's interest in the Purchase Agreement, and no party to the Purchase Agreement is presently in default with respect to the performance of such party's obligations under the Purchase Agreement.

     By accepting this Assignment, Assignee assumes and agrees to perform all of the obligations of the Buyer under the Purchase Agreement, including but not limited to any obligations to be performed after closing thereunder, and to indemnify Assignor against any loss, claim, damage or expense Assignor may incur by reason of Assignee's failure to perform the assumed obligations on a timely basis.

     As a WITNESS WHEREOF, the said parties have hereunto set the agreed terms and conditions of said contracts written agreements.

Signed, Sealed and Delivered in the Presence of

Catherine Martell

B Horne

This area for official notary seal

MARY JO PLUTNIK
COMMISSION EXPIRES
NOTARY
PUBLIC
MARCH 23, 1989
TWIN PEAKS, WA

[3] Based on what it cost him
personally, the price Horne
paid for the mill was a lot
higher than the amount on
the check—TP

The role of genuinely tragic victim here is reserved for
18-year-old Audrey Horne. The following note was left
for Ben Horne at the front desk of the Great Northern Hotel
on the morning of the explosion at the bank.[3]

Twin Peaks
The
GREAT NORTHERN
HOTEL
Washington
◀◀◀◇▶▶▶   ◀◀◀◇▶▶▶

Dear Daddy,

I know you think I've been a selfish little bitch most of my life and you're absolutely right. I've been really mean to people and treated them very badly and thought only about myself. I've been spoiled rotten. I'm not blaming anyone for that anymore and it's about time I take responsibility for my actions. So I'm making amends as of now, from this day forward, and I'm starting with this letter.

I can no longer stand by and watch as you destroy the heart of our town with your plan to close the mill and turn all our beautiful forests into tacky neighborhoods and shopping centers and whatever else you and your greedy friends are planning. (Maybe even a prison, I'm hearing.) Daddy, there is more to life than money! But I know there's no point in talking about it because you won't listen to me anymore.

◀◀◀◇▶▶▶

I won't tell you how I found out what you're planning because it doesn't really matter. And no matter what you may think, it's not too late to stop all this madness and do the right thing. So I am going to try and stop you the only way I know how, by calling public attention to your secret plans. I believe that's the only way you will come to your senses about how wrong all this is, and what a betrayal it would be to the people of our community.

I intend to give copies of your plans to the newspaper and I will be talking to people, probably news reporters and such, about all of this very very soon. You'll see.

I hope you understand that none of this is done out of hate. None of it. I also hope someday you'll realize I'm taking this step because of how much I love you, with the hope that it will help you become the man I know you can be. The man I believe you once were, the one I love and admire more than any other.

With all my heart,

Audrey

ARCHIVIST'S NOTE

Audrey's plan that morning, apparently, was to handcuff herself to the bars of the bank vault -- where her father kept a lot of his money -- after sending notes to local news organizations that they could find her there.[4]

In the weeks leading up to the accident, Audrey had been reading about social protest and civil disobedience. She brought with her to the bank copies of information she'd discovered about her father's plans that she intended to share with the news sources. Her luck was as bad that day as her intentions were good. Those copies were destroyed in the explosion before anyone could see them.

But her father did receive her note at the hotel -- too late to prevent her from being hurt, as it turned out -- but in time to make him the only person in town who knew what his daughter was doing there that day. Ben Horne never revealed the existence of that note or commented on it to anyone. Those who saw him at his daughter's bedside in the hospital afterward describe a man broken in half with grief, and, we can now also surmise, personal guilt.

Ben Horne experienced no overnight conversion, however. As noted, he went ahead with the purchase of the mill and Ghostwood from Catherine. But something did change in the man at that point.

In the months leading up to the explosion, Ben watched the calamity that befell the family of his friend and lawyer Leland Palmer with shock and horror; the murder of their daughter Laura unhinged the entire community. In its aftermath Ben went through something of a mental break himself.

[4] This "anonymous tip" must have been the source of the rumor mentioned in the *Post* article that something "big" was about to happen at the bank—TP

CALHOUN MEMORIAL HOSPITAL

DEPARTMENT OF PSYCHIATRY

PSYCHIATRIST	Dr. Lawrence Jacoby	DATE, TIME	3/22/89 2:00 PM

NAME, MARRITAL STATUS	Benjamin Horne, Married

DOB	8/4/1940	GENDER, AGE	Male / 49	HEIGHT, WEIGHT	6'1" / 174 Lbs

Patient has been recently under my care at his place of employment, the Great Northern. Daily house calls for the last week. I've insisted that he be confined to his quarters there, with no visits home that might counter the treatment plan.

Patient is laboring under an elaborate delusion that he's traveled back in time to the Civil War. He is living inside the persona of a "southern general," attempting to "rewrite" history by leading his side to victory.

This seems to me an unconscious compensation--as he's assumed the side with the untenable moral position--attempting to alter or erase his own personal, and questionable, recent behavioral history.

I've enlisted the help of his family and a few employees to "enable" the fantasy, but also gently direct him to the "truth" of the war's actual conclusion. If we are able to guide Ben to enact the actual "surrender at Appomattox," I believe we can bring him out of the delusion and onto a healing path.[5]

page __/_/_

initial __L.J.__

* Ben Horne at the Great Northern

[5] Verified. According to Jacoby's subsequent patient files, Ben Horne did "surrender at Appomattox" and find his way back to health —TP

[6] Chronologically speaking, this is one of the latest events that the Archivist references in the dossier. One possible theory is that something may have happened to our "correspondent" soon after this point. Making efforts to discover what that might have been —TP

But the larger question remained: Would the injury to Ben's daughter serve as a further wake-up call to make him more the man his daughter longed for him to be? She'd nearly died delivering that message to him, and her life hung in the balance. Only time would tell if he listened.[6]

[1] Verified. A joint FBI-DEA operation—TP

[2] Three years later—by which time the Archivist had stopped writing—I can confirm that Hank Jennings was fatally knifed in the prison weight room by a hard-core lifer who turned out to be a distant cousin of the Renault family. As we say in law enforcement and Sunday school, what goes around, comes around.

Jennings, to clear his conscience, issued a deathbed confession to all his various crimes, starting with the football game fix, up through and including his role in the attempted murder of Andrew Packard and ending with the message shown here, which was sent from prison after his death—TP

[3] After signing this note, according to prison sources, the last of the Jennings clan of Twin Peaks drew his final breath—TP

8 RENAULT AND JENNINGS

Two final loose ends tie up this section.

Jean Renault, the Canadian criminal kingpin, was gunned down in an FBI shootout -- on American soil, outside of Twin Peaks -- during an FBI-DEA joint sting operation involving narcotics that also involved local thug Hank Jennings. Agent Cooper himself took Renault out while under fire himself. [1]

Hank Jennings was then pulled in for parole violations that, in addition to international drug trafficking, also included assault and attempted murder. He pleaded guilty again and went off to serve a 25-year stretch in the state pen at Walla Walla. [2]

* Hank Jennings's last day at the RR

To my former friends
  and my former wife Norma:

You all tried to help me so many times, and get me back
onto the way of what's good and right. I'm so ashamed
to admit that I betrayed you all so many times.
I knew better. I knew I was doing wrong and couldn't
help myself. No excuses. I have nothing left to give
except to say how sorry I am for any hurt or
sorrow I ever caused you. I can't even ask for
your forgiveness because I don't deserve it.
It's too late now. I loved you all, in my own way,
as best I could, but that wasn't enough.

  I'm sorry. I'm sorry. I'm sorry.

           — Hank³

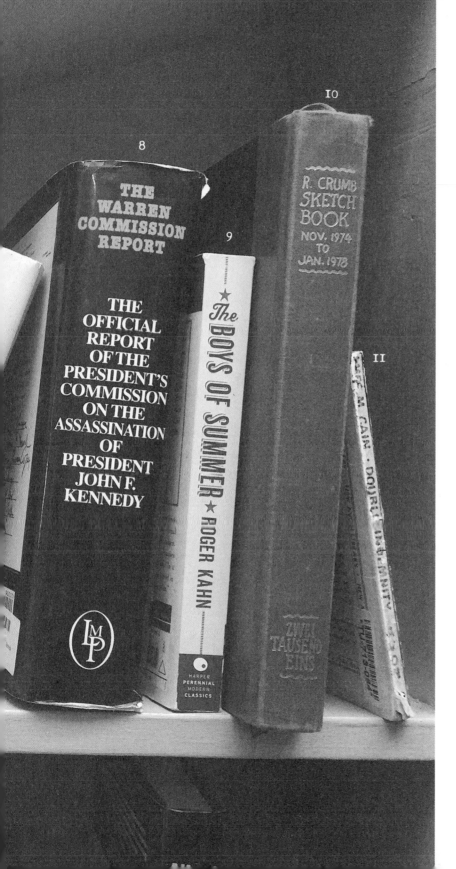

THE
WARREN
COMMISSION
REPORT

THE
OFFICIAL
REPORT
OF THE
PRESIDENT'S
COMMISSION
ON THE
ASSASSINATION
OF
PRESIDENT
JOHN F.
KENNEDY

9

The
BOYS OF SUMMER ★ ROGER KAHN

HARPER
PERENNIAL
MODERN
CLASSICS

10

R. CRUMB
SKETCH
BOOK
NOV. 1974
TO
JAN. 1978

ZWEI
TAUSEND
EINS

11

ARCHIVIST'S NOTE

Much can be learned in unexpected places. The library
at the Bookhouse is unique
in my experience as an
invaluable local resource.
This special shelf contains
the members' favorite tomes.

I. Hawk   2. Andy   3. James

4. Lucy (included because
   she buys all the books)

5. Harry Truman

6. Ed: "Read it five times; next
   time through I think I'm
   really going to figure it out"

7. Frank Truman   8. Cooper

9. Cappy   IO. Toad   II. Hank

Good literature is a mirror
through which we see ourselves
more clearly, and it's clear
to see that the people of Twin
Peaks have experienced many
a twisting turn of fate. It's
time to go back and pick up
the trail of Douglas Milford,
to learn how he moved forward
from the moment we last left
him -- 1949 -- into the world,
and town, of today.

*** THE COMING OF . . . WHAT?:

We know that after Milford presented his report on the Twin
Peaks incident to Project Sign, the "Estimate of the Situation"
that they sent to the Air Force top brass was roundly rejected.
Soon afterward Sign turned into Project Grudge, and debunking
UFOs became the order of the day.

The first case assigned to Major Milford for Grudge was mind
altering. It came to him from an oblique angle, and his work
on it took place over a three-year period, at the end of which
the polar axis of UFO investigation would shift yet again,
radically changing the focus of his work.

The case began when this letter[1] arrived at Wright-Patterson
AFB in November 1949.

[1] This appears authentic—as does the signature—but I can find no other existing copy of this letter or the transcript that follows it in official files—TP

House of Representatives

PERSONAL & CONFIDENTIAL   11/12/1949

Dear General Twining,

Members of the Joint Chiefs of Staff suggested I write to you directly
regarding the following matter.

In my ongoing capacity as a member of the House Un-American Activities
Committee (HUAC), I am charged with the investigation of organizations
or individuals, often within our government itself, who may represent
a hidden menace to the security of our nation and our way of life.

On occasion, testimony is offered to me in closed session that warns
of a grave threat at such a high level of potential risk that its
investigation requires extraordinary levels of discretion and sensitivity.
As you will find within the body of the testimony, aspects of this case
appear to fall squarely within your charter. If I may be so bold to
suggest, only your most dependable and experienced officers should be
entrusted with this.

The enclosed transcript contains unsolicited information offered to
me recently by a former Navy intelligence officer. It describes a
scandalous and corrupt personality close to the heart of an organization
that is absolutely vital to the security of the American military.

Jet Propulsion Laboratory in Pasadena, California, founded several
years ago, has become our nation's most important research and development
facility for rocket science. I believe you will agree with me that
these frankly shocking allegations are potentially explosive and demand
immediate inquiry. Please contact me at your earliest convenience after
you've had a chance to review the following material.

                                    Very sincerely yours,

                                    Richard M. Nixon

10█

TRANSCRIBED FROM INTERVIEW CONDUCTED AT THE
CONGRESSMAN'S WASHINGTON OFFICE, 10-17-49

* * * * * * * * * * * * * * * *

CONGRESSMAN NIXON: Okay, the tape is rolling now. Please state your name for the record, sir.

LT. HUBBARD: Lafayette Ronald Hubbard, Lieutenant, Navy Intelligence. Born in Tilden, Nebraska, age 38.

NIXON: Are you still on active duty, Lieutenant?

LT. HUBBARD: I was mustered out after the war, sir, but I still hold my commission. I prefer to go by Ron, by the way.

NIXON: Thank you, Ron. I see here that you were discharged for medical reasons, is that correct?

LT. HUBBARD: Yes, sir. During my years as commander of two anti-submarine vessels in the Pacific theater, I suffered from, among other ailments related to the stress of combat, ulcers, conjunctivitis, bursitis, various eye problems and something wrong with my feet.

NIXON: And I understand you're here to tell us something about your experiences just after the war, is that correct, Ron?

LT. HUBBARD: Yes, sir. Since my war service, I've pursued a career as a writer--fiction, science fiction, mostly short stories for magazines and a few novels for small publishing firms. I don't know if you'd be familiar with--

NIXON: I'm not. Sorry. Please go on.

[2] As unlikely as it sounds, this appears to be the same L. Ron Hubbard, a prolific pulp fiction author, who a short time later was responsible for the founding of the controversial "religion" of Scientology—TP

[3] Verified that Jack Parsons—a noted chemist and engineer—was indeed one of the founders of JPL. During the '30s and early '40s he was instrumental in the development of rocket fuel science, which led directly to its implementation by the military during WWII—TP

* L. Ron Hubbard, circa 1948

2 LT. HUBBARD: While pursuing my writing career, living in Los Angeles at the time--this was August of 1945--acquaintances of mine, some of them fellow writers, introduced me to a group of people living in Pasadena. This social circle revolved around a man named Marvel John Whiteside Parsons, who went by the name of Jack.

NIXON: Would this be the chemist "Jack" Parsons who cofounded Jet Propulsion Laboratory in Pasadena?

LT. HUBBARD: The very same, sir. [3]

NIXON: I am somewhat familiar with his role at JPL, yes.

LT. HUBBARD: Good. Well, after we were introduced, Jack and I became friendly. As I was going through some financial difficulties at the time, he generously invited me to stay at his house in Pasadena. I say "house," but it was a mansion, really. Known locally as, a bit of a pun, "The Parsonage."

NIXON: Yes, I see.

LT. HUBBARD: A number of people lived at the house there, you see, so this invitation was nothing out of the ordinary. But what I learned soon after moving in was that things at the Parsonage were not as they seemed.

NIXON: In what way?

LT. HUBBARD: I discovered that Parsons, for the better part of the decade, had been consorting with a peculiar cultish and self-styled religion that its adherents call "Thelema."

NIXON: I can't say that I'm familiar with it.

LT. HUBBARD: Neither was I, sir. You see, Thelema is patterned after the teachings of Parsons's friend and mentor, the notorious English mystic Aleister Crowley--

-2-

drel # 3

Congressman Richard M. Nixon and ▓▓▓▓▓▓▓▓▓▓▓	REF # 49-0351
	DATE 10-17-49

NIXON: I've heard the name.

LT. HUBBARD: Well, as a reference point, I have often heard Crowley described as "the most evil man in the world."

NIXON: You have my attention, Lieutenant.

LT. HUBBARD: You see, Crowley and Parsons and his followers believe in some very strange things. And they indulge in some extracurricular activities at the Parsonage that frankly boggle the mind.

NIXON: For instance?

LT. HUBBARD: Openly partaking of various drugs. The practice of free love and the periodic enactment of bizarre "sex magick rituals."

NIXON: All right there, smack in the middle of Pasadena.

LT. HUBBARD: Yes, sir.

NIXON: Well, did you alert the proper authorities?

LT. HUBBARD: The local police have been frequent visitors to the Parsonage, yes, sir. Especially on nights when these hijinks go on late into the night and disturb the neighbors. But my concern, and my reason for being here, isn't about disturbing the peace, but entirely about the threat that Mr. Parsons represents to the security of the rocket program at JPL. If I may, I'd like to introduce into evidence a report I've prepared for you on activities I've observed. Something, may I hasten to add, done and offered entirely in the spirit of my duty and obligations as a former Naval Intelligence officer.

NIXON: So noted and appreciated, Ron. I'm a Navy man myself, and still a proud officer in the Reserve. Let it be entered into the record.

002-45

U. S. NAVAL AIR STATION

POINT MUGU, CALIFORNIA

LOCATION: PASADENA, CALIFORNIA
FIELD REPORT: LT. L. RON HUBBARD, ret.

TOP SECRET

I had little trouble making contact with the subject of my inquiry.
Parsons is a naturally gregarious sort, and presides over his
personal and professional "duchy" in Pasadena with the beneficence
of a feudal lord. With the war over, he was somewhat removed from
day-to-day operations at JPL. A dreamer by nature and an "amateur"
at heart, Parsons disdains interest in "factory work," although he
continues to consult with scientists and engineers who were part
of what he called his "Suicide Squad" during their free-wheeling
research on advanced rocket fuels. Back then Parsons and his team
were the only ones in the country working on rockets, and the man
possessed an uncanny mastery for identifying and taming the most
combustible and dangerous chemicals known to science, producing
what he calls "alchemical elixirs"--what we more prosaically call
"fuel"--that generated the most powerful controlled and sustained
explosions the world has ever seen. Parsons today still possesses
unshakable faith that the path he's blazed over the past twenty
years--at a time when the scientific community mocked and dismissed
the idea of "rocket science" as a pipe dream, mere science
fiction--will one day result in vehicles capable of taking man
to the moon and the stars beyond.

Raised by a wealthy Pasadena family who lost their fortune in the
Depression, Parsons never received a college degree because of
financial hardship, although he briefly attended classes at three top
universities. This made him, in effect, a self-taught chemist who
from an early age possessed a burning obsession--ignited by early
exposure to authors like Jules Verne and H. G. Wells--to launch objects
into the sky. With drums of war beating in Europe, armed with little
more than chutzpah and youthful enthusiasm, Parsons talked his way
into a grant from the California Institute of Technology (Caltech)--
the foremost scientific academy in the western United States.

Seven years downstream from that investment Jack Parsons's groundbreaking work has resulted in the creation of rockets as science, with, needless to say, limitless and ongoing military utility. ("Jet-assisted takeoff," a now standard feature for Air Force fighters and bombers, being the most obviously beneficial for which he was directly responsible.) One need speak to him only once to realize that Jack Parsons is a true visionary, perhaps even a genius along the lines of past noteworthy scientists who have altered the course of human history.

There is no question in my mind that he is also stark, raving mad.

With the windfall he received from the founding of JPL in 1943, Parsons purchased his mansion on Orange Grove Boulevard in Pasadena, a street known as Millionaire's Row, where he also happened to have lived growing up. He dubbed his new house "The Parsonage," which sounds considerably more ecumenical in name than in practice.[4]

Parsons uses the house as his residence, but it also functions as headquarters for his "church," which they call "Thelema," but what I think is better described as a "coven." Parsons's interest in the occult developed after his fascination with rockets--his first contact with the "Thelema" crowd came in 1939--but in his mind, at this point, the two disciplines are intertwined. Three years later, Parsons became leader of the West Coast branch, or "lodge," and his immersion has only deepened.

At Parsons's personal invitation, I took up residence at the Parsonage and soon afterward attended a Thelema gathering. A strange, incense-laden air of debauchery, populated by a motley assemblage of leftists, bohemians and hangers-on, attended by a cadre of attractive young JPL secretaries, all of them swept up into a kind of fever cult. Many of the guests wore colorful, erotic masks, and a few were in elaborate Egyptian costumes or masks with distorted animal faces. Disturbing atonal music played from somewhere and prompted much uninhibited dancing, and by that I don't mean the jitterbug. In some back rooms, I have no doubt, there was rampant drug use; I caught the unmistakable tang of reefer wafting throughout the upper floor and I believe the punch they

were serving may have been laced with a home-brewed mind-altering
substance, perhaps absinthe. In many of these rooms, not even
behind closed doors, sexual hijinks abounded. I'm no prude, but
I've never felt more Episcopalian in my life.

For all his accomplishments, Parsons was only 31 years old, a tall,
powerfully built, ruggedly handsome man with a Barrymore mustache
and the louche air of a sybarite. Dressed in a flowing robe and
fez-like headdress, with an albino python draped around his
shoulders, he presided over his guests like a Pied Piper to all
their illicit behavior.

At one point I found myself alone in a strange room upstairs with
Parsons. The walls were festooned with crossed swords, symbols from
the Tarot, pagan artwork. It was furnished only with a skull-shaped
altar, what looked like a throne and an unnerving life-sized statue
of a bestial satyr, which Parsons told me is the demi-god Pan.
(Parsons is fond of stomping his feet while reciting a poem called
"Ode to Pan" during test launches.) I activated the small
tradecraft tape recorder I always carry with me and took the
opportunity to record and later transcribe, without his knowledge,
the following conversation:

LRH: All those photos on the wall, is that who I think it is?

JP: Yes, Aleister Crowley. "The Beast." My friend and teacher.

LRH: He died recently, didn't he?

JP: Yes. He shed his body just last year.

LRH: Well, he was a heroin addict, wasn't he? That might have had
something to do with it.

JP: Oh, he didn't need drugs. He was drugs.[5]

(Continues) I mean, look around you. It's all Thelema, you know.
That was his lasting legacy for us, his crowning achievement, and
it will live forever.

[4] The house had originally been built by one of Caltech's early benefactors, a lumber baron named Arthur Fleming. Perhaps coincidentally, with high-grade lumber imported from the region around Twin Peaks—TP

[5] Crowley was in fact a notorious drug addict who wore himself out at 72 after decades of rampant abuse of every indulgence ever cataloged by man—TP

[6] Thelema is literally the Greek word for "will" or "intention." Making it the centerpiece of an anti-Christian religion seems to have first been done in a 16th-century satirical novel by Rabelais, and was later appropriated by Crowley for his own purposes, which were decidedly *not* satirical.

But Crowley took credit for "inventing" the whole Thelema business after a series of mystical experiences in Egypt, which led to his writing the tenets of his new religion while in a kind of trance state, claiming he received them from a higher power. Like opium or hashish, for instance.

A lot of it seems inspired—i.e., lifted—from the Book of Revelation, which also strikes me as impenetrable gobbledygook. On the one hand Crowley's kind of fascinating—upper-crust Englishman, iconoclast, mountain climber, author, first Westerner to spend time studying with lamas in Tibet—and on the other he's like a sick, perverted Bond villain. They didn't call him "the most evil person in the world" for nothing—TP

* Crowley, date unknown

LRH: Thelema?[6]

JP: "The word of the LAW is Thelema. Do what thou wilt shall be the whole of the LAW. Love is the LAW, love under will."

(He recites this as if addressing a congregation, by rote, like a groove on a record. Then he turns his eyes on me and speaks more intimately.)

JP: Do you see? The power of the will is all. But without eros, or agape--love and sex, joined together--"will" is nothing but hollow, patriarchal power without direction or force. What he taught us is that both forces must exist in balance. In order to stand beside God you have to first reject the idea of "God." Then, and only then, will you come to realize that you are God. Every man and woman is a star.

LRH: I see.

(I notice he's worrying a ring on his right ring finger, a flat green stone, maybe jade, etched with some sort of inscription.)

JP: Rockets and magick: Ask yourself, what do they share? They're about transcending all limits. Acts of rebellion against the limits of gravity and inertia, and the limits of human existence. We will only be held down, earthbound, for so long. Two sides of the same coin.

(He takes what looks like an ancient silver coin from his pocket and performs some kind of sleight of hand with it; suddenly there are two coins.)

JP: Alchemy isn't only about "chemistry" or turning base metals to gold. The medieval philosophers and alchemists knew this--even Isaac Newton knew it--but their knowledge was lost until Crowley brought it back. You see, alchemy actually speaks to internal processes, and a radical revolution in our spiritual development; transforming the "base metal" of primitive man to the "gold" of an enlightened soul. Rockets and magick are both about breaking through the animal boundaries of space and time that hold us back from realizing our potential. Either, maybe both, will someday take

us to the moon and the stars beyond. I truly believe that. Magick is
just the name we've always given to things we don't yet understand...

(He stares at me a moment with his dark brown eyes, then turns his
gaze to the statue of Pan, gets a faraway look and mutters
something under his breath.)

JP: The magician longs to see...

LRH: Excuse me, what's that?

(He trails a hand along one of the walls.)

JP: I've often felt there were spirits in this wood...

(He looks at me again, suddenly focused.)

JP: You'll have to excuse me. I must attend to my other guests.

(He glides out of the room. I look at my arms; the hair is standing
on end.)

I left the Parsonage near midnight, but the party was just getting
started. People were jumping over a bonfire out by a pergola. Some
of them were naked. This was a Thursday night, by the way.
Presumably all these people were expected to show up for work in
the morning.

The next day at JPL--where Parsons himself did not show up for
work--I spoke with scientists and administrators who had not been
at the party. They expressed serious concern that Parsons is on the
verge of going off the rails. They're underestimating the
situation; I believe he slid off the rails into an amoral swamp
years ago. His scientific mind may be as sharp as ever, but the
consensus is that what was once tolerated as personal eccentricity
has overwhelmed his native brilliance. To my eyes, he now seems
about as stable as a soufflé.

* Jack Parsons at JPL, circa 1942

ARCHIVIST'S NOTE

The report offers no explanation about why Hubbard waited so long to report this to authorities. It may have something to do with the fact that, in the interim, Ron Hubbard conned Jack Parsons out of his life's savings and ran off to Florida with Parsons's hot young girlfriend, where they used the money they snookered from him to buy a yacht.[7]

During those postwar years, JPL grew into a multimillion-dollar business, occupying a central role in the aerospace industry and the emerging military-industrial complex. As his company took off, Parsons doubled down on his involvement in occult mumbo-jumbo and came under suspicion for, possibly, selling secrets of America's rocket program to a foreign government.

Soon after these charges came to light -- although he was ultimately acquitted -- JPL terminated its official relationship with Parsons. With his income gone and his professional reputation damaged, he was forced to sell the Parsonage. Struggling financially, he sued Hubbard to try to get his money back, while working as a consultant on a military missile program, when it came time to renew his national security clearance.

Which is why, soon after the foregoing report from Congressman Nixon landed on Major Doug Milford's desk, Project Grudge dispatched him to Pasadena to investigate. This is the report he soon filed in response:

[7] Confirmed. Hubbard soon married Sara "Betty" Northrup, before officially divorcing his first wife, adding polygamy to his checkered résumé. And in 1950 he published his greatest success, *Dianetics*, the book that became the basis of his own "religion," one that clearly borrowed multiple ideas and themes from Thelema—TP

RE: PROJECT_GRUDGE
        49-12-0037

PASADENA, CALIFORNIA December 3, 1949

TOP SECRET

FIELD REPORT: MAJOR DOUGLAS MILFORD

SUBJECT: JACK PARSONS

I found Jack Parsons living in an apartment near the beach, in
meager circumstances, trying to scrape together a living from a
variety of consulting and manufacturing jobs. I approached him
using cover as a journalist for a left-wing magazine, and he
agreed to meet me for an article I told him I was writing about
"what really happened to him at JPL." He welcomed the opportunity
to, as he put it, "set the record straight." He appeared fleshy
and downtrodden, and his handsome features had started to corrode.
His personal life had taken a recent turn and that was where,
in a Manhattan Beach coffee shop, our conversation began:

DM: I heard you just got remarried, Jack. Congratulations.

JP: (chuckles briefly) I wish it were that simple, but thank you.

DM: If you don't mind my asking, what's happened to your ex?

JP: Helen?

DM: I thought her name was Sara.

JP: Oh, you mean Betty--Sara's middle name is Elizabeth, that's what
she goes by, Betty. No, I was never married to Betty. She's Helen's
younger sister--half sister. Helen was my first wife, but she's
married to someone else now, too.

DM: Wow. Sounds complicated.

JP: It is. And Betty just got married. To h̲i̲m.

TOP SECRET

01

NW#: 26942   DocId: 26497209

Control No. 6947

DM: Him?

JP: Hubbard, Ron Hubbard. He was part of our crowd in Pasadena.
Showed up after the war. Navy man, intelligence, a hack science
fiction writer, maybe you've heard the name.

DM: Can't say that I have.

JP: People wandered in and out of that house all the time. When Ron
showed up, with his war stories and his wit and his polymath
brilliance, I thought I'd found a boon companion. Betty hated him
on sight. (He lights a cigarette, long exhale.) That's when I knew
she and I were in trouble.

DM: How so?

JP: Oh, within weeks they were together, Ron just drew her to him
like he had her under a spell. So she left me. But he was such a
friend--and we weren't, you know, any of us, focused on bourgeois
shit like monogamy. So I still thought of him as my friend. We were
as close as could be. I thought he understood me better than
anyone I'd ever met.

DM: Was he a member of your church as well?

JP: Oh yeah, he dove right in. Relentless, he wanted to know
everything about it. We worked together, tirelessly, for two years
on a, uh . . . on a really important project.

DM: Are you talking about rockets or magic?

JP: (lowers his voice) See, these were things Crowley had written
about. A ritual that he'd attempted in Europe--important work--but
no one had ever tried it over here.

DM: A ritual? And Hubbard was helping you with this?

(He nodded, a faraway look in his eye.)

JP: We saw things that maybe men aren't supposed to see.

DM: Where was this?

JP: Out in the desert. The desert's a perfect medium for summoning

02

...an empty canvas, a beaker into which, under certain
circumstances and with fearless rigor, you can create an
elixir that will call forth... call them what you will
....messengers of the gods...

DM: (I laughed nervously) Wow. What does that look like?

JP: Oh, they assume many forms. The grays, for instance.
You know, Zeta Reticulans.[8]

(Continues) The tall ones, now, the Nordic types, they're
different. More benign. Some say they've always been
here. Supposedly they come from the Dog Star.

(I notice he's sweating heavily as he says this and his
eyes have taken on a glassy sheen. I wonder if he's on
drugs right now.)

DM: The Dog Star?

JP: Serious.

DM: Yes, I'm serious.

(Slight laughter from Parsons, but I'm not sure why.)[9]

JP: Ever been to Roswell?

DM: Roswell, New Mexico? As a matter of fact, I have.

JP: We were near there. In the desert. A place they
call Jornada del Muerto.

DM: That's near White Sands, isn't it?

JP: Right. It means "Journey of the Dead Man." Isn't
that beautiful? The way we all move through our lives.
Eyes closed, head down, shuffling along. Dead before
our time, journeying toward the grave.

DM: That's where they tested the bomb.

JP: Yes. (The faraway look again, eyes unfocused)
Such a fertile ground for the Working.

03

8 Zeta Reticuli is a binary
star system in the constellation of Reticulum, visible
to the naked eye in the
Southern Hemisphere. Often
cited, in UFO "literature," as
the home to a race of small
gray aliens who allegedly
visit Earth—TP

9 I believe Milford missed
Parsons's reference here
to "Sirius," a star in the
relatively nearby constellation Canis Major or "Big
Dog." Often referred to in
UFO lore as another possible
source of visiting alien life.
This recalls the two
competing races of aliens
mentioned earlier in the
Ray Palmer magazine
stories—TP

DM: Pardon? What's the Working?

JP: The ritual. The Working of Babalon. Calling forth the Elemental.

DM: Could you elaborate on that, Jack?

(A car horn blares. I look outside, where an old Buick roadster
convertible has pulled up. A striking, Technicolor redhead is
behind the wheel. Jack snaps back to himself, out of his dreamy
reverie, looks at his watch and smiles.)

JP: Sorry, that's the wife. We're supposed to hit the flea market
today. Anyway, Hubbard, yeah. He really knew how to stick in the
knife. And twist it.

We shake hands, and after he leaves I drive to Pasadena.
I'd arranged to meet with one of Parsons's former colleagues,
a longtime scientific associate, calm, cerebral and sober as a
judge. I told him the truth, that I was conducting a confidential
military investigation, and he agreed to speak only on the
condition of anonymity. I of course agreed. He had worked with
Parsons from the mid-1930s as part of his "Suicide Squad," and
still had great affection for him, so he had seen changes diminish
the man he knew as well as anyone.

He took me into the Arroyo Seco near the JPL labs. The Arroyo
Seco is a forbidding and desolate 25-mile-long dry river canyon,
lined with rocks and immense boulders washed down over geologic
eons from the San Gabriel Mountains that tower above the city.
This desolate patch is where Parsons and company used to test
their fuels and shoot off rockets in their halcyon days. During
the sporadic monsoonal rains peculiar to the region, the Arroyo
Seco ("dry stream" in Spanish, named by the Spanish explorer
Gaspar de Portola in the late 18th century) becomes a raging
torrent. As the city of Pasadena grew down below, a dam was built
there in 1920, where a waterfall rumbles during the rains, to
contain the seasonal floods. They call this spot the Devil's Gate,
named for a rock outcropping at its base that many believe
resembles the face of a devil.

* The Devil's Gate, Arroyo Seco, Pasadena

[10] In a letter I've found that Aleister Crowley wrote to Parsons after he assumed leadership of Thelema's Pasadena "lodge," he tells Parsons that he had "researched" Hell Gate—he doesn't specify how—and concluded that it was one of seven gateways on the planet to hell and encouraged him to "make use of it." Make of that what you will—TP

[11] I have to concede that even for the ravings of a madman that's a little ominous—TP

[12] "The goddess Babalon" is a reference to a figure borrowed and reinterpreted by Crowley from the Book of Revelation, the odd appendage to the New Testament that was added hundreds of years after the Bible's traditional structure had been widely adopted. It is apocalyptic in both rhetoric and content, although an ongoing debate about whether it was intended as a literal or metaphorical document continues to this day—TP

[13] The timing of which could explain Hubbard's sudden urge to "testify" to Congressman Nixon—TP

* The Whore of Babylon, Sumerian bas relief

I can confirm that it does. But the name goes back farther than the
Army Corps of Engineers. The Tongva Indians, who lived in the area
for centuries, called this spot the Hell Gate because they believed
it was literally a portal to the underworld.[10]

His colleague told me that Parsons used this area for his personal
exploration of what he called "the explosive sciences, of both the
literal and metaphorical varieties"--because he believed they would
"open up the gate."[11]

So this is also where, after founding JPL, Parsons first began
enacting his bizarre "Thelema" rituals. His associate told me--
strictly off the record--those rituals were "an attempt to summon
into human form the spirit of a figure central to the Thelema
pantheon, the goddess Babalon, known as "the Mother of Abominations."[12]

I asked him what possible good could come of Parsons doing
something that sounds like provoking the end of the world? Looking
pale and uneasy, frequently glancing at the dark mouth of a tunnel
under the "devil rock," the man told me he had no idea what Jack had
in mind, but that it took two people to enact the ritual. He said
that a friend of Jack's named Ron Hubbard had been his key
collaborator in these weird rites. He described Hubbard as a science
fiction writer who had drifted into Parsons's orbit. The man I was
speaking with had immediately made Hubbard for a con man who didn't
believe any of Jack's "supernatural hoo-ha," but Parsons wouldn't
listen to his or anyone else's concerns about Hubbard. He also
recalled a conversation in which Hubbard asserted that the best and
surest way to make a fortune in America--aside from bilking your
friends, I guess--was to start a religion. Within a year of worming
his way into Parsons's confidence, Hubbard had conned him out of
twenty thousand dollars and his girlfriend Betty--his wife Helen's
younger sister, for whom he'd left Helen in 1945.

After heading east, Hubbard brazenly used Parsons's money to buy a
yacht that he lived on in Miami with Betty. When Parsons threatened
legal action to get his money back, Hubbard threatened to publicly
expose Parsons's relationship with Betty, who had been underage (17)
at the time she and Parsons became involved.[13]

[14] After reviewing Hubbard's oeuvre, I can go further than that. His "origin story" of ancient aliens—beings he called Thetans—colonizing earth in deep underground cities beneath volcanoes seems to owe a lot to Richard Shaver's wild stories of the subterranean "Lemurians"—TP

[15] Marjorie Cameron, Parsons's second wife—TP

[16] He seems to be suggesting that Parsons's ritual somehow "opened a gate" that resulted

in aliens showing up in Roswell. I'm not endorsing this jibber-jabber as fact, but I have done my own research now into the Arroyo Seco. The Native Americans who lived here were in fact wary of the place, and did call it the Hell Gate, claiming they could "hear the devil's laughter in the waterfall."

And, call it coincidence if you like, but in the decade after Parsons worked his voodoo here, four children went missing in the Arroyo Seco. Two were killed by a construction worker who'd helped build a nearby freeway. He claimed he'd heard voices that compelled him to do it and later took his own life in prison. The third and fourth victims simply disappeared without a trace and were never found. It's late, it's dark, and I'm now turning all the lights on in my office—TP

ARCHIVIST'S NOTE:

When he briefly became respectable after publishing his best-selling Dianetics in 1950, Hubbard claimed he had only infiltrated what he called Parsons's "sex cult" on assignment from military intelligence as an undercover officer. This claim is utterly without foundation. Hubbard was infamous within the intelligence community -- who were eager to see him discharged in 1945 -- as a braggart, liar, and opportunistic sociopath who made Jack Parsons, in all his crackpot glory, look like a Cub Scout. It's also clear that after his close study of the Thelema religion, many of its tenets became central parts of the work Hubbard is best known for. [14]

I asked his former associate if he thought that Parsons believed
that any of his "black magic" rituals had worked.

"Well," he said quietly, "the week after _that_ one he met the woman
he's married to now. Right after he came back from one of those
trips to the desert, just before Hubbard ran off with Betty and
most of his dough. She was actually waiting at his front door."

I realized I had seen the woman he then described to me behind the
wheel of the Buick at the coffee shop. She is apparently now
Parsons's lawfully wedded second wife.

I asked the man if he knew anything about Parsons conducting a
ritual in the New Mexico desert. He looked at me sharply, and asked
how I knew that. I said that Parsons had told me about it himself
that morning at the coffee shop, something called "The Working." The
man paused to collect himself and said that Parsons had also told
him something like that had taken place. An effort to open a _second_
gate that they'd found in the desert in order to bring across an
entity he called "the Moonchild." ***

I asked if he had any idea when that ritual might have taken place.
He said he knew _exactly_ when it happened because Parsons had asked
him to feed his cats while he was gone. Cross-checking the date, I
realized it was the weekend just _before_ the UFO incident at
Roswell, part of which I personally witnessed.

I looked back at the dam, and the tunnel and the eerie face in
those rocks. Something uncanny enveloped me, an animalistic fear
sliding up my spine, akin to the feeling I'd had that day in the
woods long ago above the Pearl Lakes.

*** "Moonchild" is both the title and subject of a 1923 novel by Crowley
about a battle between two "lodges" of black and white magicians over an
unborn child who may or may not be "the Antichrist." Crowley apparently
tried to conduct this ritual himself on numerous occasions earlier in his
own life--without success--which served as Parsons's inspiration.

Conclusions: As strange as he seems, I confess that I found Jack Parsons a sympathetic person. He doesn't seem "evil" to me, just deeply confused, a highly creative man who wants to be liked but who has sadly lost the ability to filter out the irrational or recognize those who do not wish him well.

That being said, it is the considered recommendation of this officer that the renewal of his security clearance be denied and that all associations with Marvel John "Jack" Whiteside Parsons by companies or agencies associated with the U.S. military, or any other branch of our government, be immediately terminated.

Major D. Milford

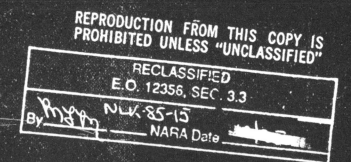

ARCHIVIST'S NOTE

So, once and for all, Parsons lost his place in the science he'd done so
much to create. Called to give closed testimony to the HUAC -- where he
named a few names, one of them his closest former colleague -- Parsons
insisted that he no longer had any contact with the "Church of Thelema,"
but did offer a spirited defense of his "usual religious beliefs."

FEDERAL BUREAU OF INVESTIGATION

THIS CASE ORIGINATED AT ▓▓▓▓▓▓▓▓▓▓ FILE NO. 65-1753

REPORT MADE AT	DATE WHEN MADE	PERIOD FOR WHICH MADE	REPORT MADE BY	
CINCINNATI, OHIO	11/22/50	11/17/50	▓▓▓▓▓▓▓▓ 67C	NJB

TITLE: JOHN WHITESIDE PARSONS, aka Jack Parsons

CHARACTER OF CASE: ▓▓▓▓▓▓▓▓▓▓

TRANSCRIPT OF CLOSED SESSION TESTIMONY

CONGRESSMAN RICHARD NIXON: Could you share something of your religious beliefs with us, Mr. Parsons?

MR. PARSONS: The only religion I practice now is the religion of individual freedom. Absolute freedom for the individual to follow his or her own path. No one can do that for any other human being, and every person must arrive at that discovery for themselves. The only restriction I would add to that is that you must do so without interfering with the path of any other person. In other words, do no harm. If there's anything more anti-fascist and anti-Communist and more American than that I'd liake to know about it.

CONGRESSMAN NIXON: So what, then, is the central belief of your religion?

MR. PARSONS: I would say it is this, sir: that everyone has a divine purpose and nature inherent within them. That every person is a divine being, but only through achieving a balance of self-will and love for all living things can one open the door to discover their own divine purpose. 17

ARCHIVIST'S NOTE

After this report, the House Un-American Activities Committee --
the engine driving the paranoid hunt for Communists in the
postwar U.S. government and military -- planted a bull's-eye on
Jack Parsons. Although he never joined the Communist Party,
by the time he came under their scrutiny, the FBI had already
compiled a 200-page file on him, focusing on the salacious
details of his private life. They decided not to prosecute, but
denied the renewal of his high-level security clearance, citing
his membership in the American Civil Liberties Union.

With the permanent revocation of his security clearance,
Parsons turned to a life of manual labor to make ends meet,
working as a mechanic and hospital orderly. Apparently using
bootlegged explosives, he eventually found steadier work as a
pyrotechnic consultant on a number of war movies that required
numerous explosions.

Parsons's downward spiral continued, but another perceived
threat he represented to national security prompted Major Doug
Milford to make a final visit to Pasadena in 1952.[18]

[17] Just a theory, but
authorities probably leaned
on Parsons to name names
by threatening to publicly
reveal that America's
number-one rocket man had
been using Satanic "sex
magick" to try and "incarnate
the living embodiment of an
ancient being called the
Moonchild." Parsons's career
was ruined, but at least he
avoided jail—TP

[18] The document on the
following page is verified.
Parsons's wife later
confirmed they were about
to permanently relocate to
Mexico—TP

PASADENA, CALIFORNIA June 15, 1952

TOP SECRET

FIELD REPORT: MAJOR DOUGLAS MILFORD

SUBJECT: JACK PARSONS

I found Jack Parsons living in the old carriage house of the Cruikshank
estate, another Orange Grove Boulevard mansion in Pasadena, just down the
street from the former location of the Parsonage, which has since been
demolished and replaced with apartment buildings, and not far from the
mansion he grew up in, also gone now. The Tudor-style carriage house sits
far back from the street, down a long winding driveway. It is an overcast
and sultry summer day, and the air smells of citrus trees, magnolia trees
and thick jasmine vines that overgrow the timbers.

Now 37, Parsons is stockier than I remember, his handsome features
sagging and bloated from, I'd hazard to guess, equal parts dissipation
and disappointment. I again present myself to him as the same left-wing
journalist, following up on the story I wrote three years earlier, which
he never asks to see. He remembers me from our previous encounter and
invites me inside. He seems distracted and anxious.

Parsons tells me he lives here with his wife Marjorie; there are pictures
of them on the wall and I recognize the same striking redhead I saw him
with earlier. He tells me he's working for the movies as a "pyrotechnics"
man, which means he's the guy who "blows stuff up." World War II movies
are all the rage, and as someone able to create and control realistic
explosions, he is much in demand.

The downward trajectory of Parsons's life is reflected in the near squalor
of his surroundings. A portion of the main room is given over to a
laboratory, lined with bottles, beakers, test tubes and barrels of
chemicals and compounds, a few labeled DANGER: EXPLOSIVES. This area is
neither clean nor well maintained and a strong chemical odor fills the
air. There's a small drafting table in the middle of the room where I
notice sketches and formulas that seem related to rocket design, which he
casually covers when I take an interest in them. When I hear people
moving upstairs, he tells me he's taken in two boarders to help with the
rent, an actor and a graduate student. I notice he's worrying the same jade
green ring I'd seen during my previous visit, on his right ring finger.

I also notice some discarded hypodermic needles in a trash can. An open box
of old printed pamphlets about Thelema sits nearby. A tall dusty stack of
science fiction magazines with lurid covers sags against one wall. A number

of strange symbols on papers are pinned to the wall above
the drafting table, some of which I recognize as related to Thelema.
Gazing through curtains into the next room I notice the back wall
has been painted pink and the rest is taken up by a disturbing painting
of a black devil's head, replete with horns and mesmerizing, slanted red
eyes. Parsons doesn't realize that I've seen this.

He tells me that having suffered a precipitous comedown in the world, denied
all avenues for work in his chosen field, he's severed his connection to the
"Church of Thelema." From what I've seen here he seems--if such a thing is
possible--to have thrown himself more fully into a private version of his
"occult" work. Tired and irritable, he's working on a rush order for a movie
and soon tells me he needs to get back to it. We move back outside. I notice
a small trailer parked nearby, loaded with suitcases, boxes and sporting gear,
and ask him about it. Parsons tells me he and his wife are packing to leave
soon for a vacation in Mexico. I shake his hand, wish him well and take my leave.

ASSESSMENT:

Recent suggestions that he may still represent a security risk seem
accurate, for the following reasons:

Parsons clearly needs money. He clearly possesses invaluable classified
information about rocketry and fuels, and is clearly still dabbling in
that area despite his security ban. He has been and remains obviously
unstable on a personal emotional level. He has also been accused of
espionage before. Although he offered that he is about to embark on a
Mexican vacation, it is my belief he may be on the verge of relocating
there permanently, where making contact with any number of foreign
espionage agents would be considerably easier.

It is the opinion of this officer that the foundational, arcane nature
of the scientific mastery he carries with him, in tandem with his
increasingly erratic personality, still renders Jack Parsons a profound
security risk. I cannot with any assurance guarantee that he won't
present such a risk in the future, at least until enough time has passed
that his technical know-how becomes outdated.

It's not for me to say how this should be accomplished, but perhaps
some form of house arrest to prevent his flight to another country
might be appropriate.

Major Douglas Milford

*** <u>L</u><u>OS</u> <u>A</u><u>NGELES</u> <u>T</u><u>IMES</u>
JUNE 18, 1952

ROCKET SCIENTIST KILLED IN PASADENA EXPLOSION

PASADENA—AN EXPLOSION RIPPED through the residence of a brilliant Pasadena scientist at 5:08 yesterday afternoon, taking the life of 37-year-old John "Jack" Parsons, one of the co-founders of Jet Propulsion Laboratory (JPL), and a key contributor to the development of rocket science in this country.

Moments after the blast, Parsons' body was discovered by neighbors under a pile of rubble in the wreckage of his apartment. He had been gruesomely injured in the blast, the origins of which police say they are still investigating, and half an hour later was pronounced dead upon arrival at Pasadena General Hospital.

In a dreadful aftermath, immediately after being informed of the tragedy at her nearby residence, Parsons' mother Ruth (63), a longtime Pasadena resident, took her own life with an overdose of pills.

Parsons' widow, Marjorie Cameron Parsons, arrived on the scene of the explosion within the hour. She was not available for comment and, it is believed, fled immediately by car to Mexico before she could be questioned.

ARCHIVIST'S NOTE

Milford did not delve into this, but a closer examination of Parsons's mysterious death is in order. Police quickly concluded that he died in an accident as a result of a mishap, caused by his mishandling of a deadly and highly volatile explosive called "fulminate of mercury," traces of which were found among the wreckage in a shattered coffee can. They presumed he'd been mixing the substance for use in the unspecified pyrotechnic he was creating, when the canister slipped from his hands, exploding the moment it made impact with the ground.

The blast atomized his right arm, no trace of which was found, broke both his legs, caused massive internal injuries and destroyed the right side of his face, suggesting that he reached down to catch the can when it dropped before it hit the floor.

Parsons was, improbably, still alive when his upstairs tenants found him, but his injuries made it impossible for him to speak. The tenants later admitted that, before police arrived, they disposed of hypodermic needles they found nearby. After police left, in the back room -- which the explosion made inaccessible by collapsing a wall -- they painted over the devil's head to protect their friend's already tattered reputation.

Too little, too late. In the days after the explosion, newspapers focused more and more on the shocking aspects of Parsons's personal life -- "Satanist," "leader of free-love cult," "black magician" and of course the Crowley connection. The public perception that resulted reached the tabloid conclusion that Parsons -- magician and scientist, like Icarus -- met a fate he deserved by pursuing dark arts that mocked and jeered at the values of civilized society. This lurid version of his story won the day; Parsons has subsequently been either written out of or marginalized in the history of the institution he cofounded, JPL -- now a respected, conservative pillar of the American scientific and military community, and a central player in America's space program -- which Parsons's pioneering work did so much to advance.

In the aftermath of Parsons's death, for the skeptical of mind, theories emerged to contradict the accident scenario, although none has ever gained enough traction to counter the prevailing narrative.

Parsons's closest colleagues argued that, while his personal life crumbled, he never lost his discipline as an experienced handler of dangerous chemicals and explosives. The idea that he would have casually twirled around and dropped a coffee can containing something as lethal as fulminate of mercury struck them as preposterous. This opens a door to the possibility that Parsons's death was not accidental. And there were rumors, some borne out by evidence at the scene, that a first explosion had initially ripped up through the floorboards and triggered a second explosion of chemicals that were already stored in the room, suggesting that perhaps a bomb had been planted and detonated in the crawl space below.

But no convincing alternate theory has emerged to explain what ultimately happened. So the death of scientist/poet/mystic Jack Parsons remains a mystery. The best explanation was offered by one of Parsons's closest friends, a science fiction writer who had known him for many years. He summed up the tragic death of the man he called "an American Byron" this way:

"Once a magician stands between two worlds, he's in danger of not belonging to either one of them. In the end, Jack danced

[1] Mentioned earlier in the dossier as part of the secret postwar program known as Project Paperclip—TP

too close to the flames and it cost him his life. Whether he killed himself, was felled by an accident or died at the hand of another is beyond the point. I believe Jack Parsons summoned a fire demon."

After WWII dozens of German scientists who contributed to the Nazi war effort avoided prosecution at the Nuremberg trials by agreeing to work with the American government on the development of rocket, aircraft and weapon systems and what eventually became the U.S. space program, all carried on after the war, in total secrecy, at White Sands Missile Range, New Mexico.[1]

In official histories some of these Axis scientists -- Wernher von Braun, for instance -- are still widely credited with the success these programs enjoyed. American-born Jack Parsons, who helped formulate the science upon which most of those successes rest, is scarcely mentioned, by virtue, one presumes, of a messy personal life and his dabbling in the occult.[2]

The Parsons case marked a turning point for Doug Milford and the Air Force's investigative efforts into the still-growing UFO phenomenon. The next chapter would bring them slowly closer to the truth, to clear and present danger, and lead back to where it may have all begun.

[2] I can update one aspect of this aftermath: The Powers That Be have recently reinstated Jack Whiteside Parsons into their accounts of aerospace history. He is now mentioned, marginally, in JPL's public relations documents.

In 1972, three years after American-made JPL rockets first landed American astronauts on the moon, they officially named a prominent crater there after him. You'll never see it, though, and neither did NASA until their satellites mapped its entire surface. It's, fittingly, on the dark side of the moon.

So what happens to the UFO program now? And what does Doug Milford do for his next act, sprinkle poison in Fidel Castro's beard? Board a UFO with Elvis? Kill JFK?—TP

*** PROJECT BLUE BOOK:

In 1948 America's top military brass officially rejected the
initial findings of Project Sign -- that UFOs appeared to be
of no known earthly origin. As we've seen, Sign's successor
program, Project Grudge, was given a specific Pentagon
directive to debunk any unresolved UFO sightings or encounters
with mundane explanations, and they used the press and
national media to do it.

After three years of sloppy, unconvincing and biased research,
Grudge offered as its official public summation a blanket
denial of the UFO phenomenon as, at best, a mild form of
"mass hysteria," and at worst, evidence of psychopathology or
outright publicity-seeking fraud in civilian witnesses.

The public's response: anger, frustration and disbelief. It
seemed the now thousands of citizens who had been through "UFO
experiences" didn't appreciate being publicly shamed, and
through letters and the media they let authorities know about it.[1]

[1] Verified—TP

In 1952, a smaller group within the government -- many of them
alleged members of President Truman's alleged top-secret UFO
task force, Majestic 12 -- asserted itself and shut down Project
Grudge in favor of a new, lower-key program that promised to
examine the ever-expanding body of civilian evidence in a more
open-minded way that embraced the scientific method without a
predetermined negative bias.

According to eyewitness Major Doug Milford, who was present
at the first meeting of what soon was publicly announced as
Project Blue Book, commanding officer General Charles Cabell
offered the following directive: "I've been lied to, lied to and

2 Verified that this
handwritten section offers a
99 percent probability match
to known samples of Major
Milford's handwriting—TP

2 Verified that this
handwritten section offers a
99 percent probability match
to known samples of Major
Milford's handwriting—TP

3 Verified that "the Wise
Men" has often been
employed as another name
for the alleged mystery cabal
Majestic 12, or MJ-12. The
"Mason" reference appears
to mean President Truman,
a high-degree Mason, who
allegedly convened MJ-12
to begin with.
  The "other path" might
then, following the message's
internal logic, refer to an
opposing "secret society,"
i.e. the Illuminati, etc.
  The Archivist admits here
to having access to Milford's
private papers, establishing
an irrefutable personal link
between Milford and the
Archivist. Not sure who "M"
is in these notes, but it likely
refers to the "White House
source" mentioned above by
the Archivist.
  Now it gets a lot
weirder.—TP

4 "Connie" was an often-
used nickname for a
Lockheed Super Constella-
tion, which happened to be
the type of plane used by
President Eisenhower at the
time, prior to it being known
as "Air Force One"—TP

lied to. I want an open mind. In fact, I order an open mind,
and anyone who doesn't keep an open mind can get out now!
I want an answer to the saucers and I want a good answer."

Major Doug Milford did eventually provide a good answer,
but it would take him an additional 17 years of fieldwork,
and it turned out to be an answer that almost nobody wanted to
hear. As one of Blue Book's original personnel -- with certified
field experience going all the way back to Roswell -- Milford
emerged as their go-to investigator on high-profile sightings
that ensued through the next two decades, and there were
dozens of them.

He also had a history of sniffing out cases that Blue Book
hadn't even heard of, leading some to believe that he had
a high-placed source within the Eisenhower White House.

The following is a private journal entry of Milford's
from 1958.[2]

Musings on a Tuesday Night

Another call from M today. Still won't commit
anything to paper. The message: "The Wise Men" operate
in the shadows. Not even sure Ike knows what
They're up to. They may have been started by a Mason
but appears They're followers of "The other path" now.

Still trying to run down M's tip on alleged '55
incident at Holloman AFB, NM. Rumors of film
depicting approach and landing of craft persist,
but no film, yet.

Have confirmed That Ike did "disappear" from public
eye during his "quail hunting trip" to Georgia for
close to 12 hours. Verified source at Holloman
swears Ike visited base during That time frame. Also
verified That during That time he had orders to "shut
down all radar." When asked why, he was told
"radar fouls up Their systems, like at Roswell."
Mentions also That "one of Them landed on a closed
far runway" near where The "Connie" had stopped
after landing.

No eyewitness directly verifies rumor that
personnel from one craft then entered the other.
M will be disappointed. One wild report that
something was exchanged — referred to in one
confidential memo as "The Yellow Book." Reported
to be advanced technological "viewer" that
displayed pictures of objects in deep space.

One source says Ike rejected "offer" —
these "Nordic types" apparently made their offer
contingent on U.S. giving up nukes. Second
meeting — time and location unspecified — followed
with "grays," who made no such demands
and offered their tech in exchange for access
to "genetic material." That source says
second offer accepted.

ARCHIVIST'S NOTE

So Milford was publicly working for Project Blue Book,
but never took his eyes off the shadows. The "incident at
Holloman" has never, of course, been officially confirmed.
It did, however, allegedly serve as the real-life inspiration
for the final sequence in the I977 Steven Spielberg movie
Close Encounters of the Third Kind.

As to the identity of "M," Milford's high-placed White House
contact, ten years later a better picture of who that might
have been emerges.

Through the I960s, Milford maintained his reputation as the
most ethical, dispassionate and trustworthy case officer in
Project Blue Book's history, despite the fact that the program
suffered from years of autocratic and irresponsible leadership
after the death of JFK, who showed strong interest in the
subject. [7]

These officers once again steered Blue Book toward dedicated
debunking at a time when sightings continued to involve
thousands of citizens a year who knew perfectly well they
weren't lying, crazy or looking for publicity.

During these years Milford received another promotion -- though
his military records, for some reason, are still not obtainable
through the Freedom of Information Act -- attaining the rank of
lieutenant colonel. [8]

After the inauguration of Richard Nixon in early I969, Colonel
Milford accompanied longtime scientific consultant of Project
Blue Book J. Allen Hynek for a secure briefing in the Oval
Office with the recently elected president. [9]

Following is Milford's account of that meeting, this time
excerpted from his "official" journals.

[5] Verified that rumors of "The Yellow Book" persist—maybe it was Steve Jobs from the future offering them a beta version of the iPad—and if you connect the dots it seems they further suggest that this was the original "take me to your leader" moment in American history.
    Then it gets even weirder—TP

[6] I hope it goes without saying that I find no official confirmation anywhere for any part of the previous statement—TP

[7] Verified. JFK was openly curious about space in general and the UFO phenomenon in particular—TP

[8] Verified. Milford's promotion came in 1966—TP

[9] Dr. J. Allen Hynek was an astronomer and professor of physics at Ohio State University who—like Milford—worked with Projects Sign, Grudge and Blue Book. Though he was, by his own admission, an early skeptic, decades of exposure to credible UFO eyewitnesses—including many fellow astronomers—opened his mind to wider possibilities. He later launched his own, privately funded line of inquiry into UFOs, and served as scientific advisor on—and also briefly appeared in—Close Encounters of the Third Kind. (Still, no matter what you think about UFOs, a classic)—TP

TOP SECRET

DEPARTMENT OF THE AIR FORCE
TASK FORCE MJ-12

PROJECT BLUE BOOK
69-02-0024.
Lt. Col. Milford

February 24, 1969

We knew before the meeting that Nixon held a strong private interest
in UFOs that went back decades. He'd been Vice President for eight
years under Ike and had pushed Ike to be copied on all our regular
updates and reports, to little effect. Ike shut him out.

In 1966, another year that featured dozens of unexplained high-
profile sightings and encounters across the country, Congress
commissioned a committee to fully investigate the phenomenon--under
the auspices of a neutral university and from a more deeply
scientific perspective--to decide whether or not the government
should continue to look into the UFO phenomenon.

That resulted in the Condon Committee, at the University of Colorado--
which already enjoyed a sweetheart relationship with the Air Force
Academy at nearby Colorado Springs--under the direction of renowned
American physicist Edward Condon. The Committee was given unlimited
access to our archives from Sign, Grudge and Blue Book, as well as any
new incoming data related to recent sightings. After two years of
study at a cost to the government of $500,000, the Committee delivered
its report to the Air Force in 1968. It was rushed into publication for
the public in January of 1969--almost a thousand pages in paperback--
and by February, with Nixon newly in office, we were there to meet
directly with the President and discuss the Committee's report.

For clarity, the core of the Committee's findings can be boiled down
to this excerpt:

> Our general conclusion is that nothing has come from the study
> of UFOs in the past 21 years that has added to scientific
> knowledge. Careful consideration of the record as it is
> available to us leads us to conclude that further extensive
> study of UFOs probably cannot be justified in the expectation

01

T52-EXEMPT (E)

5.3

DEPARTMENT OF THE AIR FORCE
TASK FORCE MJ-12

TOP SECRET

PROJ
69-C
Lt.

*that science will be advanced thereby. The problem
that confronts the scientific community is that each
scientist must evaluate the record for himself,
and that this recommendation against further
research may not be true for all time. Government
agencies and private foundations ought to be
willing to consider UFO research proposals on an
open-minded, unprejudiced basis and each individual
case ought to be carefully considered on its own
merits. Therefore we recommend against the creation
of any government program to further investigate
UFO reports.*[10]

Their final report included the committee's evaluations
of only 59 of the most troubling unexplained cases we'd
investigated, a mere fraction of our body of work. And
although dismissive of every single sighting, they were
unable to provide even the most rudimentary alternate
explanation for over a third of the cases they included.
They also acknowledged that of the thousands in our
collective files at least a third still remained "unknown."
Despite this, Condon wrote the report's foreword--
excerpted above--and dismissed the UFO phenomenon as
unworthy of scientific interest--which openly contradicted
the finding of the report itself. Unfortunately, most of
Congress didn't bother reading past his withering
introduction.

Professor Hynek, speaking first at the President's
invitation, relayed our dismayed reaction to the report:
it was singularly slanted, and it seemed perfectly clear
to us that Condon did not understand the nature and
scope of what he had been asked to study.

Furthermore, Condon had focused solely on considering the
idea of UFOs as a purely extraterrestrial phenomenon, and
when he failed to find scientific support for that single

[10] Verified as accurate
quotation from Condon
Report—TP

02

THE AIR FORCE

PROJECT BLUE BOOK
69-02-0024
Lt. Col. Milford

interpretation, he dismissed the phenomenon in its entirety.
Let me state that Professor Hynek is one of the most
impressive scientists I've ever known, and he was in rare
and passionate form on this occasion, so I was startled
when Nixon raised a hand to interrupt him. Not to argue
with the professor's points, but to launch into a
blistering personal attack on Edward Condon's credibility
and his leadership of the committee. He revealed that
twenty years earlier Edward Condon--as a nuclear physicist
with a high security clearance involved in the Manhattan
Project--had been a person of interest to and extremely
hostile witness before the House Un-American Activities
Committee, where Nixon served as a young California
congressman. As a result Nixon's enmity for this man knew
no bounds, and he unleashed a burst of epithets to describe
Condon that wouldn't have been out of place in a Navy
boiler room. The President then stood up and flung the
Condon Committee's report across the room against a wall.

That got our attention. The President is much taller in
person than he appears in photographs, and in anger he is
even more impressive.

He thanked Dr. Hynek for coming and asked him to leave the
room. He told me to stay and, once we were alone,
initiated a confidential conversation as startling as any
I've experienced in my lifetime. The President was of
course fully aware of my work in this field going back to
Roswell and we had communicated for years, but this was
the first time we'd ever met face to face.[11]

Of all our case reports he'd personally examined he said
he'd always found mine the most comprehensive and
reliable. As near as I can re-create--let me add that I
was blessed with nearly perfect recall and have sharpened
that ability over time--this is a verbatim account of the
conversation that ensued:

[11] This appears to suggest that Nixon was "M," Milford's 1950s White House contact. So "M" may have stood for Milhous, his middle name—TP

[12] Verified. The Viking program successfully put a lander on Mars in 1976—TP

● **TOP SECRET** ▸

PRESIDENT NIXON: Condon's report is a royal Chinese clusterfuck, pardon my French. The finding, the timing, all of it--and they rushed it into print for the public, you know, as soon as they saw how the wind was blowing with the election, to get it out there before I took office.

ME: Why do you think they'd do that, sir?

PRESIDENT NIXON: Because he knew I'd toss it back in his face. The man despises me and the feeling's mutual. If that pile of dogshit had landed on my desk first it would never have seen the light of day. Slipshod work, intellectually lazy, high handed and smarmy--where's the voice of intelligent inquiry? Where's the objectivity? His conclusions are completely at odds with the facts. Here we have the damnedest, most puzzling and potentially most important mystery that's confronted us in all of human history, and he dismisses all of it with a pompous wave of the hand like a goddamn fairy tale--typical ivory tower Berkeley bullshit.

ME: How can I help, sir?

(He grew calmer now. Moved to a cabinet in the corner and poured us both a drink--Cutty Sark and branch water on the rocks--in cut crystal White House tumblers.)

PRESIDENT NIXON: We're putting a man on the moon this year, Colonel. And I'm going to push through Congress requests for funding that in another five or six years will land one of our craft on Mars.[12]

(I walked over to him and he handed me my drink.)

PRESIDENT NIXON: This is the ultimate foreign policy--"out there." It was going to be a part of my agenda, I promise you that. But now Condon and his bonehead committee have fucked us all the way up to the elbow. I won't be able to squeeze one more bright shiny nickel out of Washington to keep your work going now. Blue Book will be shuttered, within months, maybe weeks. I would have shared this with the professor, but frankly he's an academic. No disrespect, but once an egghead, always an egghead, if you know what I'm saying,

Colonel, so keep all of this under your chapeau. I know you're a man who can keep secrets.

ME: I hope my record speaks for itself, sir.

PRESIDENT NIXON: You're also a man who gets things done. That's my personal opinion, and that's what I need right now. I've got a private library of over a hundred books on this subject, and I've read 'em all.

(I guess at this point I glanced around, on reflex, as if expecting to see them on a shelf.)

No, no, not here. Jesus, if I kept those here they'd think I'm some kind of a kook. Well, I am not a kook.

ME: No, sir.

(He moved closer, looming over me, lowered his voice, and I felt the full force of his formidable presence.)

PRESIDENT NIXON: We're going to get to the bottom of this thing. You'll answer to me, once the shit hits the fan on Blue Book, and no one else. We're going to pull something together, below the radar, a private task force, interagency, to keep this going.[13]

ME: What can I do?

PRESIDENT NIXON: Lay low. Draw up a roster, who you might use, cherry pick from any branch of service or agency, and a plan on how you'd most effectively proceed--though whatever you do, keep the CIA out of it. They play their own game by their own rules no matter who's at this desk. Be ready when I call on you. I need to flex some muscle first, carve out some operating room--this is a power game; I know how the system works but it takes time--and then we're going to find out exactly what these Skull and Bones "Wise Men" have stashed up their sleeves.[14]

ME: Could you expand on that, sir?

05

PRESIDENT NIXON: They've played you for a fool, Colonel,
your whole program. They let Blue Book take all the
heat on this publicly without giving you a fraction
of what they really knew. Same goes for the executive
branch. There's a shitload of military real estate
behind government chain link out there. These bastards
have been sitting on pure dynamite for twenty years.
Ike never told me what he knew--too much West Point in
the old man, God bless him, always following orders--
but he knew something, and my guess is it was a <u>lot</u> of
something. They say Kennedy was sniffing around after
whatever Ike knew but was too busy chasing broads to
give it the attention it deserved. LBJ has a cunning mind
but the curiosity of a dung beetle, too busy settling
petty scores in the shit to look up at the stars. I'd
like to change all that. A few more questions.

(He paused, looked at me searchingly, then he smiled.)

PRESIDENT NIXON: What do you think they are, Colonel?

(I gathered my thoughts. I sensed that a lot depended
on my answer.)

ME: They're not nothing.

PRESIDENT NIXON: Go on.

ME: I don't think they're just one thing, sir. Some of
them may be, but I don't believe they're all exclusively
"extraterrestrial."

PRESIDENT NIXON: Elaborate.

ME: It seems to me these things have been with us a lot longer
than we know, taking different forms at different times.
I think some or all of them may also be "extradimensional."

06

[13] Sounds like a reference to starting his own version of a Majestic 12—TP

[14] Apparently connecting the Wise Man/MJ-12 group to Yale's own secret society, which has, at various times, been linked in conspiracy theory to global organizations like the Illuminati or the Council on Foreign Relations—TP

THE AIR FORCE

PROJECT BLUE BOOK
69-02-0024
Lt. Col. Milford

It's an idea that deep water physics is starting to engage with, not that I'm any kind of expert. And I could argue it round or flat, but to my eye there's enough evidence to support both theories. At this point neither possibility should be discounted. They may both be true.[15]

PRESIDENT NIXON: Are we talking about time, or space?

ME: Probably both.

PRESIDENT NIXON: Do you honestly believe the Air Force or your investigations have gotten you anywhere near the truth?

ME: If they have, they plan on keeping it to themselves. Are you familiar with Air Force Directive 200-2?

PRESIDENT NIXON: Tell me.

ME: It prohibits the disclosure of any information about a UFO to the public unless it has first been positively identified as a familiar or known object.

PRESIDENT NIXON: Catch-22.

ME: If you were to ask me if I feel I've gotten closer to it on my own, the answer is yes.

PRESIDENT NIXON: Go on.

ME: I can attest that having one of these "encounters" is a life-altering experience. Comparable, in some ways, to ways in which people used to describe a "religious conversion." Cross that threshold, it's hard going back.

PRESIDENT NIXON: Based on your experience, do you think there's any real or effective way to contain this thing?

ME: I've done the math. We average between three and five

[15] This is the first mention of anything related to "extra dimensions" on this subject and, like Nixon, I'd really like to hear some elaboration. Will self-engage on research—TP

[16] Damn. Milford strikes again—TP

thousand domestic sightings a month. Thanks to the dismissive and often brutal way in which witnesses are treated publicly, we believe less than 3 percent of sightings or encounters are actually reported. Let's also not forget this is a global phenomenon; it's going on all over the world, every month. Even if 95 percent turn out to be explicable, that leaves us with some startling numbers.

PRESIDENT NIXON: (A brief pause; I think he was doing the math.) I believe you, Colonel.

ME: I've seen more than my share of unfamiliar and unknown things, sir.

(A moment later he smiled again, satisfied.)

PRESIDENT NIXON: You haven't disappointed me.

(He shook my hand and walked me to the door.)

PRESIDENT NIXON: We've gone from Kitty Hawk to the moon in less than seventy years. Only stands to reason that—to paraphrase the Bard—out there lies far more than we've dreamt of in our philosophies.

ME: That's what my scoutmaster always used to tell us.

PRESIDENT NIXON: Good counsel. Not a word to anyone on this. I'll be in touch.

We shook hands and I rejoined Professor Hynek, who was waiting for me outside. As we left the White House he asked me what the President and I had discussed. Fishing, I said.[16]

CLASS. & EXT. BY
DE'SCN - F

REC-7   ST-103 63-44511-

76-26

08

[17] The reader will recall that many moons earlier, back in the '20s, Milford had "shacked up" for a time with the daughter of the *Gazette*'s then owner, Dayton Cuyo. Turns out she also lived long enough to sell him the paper—TP

[18] There is more to come on their deteriorating relationship later—TP

ARCHIVIST'S NOTE

Just as President Nixon predicted, in 1969 all military funding for Blue Book was terminated and the entire project mothballed. That July, astronauts Neil Armstrong and Buzz Aldrin left the first human footprints on the moon. In the years before and after, many Apollo astronauts reported seeing UFOs while up there, but -- like most witnesses at this point -- kept it largely to themselves.

The week after the first moon landing, Doug Milford returned home to Twin Peaks, where he told people that, having reached the age of 60, he'd retired from his long, peripatetic military career. He told closer friends that he planned to take up fly-fishing and oil painting, in that order, but within weeks, following the death of editor/publisher Robert Jacoby, Milford bought a controlling interest in the Twin Peaks Gazette.[17]

Douglas took immediate steps to modernize both the operation and the look of the paper and also changed its name to the Twin Peaks Post. That fall his older brother Dwayne -- the longtime town pharmacist who'd never left home -- won his fifth election as mayor.

Douglas wrote a front-page editorial endorsing his brother's candidacy, which turned out to be the last kind words Douglas ever said or printed about Dwayne.[18]

Although it's possible that President Nixon communicated with Doug Milford throughout his first term, Milford leaves no written record of it; the next contact between them that Milford details in his journals wouldn't happen until nearly four years later.

In that time Nixon had indeed "carved out a little operating room"; his reelection in 1972 over Democrat George McGovern turned out to be the biggest landslide in American presidential history. It's also possible, but difficult to verify, that during those four years Milford began putting together a sub-rosa, interagency investigative team just as the president had requested. Records indicate he traveled extensively to the East Coast -- Washington and Philadelphia, primarily -- during this period, at a time when he was ostensibly a retired military man running a small-town newspaper.

Then, on the night of February 19, 1973, Milford was summoned to a private compound known as the Florida White House, in Key Biscayne, Florida, at the request of the White House chief of staff, for a briefing with the newly reelected President Richard Nixon.

This meeting has never been made public, and what follows is, once again, Colonel Milford's account from his personal journals.

FEBRUARY 19, 1973, KEY BISCAYNE, FLORIDA

On February 12, I arrived at my condominium in Fort Lauderdale for my customary midwinter monthlong break from the Northwestern gloom and had enjoyed a leisurely week of fishing while looking forward to the start of spring training games. One week later, on the afternoon of the 19th, I received a phone call from an old friend of mine in Tacoma, Fred Crisman, who told me he'd received a call from his old friend H. R. "Bob" Haldeman--Nixon's chief of staff--with a request that I present myself at Nixon's Key Biscayne compound that evening at 8:00 PM. I made the drive down to Key Biscayne and arrived promptly, as instructed.[19]

Aside from the usual Secret Service presence, the compound appeared to be empty. An agent escorted me into Nixon's private offices, where I was greeted warmly by the President; wearing golf togs, he had apparently just returned from an afternoon round and a dinner. He then introduced me to the room's only other occupant, who needed no introduction; I was shocked to instantly recognize ███████, the world-famous entertainer-- a longtime personal favorite of mine--who had been Nixon's companion that day on the links at his charity tournament. They both had cocktails in hand--not their first, judging by their elevated jocular spirits--and I joined them when the President quickly offered and poured me one as well. As closely as I can re-create it, the conversation that followed went like this:

PRESIDENT NIXON: So we were putting out on the 15th green today--and you have to understand we've talked about this on a few prior occasions--

███████: Only every time we play.

PRESIDENT NIXON: Over the last few years. Well, out on the course is the only time no one else is listening, isn't it? Safe to say it's a subject we share a passion for, isn't that right, ███████?

███████: My library on this stuff might be the only one bigger than his--that is to say, the only private collection. Over 1,700 books.

PRESIDENT NIXON: You have to understand, (he refers to his guest by his first name throughout) has not only read most of the same books, he built a library in the form of a spaceship to house them.

████████: For the record, the room is merely round--as is the rest of the house--because I happen to believe it's conducive to improved mental acuity, among other beneficial qualities.

PRESIDENT NIXON: Hell, he calls that place "the Mothership," what does that tell you?

(They shared a laugh. As I looked around I realized that the shelves in this room were entirely filled with books-- most of which I'd read, many based on cases I'd personally investigated--on the subject of UFOs. So this was the "private library" Nixon had spoken to me about four years earlier.)

████████: True, all true, Mr. President. Guilty as charged, if being fascinated with the most tremendous mystery facing mankind today is a crime.

PRESIDENT NIXON: In my experience, what defines a crime depends on who's getting screwed.

(Another laugh. Presidents get a lot of laughs.)

PRESIDENT NIXON: All kidding aside, ████████ has been urging me to get out in front of this issue, make a splash, as it were, lift the lid off the box and give the public a little glimpse about what we know.

████████: If anyone can and should, I believe it should be you, Mr. President. As I understand it, Colonel, you've been working on this subject your entire professional life, so what do you think about that idea?

ME: Before lifting the lid on any box, I check to see if it ever belonged to Pandora.

[19] This appears to be the same Fred Crisman, the alleged CIA "black ops" operative, who played a central role in 1947's Maury Island incident. Crisman is also known to have had a close relationship with E. Howard Hunt, the senior black ops figure in the botched Watergate burglary in June 1972 that was only now starting to crawl into public perception as a "White House problem"—TP

███████: Don't you think the public has the right to know what's really going on out there?

ME: That's a question I've never really been paid to express an opinion about, sir.

███████: Impressively evasive, Colonel, but you must have one, don't you?

(I looked at the President, who was grinning at me in a way I can only describe as sly.)

ME: I would feel more comfortable about expressing it if the "suggestion" came from him.

PRESIDENT NIXON: What did I tell you, ████████? Good man. Loose lips sink ships.

ME: But now you've got me curious. Is this something you're actually considering, sir?

(The President sets down his empty glass to look at his bookshelves, and I notice he's worrying a green ring on the ring finger of his right hand.)

PRESIDENT NIXON: I believe that on a subject as vital as this one the American people have the right--the fundamental right--to make up their own minds about what they believe. They can't do that without more information. The question that needs to be asked first is: should the public be told about what we already know, and, if the answer is yes, it then falls to us to determine how much should they know if the issue concerns our national security.

(He looks at me again, and gives a slight nod.)

PRESIDENT NIXON: So why don't you go ahead and answer (████████)'s question, Colonel.

ME: I've looked at this from every angle. My personal opinion, sir, is that while I and my fellow investigators in Blue Book ran around for two decades tracking cases, the Air Force and military had in their possession--from the beginning, and have since continued to accumulate--

03

a great deal more evidence than they were ever willing to share with us. Also bear in mind that all the other branches conducted their own investigations and they're all equally, remarkably unwilling to share results with each other.

████: That's a pisser.

PRESIDENT NIXON: That's the way of the world, gentlemen.

ME: Whatever they knew in <u>fact</u>, the Air Force used Grudge and Blue Book as a sop to public perception--because it gave them the <u>appearance</u> of meaningful inquiry into this subject, as political cover, without any intent of providing public revelation. The Condon Report was more of the same, and they used it to put the final nail in the coffin. The intellectual interest of enlightened citizens like yourself aside, it's clear to me now that the military-intelligence community's primary goal all along has been the quashing, debunking and discouragement of general civilian curiosity while, the entire time, they were pursuing their own investigation into this matter on a separate, deep dark track which had nothing to do with us. Is that specific enough for you, sir?

(████ lit a cigarette as that sunk in.)

████: That's truly shocking, Colonel.

ME: It's just an opinion, sir.

(Nixon picks up the phone on his desk and punches in a number.)

PRESIDENT NIXON: Have the car brought around to the back, please, Luis--no, the other one...no, I'd prefer that you didn't tell them, please...if they ask, tell them we're just giving Mr. ████ a ride home. Thank you, Luis.

(He hangs up and turns to us both. There's a sharp gleam in his eyes.)

PRESIDENT NIXON: In politics, secrecy is power and power is currency, but if you don't use it for anything meaningful it wastes away. Eats at you, from the inside, like a cancer. We all want answers to the big questions. I've always been of the mind that policy decisions need to be informed with fresh insight, which sometimes can only be gained from expert opinion that develops outside the dense fog of institutional influence. You need to keep at least one eye toward history on these things. I felt that about China, I felt it about detente, and the nuclear treaty with the Russians. (Pause, as he deliberated over something.) I'd like you both to take a drive with me. I'm also going to have to swear you both to secrecy.

We both readily agreed. At the President's direction, we quietly exited the library to the rear of the compound, where an unadorned black sedan was waiting for us on a back service road. It was well after 9:00 now, a warm humid night with the only pale light on the water provided by a rising half moon. There was a driver sitting inside but I saw no additional Secret Service presence. I sat beside the driver, while the President and ███████ settled in the back. We exited the compound through the service entrance. I heard the two men quietly converse during the trip, below my ability to hear, as we drove for approximately half an hour.

We eventually arrived at what I realized was a side entrance to a vast military installation that I had previously visited, Homestead Air Force Base. The sentries on duty were apparently expecting us and immediately waved us through the gate. We drove to the far end of the complex, parked outside the entrance of a large hangar, got out of the sedan and walked to a nearby door. All exterior lights had been extinguished, most likely so no one would realize who was there, and a single soldier was waiting for us at the door. I recognized him as General ████████, who I had met on a few previous occasions, and who had long been rumored to be a part of Majestic 12. (He gave no indication of recognizing me, but I find it hard to reckon that, under the circumstances, he wouldn't have known who I was.)

Few words were spoken. The General led us inside, where I realized that the belly of the hangar had been transformed into a large and complex concrete bunker. He took us to a waiting elevator—it required the use of a key he carried to operate—and we descended three levels belowground. I felt a rising level of tension that I could see the others shared; a light sheen of sweat coated the President's face, and ████████ looked pale and anxious. The General led us out of the elevator and down a long concrete corridor with rooms on either side. Through the windows I saw a number of what appeared to be labs or clean rooms. He took us into one of these rooms, a large blank space.

Varying-sized pieces of strange metallic debris were laid out all
around the center of the floor; it appeared to me similar to an FAA
crash retrieval, where investigators attempt to re-create the shape
of a crashed plane. In this case, the shape it conformed to on the floor
bore no resemblance to a plane or jet. This was more triangular than
circular, with a wingspan of approximately thirty feet. Neither the
General nor the President offered any words of explanation. We stood
looking at it for a while. ██████ and I exchanged a look. I felt he was
asking me whether I thought this was "authentic." I shrugged slightly;
"no way of knowing." Without closer examination, for all I knew it could
have been the shattered and rearranged remains of a Pontiac Firebird.

Without a word, the General led us back into and down the corridor
outside until we reached a heavily secured steel door and paused while
the General punched a code into a numeric keypad. The door opened, we
entered another corridor, then passed through a door on the right into a
plain, rectangular paneled room. A long wooden console and chairs faced
a window that ran the length of the room and was currently obscured by a
shade. No other personnel were present. The General dimmed the lights
and indicated we should be seated. At a signal from the President, the
General pushed a button on the console and the curtain started to rise.

We were looking into a very dimly lit room that appeared to be empty.
Then, in roughly the center of the room, I realized a shape, small and
pale, appeared to be sitting or squatting, turned away from us, showing
only a grayish-greenish-white spiny back. Then it disappeared entirely.
Moments later it reappeared, as if a concealing shadow--or a magician's
cape--had simply passed over it. But it hadn't moved and I still
couldn't tell if it was inert or animated. Whatever it was then phased
in and out of my view a second time. The General flipped a switch on
the console and tapped twice on a microphone; the sound of which we
could hear through a speaker as it was conveyed into the room.

I saw the shape react, stiffen. Then it turned to look our way through
the window--it seemed to me likely that it was one-way glass, mirrored
on the interior side--and for a brief moment the shape of its face was
visible. The glimpse we got was extremely brief before it vanished again,
and I wasn't entirely sure of what I saw, beyond a vivid impression of
large oval black eyes, pinched to the point of nonexistent mouth and
nose, and a smooth bulbous head. Then it was gone.

But what lingered longer than the persistence of the image was the
visceral feeling that seemed to emanate from the figure; what clawed at
my gut and the base of my skull was a sickly sour wave of such pure and
uncanny malevolence that for a moment I thought I might lose consciousness.
A paralyzing fear ripped through the most primitive parts of my brain
and I couldn't move, except to glance over at ▮▮▮▮▮▮ and I instantly
recognized he was just as pole-axed as I was; pale and covered with sweat.

Then the thing was gone and it didn't reappear. The room went dark.
The General and the President did not react--I'm guessing they'd seen
this before--although Nixon wiped the sweat off his upper lip. Moments
later, the curtain came down again. I knew perfectly well that what we'd
just seen could have been conjured up for our benefit with the simplest
of smoke and mirrors. As a kid I'd seen the trick a dozen times in
carnivals and county fairs. But the feeling persisted. I felt shaky
and nauseated. ▮▮▮▮▮▮ leaned forward to grab the back of a chair to
steady himself. Not a word was spoken. The General and the President
walked out of the room. Moments later, ▮▮▮▮▮▮ and I followed. We rode
the elevator back up in silence.

When we walked back outside, I saw my car waiting on the tarmac beside
the black sedan. The President shook my hand and said quietly that we
would speak soon, then he and ▮▮▮▮▮▮ got back into his car. ▮▮▮▮▮▮
didn't look at me again; he appeared to be in shock. They drove off and
I followed them back out through the same gate through which we'd
entered. Once we were back on the streets they soon turned and drove
off in a different direction, while I headed back toward the highway
that would take me home.

I wouldn't hear from the President for over three weeks. Although we
had made plans to speak again, I never saw ▮▮▮▮▮▮ again in person,
so I don't know if he continued to advocate that the President publicly
disclose any of what we'd seen. I can't imagine that he would. To this
day I'm uncertain of what the President's motives were that night:
Was he earnestly seeking our opinion about disclosure, or did he mean
to terrify us enough to buy our enduring silence? To my knowledge,
▮▮▮▮▮▮ never spoke about it to anyone and, naturally, neither did I.

295-3784

ARCHIVIST'S NOTE

If the president still harbored any thoughts about going public with whatever he knew -- and whether or not this was an "authentic" encounter of the third kind remains an open question -- the problems he was about to face in the real world soon overwhelmed every other aspect of his remaining ambitions. Within a month the lid blew off his attempt to cover up the previous year's "third-rate burglary" at the Watergate headquarters of the Democratic Party. Although no evidence ever surfaced in the subsequent congressional hearings that Nixon had given the initial order for the job -- apparently he did not -- his actions in trying to contain it and obstruct the ensuing investigation were decidedly criminal. Within a year this led to his resigning the presidency in disgrace, which forever blackened his name in history.

One of the few stones left unturned from Nixon's five and a half years in office concerns what Air Force Colonel Doug Milford, soon to be retired, went on to do with the job Nixon had given him.[20]

[20] They did, however, leave a clue to the identity of their unnamed companion that night at Homestead AFB. Those numbers scrawled on Milford's journal entry—which I'm assuming he wrote in the immediate aftermath of this experience as part of their "plans to speak again"—correspond to an unlisted phone number from 1973 in Hialeah, Florida. If records from the period are accurate, that number belonged to the actor and entertainer Jackie Gleason. Remembered today primarily for his work on the early TV sitcom he created, *The Honeymooners*, during the 1960s Gleason was a showbiz titan, working in movies, television and music.

I have also confirmed that Gleason did indeed, a few years prior to their meeting, build a circular house in Peekskill, New York, that in more than one interview he referred to as "the Mothership." Equally true is the reference to his massive private library of books on UFOs and many

continued

other occult subjects; such a collection was donated by Gleason's estate to the University of Miami after his death in 1987.

As for the encounter at Homestead Air Force Base, years later Gleason's wife at the time of the incident made reference to it in an unpublished memoir, saying that Gleason eventually shared with her some of the chilling details about "something" he'd seen that night with the president and that it plunged him into a serious, disorienting depression for many weeks. At his request she never published the book, but word about the Homestead incident leaked out. Gleason made an oblique reference to the incident himself in an interview not long before he died.

I don't know about you, but this gives a whole new meaning to the phrase "To the moon, Alice!"—TP

As far as we know, despite his mounting legal difficulties, Nixon was able to make good on his promise to Doug Milford, earmarking an untraceable source of funding -- known in intelligence circles as a "carve-out" -- for his plan to carry on some deeper and more independent investigation into the UFO phenomenon without any official military or political involvement or oversight. Milford proceeded to use his four decades of discreet interagency experience to engage with a small number of individuals he trusted from different backgrounds and organizations.

The last known direct contact between Milford and Nixon took place near the end of his presidency. On the night of July 24, 1974, Nixon placed a call to Milford at his Twin Peaks residence on a secure line directly from the Oval Office. The following entry from Milford's personal journal is his reconstruction of their conversation:

JULY 24, 1974, 8:30 PM, PDT

ME: Hello?

PRESIDENT NIXON: Can you guarantee that this is a secure line on
your end?

ME: (instantly recognizing his voice) Yes, sir, I can.

PRESIDENT NIXON: No names. God knows if any members of the Inquisition
have tapped me here--I have the room swept every day--but it's a chance
we'll have to take. And, believe me, this is one conversation I am most
certainly not recording on this end.

(I wait. I hear the sound of ice cubes rattling in a drink; from past
experience he sounds as if he's been drinking heavily.)

PRESIDENT NIXON: You've heard the news, I suppose.

ME: The Supreme Court.

PRESIDENT NIXON: Shot down our argument of executive privilege. 8-0.
I put three of the bastards on that bench myself and this is the thanks I
get. Only Rehnquist recused himself. We gave Congress all the
transcripts--more than 1,200 pages--but no, that's not enough for them.
Now they'll get the tapes, just as they're preparing to vote the
articles of impeachment.

ME: I'm sorry to hear that, sir.

PRESIDENT NIXON: Well, you can't just stick your head in the sand about
it. Got myself on the wrong side of the wrong people--it's a global
conspiracy, Colonel; go after their secrets, they play the game with
live ammunition. And I'm about out of bullets.

ME: How can I help?

PRESIDENT NIXON: Listen to me now, it's even worse than we thought.
Worse than I ever imagined. They never told me a fraction of their
plan--and it was what they were planning all along, after Blue Book.
You were dead-on, Colonel, Blue Book was a misdirect from the start,
nothing but a cheap feint to draw the eye and tamp down public opinion.
The real action started in '53--I don't even know for sure if Ike knew
about it, if he did he never told me--they called it Gleem then. They
renamed it Aquarius in '66, one big fat fuck-you to the hippies, I
suppose, and it's still going.

ME: What is it?

PRESIDENT NIXON: A parallel program shadowing Blue Book, in place from
the start. The Wise Men are running the whole show at this point--not
even a pretense of public interest. They had full access to all your
records, and the cases that popped, the ones that really stood out, all
went to them. They left you to sift through the 90 percent that were
mostly horseshit. Truman or Ike probably set it up this way for security
reasons, but the net effect is they were not at any point answerable to
the executive branch, still aren't, and now it's out of control. As far
as I can tell they never answered to anyone.

(He lowers his voice, as if there's someone in the next room.)

PRESIDENT NIXON: And I can tell you exactly why they shut down Blue
Book--because they'd already made contact, and they were terrified
somebody down the chain--somebody whip smart, Colonel, like you--
might find out and blow the whistle. I didn't know that at the time
or I never would have shown you Homestead, but I'd only just found
out about it and I thought...well, it doesn't matter what the hell I
thought anymore.

ME: Why would they do this?

PRESIDENT NIXON: (He lowers his voice to a harsh whisper) It wasn't
just bodies at Roswell. There was a craft. There was another crash in
'49, then a third in '58. With a survivor. That was the one you saw,

that thing was real, Milford. They've been secretly trying to reverse-engineer the technology they found at these sites ever since.

ME: Who has?

PRESIDENT NIXON: The Gleem/Aquarius group. Like I said, they use different names for it now: the Wise Men or the Study Group, or sometimes just "the Group." Headed by someone they call the Caretaker.[21]

I don't even know who that is. CIA was in on it from the start. Jim Forrestal ran the Defense Department then, he was part of this thing to begin with, under Truman—Jim was a friend of mine—but he didn't like where the Agency was taking it and he tried to blow the whistle. You know what happened to Forrestal, Colonel?

ME: (I paused) Yes, sir.

PRESIDENT NIXON: So they're calling the shots now, and they'll drown every last damn cat before they let one out of the bag. It's not just that thing I showed you. I'm told there's more than one kind, too, different species, maybe as many as six. We don't know what they want. Hell, some might be nothing more than the equivalent of long-haul truckers. But a few of the others, they've got agendas. I've heard all sorts of batshit crazy ideas, that they built bases, vast complexes, all underground. Here—in Nevada, Washington State, in Dulce, New Mexico, at least one in Australia they call Pine Gap, way out in the desert, the outback. A goddamn kangaroo couldn't find it.

ME: Who built them?

PRESIDENT NIXON: Our own people, they say. The ones on the inside, the Wise Men.

ME: For what purpose?

[21] Verified that these are often-used synonyms for Majestic 12 TP

03

PRESIDENT NIXON: That's up to you to find out now. I can't help you anymore from here. Captains go down with their ships. (He lowers his voice again) But I can tell you these things are part of something even bigger, something old and dug in, and it's been here all along. Watching us. More than that. Manipulating. We're all so caught up with our own petty preoccupations we can't see what's got its hand stuck up the back of our shirts. We've all been barking up the wrong tree. Which, take it from me, has been their objective all along. Distract us with bullshit so we never see how they're really and truly fucking us.

ME: What can I do? Where do I start?

PRESIDENT NIXON: You have to listen. Over time. In the right places, and you better be smart about it. Dig deep. And for God's sake, go slow in case they're watching you, and stay low in your foxhole, because they probably are.

ME: Who can I trust?

PRESIDENT NIXON: (He pauses) There's a man at the FBI, the one I told you about.

ME: I have his contact.

PRESIDENT NIXON: He's the only one. Wait awhile and then set a meeting. Face to face. Nothing written, nothing on the phone. CYA, Colonel. You'll have to figure it out from there. They all have code names, by the way, the ones at the top of Aquarius. Birds. I hear the Caretaker's name is Raven--(A loud knock is heard.) Shit, someone's at the door. Best of luck to you, Colonel. We'll never speak again.

(He hangs up abruptly.) [22]

[22] JESUS. We knew Tricky Dick was cracking toward the end, but this is Humpty Dumpty territory. As Doug Milford claims to be recalling the conversation from memory alone there is, of course, no way to verify the contents. But just because you're paranoid doesn't mean they aren't out to get you. Oh, by the way: James Forrestal. The country's first secretary of defense, appointed by Truman in '48. Long rumored to be one of the original members of Majestic 12, which may or may not have been real and which may or may not have been behind what Nixon referred to as Project Gleem. Forrestal resigned a year later, 1949, and soon after, although no longer in the military, he was confined in the psychiatric ward of Bethesda Naval Hospital for "nervous exhaustion." In what they called a "VIP suite" on the 16th floor. Six weeks later they found an open window across the hall from his room and his pajama-clad body on the roof of the third-floor kitchen below. Ruled a suicide, but they found severe abrasions around his throat and broken glass in his room suggesting a possible struggle. He was 57—TP

ARCHIVIST'S NOTE

Three days after Milford last spoke to Nixon, Congress
passed the first of three articles of impeachment against the
president, for nine acts of obstruction of justice. Less than
two weeks later Nixon resigned from office and retreated into
deep seclusion at his home in San Clemente, California, from
which he would only rarely emerge. President Gerald Ford,
the handpicked vice president who succeeded him, pardoned
Nixon the following year, but over 40 of his former aides
and associates eventually went to jail. President Ford, who
years earlier had attempted to expand the investigation into
UFOs while still a Michigan congressman -- there had been
frequent and disturbing sightings in his home state; he was
rumored to have had a sighting of his own -- turned over
that responsibility to his new secretary of defense, Donald
Rumsfeld, and the man Ford had just chosen as his chief of
staff, Richard Cheney.[23]

Doug Milford laid low as well. After waiting for over a year,
as the president had advised, Milford cautiously went to work.
During that time he pulled together the strange history of
the region around his hometown -- which comprises the early
sections of this dossier -- including the accounts of his own
youthful experiences in the woods around Twin Peaks.

I can also confirm that the funding for the secret program
Milford discussed with the president came through -- apparently
set up in untraceable offshore accounts in the Cayman Islands.[24]

[23] And I'm guessing that
was most likely the end of
anyone on the outside ever
hearing about any of this—TP

[24] So this establishes that
Milford himself compiled the
early research for the dossier,
and then somehow passed
it on to the Archivist,
who—apparently in response
to Milford's work—wrote all
of the interstitial commen-
taries. The Archivist also
professes to know about
Milford's secret funding,
which I assume he could
have learned about only
from Milford himself.
    But what exactly had
Nixon empowered Milford
to do, and how did he go
about it?—TP

*** THE SEARCH FOR INTELLIGENT LIFE:

I BLUE PINE MOUNTAIN

Habits of secrecy established by decades of working with classified intelligence are hard to break. Doug Milford did, apparently, make contact sometime in the late I970s with the FBI man that the president referenced in their final conversation. On a parallel track, perhaps acting on a tip from the FBI or his existing contacts within the Air Force, he also opened a second operational front in I982.

A young officer stationed at Fairchild Air Force Base in nearby Spokane moved with his family to Twin Peaks that year on special assignment. Here is the small item Milford ran about it in the editorial section of the July I5 edition of the Twin Peaks Post:

issued on strictly need-based criteria.   role in your life.   sn

Welcome to town!

by DOUG MILFORD, Publisher

I F YOU'VE BEEN SEEING a little more blue with your "scrambled eggs" around town lately, there's a good reason for that, and it's not on the menu at the Double R. Your United States Air Force has just posted one of their best and brightest consultants to our local airport, Unguin Field, to help us upgrade our runways, communications and security systems

to modern standards—sorry, Charles Lindbergh, the milk run for the morning mail doesn't stop here anymore! We're happy to know that Unguin Field will soon be a regional airport, transformed into a source of pride for our entire community. So if you see a snappy, smart-dressed man in blue about town—or his lovely wife Betty, and their bright-eyed twelve-year-old boy Bobby—be sure to say hello to Major Garland Briggs and his family with a hearty handshake or a crisp salute. Welcome to Twin Peaks, folks, we're happy to have you with us!

my
de
ofl
mi
on
all
qu
sc
sc
se
th
sc
c
e
s
i

CASE FILES   consider the things that makes you

[1] Rodd appears to be suggesting that the "Illuminati" strain continues to this day in the guise of the Bohemian Grove, a 150-year-old "secret society" located near San Jose, California. Their sprawling, heavily secured rural forest compound is the location for an annual gathering of its members, a roster which includes a staggering number of establishment heavyweights, former presidents, statesmen, military leaders and industrial tycoons. Their two-week summer retreat kicks off each year with a huge bonfire known as "the Cremation of Care," conducted before a gigantic statue of a horned owl. It is the inspiration, perhaps justifiably so, for a long list of American conspiracy theories. Photo follows—TP

[2] The reader will recall Carl Rodd as one of the three children allegedly "abducted" in the incident witnessed by Doug Milford back in '47.

Doug Milford's brother Dwayne—the pharmacist and former scoutmaster—was by this time serving his sixth term as mayor of Twin Peaks—TP

ARCHIVIST'S NOTE

The reason for this newcomer's arrival, you may have already surmised, had considerably less to do with the upgrades at Unguin Field -- although they did take place, providing a very convenient "day-job" cover -- than it did the actual intent of the mission at hand.

As the work at Unguin Field proceeded slowly -- very slowly, by design -- a squadron of full-time personnel were also diverted from that job site and put to work building a much smaller, top-secret facility high up on Blue Pine Mountain. The area, a secluded 25-acre section of Ghostwood National Forest, had been quietly acquired by the military through the use of eminent domain. This detail was never reported by the newspaper, although one nosy neighbor wrote the following letter to the Post, which only made it into print because the publisher was out of town that week on business:

"We Get Letters!"

An Open Letter to Mayor Dwayne Milford:

I don't know what you people think is going on around here, but I can tell you it's a whole lot worse than you know about. Every morning and every evening I take my walk through the woods, rain or shine, and I can hear the sound of construction going on way up the mountain just about around the clock. It's steep as hell up there. Strange lights at night! Graders driving in, cutting new roads, black jeeps and helicopters and a whole lot of cement trucks! Of course it's all fenced in with those "no trespassing or else" signs like it's theirs to do with as they please even though it's supposed to be our national forest! Armed guards, too, so any nimrod can see it's military, but you won't see any unit insignias on them anywhere. No sir. I don't know if it's the Knights of Columbus, the Knights Templar, the Illuminati or the Tri-Lateral Commission—it don't matter, they're all the same bunch in

different costumes anyway, always have been. Ever wonder why the symbol of the Bohemian Grove is an owl? A big giant statue of one standing out in the woods, like some ancient Sumerian deity? [1]

It's a story old as time: if you don't know who's really in charge, you'll never figure out how they're screwing you sideways. And I can tell you from personal experience there's plenty enough strange goings-on in those woods without a bunch of jackbooted spooks pouring concrete. Well, the price of freedom is vigilance. So what are we going to do about it, Mr. Mayor?

Sincerely,

[2] **CARL RODD,**
*Manager, Fat Trout
Trailer Park*

Keeps Me Going

I am a 61-year-
have been skii
cause of m?
running a
te

Terror in the

foun
thro
bala
scho
assis
fem;

A
plac
scho
and
gra
ally
see
cac
par
hel

my
def
offe
mc
on
gui
fina
scho
mak
mif

BOHEMIAN GROVE OWL,
circa 1930s

—TP

The first thing Doug Milford did when he returned from his business trip, after realizing this letter had made it into print, was fire the assistant editor who put the edition to bed without telling him about it. The second thing he did was pay a visit to his brother, the mayor. Tension between the two had been building ever since Douglas retired and moved back to town -- or, to trace it more precisely, ever since Douglas was born. This editorial that Douglas ran the day after Nixon resigned the presidency in 1974 certainly didn't help:

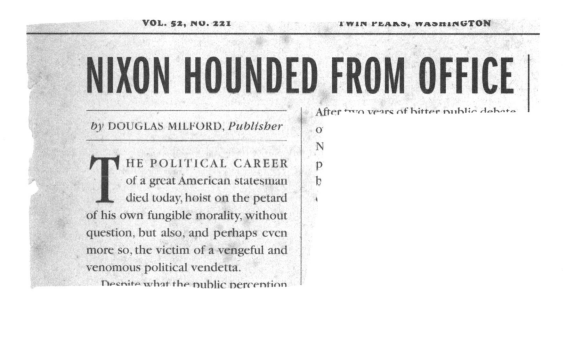

VOL. 52, NO. 221   TWIN PEAKS, WASHINGTON

NIXON HOUNDED FROM OFFICE

by DOUGLAS MILFORD, *Publisher*

THE POLITICAL CAREER of a great American statesman died today, hoist on the petard of his own fungible morality, without question, but also, and perhaps even more so, the victim of a vengeful and venomous political vendetta.

Despite what the public perception

After two years of bitter public debate

o
N
p
b

And so on -- you get the idea. It may not have been the smartest or most popular stance to assume publicly, given Doug's own high-risk, covert relationship with Nixon -- although one could argue that, from a tradecraft point of view, if you wanted to hide your affiliation with Caesar, what better way to do it than to praise him in print, rather than bury him along with the rest of the ink-stained wretches with whom he'd suffered such a long, bitter and contentious relationship.

In any event, the local flap generated by Doug's opinion piece lasted only a few days, but his brother Dwayne, the perpetual mayor -- a lifelong, dyed-in-the-wool Roosevelt Democrat -- never forgave him for it. From that day forward, Dwayne couldn't requisition a pencil in office without Doug flogging him in print about wasting taxpayers' hard-earned bucks, while Dwayne practically based his biannual campaign platform on the fact that the Post and its "crackpot publisher" irrationally despised him. This juicy fraternal rivalry evolved into a reliable staple of local entertainment, providing endless and irresistible grist for the gossip mills at the barbershop, the salon and the Double R. In other words, like a lot of modern politics, people viewed it about as seriously as they do televised wrestling.

As for Carl Rodd's letter, in response Dwayne publicly promised a thorough investigation into the questions it raised about the mysterious construction project up on Blue Pine Mountain. To Dwayne's surprise, when Douglas came to his office a few days later, it was to volunteer his services in facilitating that inquiry. He even offered to contact the FBI personally, and Dwayne took him up on it. A few days later, a regional FBI supervisor and one of his special agents paid Dwayne a visit, hung around for a few days to conduct what they promised would be a "thorough investigation," and a week later submitted a copy of the following report to Mayor Milford.

[3] I can verify that this letter is authentic. Confirmed that alleged SDI connection was intended as a misdirect. Since this directly involves one of my superior officers, I am seeking independent verification from elsewhere in the Bureau—TP

U.S. Department of Justice

Federal Bureau of Investigation

In Reply. Please Refer To
File No.

Washington, D.C.
May 28, 1983

To Mayor Dwayne Milford:

    This communication is FOR YOUR EYES ONLY and classified "SECRET."

    After three days in the field, we have been able to confirm various eyewitness reports that a government-sponsored construction project is indeed under way on the upper slopes of Blue Pine Mountain.

    We have spoken directly to the project supervisor, Major Garland Briggs, and to his superiors at Fairchild AFB and the Pentagon. The project in question involves the authorized installation on legitimately government-owned and -controlled property of a state-of-the-art radar and weather forecasting facility.

    This facility is directly related to President Reagan's recently announced Strategic Defense Initiative (SDI).

    As such, it is rated classified/top secret and no further details for public release can or will be forthcoming. Please extend our thanks and appreciation to those concerned local citizens whose perfectly natural and responsible curiosity brought this to the Bureau's attention. We hope that this information serves to satisfy the patriotic spirit of their inquiries.

Respectfully yours,

3 FBI Regional Director Gordon Cole   *Gordon Cole*

Special Agent Phillip Jeffries   *Phillip Jeffries*

SECRET
CLASSIFIED BY G-C
DECLASSIFIED ON CADR
X   X

[105-355 639-12]

[4] This points more or less directly to then–Regional Director Gordon Cole—who, as I recently pointed out, is one of my superior officers—as the "FBI man" initially recommended to Doug Milford by none other than Tricky Dick himself. I have to admit I find this troubling, but then, Director Cole's admonition to me was "follow the trail wherever it may lead."

As for the inclusion of "Special Agent Phillip Jeffries" on that letter, I can find only the following about him in official FBI files:

He went through Bureau training at Quantico with Gordon Cole, where they graduated as the top two agents in their class of 1968.

continued

ARCHIVIST'S NOTE

The FBI's swift and sure response brought a quick resolution to Mayor Milford's crusade for the truth. In other words, Dwayne swallowed it hook, line and sinker. The Blue Pine project would now proceed without any further nosing around from chatty locals, and the facility itself went live and operational in November of 1983. It did not, however, have anything in the slightest to do with the Strategic Defense Initiative -- or "Star Wars," as the mainstream press derisively called it in print.

The project known officially as SETI ARRAY 7-I -- or, as those on the inside more commonly referred to it, Listening Post Alpha (LPA) -- was in fact the centerpiece of Doug Milford's top-secret, ex-officio, post-Nixonian effort to plunge deeper into the post-Blue Book miasma of UFO investigation.

What the facility housed, in fact, was the most advanced deep-space, multispectrum search-and-receiving station ever constructed. And through the entirely plausible SDI cover offered by Doug Milford and his FBI colleagues, it began, remained and operated completely off the books of any official government or military oversight once it came online in late 1983. [4]

With Major Briggs as the only officer on site, work proceeded at the LPA through the second half of the 1980s -- slow, methodical and extremely technical; combing the haystack of space for needles, searching for signs of intelligent life in the universe at large. At the direction of Doug Milford, the sophisticated intelligence-gathering array at LPA was also pointed in the opposite direction, toward the environs of Twin Peaks.

At which point, almost to the day, a series of tragic events began to unfold in the town that, at first, seemed entirely unrelated -- until they eventually began to shed light on the bigger picture.

Twenty years into a distinguished career, Jeffries disappeared without a trace while on assignment in Buenos Aires, Argentina, in 1987. I also came across a vague reference, in a Bureau station log from that period, to Jeffries making a sudden reappearance in 1989— apparently in Philadelphia— followed by another disappearance which continues to this day. To dig deeper I need to requisition reports that are currently classified beyond my reach in the deputy director's files.

I'm beginning to wonder if I'm going to be able to show this to anyone without getting fired. The world of Doug Milford is like a hall of mirrors. Frankly, I could use a drink—TP

2 M A R G A R E T L A N T E R M A N

*** T W I N P E A K S P O S T
O C T O B E R 2 8 , 1 9 8 6

Weekday Edition
$1.00

PUBLISHED
IN THE STATE OF
WASHINGTON
SINCE 1922

TWIN PEAKS
POST

VOL. 64, NO. 301   TWIN PEAKS, WASHINGTON   TUESDAY, OCTOBER 28, 1986

IF THESE WOODS COULD SPEAK,
and, Trust Me, Sometimes They Do

by ROBERT JACOBY, *Editor*

YOU MIGHT ENCOUNTER her hiking one of the many paths she favors through our surrounding hills and forests—paths she helped create, you'll be interested to learn. You might recognize her from community meetings at the Grange Hall, a constant presence, flicking the lights on and off to make sure they start and end as scheduled. The rest of the time she's at her cabin in the woods—a bonus fire ranger, if you will—watching and listening like a wolf, alert to any dangers to our local environment, and—you would quickly realize—never shy to sound the alarm. You might find yourself sitting next to her at the counter of the Double R as she enjoys a late-night slice of Norma's pie—well, not right next to her, she's eating for two, as it were. There's a log on the seat next to her.

I'm speaking, of course, of my dear friend of over forty years, Margaret Lanterman. You probably know her only as the Log Lady.

There's one in every town, you might say, trying to explain Margaret to a stranger. A loner, cut from a different cloth, who doesn't care to conform to our cozy, collective view of

Psychiatrist says Margaret Lanterman "is the sanest human being I've ever met."

how "normal" folks are supposed to properly conduct their neat little lives. There's something unsettling about a person who gives you such undivided attention, looks you in the eye with such unblinking clarity, who clearly doesn't care what *you* think of *her*—or her log—but is interested, it seems, in only one thing: speaking deep and thoughtful truths.

I've reached a ripe old age where I don't give a rip what people think or say about me either. And one of the chores at the top of my to-do list is to set the record straight about Margaret. I've heard all the wild stories about her down through the years, more nonsensical variations than Heinz has varieties. She's a witch, they say, the kind they would have burned at the stake in Massachusetts three hundred years ago, if they could pull her off her broomstick. No, that's not it, she's a mental patient who walked away from the home, off her meds, communing with the trees, talking and listening to her ever-present wooden companion. Well, let me quote for you what my brother says about her—that's Dr. Lawrence Jacoby, our town's only licensed shrink, if you're not familiar with him: "Margaret Lanterman is the sanest human being I've ever met."

I happen to agree with him.

But with difference comes misunderstanding, which leads to assumption, which makes a you-know-what out of "u" and "me." So please allow me, your longtime public custodian of the local Fourth Estate, to set the record straight.

"These Woods" continued on pg. 22

Surviving Family Members of

annual labor of every nation is the

"These Woods" continued from pg. 1

Maggie Coulson was a bright, lively and curious young gal, always tall for her age—sometimes awkwardly so—when we first met in third grade in Mrs. Hawthorne's class at Warren G. Harding Elementary. Taller than me, that's for sure, and I was seated behind her, until one day, as she noticed me craning my neck to read the blackboard, she kindly offered to change seats with me. Obviously intelligent, a little reserved, maybe—I preferred to think of her as dignified—but no different than the rest of us. She sought happiness and, like all kids, the approval of others in equal measure.

One night in 1947, during a school outing, Margaret and two other classmates disappeared overnight. They were found the next day, safe and sound, but not unchanged. She didn't speak of what she'd been through— none of them did—but she was quieter afterwards, in class and out. Not as playful. More watchful and internal. She wouldn't confide in me what she'd seen or heard out there—and we were quite good friends already— but I sensed she remembered more than she was willing to share.

We remained friends through high school, but Maggie stood apart from us in a way that's hard to convey. She wasn't unfriendly, but as we all struggled through the turbulence of adolescence she seemed unaffected, self-contained, observant and utterly serious. Her focus, I believe, was never on her own internal troubles, but remained fixed on the outside world. Watching, without anxiety or judgment, always watching. We went on a couple of dates in high school, taking in a movie every now and then at the Bijou, going for burgers after at the Double R. She found it hard to engage with artificial entertainment, as if she had no desire to "escape" reality and was puzzled by others' need for it. But she was deeply affected by an unsettling science fiction film we saw called *Invaders from Mars*. We spent hours talking about it, pondering the idea of life on other planets—or as she called it "life from other places"—and wondering what, if any, interest *they* might have in us.

That turned out to be the last time I saw Maggie for a while. Our family had moved to Hawaii when I was a small child—my father was an army officer who'd been posted to Pearl Harbor. Our parents divorced soon afterward, and I moved back to Twin Peaks with my father, who'd been reassigned to the air base in Spokane, while my mother and younger brother stayed in Hawaii. We didn't see each other during the war, but once it ended I rejoined them in Honolulu for the last semester of my senior year, so I missed graduation— but I did learn to surf, a little. (By this point my younger brother Lawrence could ride the waves like a dolphin.) After that remarkable summer I returned to Washington for college (Gonzaga, journalism) and by the time I made it back to Twin Peaks with my degree five more years had gone by.

Maggie—she preferred Margaret now—had studied forestry at Washington State and hoped to work for the U.S. Forest Service. She'd grown into a tall, strong and handsome woman and her devotion to the woods and natural resources of our state defined her in a striking and positive way. Margaret was the first person I knew who'd developed an ecological consciousness about the future of the natural world. Over coffee at the Double R one night— early '60s now, a decade before the first Earth Day—she convinced me the greatest danger facing earth wasn't nuclear war, but man's threat to our own environment. She asked me to chip in twenty bucks for some worthy cause to that end, which as a struggling journalist I couldn't afford but promptly proceeded to hand over. I paid for the coffee, too. I never could say no to Margaret.

"...her devotion to the woods and natural resources of our state defined her in a striking and positive way."

Sound crazy to you? I didn't think so either.

I saw her around town from time to time. She had applied for work with the Forest Service, but all they offered women at that point was secretarial pool stuff. Would it surprise you to learn Margaret also qualified as an early feminist, before the word had been coined? Sitting at a desk typing some bureaucrat's letters didn't interest her—she wanted to be out in the field, among the trees—so she turned them down, claiming she could outwork any man they put her up against. She restored an old Ford pickup and worked in the town library while raising money for the Sierra Club.

That's where she met Sam Lanterman. Sam was a decade older than us, already a legend in our parts. At one time he'd been the youngest lumberjack in the history of the Packard Mill, and a glance would tell you why. If he'd been born a century earlier he

might have been Paul Bunyan or Pecos Bill. Like any good folk hero, he was bigger than life: six foot five, 240 pounds. (His full name was Samson—his parents were a little clairvoyant about how he'd turn out—although no one ever called him that.) He was a third-generation woodsman; the Lantermans had been living and working among the trees since the industry began. They were all big, sturdy types, but Sam—the oldest of five brothers—represented the apex of their family tree. The things he could do with an axe and saw defied imagination. He'd started competing in lumberjack competitions at fifteen; three years later he held every record they kept track of; after ten years he offered to retire so somebody else could win something. Sam and his brothers were the first in their family to go to school, because the law said they had to, but a funny thing happened: Sam fell in love with poetry. That fed and nurtured the sensitive side of his brawny soul. Throw in the square jaw, chiseled features and well-tended beard and no wonder Margaret fell in love for the first, last and only time in her life.

They met at Haw's Lumber Yard down by the river on a bright spring day. Margaret was picking up a load of two-by-sixes for the eaves on the first cabin she was building—saving on rent so she could afford to spend her time on volunteer work. Sam, who didn't get into town that often, was dropping off a load of reclaimed timber from a barn he and his brother had salvaged. Sam had already built two houses from scratch in the family compound up on Blue Pine Mountain. He saw Margaret loading up her truck and, naturally courteous, went over to give her a hand. His brothers said they knew Sam was a goner the moment they locked eyes. He wasn't exactly inexperienced in the field of female companionship, and he could quote Wordsworth and Yeats by the yard to excellent effect, but the sight of Margaret lifting a pallet of fresh-cut lumber with her own strong sinews left him thunderstruck. Margaret did most of the talking that day, the brothers said, and Sam followed her around like a puppy. She was calm and sensible as always—even knowing she'd just met the love of her life—and before Sam knew what hit him, Margaret had arranged their first date and made it all seem like his idea.

A courtship right out of the 19th century ensued. Margaret didn't have family; she was an only child, and her parents had died young. She believed the important things in life needed to be done a certain way, and although she was on the wrong side of thirty and love and marriage had never been high on her list, she knew there was a time and place for everything and this was it. Sam was to present himself at her place that Saturday at such and such a time, and a bath prior was mandatory, not optional. I saw them a number of times during the yearlong courtship that followed, and they were always so proper it looked like they were being watched by an invisible chaperone, but there was no mistaking that they were entirely meant for each other.

They became engaged a year to the day after they met and a wedding date was set one year to the day after that. Margaret told me Sam had proposed at a special place in the woods above Pearl Lake near Glastonbury Grove that she called "The Heart of the Forest." [1]

"These Woods" continued on pg. 24

Girl
Offe
Sch
for I
Inco

Gender in
male-domi
of foundati
philanthro
greater bal
offering sc
educationa
exclusive t

As they
their place
ment roles
access to s
continuing
from unde
levels. Trac
profession:
representa
trained wo
educationa
them succe

Scholar:
myriad of
defined by
offering th
merit-base
on strictly
find all the
you qualify
high schoc
your schoc
you search
the things
scholarshij
church, yo
employer,
some othe:
a role in yc

Some ar
others are

[1] The same location where Margaret experienced the strange overnight encounter witnessed by Doug Milford—TP

"Give Peaks
a Chance"

a thriving community that has a lot to offer. In addition to the dynamic landscape and diverse local businesses, the rich, colorful history of Twin Peaks is enough to "peak" the interest

"These Woods" continued from pg. 23

The small and simple wedding at the Chapel-in-the-Woods was attended by Sam's family and a few friends, myself included. The depth of feeling between them that day went far beyond romance and if I go into specifics I'm going to end in tears, but I will say this: Having attended more than my share of nuptials over the years, I've never seen a couple so plainly, sincerely and unabashedly in love. If you don't know what happened next, we may end up in tears together.

A thunderstorm swept toward the area that afternoon, rumbling throughout the ceremony. It had been a dry summer and a lightning strike up the mountain started a fire that swept down the ridge toward Blue Pine, an area of woods that hadn't burned in decades, since the Fire on the River. Sam, the volunteer fire chief, rushed to help when the alarm sounded while we were at the reception. Their truck was loaded and decorated and ready to leave for the honeymoon—they were about to drive up to Lake Louise for a stay at the grand hotel. Sam changed out of his only suit, told Margaret he wouldn't be long and drove off with his father and brothers toward the fire. I'll not forget the look on Margaret's face as they parted as long as I live. She knew, I'm convinced of it, what was going to happen. She also knew, given the circumstances, Sam could no sooner stay behind than sprout wings and fly.

When word came the next morning that he'd fallen—a savage gust of wind, an inferno, a funnel cloud of fire that rose up and swept Sam off a ridge into a burning ravine—Margaret, who'd worked all night at the Grange Hall in

Aftermath of the fire that killed Margaret's husband

"I'll not forget the look on Margaret's face as they parted as long as I live. She knew...what was going to happen."

her wedding dress, where people evacuated off the mountain came for food and shelter, received the news calmly—again I suspected somehow she already knew. She said nothing, excused herself briefly, packed her dress in a suitcase that she set by the door, and went back in to help serve breakfast. When I offered my condolences she simply nodded and smiled, without a word, and went back to work. The fire subsided the following day when another storm came through. They recovered Sam's body from the ravine—he was the only casualty—and Margaret buried him two days later, in a plot behind the house they'd been building together for the last six months up on the mountain.

They say she went up to visit the Heart of the Forest again the next day. Although dozens of acres had burned around it, the small grove of sycamores

there was still standing. Nearby, a magnificent old-growth Douglas fir had fallen during the conflagration. When Margaret came back down she carried a piece of that great tree with her, cradling it like a newborn babe. She knew exactly which part of the great creature to take—it told her as much, she said—and from that day on Margaret and her log were inseparable.

Over the years, I've borne witness as our generation ages, slows and slips apart, as time strains the fabrics of our narrative—that's been my life's work, you might say—and I've seen many come along after us who don't know Margaret's story. I've heard all the crackpot theories, behind-the-back snickers, all the cruel jokes whispered—often in her presence—at her expense; this is the price she's paid for surviving unthinkable loss the only way she could without a care for

SHOCK WAVES HIT
BUSINESS COMMUNITY

what others think of her. I believe this callow disrespect bothers her not at all. Her mind is on other matters.

But it bothers me tremendously.

What would life be like if all of us, I ask you, were committed to seeing, hearing and speaking the truth? I mean our personal truth, what we know to be true inside, about what we feel, and what we see and hear around us. Because, I submit, it would be impossible to sustain such an effort without learning to care deeply for the welfare of others. If I've learned nothing else it's that there are many ways of knowing, not just the ones they taught us in school or church, or that you see on TV or read about in a book. I believe Margaret recognized that this art of knowing comes as close as any human quality to embodying the purpose of life, and she's embraced that purpose more fully than anyone I've ever known. A tragedy that might well have splintered most people in shards opened her heart and soul to a deeper truth. Grief can lead to madness, but it can also lead to clarity. It doesn't matter whether it comes to you in the form of a burning bush, a lamp by the side of the road or a voice from a piece of wood. What matters is

Margaret's precious log, from which she is inseparable.

Photo courtesy of Margaret Lanterman

whether or not you listen. And then, of course, you have to act on it.

So why am I telling you this, you have every right to ask. Chronicling the lives and stories of the people of our town has been my honor and privilege for nearly fifty years now. I like to think I've taken this responsibility seriously, but as far as I'm concerned setting the record straight on Margaret Lanterman was long overdue and for that I feel more than a little remorse. I hope it makes an impression. But it's also time for some fearless truth telling of my own.

This is my last column for the *Post*. I'm facing challenges of my own in the days ahead, related to that final destination we all bought tickets for on our way in. I've spoken about this with Margaret, recently, and from what she tells me I have nothing to fear. I don't doubt she knows when her own time will come, and know it doesn't trouble her in the least. I'll try, as best I can, to live up to her example. It seems not to matter how long you live because, near the end, everyone reports the same; that it all went by so quickly, water slipping through our hands. There's no answer for it. Live *now*, that's my only advice to you. I leave not willingly, and haunted by the thought that my job—writing down stories, bearing witness to our mutual journey through time and space—is far from done. But even in this dark moment I take some comfort in a truth I'm now forced to accept: Storytellers don't run out of stories, they just run out of time. It's someone else's job now.

Truthfully and respectfully yours,
ROBERT JACOBY

Lawyers ask for review of

ARCHIVIST'S NOTE

Three weeks after posting this column, Robert Jacoby passed away from complications of multiple sclerosis. His brother, Dr. Lawrence Jacoby, spoke at services he presided over at the Chapel-in-the-Woods, where over 200 people turned out, before scattering Robert's ashes nearby on the steel blue surface of Pearl Lake. With the congregants assembled by the shore, Margaret Lanterman asked to say a few words of her own. As best as this correspondent can remember, this is what she said: [2]

[2] So we know the Archivist was at the funeral that day. I'm attempting to locate the church's guest register that may list all the attendees' names—TP

[3] So I now have a sample, I believe, of the Archivist's handwriting, and perhaps fingerprints as well—I'm checking the program—which up until now we've been unable to find on the dossier. I'm going to check names against the register and then track samples. I believe that discovery of the Archivist's identity should soon follow—TP

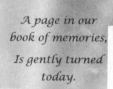

A page in our book of memories, Is gently turned today.

In Loving Memory of
Robert Jacoby

BORN
May 8, 1931

DIED
November 19, 1986

SERVICES
Saturday, November 22, 1986
11:00 A.M.
Chapel-in-the-Woods

OFFICIATING
Dr. Lawrence Jacoby

EXPRESSION OF GRATITUDE
FROM THE FAMILY

On behalf of the members of the family, we wish to express their gratitude for your many kindnesses evidenced in thought and deed and for your attendance at the Memorial Service.

Margaret holds her log and looks around, really looks, for some time before speaking:

"This is 'now,' and now will never be again. Blue sky, cool air, and green, green forests. Mountains, lakes, and streams. The wind, the wind. Water, earth, air, and fire; red, yellow, purple, and white. We come from the elemental, and return to it. There is change, but nothing is lost. There is much we cannot see. — air, for instance, most of the time — but knowing our next breath will follow our last without fail is an act of faith. Is it not? Dark times will always come, as night follows day. A dark age will test us all, each and every one. Trust and do not tremble in the face of the unknown. It shall not remain unknown to you for long. Robert knows this now, as will we all in the sweet by-and-by."

3

Arrangements by

Chapel-in-the-Woods

Courteous and Sympathetic Service
112 Doyle Road, Twin Peaks, WA 98065
Donald and Donna Mulligan, Owners

3 LAURA PALMER

The "dark age" Margaret mentioned arrived sooner than we
imagined. The first seeds of this story broke the surface in
1988, one county to the west in the nearby community of Deer
Meadow, Washington, with the murder of a young woman named
Teresa Banks. A depressed, working-class town devastated by
the decline of the logging industry, Deer Meadow was everything
Twin Peaks was not; sullen, sinking and hostile. Two FBI agents
were sent west by Gordon Cole -- by this time chief of the Bureau
office in Philadelphia -- to investigate: Special Agent Chet
Desmond and forensic specialist Sam Stanley. Why send FBI
agents all the way from Philadelphia to investigate a murder
in eastern Washington? You might well ask.[1]

Despite the FBI presence, the Teresa Banks investigation yielded
little. One of their only significant findings: The agents
discovered that a distinctive jade green ring Teresa had been
photographed wearing close to the time of her death was missing.
They also found that, postmortem, a small printed letter "T" had
been inserted under the ring finger of her right hand.

Then, a calamity. One day during the course of his investigation
in Deer Meadow, Special Agent Chet Desmond disappeared without
a trace. Special Agent Dale Cooper was sent west to find him, but
Desmond left no trail, the Banks case had gone cold and Cooper
returned empty-handed. The Banks case remained listed as open.
After returning to Philadelphia himself, forensic expert Sam
Stanley suffered some sort of unspecified breakdown -- perhaps
related to alcoholism -- and was placed on administrative leave.
I find no record of him returning to active duty.[2]

[1] The names of these
agents also appear on a
short list from an erased
document I recovered from
a secure server in the FBI's
Philadelphia office. I ran
a search for Desmond
and Stanley and came up
with this:

Gordon Cole
Phillip Jeffries
Chet Desmond
Sam Stanley
Windom Earle
Dale Cooper
Albert Rosenfield

I can't determine whose
computer this was on.
Nothing else was on the
page. Just those names.
I have no idea what it
means or implies. Checking
this out now—TP

[2] Confirmed—TP

You will recall that, as previously mentioned, Special Agent Phillip Jeffries had gone missing in Buenos Aires under similarly inexplicable circumstances two years earlier. A double vanishing act that defied explanation. Shortly thereafter, Special Agent Windom Earle -- a veteran, decorated agent who earlier in their careers had been Agent Cooper's mentor and partner -- suffered a catastrophic breakdown of his own; he murdered his wife, Caroline, shot Agent Cooper and was confined to a psychiatric hospital for the criminally insane.[3]

One year after the Teresa Banks murder, a fully recovered Special Agent Dale Cooper returned to Washington to investigate the murder of another young woman, this time in Twin Peaks, the girl named Laura Palmer. At this point, all manner of hell broke loose.

A review of the Palmer case, by the local mental health professional who knew and treated the family, sums it up this way:[4]

[3] Confirmed. We can safely conclude the aforementioned list is clearly not a very good one to be on. But what did it signify? If it's a list of agents who've suffered terrible fates, Gordon Cole and forensic expert Albert Rosenfield remain notable exceptions; both are healthy and on the active duty roster. There has to be another link—TP

[4] The following is verified—TP

Dr. Lawrence Jacoby

WASHINGTON STATE
LICENSED PSYCHIATRIST

LAURA PALMER, FINAL CASE NOTES
DR. LAWRENCE JACOBY,
PRINCEVILLE, KAUAI

MARCH 19, 1989

As an excruciatingly manipulative and staggeringly popular novel of the 1970s once began—I'm paraphrasing, the insufferable "heroine" in that story was a little older—What can you say about an eighteen-year-old girl who died?[5]

I'm watching the combers roll in across Hanalei Bay on a cool, cloudy spring day. Isolated patches of blue. The trades are blowing. Dolphins feeding just off shore. My mother's ashes were scattered not a hundred yards from the porch where I'm sitting. I brought along some of my brother Robert's "cremains"—there's a fun new hybrid word—as well and he'll join her soon in the bay he dearly loved to surf, once I get my old longboard out after the breeze dies down.

The facts say her father killed her. Leland Palmer, 45. Pride and only son of a wealthy Seattle family. Private schools. Summa cum laude, University of Washington, 1966, president of the Law Review. Outstanding professional career, culminating in an eight-year run as chief counsel to the Horne Corporation, which is what brought the Palmers to town. No drugs, no alcoholism, no criminal record or history of mental illness. Happily married twenty-one years to Sarah Novack Palmer, 44. Political science major. College sweethearts.[6]

One child, Laura. Homecoming queen. The golden girl next door that the whole town adored. Myself included.

Dead at eighteen.

The facts say Leland then killed Laura's first cousin, too; his niece, Madeleine Ferguson, from Missoula, Montana, on the mother's side. There's no question that Laura—in more than one way, for many reasons—danced with the devil and paid a terrible price. Madeleine was an innocent who came to help the family in the wake of Laura's death. (Leland also smothered a villain named Jacques Renault who'd harmed his daughter, an act I inadvertently witnessed as a cardiac patient, sedated in a nearby bed.)[7]

* Laura Palmer

5 Jacoby here is referencing the novel *Love Story*—TP

6 Verified—TP

7 Verified. Palmer was suspected of Renault's murder, but never formally charged—TP

And then, after his arrest, while in custody, confronted with the enormity of the crimes he at first claimed not to remember, Leland took his own life.

I had frankly lost interest in my practice prior to Laura entering my life. The years I'd spent among authentic native people had left me bored to death with the garden-variety neuroses of "modern Americans." The maladaptations of disaffected housewives and hostile teenagers were symptomatic to me of a larger, collective societal disorder—all right, I'll Cliff Note them for you: rising corporate greed, enabled by institutional corruption, fueled and distorted by dirty money, leading to generalized rampant materialism, militant ignorance, military triumphalism and widespread loss of spiritual authenticity—that was eating away at the foundation of our culture.

I'm not trying to excuse my own negligence: Nobody held a gun to my head, told me to hang up that shingle and then give up on my patients. That choice is on me entirely and by the end I was doing those poor people a disservice. Clearly, with the death of my brother Robert—my last living relative—my reason for being in Washington was gone. I knew that my time in my hometown was drawing to a close. Then she walked into my office.

I treated Laura privately—and, at her request, without her parents' knowledge—for six months prior to her murder. (She first came to see me the day after her 18th birthday—the point at which she'd be treated as an adult, with no legal obligation on my part to inform her parents; this was not a coincidence. Laura was brilliant.) What emerged did not immediately present as a case of parental sexual abuse, although that's what the facts—and her explosive diary—tell us happened. I'm trained to recognize these signs. For the longest time, I didn't see them. Because I should have, I hold myself responsible for all that followed. Emotionally, circumstantially, legally. Whether the Washington State Board of Review currently deliberating these facts, and others equally damning, agrees with me—and suspends my medical license—I'll know soon enough.

The outcome doesn't matter. I know what I've done, what I should've done, what I didn't do to help her. I barely survived the heart attack it already cost me. Whatever the Board's ruling, living out my life with that knowledge will be, rest assured, punishment enough.

I conducted an intake evaluation with the father, just after Laura's death. A few bursts of mania were the only tangible symptoms, which I attributed to grief. That was it. The mother almost immediately began a slow, steady slide into alcoholism and prescription drug abuse. There may be some trauma in her background that created a vulnerability—just a theory—but aren't the facts of what happened in her family alone enough to unspool her? Could you survive that torment? I wasn't able to pump the brakes on the poor woman's descent, or answer her burning question: Why? Why Laura? The question that will haunt the rest of her days, and mine.

Nightmares like this don't take root in native or aboriginal homes. *Ever.* In affluent, urban American families it's, increasingly, a specialty of the house. Strange, isn't it? All those "gifts" we think of as advantages, the ones we're socially programmed to strive for, the "dream" no one questions because it looks so seductive on television or in the pages of glossy magazines. But my own prejudices and predispositions got in the way. I'd never seen an anomaly like Laura's family up close before. I plain missed it. I'm still convinced I don't know the real story.

Why is harder to answer. Part of it's baked into the culture. We're so upright, so sure of ourselves, so invested in "progress," "optimism," "hope." "Can-do" is part of our DNA, reflecting back what we want to see in every angle of the hall of mirrors we inhabit. (It's also endemic to the medical profession.) When something this unspeakable happens we're quick to condemn the individual, indict society, distance ourselves with "it couldn't happen here." It's clear to me now that's part of our problem. When tragedy strikes we need to sit still and rock in place, wailing, keening, or crawl on our hands and knees gnashing our teeth the way native people yield absolutely to their grief. Embrace it, take it into your soul until it breaks and remakes you. There are no words, no lasting comfort to be found in avoiding pain. It's a primeval, painfully physical, animal process and you'd best get about it until it's done with you. You'll know when. At which point you have to say fuck analysis.

And yet.

Leland spoke of "possession." Laura wrote in her diary about an entity she called "BOB," all caps. A malevolent being she claimed to "see"—in her father's stead—whenever he assaulted her. Leland had no memory of his dreadful acts till the very end. A masking memory, for both of them, our "professional training" would instruct me to label it, a way for their minds to protect themselves from the unendurable truth. Or, in other words, whistling through the graveyard.

A medicine man in the Amazon would take them both at their word, believe the story at face value and treat it accordingly. *Possession.* An entity. Why is that any less plausible or relevant than the safe, sanitized, pre-packaged bullshit of an armchair diagnosis made solely from the neck up? What is that but a shield hoisted to protect us from the unholy terror of glimpsing ourselves as we truly are: creatures of unknown origin, trapped in time, pinned to a hostile rock whirling through indifferent and infinite space, clueless, inherently violent and condemned to death?

There is more to Laura's story than the facts. More than meets the eye or ear. A third rail lurks here in the shadows that's deadly to the touch. There's only one way to find it. The shamans I've worked with know how to pierce the veil and see beyond the membrane of our poorly perceived and shared "reality." (They'd use the word "illusion.") They've shown me, I've experienced these things with them, I've seen through the veil, and traveled the world in pursuit of that knowledge. Dedicated my life to this search, personally and professionally.

But the truth is Laura's death has broken me. My own belief system—the fantasy that I could hold these two worlds in balance—inner life, outer reality—and bring the truth of one closer to the other, like some free-thinking hippie Prometheus, is shattered. What a hapless fool I've been. Actions have consequences. Whatever happens from here, whatever the "squares" decide about my professional fate, if I can survive this ordeal, find the strength to dig my way out of it, I make this vow: No more lies. Only truth. Straight up. To everyone.

But where to begin? "Medice, cura te ipsum." Physician, cure thyself. I can't heal the world unless I first heal myself. There are native practitioners I grew up with here on the islands who are elders now. I'll be turning to them for help.

We are creatures of darkness and light, capable of barbarism and limitless cruelty, and also love, and laughter and the creation of the most sublime beauty. We are both these things, clearly, but which are we more of? I don't know the answer. Is "evil" a thing—independent, outside of us—or is it an essential part of who we are? I don't know the answer.

Life is but a dream from which we seem able to only rarely awaken. Whatever it means is beyond words. Words lose their meaning when you look at them too long. "God." "Science." "Meaning." Everything melts into silence.

The trades have eased. The whitecaps are gone and there's sunlight on the water. I'm going to go bury my brother now.

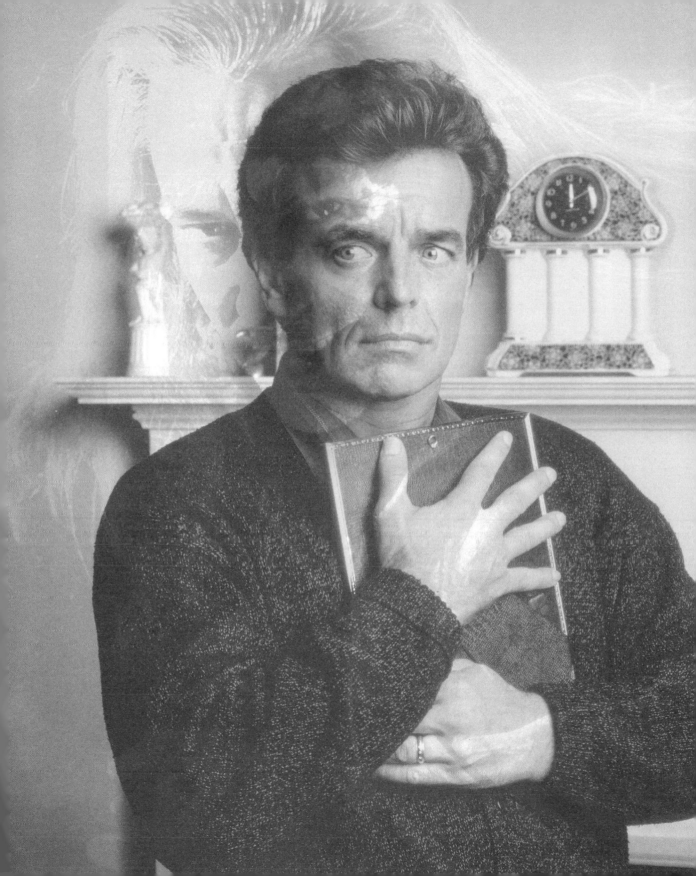

[8] Verified. Lawrence Jacoby, no longer a doctor, decided to settle in Hawaii and begin work on his memoirs
—TP

ARCHIVIST'S NOTE

Less than a week later, Dr. Jacoby received his answer:

WASHINGTON STATE MEDICAL ASSOCIATION

March 26, 1989
Washington State Medical Association
243 Israel Rd SE, Tumwater, WA 98504

Dear Sir,

After consideration of your case, the State Medical Review Board has decided to indefinitely suspend your license to practice medicine as a psychiatrist in the state of Washington.

Please be aware that any violation of this revocation, or any subsequent attempt to practice medicine without a state-issued license, can and will result in criminal charges.

Please remit immediate notification of your receipt of this letter to this office. [8]

Thank you.

███████████████ Chairman

4 COLONEL DOUGLAS MILFORD

Every man has his weakness. By the late 1980s, as members of
their generation began exiting the planet in greater numbers,
few citizens were left in town who remembered Doug Milford's
early troubled years or even his decades-long military career
away from Twin Peaks.

Most knew him now only as the friendly, avuncular and somewhat
eccentric owner and publisher of their local newspaper. He was
often spotted driving around town in a forest-green two-seat
convertible Morgan, an antique British racing car, wearing
scarf, goggles, racing cap and gloves. As he aged Doug lost his
hair, wore a bad toupee for a time, then lost his vanity, ditched
the rug and settled on a jaunty beret. His conservative politics,
particularly during the Reagan years, had moved slowly closer
to the middle, or rather should I say the middle had moved
closer to him.[1] His long, deep undercover career as a key
figure throughout the shadowy history of Air Force intelligence
and UFO investigation, or his even stranger later years as
an independent operative supervising an undercover mission
assigned to him by a disgraced former president, remained
a secret he kept from every single soul he encountered.

Except one. More on that in a moment.

By all appearances, Doug Milford had money. He lived in a big
house on a five-acre spread outside of town. He owned a small
fleet of luxury automobiles -- including the aforementioned
Morgan -- which he stored in a custom garage. An urbane,
sophisticated figure, he wore fashionable bespoke clothes and
left sizable tips at local restaurants. No one knew where his
fortune came from -- well beyond what one would expect for
a retired colonel living on an Air Force pension -- or, even
more mysteriously, how he'd managed to hang on to it through

[1] Significant that the
Archivist is now using the
word "I"—TP

* Mayor Dwayne Milford, 1989

four divorces. (As I said, every man has his weakness.) By the late 1980s, Douglas had become a pillar of the community, and the curiosity aroused by his apparent fortune subsided.

For everyone, of course, except his brother Dwayne, the perpetual mayor, who remained convinced that Doug had acquired his pile from some sort of unholy swindle, or perhaps from the stock market, which to Dwayne's mind meant the same thing. (As he aged, Dwayne had countered his brother's move to the right, edging closer to what he himself called "socialliberalism," which made his brother's public conservatism, and lavish lifestyle, even more irksome.)

By 1989, Doug was closing in on his 80th birthday. Aside from the year he'd spent living with Pauline Cuyo in the late 1920s, he had, by his own admission, never formed a long or lasting intimate relationship with any woman in his life; he often brought up the four failed marriages on his résumé to prove it, three of them alone in the years since he'd returned to Twin Peaks. But after his most recent misadventure, with a Bolivian flight attendant -- which ended in annulment after only three weeks -- he swore up and down that he'd finally learned his lesson. From that point forward, Doug took a vow that he would only rent, not buy.

His impending 80th -- and whatever thoughts, feelings or lapses attended that milestone -- brought with it, in the matrimony department, what we must charitably term one final relapse in judgment.

Her name was Lana Budding; at least that was the name on her driver's license. She claimed to be 19, although a later, more diligent vetting of her available records put the actual number six integers north of there. Lana was a new arrival in town -- her accent said southern, and the license said Georgia, but aside from that she never elaborated -- and she'd drifted in on a breeze -- no one could recall exactly when, but it was recent. Lana's form was her fate: She had the legs of a chorus girl, the chassis of a sleek jungle cat and a face poised precisely between perky and provocative.

Soon after securing a job at the Twin Peaks Savings and Loan-- where, one assumes, she assayed a glance at Doug's balance sheet-- Lana locked onto her target like a Hellfire missile from the moment he entered her sights. She proceeded to conduct the kind of purposeful campaign to bring down her prey that the younger Doug Milford would have recognized, professionally appreciated and avoided like dengue fever. This was not the younger Doug Milford.

They met "cute," as they used to say in pictures, on a visit to his safe deposit box. There was a mix-up with the keys, and Lana and Doug ended up locked in the vault for an hour -- and by the time the staff opened the door again Doug was a goner. Before long they were tooling around town in his Morgan and canoodling over cocktails in the dimly lit nooks of the Waterfall Lounge at the Great Northern. Even those of us familiar with Doug's predilection for the fairer sex were stunned by his abrupt capitulation to Lana's charms. His refinement, sense of dignity and self-containment -- qualities he'd maintained throughout all his prior failings -- fell away like empty booster rockets. Even he recognized the absurdity of his situation. "There's no fool like an old fool," he said to me once, wearing a wolf's grin as he watched her sashay out of the room.

Whatever erotic power Lana exerted over him -- take it from me, the effects were in no way confined to Doug alone -- most of his male friends found it hard to begrudge a man in the late November of his days, who'd dedicated his life to the disciplined service of his country, embarking on one last personal mission and, to quote Doug directly, "putting some sugar back in my sap."

Well, I think we know who the sap was. After their whirlwind courtship -- no longer, if that, than three weeks -- Doug announced their engagement at Leland Palmer's wake; awkward at the time but, in retrospect, more than appropriate. (The news also nearly prompted a fistfight with Dwayne.) The truth is, Doug Milford loved romance more than life itself, and certainly more than he'd loved any of his wives. Always an endorphin addict, he'd just taken one last spectacular tumble off the wagon.

Soon after, Doug and Lana tied the knot at the Great Northern. A grand soiree followed, another inevitable part of his addiction cycle. (His weddings provided such reliable business, the hotel gave him what they called "the Milford discount.") Lana looked bewitching. Doug looked bewitched. (Dwayne looked apoplectic.) The last words Doug spoke to me that night, with one of his patented grins and a wink, just before they retired to the bridal suite: "Good thing I kept the minister on speed dial."

* Doug's and Lana's wedding

Weekday Edition
$1.00

PUBLISHED
IN THE STATE OF
WASHINGTON
SINCE 1922

POS

VOL. 67, NO. 72   TWIN PEAKS, W

HE DIED WITH HIS BOOTS ON

THE ENTIRE TOWN of Twin Peaks mourns today the sudden passing of the *Post*'s owner, publisher and editor-in-chief, Douglas Raymond Milford, 80.

A few scant hours after the joyful occasion of his marriage, in the morning Mr. Milford was found to have passed during the night, peacefully, in his sleep, of natural causes, announced Great Northern owner Ben Horne.

Mr. Milford will be remembered not only for his selfless service to our community and various charitable causes, but also for his long and distinguished career as a senior Air Force officer. He is survived by his widow, Lana Budding Milford, and his older brother, Dwayne Milford, our mayor. We share their sorrow. Funeral arrangements are pending.

STORM L
THE GRE
NORTH-

DRENCHING STORM
slides and flooding i
northwest on Wedr
out power to thou
and leaving two wor
Peaks, authorities ar
ported.

Twin Peaks has e
5 inches of rain in th
much as all of Dece
year, and Seattle exc
December rainfall ta
the National Weathe

The service said r
of Twin Peaks and r
ington state, where C
a state of emergen
have received more

The record-breaki
sinkholes in seve
caused rivers to spil
and closed roads a
third day in the wor

DONUT EATING

ARCHIVIST'S NOTE

In other words, Lana went to sleep a newlywed and woke up a
widow. After he was escorted in to view his brother's body in the
honeymoon suite that morning -- wearing only a smile no mortician
in his right mind would try to remove -- Dwayne tried to persuade
Sheriff Truman to press homicide charges, claiming that a copy
of the Kama Sutra found at the scene was the murder weapon.
That was *grief* disguised as bluster; Dwayne, I believe, despite
their quarrelsome differences, truly loved his brother. Of course
nothing came of Dwayne's talk about manslaughter. If anything,
as news of the circumstances of his death leaked out, there was --
among his male friends -- universal envy that Doug Milford had
stage-managed the perfect exit from the cockeyed caravan of
life. As one of them -- who shall remain nameless -- said to me
that day: "If that was manslaughter, sign me up."

Doug had, it may not surprise you to learn, neither insisted on
nor signed a prenuptial agreement, so if fortune hunting was
indeed Lana's game, she bagged her limit. But let's give the widow
Milford the benefit of some doubt; she stayed in town the better
part of six months after Doug's death, until probate closed, and
apparently provided, ahem, great comfort and emotional support
during that time to our grieving mayor. Once the check cleared,
of course, she was gone like the Hindenburg. (But not before
providing a thrill the whole town wouldn't soon forget with her
performance of "contortionistic jazz exotica" at the Miss Twin
Peaks Contest.) She allegedly fled to the Hamptons, and briefly
dated a bizarrely coiffed real estate mogul before marrying a
hedge fund manager -- sounds about right.

There also occurred to my mind, alone, a stray thought which
I've never been able to either prove or entirely dismiss: that

2 The Archivist is speaking
openly and clearly in his
voice. Any pretense of
objectivity or journalistic
distance is gone. We're about
to learn what we came here
to find—TP

* The widow Milford

"Lana" may have been a paid assassin, sent by unknown figures from Doug's past, to silence a voice that knew far too much. I offer no evidence for this intuitive suspicion, although if true she was certainly well paid for her trouble, but as anyone who's parsed the dossier to this point can attest, in Doug's life, stranger things have happened.

Per the instructions in his will, after the funeral we scattered Doug's remains up the mountain, near the old campsite by the Pearl Lakes, not far from the entrance to Ghostwood Forest and Glastonbury Grove, where, as a young scout, the enduring mystery that set him on the path of his life's work had begun more than 60 years before.[2]

*** L I S T E N I N G   P O S T   A L P H A :

I   R E V E L A T I O N S

The death of Doug Milford marked the end of an era. It also denotes
a sharp transition in the narrative of the many mysteries he
sought to answer in his work. That job would fall to me now, alone.

I am the man that Colonel Milford, in his capacity as commander
of Listening Post Alpha, handpicked to succeed him. He brought
me here to build, develop and run Listening Post Alpha without
at first telling me much of anything about it. My name is Major
Garland Briggs, USAF.[1]

At first I too believed our work here was part of the Strategic
Defense Initiative, so a high-security profile seemed perfectly
appropriate. It was only after construction was complete, with
all the technology and equipment installed and operational, that
I came to realize the real intent of the mission.

Doug had been training me for my mission throughout the process,
in a way that sometimes seemed random or haphazard: dropping the
"casual" startling remark, leaving documents lying around the site
where he knew I'd find them, waiting to see what I made of them. All
a test to determine my worthiness to follow him in his work.

Then there came a fateful day, not long after the work was
finished -- May 17, 1985 -- when the two of us enjoyed Cuban cigars
and a fine red Bordeaux he'd brought along to celebrate on a
concrete patio outside the control room, overlooking the Pearl Lakes.

Without my knowing, Doug recorded our conversation. I found this
tape the day after he died, sitting on my desk, where he'd left
it for me. I here include the transcript from that point in our
conversation forward.

[1] There it is. We've found our Archivist—TP

* My faithful Corona

MILFORD: The unknown, Garland. Respect for the unknown. We all know what we know. Most fear or ignore what they don't. But if you seek the truth you must approach the unknown. Lean into it. Wait for it to speak to you. Are you willing to pass that threshold?

BRIGGS: I'll admit to a certain reticence in my character. A shying away, if you will.

MILFORD: Why do you suppose that is?

BRIGGS: Habit. Twenty years in the service. Reticence to questioning command-level decisions.

MILFORD: A prized quality in the military, no doubt; an order is given, your job is to do it. Highly prized in career officers among the conventional ranks. Do you suppose that's why I selected you for this detail?

BRIGGS: I don't imagine so, no.

MILFORD: Be truthful now. That's not who you really are, is it?

BRIGGS: (a pause) Well, I'll confess that while I've been able to present this characteristic to my superiors --

MILFORD: And been rewarded for it. Go on.

BRIGGS: I've always, almost willfully, retained an internal independence of mind.

MILFORD: There you go. And to what do you attribute this?

BRIGGS: In part, my dear departed parents --

MILFORD: Tell me about them.

BRIGGS: Catholic, but Bohemians at heart. He was a concert violinist, she a Parisian-born Montessori school teacher.

MILFORD: Good. Contradictions. Very helpful. So you went to Catholic schools?

BRIGGS: Where my Jesuit education ingrained in me the value of fealty to an established order while retaining a private allegiance to the truth.

MILFORD: Precisely. Excellent. A spiritual nature.

BRIGGS: That's the lens through which I view the world. Privately, of course.

MILFORD: Catholics, real ones, are all about the mystery.

BRIGGS: What about you?

MILFORD: Oddly enough, I'm a meat-and-potatoes man. Facts. Figures. What I can see with my own damn eyes. Women, for instance. Mysteries, in and of themselves, are a dime a dozen.

BRIGGS: How so? I thought you said --

MILFORD: Their real value lies in their ability to create within us wonder and curiosity. That, and only that, spurs us to seek understanding of the ultimate truths.

BRIGGS: I disagree. I see mysteries as the truth itself; that they're the essence of our existence, and aren't necessarily meant to be fully apprehended.

MILFORD: So we're consigned to ignorance, is that it?

BRIGGS: No. But that final barrier can be breached only by faith.

MILFORD: (laughs) That's just your Catholic slip showing, Briggs.

BRIGGS: In what way?

MILFORD: The truth can be seen. Directly. The question is, are you willing to accept what it tells you?

BRIGGS: Give me an example.

MILFORD: You've had a sighting.

BRIGGS: How do you know that?

MILFORD: Don't be naive. Tell me.

BRIGGS: (pause) Routine reconnaissance flight over western Montana, August 1979. As copilot of an F4 Phantom, I spotted an unknown silvery craft in a distant cloud formation above the Bitterroots. First on radar, then visually. I saw it for about 20 seconds, crescent shaped, hovering, wobbling slightly, then it vanished vertically, at tremendous speed, like a rocket. My pilot saw it as well. We did not give pursuit and he advised that we not report it. Too much paperwork, too many damn questions, he said. And it puts _you_ on _their_ radar.

MILFORD: Interesting.

BRIGGS: I didn't ask whom he meant by that, but his tone of voice raised more hackles than the contact itself.

MILFORD: A sighting of the first kind. Did you follow his order?

BRIGGS: I complied with his directive, but something essential in me recoiled from this code of silence. So, soon afterward I filed an anonymous report with MUFON and thought that would be the end of it.[2]

MILFORD: And that put you on _my_ radar.

BRIGGS: So you were responsible for my transfer to Fairfield?

MILFORD: You checked all the boxes. I'd been looking for years. Background in structural engineering and architecture at the Academy. Extensive flight experience. Your sighting. More importantly: an open mind and a willingness to question authority. Sightings often do that, you know. They're closest in impact on the personality to what we used to categorize as "religious experiences."

BRIGGS: You're not who I thought you were.

MILFORD: I'm the white rabbit, drawing you closer to the rabbit hole. And like the rabbit, I'm late for a very important date. You're my replacement, Garland. You're going to become the Watcher in the Woods.

(The colonel rolled up his sleeve, revealing a series of three triangular marks or tattoos on the inside of his forearm.)[3]

ARCHIVIST'S NOTE

He began by relaying to me, in his sophisticated, matter-of-fact way, the many strange experiences he'd had in the surrounding woods as a young scout. Drawing me in gradually, sprinkling a trail of bread crumbs straight out of the Brothers Grimm -- who I've since learned drew inspiration for their stories from real events in their own dark woods -- until, by sundown, I realized I'd followed him all the way to the heart of the forest.

He talked me through his hair-raising exploits with the various investigative USAF bodies. He showed me raw data from the many cases included here, from Roswell to Nixon. He shared with me the dossier he'd compiled of the town's history. Turning it over to me, he said, "This is your job now."

I didn't respond. Overwhelmed. The approach of night sent a chill through me, but I couldn't move. We sat in silence. Somewhere an owl hooted from a treetop.

Finally he said: "Ask me two questions about everything I've given you. Make sure they're the right ones."

I thought about it for a moment: "Did you choose this life, or did it choose you?"

He grinned. "I lived a wild, dissipated youth. Brought on by emotional problems caused by the disturbing experiences I had in these woods as a kid. I didn't know how to begin to handle what I'd seen or felt, so I tried to drink them away. For the better part of a decade I was little more than a drifter. The war and the Army gave me a structure to hang a life on.

"As a result of those misspent years I had developed, shall we say, a gift for dissembling. This caught the eye of a superior officer, who instead of sending me to the brig -- which he could have done, had he followed the book -- recommended me for intelligence work; I'd found my metier. When news of these unsettling sightings in the skies began filtering out of

[2] MUFON—the Mutual Unidentified Flying Object Network—is the world's largest group of amateur civilian UFO enthusiasts, who maintain, and investigate, a massive international data bank of sightings and information —TP

[3] I believe we are to conclude from this that, while still a young man, Milford experienced his own abduction in the Ghostwood Forest—perhaps with the "walking owl"—similar to those of the other victims —TP

New Mexico -- where, at the time, the Manhattan Project was our number-one security priority -- they sent me in undercover. Kismet. What I witnessed at Roswell connected me back to events I'd witnessed here. That performance earned me a promotion and a more meaningful job: following the saucers. I'd found my path, it opened up before me and I didn't question it. I never have. In other words, I believe it chose me."

Many of the colonel's experiences made their way into the middle and later sections of this dossier, accompanied by my modest attempts at interpretation. Modern sections about the people of Twin Peaks we contributed together.

"Why am I telling you this?" he went on. "A secret's only a secret as long as you keep it. Once you tell someone it loses all its power -- for good or ill -- like <u>that</u>, it's just another piece of information. But a real mystery can't be solved, not completely. It's always just out of reach, like a light around the corner; you might catch a glimpse of what it reveals, feel its warmth, but you can't know the heart of it, not really. That's what gives it value: It can't be cracked, it's bigger than you and me, bigger than everything we know. Those tight-ass suits can keep their secrets, they don't add up to anything. This deep in the game, pal, I'll take mystery every time. Ask your second question."

"What is our mission here?"

"Monitor our array of equipment in order to detect signs of intelligent nonhuman life not only in deep space, but here on earth, in our immediate surroundings. Attempt to discern their intentions and keep a watchful eye for signs of imminent attack."

My astonishment was complete, my sense of responsibility enormous. I bent my shoulder to this solitary task with dedication and never breathed a word to anyone about the true nature of the work, not to my superiors back at Fairfield, nor to the many friends I'd made in our new community, not even to my family. For nearly five years nothing of consequence appeared in the data I collected. An occasional anomaly surfaced, but nothing that seemed to justify the expense and effort we'd made to create the LPA in the first place. I grew discouraged, and during this time the colonel himself seemed to lose interest; he made fewer and fewer trips up the mountain.

My career sank into limbo. At Fairchild, officers junior to me began receiving promotions that, given the length and quality of my service, should have gone to me. I began to wonder if I'd made the worst mistake of my life. Making colonel, something I'd felt would one day surely come my way, seemed out of reach. I struggled with despair, and buried myself deeper in what began to seem like meaningless routine. Dedication to duty, without questioning the purpose, that's the life of an officer, I told myself.

Until one morning I awoke to the realization that this compensation had distanced and alienated me from my now teenage son; during the crucial years when he most needed my support and guidance, I was hiding myself away up the mountain, working late into the night. My wife tried her best to alert me that trouble was brewing for Robert, but still I made excuses -- he was a good student, quarterback of the football team -- and refused to see what was right in front of my eyes. It took an unspeakable tragedy to return me to my senses.

The murder of Laura Palmer, my son's girlfriend at the time, changed everything. At first, when suspicions swirled around Robert, the guilt and responsibility I felt for the years I'd neglected him brought me to the edge of an abyss. Although he was cleared, our relief was short-lived as we came to realize Robert had drifted into recreational drug use and interactions with the local criminal element. Our son had become a stranger to us, and his future, his very life was imperiled. My wife and I felt more powerless and afraid than at any time in our life together.

2 SPECIAL AGENT DALE COOPER

The appearance of an unexpected ally provided help unlooked for: FBI Special Agent Dale Cooper arrived to investigate Laura's death; a stalwart, trustworthy man, stout of character, foursquare in thought and nature. Although he remained focused on solving that horrific crime, I soon realized that the scope of Cooper's interest in what had happened to our community encompassed a much broader field.

Colonel Milford confided in me that Cooper's presence here -- and his association with secret allies of the colonel's -- signaled a raising of the ante of our stated mission. Our zone had suddenly gone hot; the data I was monitoring went from zero to sixty. Strange phenomena -- of the sort frequently encountered by the colonel throughout his life -- cropped up with regularity, registering seismically on my instrumentation. From the start, Cooper himself experienced turbulent phenomena: sightings in the woods, mysterious encounters, troubling dreams. A wave of darkness that threatened to engulf us had awoken. My labors became animated with newfound purpose; perhaps, at last, the answers we'd come looking for were within reach.

Suffice it to say that, in the conventional sense, Cooper "solved" the crime; Laura had been killed by her own father, Leland Palmer. Unspeakable violations preceded this despicable act and it ended with the desperate man's suicide. A web of evil, like a viral contagion, had spread from this vile act throughout our community, a dark eldritch leviathan rearing its head. But with Leland's tragic resolution, it seemed, the fever gripping our town had broken. The leviathan slowly submerged.

Throughout this ordeal, and its aftermath, I befriended Cooper. We shared many enjoyable discussions -- without either of us revealing the covert connections we shared -- and found solace in each other's company.

Then, one night soon afterward, most unexpectedly, came a breakthrough at the LPA. A message received loud and clear through the chatter and chuff droning through my instruments. Three words, plain English, in a sea of random signals:

Cooper . . . Cooper . . . Cooper

I traced it to its source, stunned to realize it did not issue from the vastness of space, but from somewhere in the surrounding woods of Ghostwood Forest. I wanted to tell Cooper about this message -- a clear violation of my charter, but when I raised the idea with Colonel Milford he wholeheartedly agreed.

He also told me the LPA would be my responsibility now, alone, until my new control arrived. He'd found one last chance for happiness in this new marriage and he was taking it. He held no illusions this young woman was the great love of his life but knew she was assuredly the last.

I sought out Cooper and shared the message with him -- dispassionately, curiously, as a man of science -- and in that spirit he considered it. As a bond of friendship, I invited him to join me on a camping and fishing trip into the Ghostwood and he accepted. We left that very afternoon. Late that night, during a delightful conversation before the fire, he went to answer a call of nature. Before he returned, the leviathan came for me.

My memories of the event, to this day, remain a hazy jumble: blinding white light issuing from a suggestion of some mass or object above me, a silent dark-robed figure beckoning. Paralyzed with terror, I seemed to move without volition to some other space. Alone but in the presence of some immense, overwhelming force, as if gravity had increased a thousandfold. A flood of words sluiced through my mind, words not my own, nor in any language known to me, a voice metallic, ringing and bitter. This was knowledge, I sensed through my terror, from some unknown order, of a higher vibrational quality beyond my ability to process, uncanny, perhaps electromagnetic in nature and not in the remotest way human.

But what <u>was</u> it? What was it trying to show me? Whatever I'd been sent into these woods to find had after all this time found me first, roughing me up like a midnight dockside beatdown. Whatever this presence might be, it possessed nothing benign or benevolent in form or content, only a cold, crushing, calculating pressure. Time itself stood still, as if whatever place they'd brought me stood outside it. Throughout the ordeal I clung to one vague hope: If I survived, did this test hold some promise of revelation? I not only feared for my life; I feared the annihilation of my soul.

I saw many things I don't remember. I heard other voices I can't recall. All around me colors constantly phased through the spectrum, blue to green, red to violet, black to white. I felt alternately like a ragged empty doll, then nothing but searing pain that rent my flesh with sadistic ease. I saw eyes, watching, felt pressure in my mind, as if thoughts were being forcibly inserted. I'm fairly certain I journeyed back and forth through time, watching it unspool like some immense, omniscient recording.

Then I was back in the woods alone. Not far from our campsite, fire cold, deserted. Pale daylight, which my mind, coming back to itself, recognized: morning. That small shard of human experience became my lifeline, and I followed it back to what I used to think of as reality. I rested awhile, listless and spent. Found a stream and drank from it, splashed water on my face, breathed good air again, felt the sun on my face and realized: I'm alive.

[1] Verified by Cooper's notes that this camping trip and Briggs's subsequent disappearance occurred—TP

Somehow I made it down the mountain, which took all day. As night fell I staggered into my home, to my wife and son. So grateful to see their faces, determined to never take them for granted ever again. My wife told me I'd been missing for three days. Cooper had returned to town and initiated a search. They'd begun to fear they'd never find me. I ate, sparingly, then almost at once fell into a deep, dreamless sleep.[1]

I slept I6 hours, awoke and found myself back in time again, feeling it infuse its familiar rhythms back into my skin and bones. Ate ravenously, like a starving animal. I felt a dull, throbbing pain on the back of my neck. Betty noticed there were marks, symbols really, carved, burned or branded there. Interlocking triangles.

I'd seen these marks before. On the bodies of other "abductees" -- the three children who'd been lost in these woods: Margaret Lanterman, Carl Rodd and another boy who'd moved away and since passed on. And Doug Milford. Now whatever force or thing this was had placed its mark on me. Yes, I thought, as resolve flooded back to me, I'd discovered what the colonel had brought me here to find. The source itself had "chosen" me as well. I needed to tell him.

Then I learned that Colonel Milford had died at the Great Northern Hotel three nights earlier. When I returned to the LPA later that day, I found an encrypted message waiting on my computer, written and sent on the night I went missing:

I am hoping and praying you will soon safely return and be able to read this. As much as I have appreciated your relentless, dedicated work on our project, tonight I feel crippled with regret that I ever drew you into it. I've never had children, or a wife in the truest sense, but you are a family man, Garland, through and through, and your wife and son need you more than I do, or this work does. I offer this as I'm looking back now at forty-five years of my own fruitless labor, an old man filled with loss and sorrow, without a family or true friends--although I would count you, alone, in that number, Garland--and for what? I have no answer, but I've come to realize that I owe you, at least, the full truth as I've come to view it, in the chance you'll one day see this.

Portions of the government we both served with pride have failed us. They have lied, withheld secrets, acted in their own selfish interests at the expense of their citizens. And don't believe anyone who tells you this all began in Roswell in '47. I'm convinced now that whatever I've glimpsed or encountered and spent my life tracking has been with us since humankind came down out of the trees. It is not something "out there"--in the president's words. They may well have once been our "neighbors" from some distant star, but I believe they were here before us. I believe that were we able to look deeply at the whole of human history we would see that they have always been here. I believe they have observed, helped, haunted, tormented and teased us since the beginning of time for reasons entirely their own. I believe that they are a multitude, and that their true nature is singular and energetic, not physical, evolved in some way light-years beyond our ability to understand, and as a consequence our limited, linear sense of time means nothing to them. A few of us were chosen, for some strange purpose, to learn more about them. Or perhaps for other reasons.

I believe their presence fills more than the skies or these woods; they lie at the root cause of every extranormal or paranormal experience our species has recorded: religious, spiritual, scientific, ghostly, inspirational, angelic and demonic. From the burning bush to Fatima and Lourdes, to "vampires" and sky people, monsters and abductions in the night and Roswell and Homestead and all those strange lights and crafts seen for millennia by so many of us in so many skies, I believe all these phenomena that our puffed-up egos and busy ant minds persist in trying to label, categorize, penetrate and comprehend, all spring from this same uncanny source. This is the mother of all "others," and were we ever able to set our eyes on its ultimate nature we would find it as foreign, incomprehensible and indifferent to us as ours would be to bacterial microbes swimming in a drop of water.

These final truths you must never forget: we are utterly incapable of knowing their true intent, and their true intent may not be to wish us well. It may be that they're here to guide or even aid our evolution; it's equally possibly we may matter no more to them then those random protozoa in our tap water do to us. In other words, by our meager moral definitions, they may be both "good" and "evil," and those precious distinctions of ours mean nothing to them. There may even be a "good" and "evil" side at play here, and we, our human race, is the game!

Let me hasten to add I hope I'm wrong, that this work--being "chosen"-- has deranged me, but Garland, I fear that I am right and in my right mind. The owls may indeed not be what they seem but still serve an imperative function: they remind us to look into the darkness. Whatever steps you take from here, do not act alone: wait for your next control to appear.

Your true friend,
DOUGLAS MILFORD

9:50 a.m. March 15 1989

If I hadn't so recently experienced my own private nightmare in the woods the colonel's last words would have made little sense to me. Now they seared my soul.

Doug left no instructions in his will about how to dispose of his remains -- I think some part of him believed he would live forever. His brother Dwayne suggested cremation and scattering his ashes near the Pearl Lakes, where not so long before we'd put Robert Jacoby to rest. So that's what we did, a small group of us, "grieving" widow not included.

Afterward I repaired to the LPA and set about securing the dossier Doug and I had created. I crafted a custom protective case and prepared a hiding place. I scrutinized Doug's final words to me; he had been my "control," and now that he was gone, a new control would appear. An ally who knew the score, but I had no idea who this might be, or from where they might come.

I awoke before dawn the next morning with a stark and startling revelation. During the night, my subconscious mind had made a breakthrough, sifting through the jumbled wreckage of numbers and strange language and my lost time in the woods until all the pieces fell together and I felt with swift and utter certainty that I knew how to proceed toward the answers that Doug had been so certain we could never find. The answer, in other words -- as best I can describe -- had been "downloaded" into my mind during my "abduction," and left there for me to sort it out. Which against all odds I had done.

So I awoke knowing that the identity of my "control," the person I needed to complete our mission, was right in front of me, in the mysterious message I'd already received:

Cooper.

Of course. Perfect sense. It must be Cooper. All the stars aligned. Why else would Gordon Cole have sent him here? Maybe Cooper wasn't yet fully aware of the whys or wherefores himself, but I'd learned by now that "chance" events often prove providential, convincing myself that Special Agent Dale Cooper would be the one with whom I'd carry on this work.

I reached out to him that morning. Called his room at the Great Northern. No answer. I tried the sheriff's station. Lucy informed me that Cooper had gone off with the sheriff the night before on some mission into the woods. Alarmed, I asked her to connect me by radio to them. She did so. Truman wouldn't reveal the purpose of their trip over the air, but told me that, once they'd arrived, Cooper had disappeared during the night. They had no idea where he'd gone and were still waiting for him. They were at a place not far from where Cooper and I had gone camping called Glastonbury Grove. That news, and a slight tremor in his tone, alarmed me beyond reason.

I feverishly set to work at the LPA, preparing our elaborate "mayday" protocols. During my work that day I received a call from Truman telling me Cooper had finally returned to the same spot where he'd left them. He didn't say what happened to him in the interim -- I don't think he knew -- but they were taking him back to the Great Northern. Cooper said he needed rest.

Greatly relieved, I asked Sheriff Truman to have Agent Cooper contact me at my home. As soon as I could manage, I wanted to share this dossier with him and present a full picture of what I've discovered. If he responded as I hoped he would, I'd take him to the LPA and share with him what I'd discovered.

Only moments ago, while writing the previous passage, Cooper called, as I had requested. He's on his way to the house right now -- the bell just rang, he's here. Betty is letting him in...

I2:05 PM MARCH 28, I989

He just left. Something's wrong. The message holds the answer, just as I thought, but I've misinterpreted it. Protocols are in place. I must act quickly.

I'm heading to the LPA alone.

                    * M * A * Y * D * A * Y *

THE DOSSIER ENDS

HERE

I don't know what happened to either Major Briggs or Agent Cooper at this point. There are files on Briggs, at both the FBI and Air Force, and on Cooper, at the FBI, that are designated many levels above top secret. Out of my reach. I've taken my analysis as far as I can. My instructions are clear: I'm to turn over the dossier with my findings to the Director's office and wait for their response. Deadlines are pressing.

I'm guessing that if, and only if, they find my work to date acceptable they will have me begin breaking down the other data, which I have not yet seen.

The rest is out of my hands. I'm still listed on the duty roster as "on assignment" but, as far as I can determine, have been removed from active service until that decision is reached. As Director Cole once told me, that time he took me out for coffee, a big part of this job—and, for that matter, life itself—is waiting for the right moment.

—SPECIAL AGENT TAMARA PRESTON

Tamara Preston

INITIAL *TP*   DATE / /

THE OWLS MAY INDEED NOT BE WHAT THEY SEEM,
BUT STILL SERVE AN IMPERATIVE FUNCTION:
They remind us to look into the darkness.